DUDLEY PUBLIC LIBRARIES

The loan of this book may be renewed if not required by other readers, by contacting the library from which it was borrowed.

Louise Fuller was once a tomboy who hated pink and always wanted to be the Prince—not the Princess! Now she enjoys creating heroines who aren't pretty push-overs but strong, believable women. Before writing for Mills & Boon she studied literature and philosophy at university, and then worked as a reporter on her local newspaper. She lives in Tunbridge Wells with her impossibly handsome husband Patrick and their six children.

Pippa Roscoe lives in Norfolk, near her family, and makes daily promises to herself that this is the day she'll leave the computer to take a long walk in the countryside. She can't remember a time when she wasn't dreaming about handsome heroes and innocent heroines. Totally her mother's fault, of course—she gave Pippa her first romance to read at the age of seven! She is inconceivably happy that she gets to share those daydreams with you. Follow her on Twitter @PippaRoscoe.

000003111282

THE CHRISTMAS SHE MARRIED THE PLAYBOY

LOUISE FULLER

THE GREEK SECRET SHE CARRIES

PIPPA ROSCOE

MILLS & BOON

First Published in Great Britain 2021
by Mills & Boon, an imprint of HarperCollins*Publishers* Ltd,
1 London Bridge Street, London, SE1 9GF

www.harpercollins.co.uk

HarperCollins*Publishers*
1st Floor, Watermarque Building,
Ringsend Road, Dublin 4, Ireland

The Christmas She Married the Playboy © 2021 Louise Fuller

The Greek Secret She Carries © 2021 Pippa Roscoe

ISBN: 978-0-263-28269-6

11/21

MIX
Paper from
responsible sources
FSC® C007454

This book is produced from independently certified FSC™ paper
to ensure responsible forest management.
For more information visit www.harpercollins.co.uk/green.

Printed and Bound in Spain using 100% Renewable Electricity
at CPI Black Print, Barcelona

THE CHRISTMAS SHE MARRIED THE PLAYBOY

LOUISE FULLER

MILLS & BOON

CHAPTER ONE

'EXCUSE ME, YOUR GRACE, I'm sorry to bother you—'

'Then don't.' Eyes shut, Louis Albemarle, Tenth Duke of Astbury, burrowed away from the steward's coaxing voice, pulling the quilt over his floppy brown hair.

'But, Your Grace—'

'Is the plane on fire?' Louis muttered irritably, shifting onto his side.

'No, sir.'

'Have the wings dropped off?'

'No, sir.'

Opening his eyes, he winced into the light, pain blooming inside his head. He glared at the steward. 'Then why have you woken me up? I said I didn't want breakfast. I said I didn't want to be woken until we got to Zurich.'

The steward nodded soothingly. 'We are in Zurich, sir. We just touched down a moment ago.'

Touched down? Surely they couldn't be here already? It felt as if he'd just put his head on the pillow. In fact, it felt as if his head *was* a pillow. And he couldn't seem to feel his jaw...

'Right. Fine. Whatever.' Holding up his hands to fend off any further interaction, he rolled onto his back. 'Just give me a minute—'

As he watched the steward retreat, Louis ran a hand over his face, the rough skin on his fingers snagging on the two-day stubble. Even the tiniest movement made him feel as if rocks were rolling around inside his head, but he just wanted to make sure his face was still there.

He stifled a yawn. Actually, what he really wanted to do was sleep for about a hundred years.

The last seven days had been another lost week of non-stop partying. Behind closed doors, so it should stay under the radar.

Not that he cared what people thought, but it just meant his voicemail wouldn't get filled up with messages bleating about his behaviour from the Callière chief marketing officer Nick Cooper.

Messages that he simply deleted.

His lip curled. Why the hell would he take any notice of them? Nobody told him how to behave in private or in public, and that included his CMO and the shareholders.

Stretching an arm over his shoulder, he swung his legs out of bed and began dragging on last night's clothes.

What he needed was a long, hot shower, and then he was going to take a sleeping pill and crash. With any luck he'd wake up just in time for the Christmas party at the Haensli—the legendary Christmas party at the equally legendary and jaw-droppingly exclusive Hotel Haensli in Klosters. It was the grandest ski palace in the Alps, and it was the one party his CMO had given the green light for.

Understandably. It was like a festive and infinitely more fun version of a Davos forum. One night when an extraordinary roster of billionaires and global aristocrats joined a dazzling guest list of big names from the entertainment world to play.

In other words, the kind of people who should and did wear Callière jewellery—which was why they were gifting each female guest a pair of diamond earrings in the lavish goodie bag.

It had been a last-minute idea—*his*, of course. But the shareholders had loved it. So would the guests.

His mouth twisted. So maybe for the first time in three months his business would be making headlines for the right reasons, and he might finally be one step closer to being able to own the business entirely.

But first he had to get to the hotel.

After the warmth of Abu Dhabi, the crisp Alpine air made his eyes water. He hunched his shoulders against the chill, a beanie pulled low over his forehead, his blue eyes hidden behind a pair of ludicrously expensive vintage sunglasses.

Not that he needed to worry about being recognised. This terminal was for private charters only. There were no commercial flights, and that meant no nosey holiday-makers with smartphones looking to make a quick buck with a photo of some celebrity tumbling off a plane.

It was why he always travelled first class.

But nothing beat a private jet for…well, for keeping your private life private. And, frankly, he needed to lie low right now, so when Henry had offered him the use of his jet, naturally he had jumped at the chance.

Unfortunately, even a private jet could only take him so far. This next part of the journey had to be done by helicopter.

Ah, there it was: his ride.

He greeted the pilot and climbed into the sleek black helicopter. This time the flight took just over half an hour and, resisting the urge to sleep, Louis stared down at the picture-book snow-covered serenity of the Swiss Alps.

It reminded him of Canada, the place he'd called home for the last ten years. But even though he loved the endless expanse and wild beauty of Alberta and the Northwest Territories, it was not his home.

For him, that could only ever be Waverley.

And yet even now, when he could reasonably claim the house and the estate back as his own, he hadn't done so. He wasn't sure if he ever would.

His father's death should have been like a door closing. Or was it a weight lifting? He stared moodily through the window, twin pulses of resentment and bitterness beating across his skin as they always did whenever he let himself think about his parents and their actions.

Their betrayal.

Instead, his father's death had seemed to unleash a kind of fury in him that couldn't be satisfied—along with two other emotions, both of which were entirely unwelcome: guilt and regret.

Maybe it had been the shock of realising that he was now the Duke of Astbury, with the title of the man he'd spent so long hating, but all the old demons had awoken, together with a few new ones, and he'd basically spent the last three months partying so hard he couldn't stand, much less think about the past.

At Davos, a text from Henry and a flurry of snowflakes greeted him as he walked towards the heliport terminal.

No doubt Henry Sr was giving his son a hard time for handing over the family jet, but Henry Jr owed him big-time for what had happened in Cannes in the summer, so now they were quits.

A muscle twitched in his jaw. A lot of people owed him for what happened in Cannes, but as usual he'd taken the blame.

Why wouldn't he?

It wasn't as if he had a reputation to lose, he thought, his lip curling as he sidestepped a young couple kissing passionately.

He might run one of the most successful, sustainable and ethical diamond businesses in the world, but if everything he read in the media was to be believed, that was the only ethical thing in his life.

Or at least that was what most people seemed to think.

Including—unfortunately, but not that surprisingly—those closest to him.

His shoulders tensed.

It had taken ten years, but Callière had gone from being a niche diamond mining and retail business to a sought-after cult jewellery brand favoured by A-listers across the planet.

He had made that happen.

It was his company, his brainchild. He was the CEO and soon the business that bore his beloved grandmother's name would be fully under his control and he would be able to forget all about the damn shareholders and their concerns.

He felt a sharp needle of resentment between his ribs.

It wasn't fair that he had been put in this position in the first place. He was the Duke of Astbury. He shouldn't have had to borrow money and he shouldn't have needed to. But there had been no alternative after his father had cut off his allowance.

If Glamma hadn't helped him he wouldn't have had anything. Not even a roof over his head.

Across the concourse the scent of hot coffee was a welcome, enticing distraction from the well-trodden path of his thoughts, and he was turning unthinkingly towards the low-lit luxurious lounge area when his brain did an emergency stop, closely followed by his feet.

Only why?

It was just a woman, wearing a white fur Cossack-style hat, with some kind of pastry in her hand, standing next to a trolley full of luggage. A lot of luggage, admittedly, but not enough to snag his gaze and hold it captive.

No, that would be her legs.

His pulse ticked.

Sheathed—and that was the only word for it—in form-hugging dark jeans, they seemed to go on for ever. Or at least to where a frustratingly obscuring navy puffer jacket skimmed over the mouthwatering curve of her bottom.

Damn. He felt his blood divert sharply to his groin and for a moment he forgot to breathe as his eyes locked on to her bottom. And now that he was looking it was almost impossible to look away. Impossible not to wonder what else lay beneath that stupid jacket. Could the rest of her be as tempting?

At that exact instant, the woman in the hat looked up, as if she had heard his thoughts, and he caught a glimpse of a snub nose, bee-stung lips and Arctic blue eyes several shades lighter than his. It was only a glimpse, but the pull between them was so instant, so intense, that he was already moving across the concourse before he remembered that he didn't know her.

His feet slowed.

Throughout his adult life, he'd grown used to being the object of a universally admiring female gaze, but this woman was staring past him. No, make that *through* him—almost as if he wasn't there, he thought, with a beat of disbelief.

As if to prove his point, she smiled coolly at one of the uniformed porters who had come scampering over to help her and then, without so much as blinking, she was sashaying past him, following her teetering trolley of luggage towards the exit.

He watched in silence. *She was quite something.* A real ice maiden. His stomach tensed with a momentary pang of regret that she was leaving.

It wasn't just those legs.

After the party, he had planned to spend his days pitting himself against the snow-covered curves of the Alps. But he would have been happy to spend a night or two exploring other softer, warmer curves. The fact that he might have had to apply a little extra heat to melt the ice first would simply have added to the challenge.

Only it was not to be and, flipping the collar of his jacket up around his neck, he walked through the sliding doors, squinting through his sunglasses at the limousines waiting patiently like a pack of dogs in the bright Alpine sunshine.

He spotted the discreet Haensli logo on the nearest car, and without removing his sunglasses greeted the uniformed chauffeur with a lazy upward flick of his head. '*Grüezi*. They're bringing the luggage. Shouldn't be long. *Tschuldigung*—'

He broke off, frowning, as his phone rang in his jacket. Fishing it out, he answered it without thinking.

'Louis?'

He swore under his breath. For the last few months—pretty much ever since his father had died and he'd gone on the mother of all benders—he'd stopped taking his CMO's calls, so the surprise in Nick's voice was more than justified.

But it was overshadowed by his own rush of irritation at being distracted enough to pick up. 'Nick...how can I help you?'

'Good morning—or should I say, *guete morge*?'

Louis winced. He didn't know what was worse. Nick's appalling Swiss German accent or the faux bonhomie in his voice.

'Something like that. Look, Nick, I've only just landed and there was turbulence on the flight,' he lied. 'I didn't get much sleep, so can we do this later or is it something urgent?'

'I don't know, Louis. You tell me.'

'What does that mean?'

He didn't bother hiding the exasperation in his voice and he heard Nick take a breath. He could almost picture his square-jawed CMO bracing his shoulders.

'You know what it means. I've been jumping through

hoops these last few months, cleaning up the messes you leave behind.'

'So don't. That's what Housekeeping is for,' he said curtly.

'I'm not talking about an unmade bed or two, Louis.' Nick's voice was vibrating with barely contained frustration. 'I'm talking about your behaviour and how it impacts the brand.'

His hand tightening around the phone, Louis rolled his eyes. 'Yes, you are, but I fail to see why,' he said, with the chilling disdain he'd inherited along with his title. 'Callière is my business. I am the brand, and my behaviour is nobody's concern. But if you're worried, I don't have to go to the Haensli party.'

He knew it wouldn't come to that. As he'd just said, *he* was the brand. Without him, Callière would be just another upmarket jewellery business.

'That won't be necessary,' Nick said pacifyingly, as Louis had known he would. 'We want you to go to the party. I just need to be sure that you're going to bear in mind your responsibilities.'

Louis gritted his teeth. Could there be any word he disliked more than responsibilities? His mouth twisted. He could think of a few: relationships, love, wife—

Feeling a familiar push-me-pull-me lurch in his stomach at the mere thought of matrimony, he took a steadying breath. 'Then be sure,' he said, in the same cold tone. 'I know the score, Nick. No headlines. No scandal. No compromising photos.' *No fun*, he might have added. 'Trust me. I know what's at stake.'

He did, and Nick was overreacting.

He wasn't about to curtail his behaviour behind closed doors at the party of the year.

'Good,' Nick said quietly. 'Because I've stuck my neck a long way out for you, Louis, and I'm getting tired of trying to convince the world that your behaviour is the sign of a desperately romantic man searching for the right woman. I'll call you after the party.'

Louis stared across the heliport as his CMO's voice faded, no longer seeing the snow-covered peaks but his father's study. And just like that he was back at Waverley, facing the Duke's furious disapproval.

Fighting a queasy mix of resentment and humiliation, he hung up.

Great! So now he was supposed to be responsible for Nick's neck as well as everything else.

He swiped off his sunglasses and ran a hand over his face. Maybe he should have just stayed in Abu Dhabi.

He hated feeling like this—as if everything was being decided for him and his life wasn't his own. It made him feel desperate and trapped, so that suddenly it was hard to head off the memories. His breath caught in his throat. Normally he could keep them in the shadows. Now, though, he could feel them lining up inside his head, waiting to ambush him.

Jamming his phone back in his pocket, he nodded curtly at the chauffeur who was still waiting in front of the car, seemingly mesmerised by the ice-covered peaks.

'Let's go,' he snapped, turning towards the limo.

And then he froze, as if he himself had turned to ice. There was a woman sitting in the back seat of his limousine. And not just any woman.

His gaze leapfrogged swiftly over the white fur hat down to a pair of unmistakable slim denim-clad thighs.

It was the ice maiden.

So she had seen him. She'd just been playing hard to get. But she was definitely here to play.

A pulse of heat darted across his skin. This was not a situation he was unfamiliar with, and normally he wouldn't have thought twice. But now, here, was the wrong time, wrong place.

He turned towards the chauffeur. 'What is she doing in there?' he demanded.

The chauffeur's eyes darted nervously towards him. 'I don't know. I thought she was with you, Your Grace.'

'With me?'

'She said she was going to the Haensli, so I assumed—' The man broke off, not willing to say anything more… not needing to.

Louis swore under his breath. The chauffeur might not know the name of the woman sitting in his limo, but he knew his name, knew his reputation, and so he'd done the maths.

A little something for the weekend, sir?

'Is there a problem?'

The question, asked by a husky but distinctly female voice, made him jerk round and, glancing across the roof of the limo, he felt his breath catch in his throat.

The woman had got out of the car and, to answer his earlier question, she was every bit as tempting up close as he'd imagined. More so, even.

Heart hammering, he stared at her in silence, drinking in her wide apart blue eyes, her regal arching eyebrows and, as she swept the hat off her head, the mane of glossy dark hair that fell about her shoulders like some advert for shampoo.

Caught off guard by his somewhat intense response to a complete stranger, he frowned. 'Yes, there appears to have been a bit of a mix-up.'

More than a mix-up. It was the last thing he needed, to be spotted hooking up here with some random woman—particularly as he wasn't even hooking up with her.

'What kind of a mix-up?'

The confusion on her face was distinctly shaded with irritation and, aware that people were turning round and lifting up their sunglasses to look at them, he felt his own irritation spark. His voice was diamond hard as his eyes met hers.

'The kind that's easily remedied. Basically, you need to find yourself another limo. This one's taken.'

Another limo...?

Santa Somerville stared at the man standing on the other side of the car, her pulse racing, her head spinning as if she'd just finished one of her skating routines.

But it wasn't the outrageousness of his remark, or even the arrogant gleam in those distractingly blue eyes that was making her heart thump against her ribs.

It was him. This man. This stranger.

Except he wasn't quite a stranger.

She had seen him before—just now, inside the heliport. And even then he had seemed vaguely familiar.

As her gaze hovered over his stubbled jaw, then tracked down over his padded jacket to his crumpled black jeans, she felt hot suddenly. It had been so long since she'd looked at a man—*really* looked. After Nathan, she had not allowed herself to even glance. It had been too painful even just thinking about where looking had led, and where it would inevitably lead again.

Only with this man there had been no question of allowing herself to do anything. Her body had simply overridden her brain and she had felt an almost overwhelming urge—not to look but to touch.

She felt her face grow warm as she remembered the exact moment when she had first become aware of him.

Standing next to her mountain of luggage, she had been suddenly and randomly conscious of the hammering of her heart—and, even more randomly, of the pastry she was holding.

It hadn't made sense until she'd realised that one part of her brain was thinking about walking over and caress-

ing the shadowed curve of his jaw, only her fingers were
sticky...

And now she was thinking it again—not the sticky fingers part, but the wanting to touch his face.

He was so handsome that she couldn't quite believe
she was awake.

Real men in real life just didn't look this good.

Since getting sponsored by Bryson's Ices she'd actually met quite a few famous actors, and to be honest most
of them had disappointed in the flesh.

Only this man far from disappointed.

On the contrary, he over-delivered.

He was matinee-idol-handsome, those dazzling blue
eyes perfectly offset by messy brown hair and the kind of
clean, sculpted bone structure that made everyone around
him look smudged.

As for his body—

Her mouth was suddenly dry. Professional ice skaters
trained for around five hours a day, on and off the ice, so
she was used to strong thighs and muscular shoulders. But
that was just athleticism.

Whoever this man was, he had something more than
muscle. He had an energy that made the air grow kinetic
around him, like a static storm, and made her breathing
lose its rhythm.

And that was why she'd deliberately turned away, ignoring both his intense blue gaze and the sharp ache of
desire twisting her stomach.

It had been the only and the absolutely necessary response for someone like her—someone who had not just
failed to deliver but had been exposed for doing so.

A familiar nausea clutched at her stomach and, pushing the memory away, she gripped the side of the door.
'On the contrary,' she said, in the clipped, cool voice that
had helped earn her the nickname of Snow Queen on the

skating circuit. 'You need to find *yourself* another limo. You see, this one is for guests of the Hotel Haensli.'

There was a short, pulsing silence as his eyes narrowed, and then he was moving, walking round the car and stalking towards her with such a sense of purpose that she took an unsteady step backwards.

'Yes, it is,' he said silkily as he stopped in front of her. 'And I think you'll find it was sent to meet *me*.'

She couldn't place his accent. One minute it was posh London schoolboy, the next it seemed to meander into a kind of transatlantic twang. But either way there was an unmistakable authority in his voice—an assumption that he would get his own way.

Probably because he always did.

After all, if he was a guest at the hotel he must be seriously rich, and that kind of wealth coupled with looks like his pretty much guaranteed that he'd never encountered rejection or failure.

Until today, she thought with a flare of anger.

'You're not the only guest at the hotel,' she snapped. 'But I suppose it wouldn't occur to you to think about anyone but yourself.'

'What's that supposed to mean?'

His handsome face tensed with what she imagined was a mixture of disbelief and anger.

She clenched her teeth, but didn't drop her gaze. If he thought he could intimidate her then he could think again.

'It means that you are a spoiled little rich boy in a man's body. It means that you're not even the tiniest bit grateful for your wealth and privilege. In fact, you think you deserve it, and that everyone else is just here to do your bidding.'

She heard the chauffeur's startled grunt, but the man in front of her didn't so much as flinch. Instead, he started to clap slowly.

'I'm impressed,' he said. 'It usually takes most people

a good couple of hours to work that out, but you nailed it in…' he flicked his cuff back and glanced at the heirloom watch on his wrist '…four minutes.'

She glared at him. 'You're not funny.'

'Wasn't trying to be.' Now his eyes narrowed. 'What would be the point? I mean, it doesn't seem as if fun plays a major part in your life.'

She felt a shaft of pain as his words pressed against a memory she had tried and never succeeded in forgetting.

'Is everything okay, sir?'

Turning, she saw that one of the other drivers had wandered over. Behind him, other people were starting to gaze curiously.

'What the—?' Glancing round at their audience, her blue-eyed tormentor swore under his breath. 'This is all I need,' he muttered.

Jerking his head at the chauffeur, he yanked open the limo door and then, before she had a chance to register what he was doing, much less react, he had hustled her inside the car, sliding in beside her.

She felt a jolt of static like an electric current as his warm, muscular thigh slammed against her leg. Suddenly her throat was so tight she couldn't breathe, and she was leaning into him like a flower bending to the sun.

Horrified by her body's response to his, she jerked backwards and slithered as far away from him as physically possible, her pulse racing as if she'd accidentally sat down next to a rattlesnake.

As the limo moved smoothly away from the kerb she turned to him, her eyes flashing. 'What the hell do you think you're doing?'

Slouching back against the seat, he stretched out his legs. 'Look, baby, you wanted a ride to the hotel, didn't you? Well, you've got one—so maybe you could try and be a little less snippy.'

Snippy! She glared at him, her hands clenching at her

sides. Her skin was still prickling from that whisper of contact and she hated it that her body had responded so intensely to someone so utterly appalling.

What was wrong with her?

Had she learned nothing from what had happened with Nathan?

Her stomach knotted at the memory of how astonishingly and unforgivably stupid she'd been. But even if her taste in men apparently hadn't changed, she was different now.

Taking a quick, steadying breath, she glanced across the car. It was tempting to tell him exactly where he could stick his ride, only she wouldn't put it past this man to dump her by the roadside. Particularly if he found out she wasn't even staying at the hotel.

Her spine stiffened against the smooth leather upholstery. Merry had asked one of the drivers to pick her up as a favour, but officially the limo service was reserved for guests of the Haensli—not friends of the staff.

The last thing she wanted to do was get her best friend into trouble. Especially after everything Merry had done to make this happen—not just the ride in a limo but inviting her to stay at her chalet and even wangling her a ticket for the hotel's party…a party that had a guest list like a royal wedding.

Best of all, the hotel had its own private ice rink, so she could keep up with her training schedule.

She felt a sudden surge of anger. She had been so looking forward to this trip. It was the first real holiday she'd had in so long. Actually, it was pretty much the first real holiday she'd ever had.

Training to become a professional skater meant that there was little time for holidays or parties or any kind of fun, really. And anyway, not everyone was like Richie Rich over there.

Some people—most people, in fact—had to work hard

for the things they wanted and needed. Her throat tightened as she pictured her small, shabby home. Her father and Kate had already sacrificed so much to make her dream a possibility, but at least now she had the Bryson's sponsorship.

Without it, she didn't know what she would do. At this level of competition there were just so many expenses. But she did know she wasn't going to let her family take care of her for the rest of her life.

'So you're staying at the hotel.'

It was a statement, not a question, but even so she felt her stomach clench in panic as she stared at the man sprawling languidly on the seat beside her. Had he guessed that she wasn't a guest?

Lifting her chin, she returned his gaze full-on. 'For the party.' That was true, not that she owed him the truth.

His gaze travelled over her face, level and considering, almost as if he could sense that she was not lying, but also not being completely honest.

'Then we have something in common, Ms...?' He let the silence fill the space between them as he waited for her to say her name.

'Somerville. Santa Somerville.'

Her real name was Santina. She was named after the little town in Italy where her parents had first met by chance on their way to Cortina. When she had been born in December it had been shortened to Santa. Only she wasn't about to share any of that with this stranger.

His blue eyes were intent on her face and her throat felt dry, tight, so that it was hard to swallow. And then she felt her face grow warmer as his mouth kicked up at one corner.

'Santa baby...' he sang softly, 'I really do want a yacht as it happens.' His smile widened. 'Actually, what I really want is a private jet. Do you think you could slip that under the tree for me?'

There wasn't a single version of that line that she hadn't heard before and, judging by that taunting smile, she was pretty sure Louis knew that. And yet there was something about the way he delivered it that sent a jolt of sexual electricity across her skin, so that suddenly she was struggling to speak.

Or maybe it was the slow, teasing smile that accompanied it.

Or the way his blue eyes held hers in a way that made her feel as though he was looking into her soul.

She felt her skin heat, and a small shiver wound through her body. She buried her fingers in the fur of the hat in her lap.

'I'm afraid not,' she said stiffly. 'I'm right out of private jets, Mr—'

'Albemarle. Louis Albemarle.'

She blinked.

Outside the limousine, she could see the picture-postcard-perfect Alpine village of Klosters, with its snow-covered shops and horse-drawn sleighs, but she barely glanced at it. She was too busy staring at Louis.

Where had she heard that name before?

Her breathing stalled, her brain scampering feverishly through facts and faces as Louis leaned forward and knocked on the window behind the driver.

'Just drop me over there. I'll walk up.'

The driver nodded. 'Yes, Your Grace.'

Your Grace.

Santa frowned. With most people the more time you spent with them, the more you understood them. But this man was making less and less sense.

'Why is he calling you that?' she asked slowly.

She felt pinpricks of heat on her skin as his glittering blue eyes locked with hers.

'Because that, Santa baby, is how you address a duke.'

And just like that everything fell into place. Her brain

lit up like a row of lemons on a fruit machine as a buzz of shock went through her body.

No wonder he had seemed so familiar.

Unlike Kate, her stepmother, she didn't follow the lives of celebrities, but she would have had to live in a cave or maybe on the moon not to have heard at least *something* about this man's life.

Louis Albemarle, the Duke of Astbury, serial philanderer, breaker of countless women's hearts, the notorious owner of Bijoux Callière and the subject of countless splashy headlines.

Her heart began hammering against her chest.

She'd actually read a kiss-and-tell story about him the other week, when she'd been waiting for a session with the physio. Some poor model he'd dated then dumped, pouring her heart out.

Her spine tensed. The woman must have been out of her mind to think she could trust a man like Louis, given that he had famously and cold-bloodedly jilted his bride at the wedding of the decade when he was just twenty. And, judging by that magazine story, his treatment of women hadn't improved over the last ten years.

'You're the Duke of Astbury.' She shook her head. 'Well, that explains a lot.'

He shifted forward in his seat and she felt a shiver run down her spine. His face had hardened, the teasing smile was gone and tension was visible in every angle of his muscular body.

'Only if you're naive or deluded enough to believe everything you read on the internet,' he said coolly.

'Not everything.'

She stared into his cold, handsome face, her insides lurching with shock and self-loathing as the limo started to slow.

Idiot.

The word ricocheted inside her head as she met his blue

gaze. Remembering the way her body had wanted to sink into his, she bit into the side of her cheek.

Why was she so weak and foolish when it came to men?

It was bad enough that she was so susceptible to a handsome face and a few flirtatious remarks, but to be susceptible to this particular man?

'But you know what they say—there's no smoke without fire.'

His eyes narrowed fractionally. 'They also say innocent until proved guilty. But you clearly believe in trial by tabloid.'

'As opposed to what? Believing you?' She gave a humourless laugh. 'Why would I do that? You've already proved that you're not what you claim to be.'

His dark eyebrows snapped together. 'You know nothing about me.'

'I know that you're a duke, and that supposedly makes you a gentleman.' She gave him an icy stare. 'Only you didn't exactly behave like a gentleman earlier, did you?'

Santa felt the hairs stand up on the back of her neck as he leaned in closer.

'Would it have made any difference if I had?' His face hardened. 'You'd already made up your mind that I was a spoiled little rich boy in a man's body.' Thick dark lashes shielded the expression in his eyes, but his breathing wasn't quite steady as he spoke. 'But, just so you know, I'm as disappointed in you as you are in me.'

Her head jerked upwards and she felt her face drain of colour. 'What do you mean?'

His gaze didn't flicker.

'Just that you're one of the most beautiful women I've ever met. Your face is so expressive, and your eyes have this incredible *chatoyance*... Only all that radiance and sparkle means nothing...' he bit the words out softly '... because there's ice in your veins. In fact...' his fingers curled over the door handle '... I'm going to go and warm up outside.'

Her heart was in her throat and she felt raw inside. 'That suits me just fine,' she said hoarsely.

He smiled in a finite way. 'I'd wish you an enjoyable stay at the Haensli, Ms Somerville, but somehow I think that might be a bit beyond you.'

And then he was out of the limo and the door was slammed shut. And she was alone on the smooth leather seat with a frown and a head full of scattered, unspoken retorts.

CHAPTER TWO

PICKING UP HER cup of coffee from the kitchen counter, Santa walked into the living area of Merry's chalet and stared out of the window at the blue-white mountains, wishing once again that her friend was there and not on a train somewhere in Europe.

Just fifteen minutes' walk from the hotel, it was a lovely, cosy little cabin, nothing like the glamorous Haensli, with its wood-panelled walls, leather sofas, opulent gold lamps and equally opulent Christmas tree.

When she'd walked into the hotel's vast reception area to pick up the key Merry had left for her, her legs had been shaking, her hands too. Only she hadn't been able to blame the opulent *hygge* interior. Or the nonchalant, cosmopolitan hotel patrons in their sleek down jackets, cashmere jumpers and shearling-lined boots.

'There's ice in your veins.'

Her lips formed a moue of annoyance.

No, the blame for her nervousness lay solidly at the feet of the Duke of Astbury. It had been his barbed words, so casually tossed at her just as he got out of the limo, that had made her stomach knot with a familiar panic. And those same words were still echoing inside her head now.

But why?

Fingers tightening around the cup, she shivered.

Louis didn't know her. He didn't know what had happened with Nathan.

She'd never told anyone. Not even her best friend. Merry had already left to go to college by then, and it had seemed ridiculous to dredge it up when she'd finally come home to visit.

A knot tightened in her chest. Plus, she'd been ashamed—and scared. Scared to look into her friend's eyes and see not just affection and concern but an acknowledgement that Nathan was right.

She bit her lip. So she hadn't said anything, and probably she wouldn't say anything about Louis either.

And not just because of what he'd said.

Her pulse missed a beat and another shiver skimmed over her skin, this one hot, not cool. There had been that other thing too…that tension between them in the limo.

She gritted her teeth, trying to give it a name. She wanted to call it hate, but hate was so unequivocal. It had been more like a battle of wills—a kind of virtual tug of war, with neither of them willing to let go of the rope.

It was like nothing she had ever felt before. But then Louis Albemarle wasn't like any other man she'd met.

He was a stranger, and yet he didn't feel like one. And, more confusingly, even though she disliked him intensely, she had never felt so attracted to a man. It was both baffling and irresistible. Maybe that was why it had made her feel so out of control and inadequate. Just like before. Just like with Nathan.

Her throat tightened at the memory.

She'd been so naive back then. So trusting and hopeful and eager. *And stupid.* What other explanation could there be for how she'd acted? What she'd accepted?

But it wasn't going to happen again. Particularly not with a man like Louis. She didn't want or need that kind of complication in her life—and besides there was no room.

No, what she needed was to skate.

Unzipping the sleek bag that had cost more than her plane ticket, she pulled out her skates, her fingers pressing into the smooth white leather.

Skating was her passion, but it was also the matrix of her life. Everything fitted in around it and had done so ever since she was three years old. She wasn't academic like her father, or artistic like Kate, nor was she outgoing like Merry. Skating was what she did. It made her feel confident and sure of herself.

She had wanted to go onto the rink earlier, but by the time she'd picked up the keys and unpacked and had lunch it had been too late. The rink would have been too crowded.

With that many people there was too great a danger of someone banging into her, and she couldn't risk getting injured. Not with the International Figure Skating Championships just under two years away.

She had come twelfth in the last competition and, given her age, realistically this would be her last chance for a medal. She wasn't going to do anything to jeopardise that.

Her mouth thinned. And that included getting all hot and quivery about somebody as vile and up himself as Louis Albemarle...

Without Merry's company, Santa had thought she might be at a loose end. But her days had fallen effortlessly into a pattern of mooching around the shops, drinking *kaffeecreme* at one of the town's many small restaurants, and of course skating. And she was surprised to find that she was enjoying her own company—enjoying herself full-stop.

So much for that being beyond her, she thought coolly, remembering Louis's parting shot in the limo. Not that she had seen him since that tense encounter. And she had no wish to do so, she thought, bending her knee and pushing off onto the ice.

It was the first time she'd had the rink entirely to herself and, gazing up at the blue sky and the glittering peaks, she felt a rush of exhilaration. She loved competing, but there was something special about skating here, surrounded by the majesty and untamed beauty of the mountains.

She could feel her body growing weightless, her mind emptying of everything and, moving forward, she gave herself up to the ice and the rush of crystalline air.

Weaving his way through the café, Louis scowled up at the pristine blue sky, cursing Nick under his breath.

Despite having said he would call after the party, for some reason his CMO had rung him at midnight last night. Make that midnight in Toronto. It had actually been six o'clock in the morning here.

Six.

In the morning.

Nick had left a message apologising, claiming it was a 'handbag call', but it hadn't been. Louis scowled. His CMO had been checking up on him.

Pushing back his beanie, he dropped into one of the café chairs and pulled out his phone. He felt a stab of satisfaction as the screen turned black.

'*Grüezi.* Good morning, sir. How may I help you?'

Without bothering to look round at the waiter, he said tersely, '*Kaffee-creme, bitte.*'

He'd tried going back to sleep. He'd even taken a pillow and hugged it against his stomach, like he'd used to at boarding school when he'd felt hollowed out with homesickness.

His spine tensed against the back of the chair. He hadn't done that in years, and he wished now that he hadn't done it this morning.

Pulse accelerating, he leaned forward, reaching for the coffee the waiter had discreetly placed on the table. It had been fine at first, but then, at some unspecified point, the soft, down-filled pillow had inexplicably turned into the soft curves of Santa Somerville.

Sucking in a sharp breath, he stared moodily across the ice rink to the panorama of mountains.

He wasn't crazy. He had known it wasn't her. And yet with his eyes closed and warmth spreading through his body it had been easy to pretend, to press closer—

His lip curled. Maybe if it had been a one-off, he might have ignored it, but Santa had been popping into his head at annoyingly frequent intervals throughout the last few days. More annoyingly still, he kept seeing her everywhere.

Sashaying towards the lift.

Turning away so that her shimmering dark hair swung like a cape around her shoulders.

Lowering her head over a menu in the restaurant.

Except it wasn't her.

It was just his mind playing tricks on him. Only he couldn't remember this ever happening before...this being so *fascinated* by a woman that he actually conjured her up from nothing. He gritted his teeth. Not for a long time, anyway. Not since Marina.

But at least that had made sense. He had known Marina since childhood, dated her for a year. Their families even shared some ancestors.

Santa made no sense. There had been a total of only about thirty minutes from the moment she had first spoken to him at the heliport to when he had climbed out of the limo.

Why, then, had he been thinking about her on and off for the last few days?

Probably because of what she'd said to him.

It had stung.

It still did. Almost as much as disdain.

He might be allergic to commitment and a magnet for trouble, but that didn't seem to put most women off. On the contrary, it usually made them even more eager to make his acquaintance.

He felt his body respond to the memory of just how eager. And that was fine by him. He wanted women to beg him for sex, and they did.

All except Santa Somerville.

And maybe that went a long way to explaining why she kept popping into his head. The fact that she was neither begging nor likely to beg any time soon.

A muscle pulled in his jaw. Not that she hadn't wanted to.

He knew enough about women to read the signs, and while Santa might have spent the entire limo ride hurling insults at him, her eyes had said something entirely different. He had seen the flicker of curiosity, the flare of heat there that had had nothing to do with fighting and everything to do with damp skin and tangled sheets.

Picturing her face in the limo, lips parted, eyes wide, the blue irises vivid against her flushed cheeks, he felt his groin harden.

She had wanted him as much as he'd wanted her, and if she'd been any other woman they would have retired discreetly to her room and stayed in bed until they'd been too exhausted to argue.

Instead, she'd had to turn everything into some kind of battle of wills.

Shoulders tensing against the ache of frustration in his groin, he let his narrowed gaze follow the progress of the skater out on the rink.

She was dressed in black sweatpants, a black beanie, a short hot-pink fur-trimmed jacket and white boots. He watched, mesmerised, as she performed a faultless triple axel followed by a double toe loop. He loved the rush and rhythm of skiing and snowboarding, and excelled at both, but skating had always seemed too much like hard work.

Only this skater made it look effortless, organic, like a snowflake spinning on a breeze.

He leaned forward.

She was breathtakingly good.

There were usually one or two skaters on any rink who caught the eye, and this girl had all the jumps and spins. But she had more than just technical skill. There was an emotional quality to the way she moved, an uninhibited rapture in her body's flexibility and power and grace.

She knew how to skate.

And he wasn't the only one who thought so.

Glancing round, he saw that there were quite a few people watching her now. Some were even holding up their phones, and as the skater finished up with a one-foot spin there was a smattering of applause.

He watched her skate towards the café and then, as she stepped off the ice, she pulled off the beanie and he swore softly as he saw who she was.

But of course it would have to be Santa, he thought, his gaze tracking down her legs as it had tracked her progress around the rink. He'd just been too caught up in the way she'd moved on the ice to really register her separate body parts.

Now that he had, he made up for lost time by letting his eyes linger on her toned thighs. It took approximately three seconds for him to picture them wrapped around his waist, and then he dragged his gaze up to her face.

He felt something warm and silvery snake across his skin. Her chin was jutting out combatively and instantly he sat up, his earlier lethargy vanishing like Alpine mist.

'What are you doing here?' Santa was looking at him coldly, her surprise distinctly stippled with irritation.

'I'm enjoying the view.' Raising an eyebrow provocatively, he gestured past the curve of her bottom to the mountains. 'I'm also enjoying this coffee. In fact, why don't you join me?'

Before she could reply, he glanced at one of the waiters and held up one finger, relishing the cool anger in her eyes almost as much as the curve of her bottom.

'I don't think that's a good idea,' she said crisply.

'Why? Are you worried you might give in to temptation?'

Her eyes locked with his. 'Only the temptation of thumping you.'

The coffee arrived, and he watched the play of emotions on her face as the desire to tell him where he could shove it waged war with natural good manners. Of course good manners won and, not bothering to hide his amusement, he watched her sit down, tucking her legs primly under the table.

Pulling out her phone, she glanced at the screen. 'I have ten minutes. And this is just a coffee,' she said icily.

Was it?

Looking up at her through thick, dark lashes, he saw that same flicker of heat in her gaze as he had on the limo ride—a heat that had nothing to do with irritation.

'Absolutely,' he agreed. 'There will be no pastry consumption.'

As she rolled her eyes he glanced down at her skates. They were not new, but they were expensive. Custommade, probably. He gently pushed the one nearest to him with the toe of his boot.

'Nice skates.'

She jerked her foot away.

'Do you mind?'

'Not if you don't.'

There was something about this woman that made him want to get a rise out of her, and she was so delightfully easy to provoke, he thought, watching her cheeks flood with colour.

'I knew this was a mistake.' She started to get up, and he hooked his foot around the leg of her chair to stop her.

'Okay, okay...' He held up his hands. 'I'm sorry. I was just teasing. Please. Stay. If not for me then for Herr Frisch. If you leave he'll think that you don't like his coffee, and he'll be so upset it could set back his recovery.'

'Fine,' she snapped, sitting back in her seat. 'But move your foot.'

He stared at her in silence. How did she do it? How could she be so uptight, so stubborn, so haughty, so maddeningly infuriating, and yet still make him feel this hard and hot and hungry?

Shifting in his seat, needing to recalibrate the balance of power, he put his feet up on the chair beside her and met her gaze.

'So how long have you been skating?'

She hesitated, her expression still frosty. 'Since I was three.'

'Well, that explains a lot.' He'd picked his words carefully, wondering if she would remember saying exactly the same sentence to him in the limo. Watching her glacier-blue eyes narrow, he knew she had.

'Meaning?'

Meaning that it was no surprise. Because she was so at one with herself when she skated. She was an ice princess, and the rink was her realm, he thought, his gaze taking in her shining dark hair and the flush of colour on her amazing cheekbones.

Glancing down at her clenched hands, he sat forward, reaching for his coffee. Probably best not to say that. The last thing he needed was to turn up at the party tomorrow with a black eye.

'You seem at home on the ice. Let me guess... Your parents skate?'

'My mother.' Her voice was as cool as the clear mountain air, but something in the tilt of her head made his pulse accelerate.

'And did you inherit your looks from her as well as your talent?'

Giving him a withering look, she jerked the chair beside her backwards, so that his feet fell to the floor.

'I don't know. Did you inherit your arrogance and general air of entitlement when you became a duke?'

Wow, he thought. She might look like a porcelain doll, but she punched low and hard.

'Unfortunately not,' he said softly, hooking the chair and drawing it closer again, to put his feet back up on it. 'My father only died three months ago, but I've always been this arrogant and entitled.'

Her lip curled and she tutted under her breath. That amazed him. He didn't know anyone who still tutted their disapproval. Most people these days just swore routinely.

'Is that why you chose the Haensli? Because of the rink?'

She glanced away, a flush of colour creeping over her cheeks. 'Not particularly. But it's a bonus. I like to skate every day.'

He watched as she leaned forward and began tugging at the laces.

'Every day? That's a serious hobby.'

'Well, you know me.' Sliding her feet into hiking boots, she raised perfectly groomed eyebrows. 'Fun doesn't play a major part in my life.'

He stared at her in silence. His remark had clearly got under her skin, and the trickle of excitement that had started when he was watching her skate surged. Actually, he didn't know her—but he wanted to.

Or at least he wanted to know what lay beneath that padded jacket and how he could make her body arch like it had out on the ice.

'But skating does?' he said.

Her hair was tied up today, and as she nodded her ponytail swung in time to the movement of her head. There was a pause, and he could almost see her calibrating her thoughts, choosing what to give away, what to conceal.

Finally, she sighed. 'I'm a figure skater.'

Now that he knew, it made perfect sense: the poise, the sense of purpose.

And the mother.

Not many three-year-olds were articulate enough to demand skating lessons, and in his experience talented sportsmen and women usually had supportive parents behind them. The kind of parents who put their own lives on hold to encourage their children.

His chest tightened.

Not that he would know anything about that personally. After he'd stood Marina up at the altar his parents had not only failed to support him, they had banished him from their lives—privately, anyway.

Even though they knew the truth.

Even though he was their son, their only child.

He felt it inside—that familiar rush of rage and resentment and hurt...a hurt he didn't usually allow himself to feel. But it was hard to ignore it when he met someone like Santa—someone who had two parents who actually loved her.

'So that was a routine?' Blanking his mind, he gestured towards the rink.

She hesitated again, and he stared at her mouth, watching her bite into the soft cushion of her lower lip.

'It was part of a routine.'

He frowned. 'Don't you need music for that?'

'Usually. But I can't wear headphones when there could be other skaters on the ice. It would be dangerous.' Her slim fingers smoothed out a crease in the napkin that had come with her coffee and he felt a pulse of heat beat across his skin. It was all too easy to picture those same fingers moving smoothly over his body.

'So what do you do instead?'

She looked startled, her forehead creasing as if his question had surprised her, and he fought the urge to lean over and smooth away the furrows.

'I don't do anything. I just skate,' she said simply.

He stared at her, envying both the light in her winter ice eyes and the tightness of her focus. Everything about her was the opposite of how he felt about himself. His life seemed so aimless, so reactive. So curtailed...

Taking a breath to ease the sudden tightness in his throat, he shook his head. 'No, that wasn't "just" skating. Skating is a discipline. You have to learn how to move on the ice. What you did out there...how you moved... No one could learn that. It was unthinking. Like water flowing—'

She blinked. 'What?'

With her legs concealed beneath the table, and her body hidden under that quilted jacket, it should have been easier for him to think clearly, but apparently not. And as her gaze sharpened on his face he shifted back in his seat, his gut knotting, feeling suddenly on edge and exposed in a way that he hadn't allowed to happen for years.

Like water flowing. Where the hell had that come from? More importantly, what on earth had possessed him to say it out loud?

The café was filling up now and, looking across the tables, he noticed a group of young women staring over at him appreciatively.

He felt his pulse jump. Women like that—women with endless smiles and short attention spans—were reassuringly straightforward. There was none of this frustrating getting the wrong end of the stick, like with the woman sitting opposite him.

Eyes narrowing, he met their collective gaze, his smile automatic, unfiltered, inclusive, and then, still smiling, he returned his attention to Santa. 'What I'm trying to say is that you're good. Very good. Seriously. You have a real talent.'

That was better. It was true, but it was also the kind of generic remark anyone might make.

Only he knew as soon as he'd spoken that he'd said something wrong.

She tensed, her face not so much hardening as turning to stone. 'You don't need to say that.'

His lazy smile felt suddenly stupid and inappropriate, like a clown's bowtie at a funeral, and he felt his own face tense too. 'I know I don't.'

'No, I mean you don't have to tell me that just because you want to go to bed with me.'

'That's not why I said it.' He felt a flash of rage as she gave him one of those snooty little looks she seemed to specialise in.

'Of course it wasn't,' she said tartly, her eyes narrowing, one small boot tapping impatiently on the floor. 'I don't know which is more ludicrous. Your thinking we might sleep together, or the idea that I would actually fall for your half-hearted attempt to flatter me into doing so.'

Now his temper didn't so much fray as rip in two.

'Okay—just so we're clear—I don't need to use tricks or flattery to get women into my bed. Believe me, baby, most times I don't even have to open my mouth.'

She was staring at him as if he had suddenly grown scales. 'If only this moment was one of those times.'

Anger rolling through him like an avalanche, Louis watched Santa reach into her pocket and pull out a cluster of notes.

'You know, just for a moment there I thought you were almost nice.'

'Yeah, well, just for a moment I thought you were almost human,' he snarled. 'But I was wrong. You really do have ice in your veins.'

'And you have a one-track mind, Your Grace.' Snatching up her skates, she rose from her chair like a queen from her throne. 'But you'll have to find someone else to be one of your pitstops on this particular journey, because I'm not interested.' She glanced pointedly at the group of giggling women. 'Enjoy the view.'

Louis stared after her, fury and disbelief pounding in his veins. That was the second time she'd given him the cold shoulder—metaphorically and literally—and the second time she had blamed him for something he hadn't done.

Well, now he was done with her.

Done with her strange swerves of mood and her willingness to judge him.

She thought she was all that, with her glossy dark hair and those mouthwatering legs. But even if his life had been his own, and Nick hadn't been keeping him on such a short leash, he wouldn't have remotely considered hooking up with a woman like Santa. Why would he? She wasn't even his type. She was too tense. Too serious. And no fun. He was just bored, and frustrated, and looking to be distracted.

A slow, curling smile tugged at the corners of his mouth.

Fortunately, it just so happened that the perfect distraction would be taking place right here, tomorrow evening. After all, how long could it possibly take for a party chock-full of beautiful women to erase the memory of Santa Somerville?

Heart thumping, Santa made her way through the café and into the street. Panic was rising in her head like neat alcohol.

She was shocked by how close she had got to letting down her guard with Louis. A few questions here…a smile there. Was that all it took for her to forget everything she knew about him? Everything she knew about herself?

She left both those questions unanswered as she walked swiftly up the street to Merry's chalet.

Her heart was pounding like a drum and she felt unbearably conscious of her inadequacy as a human—as a woman.

Probably Louis had just been spinning her a line, but what had scared her was the thought that he wasn't. That he might have meant what he said. Because then she would have to make a choice.

Only there was no choice—not really. She wasn't that brave. But it hurt so much to admit that, and as she pushed the key in the lock she wished suddenly that Merry was there to make her laugh—

The door opened.

'There you are. I was just coming to look for you.' Glancing down at the skates in Santa's hand, Merry rolled her eyes. 'I knew you wouldn't be able to help yourself. Honestly, this is supposed to be a holiday.'

Santa blinked back her tears and hurled herself into her friend's arms. 'It is now.'

Walking into the Hotel Haensli felt very different this time round, Santa thought, carefully lifting the hem of her skirt so that she didn't tread on it.

For starters, Merry was here. *Merry*. Her friend—her best friend—the one person outside of her family who had always looked out for her and looked after her.

It also helped that they were using the staff entrance.

'Are you okay?'

Merry was looking at her anxiously.

Injecting a bright note into her voice, she nodded. 'I'm fine. Truly. And I'm going to have fun tonight. I promise.'

Smiling, she gave Merry's hand a reassuring squeeze. She knew why her friend was worried about her. As a child she'd been paralyzingly shy. She still was inside, and she didn't have—would never have—Merry's confidence. Fortunately, skating competitively had forced her to meet so many strangers that at least now she could string two words together.

She still wasn't good at big events, but just for once Merry didn't need to be worrying about her—particularly as her friend didn't seem to be her usual serene self. In fact, after their initial joy at seeing one another had faded, for the first time in their lives they had struggled to keep the conversation going.

Probably, she told herself sternly, because Merry was tired after her trip and had a lot more on her mind than Santa. Like helping to organise the biggest, most glamorous party in Europe.

She slipped in her shoes and almost lost her balance, and Merry giggled. It was a running joke between them that Santa moved like a swan out on the ice but a duck on dry land, particularly in heels. But it wasn't just her heels that were making her feel unsteady. There was every chance she was going to see Louis tonight, and she would be lying if she claimed that thought didn't agitate and unnerve her.

Not that Merry could know that.

As predicted, she hadn't told her anything about Louis other than that they'd shared a limo and he had been unbelievably arrogant, and she felt a flicker of guilt at not confiding in her friend. Only she couldn't even begin to think how to lead into that particular conversation. And she didn't have to. Not here and now anyway.

'Will we do?'

Merry was smiling at her. She had borrowed a dress, but it looked as if it had been made for her. She looked beautiful, her pale pink gown offsetting her delicate beauty perfectly.

Santa pretended to consider. 'I think so.'

They were still giggling as they reached the doors of the ballroom. As they embraced one another tightly, Santa swallowed. Her throat was dry and tight, and her hands felt shaky.

As if sensing her nerves, Merry whispered, 'You don't

have to hide in the shadows—or in the bathroom! Stay with me as much as you want.'

But that wasn't going to happen. Not tonight.

Santa shook her head and forced her smile to widen. 'Don't you worry about me. Just go to work before you get into trouble.'

Smile stiffening, she watched Merry scamper away through the throng of guests. Taking a deep breath, she smoothed her dress with a slightly unsteady hand. She had made Merry a promise and she was going to keep it.

Tonight she was going to have fun. She was going to enjoy herself. In fact, she was going to be so busy enjoying herself that she wouldn't even notice if Louis Albemarle was at the party or not.

CHAPTER THREE

SANTA STARED DAZEDLY around the Haensli's ballroom. It looked like something out of a children's picture book—a fairy tale winter wonderland, complete with snow-flecked Christmas trees and a backdrop of spinning snowflakes that looked as if they were made of real diamonds.

Even without the stunning decor it was a beautiful room, high-ceilinged and with huge windows along the length of one side that offered a world-class view of the mountains. It was the perfect setting for the perfect Christmas party.

And she felt like a fraud…an imposter.

Despite her promise to Merry, since her friend had scampered off to work Santa had hardly spoken a word to anyone, and in desperation she took a sip of her cocktail, hoping it might shift the knot of nervous apprehension in her diaphragm.

It ought to. The Figgy Fizz was a delicious festive mix of vodka, Cointreau, plum liqueur and Prosecco, garnished with edible gold spray.

It was also very potent.

She took another cautious sip. Her training schedule more or less made drinking impossible, so she wasn't used to alcohol. Not that she would ever drink much anyway. Growing up, she'd listened to everyone talking about 'getting hammered' and sometimes had thought about doing it. It would certainly have made it easier to fit in.

But she'd always been too scared of the consequences.

How could she get drunk after what had happened to her mother?

She couldn't have looked herself in the eye, much less her father.

Only surely tonight was an exception?

She was on holiday, and Merry was here somewhere. What harm could there be in having a bit of fun? Or even a lot? In fact, now she thought about it, she was absolutely committed to having a whole lot of fun tonight.

She'd show the Duke of Astbury just how wrong he'd been...

She sucked in a breath, a flicker of irritation snaking up inside her. What was he doing in her head?

Back in her head, she should say.

Since she'd left the café yesterday Louis had appeared with frustrating regularity in her thoughts.

Not just his words. Everything about him. Like the way it had seemed the entire café had surreptitiously and collectively focused its attention on him as he'd nudged her foot with his toe...the way he'd brushed his thumb against the rim of his coffee cup...and of course his face—that absurdly handsome face.

How was anyone supposed to *not* think about that face?

She swallowed hard, her throat suddenly dry. After today's session on the ice she was going to have to try. It had been the worst she'd ever skated. She had kept losing focus, making stupid mistakes, and stumbling more than once.

Even now, most of her nervousness was down to the thought of bumping into Louis. As if to prove her point, she felt her eyes dart across the room, involuntarily seeking one particular dark head among the sea of other heads.

But she wasn't going to let this strange, errant attraction get in the way of her goal. She was stronger than that. She would do whatever it took to get him out of her head for good.

And she didn't really have to worry about seeing him at this party. Men like Louis Albemarle were late for everything and women like her always left early, so their paths wouldn't overlap.

She felt her insides tighten as a group of men in immaculate evening dress and women swathed in sequins and satin greeted one another with a flurry of air kisses and, 'Where did you get that dress, darling? You look amazing!'

She felt as if everyone knew each other except her.

But, really, what difference would it make even if she knew every single person here? Look at school. Most of the other students had ignored her, a couple had tolerated her and a loud-mouthed few had pointedly disliked her. Her social life had been limited to a handful of parties, where she'd spent most of her time hiding in the bathroom.

Merry had told her that they were all jealous because she had everything they wanted. Looks, brains, talent... But at school she had been small and skinny, with a brace—she still wore a retainer some nights. As for brains... She had been okay at some subjects, but she certainly hadn't been top of the class. And most of her classmates had never even seen her skate. All they'd known about her 'talent' was that she got to have days off school for competitions.

Merry was just being a good friend, as usual.

Her hand felt cold against the glass and she stared around the room, wishing suddenly that Merry was there with her. But she was a big girl now, and Merry was working. She couldn't expect her to be her babysitter all night.

Taking another sip of her cocktail, she edged away from the excited throng of guests and made her way to the tall windows.

If only she could somehow transfer the poise she found on the ice into real life. Out there, she didn't need alcohol to feel confident. When she skated, she felt powerful and strong and free.

Her heartbeat stalled.

She didn't know how, but Louis had been right about that. It *did* feel as if she was flowing…the stretch of her muscles was unthinking. It was something over which she had no conscious choice, like breathing. It wasn't snarled up with fear of fitting in or saying the wrong thing.

'Excuse me?'

It was an American voice, female.

She spun round, her eyes widening, to find two young women, one blonde and one brunette, staring at her as if they had stumbled across a unicorn.

The blonde, who was wearing a low-cut white dress that oozed over her body without a ripple, bit into the smile curving her scarlet lips. 'You're that skater, aren't you? Santa Somerville.'

Santa felt her face grow warm. She didn't often get recognised away from the rink.

Figure skating was only really on most people's radar during the big, televised competitions, and even then, not everyone connected the make-up-free young woman in casual clothing with the poised skater in her competition costumes with her hair pulled back into a bun.

But tonight, courtesy of Merry's nimble fingers, her hair was in some kind of complicated twisted updo, and as well as wearing mascara and smoky eyeshadow she had painted her lips the colour of ripe berries to match her dress.

'Yes, I am.' She smiled stiffly.

'I knew it,' the brunette said triumphantly. 'I saw you skating yesterday at the rink and I thought I recognised you. You are amazing. I totally loved your last routine.'

Santa smiled. 'Thank you. I wish you'd been one of the judges.'

'Honestly, you're an incredible skater. I look like Bambi when I skate—you know, with my legs going in opposite directions.' As Santa laughed, the brunette waggled her drink. 'The only kind of ice I'm comfortable with comes in a glass.'

'Yeah, you should have one of these.' The blonde held up her own glass. 'It's called an Iceberg. Pastis and vodka. It's absolutely lethal. I'm Lauren, by the way.' Giggling, she clinked glasses with the brunette. 'And this is Chloe.'

'I love your dress.' Chloe sighed. 'You have such great legs.'

'Thank you.' Smiling, and desperate to think of something to say, Santa said quickly, 'I love your bracelets.' Both women were wearing identical bands studded with diamonds around their wrists.

Lauren giggled. 'We gave them to each other last Christmas. We have earrings to match, but we're not wearing them tonight.' She lowered her voice. 'You know the goodie bags they give you when you leave? Apparently Callière is giving away diamond earrings.'

Chloe fanned her face. 'I'd rather have the Duke of Astbury in my goodie bag. He is so hot—and he really knows how to party.'

Santa felt her pulse thud inside her head. It was the first time she had heard his name spoken out loud and her body froze. She felt suddenly like a hunted animal at the thought that he might be somewhere here in the huge ballroom.

Resisting the urge to glance round and check, she smiled as Lauren nodded. 'I know he's wild, but who doesn't love a bad boy?'

Me, Santa thought. *I don't*. What was there to love? Louis was rude and arrogant and spoiled and selfish. And beautiful, and sexier than any man had a right to be, her brain unhelpfully finished.

As both women made enthusiastic noises Santa kept her smile pasted to her face, but their reaction had sent a burn of jealousy through her body.

Only why?

She might be able to admit that Louis was stupidly handsome—privately, at least—but she didn't want him in her life, much less her bed. And yet for some incomprehensible reason it hurt to think of him with another woman.

'Speaking of which…' Catching her eye, Chloe winked. 'There's a private party in one of the suites, and we were thinking we might go and hang out upstairs until it kicks off down here. You should come with us.'

Santa stared at her mutely, her pulse beating out of time. At school and college she'd always been at the bottom of the ladder when it came to the social hierarchy, and she knew that her feeling of exhilaration at this invitation merely proved how uncool she was. But she couldn't stop the warm rush of pleasure from unfurling inside her at being neither an observer nor an intruder.

Oh no—

Her whole body tensed.

The noise in the ballroom was swelling, like an orchestra warming up. But somehow, through all the chatter, she heard quite distinctly the high, purring laughter of not one but several women. More specifically, the blissed-out purr of women who had just opened their stockings on Christmas morning to find not just the deeds to a diamond mine but the mine's owner.

She gritted her teeth.

There was only one man who could cause such a stir among members of her sex.

Her heart lurched. She could practically see Louis, his taunting blue eyes drifting over the women in their brightly coloured dresses, enjoying the view. No doubt he was planning on taking a closer look later on. Not that she cared. They were welcome to him.

But as she turned her head she caught a glimpse of brown hair, and just like that her bravado drained away.

Downing her drink, she snatched another from a passing waiter and turned to Chloe, smiling brightly. 'I'd love that. Shall I follow you?'

By the time they reached the lift her glass was already half empty and the alcohol was rising to her head in a rush. But now that they had left the ballroom, and the chances of bumping into Louis were fading, she felt calmer again—and a little bit euphoric. She had never been invited to a private party before. Or at least not one that wasn't either a family event or part of her job as a Bryson's Ices ambassador.

She felt a tiny prickle of guilt that she was leaving the ballroom. Merry had gone to so much trouble to get her a ticket. But she knew her friend would understand. And it would only be for a short time. Maybe she would take a selfie to show her, she thought, as the lift arrived and Lauren grabbed her hand and dragged her inside.

She barely registered what floor they were on as the lift stopped and the doors opened. Her head was spinning, and she was too busy trying to make sense of what Lauren and Chloe were saying.

As they stopped in front of a door it opened abruptly, flooding the hallway with a pounding bassline and a buzz of conversation as a tall blond man with a sharp, pale face swayed towards them.

Chloe gave a scream. 'Oh, my goodness, Sebastian! I didn't know you were here.'

Everyone except Santa screamed too.

'She used to date Sebastian back in the day. They were at Beau Soleil together,' Lauren said loudly in her ear as they made their way through a throng of people into the room. 'His father's a prince of somewhere with a really long name that I can't pronounce.'

Santa nodded wordlessly, but she wasn't really listening.

So this was how the other half lived.

She gazed across the room, her heart hammering hard. It was a microworld of enviable luxury. Pale grey walls, an immense fireplace with an actual fire, and a deep private balcony with breathtaking views of the snow-covered peaks outside.

Not that anyone was looking at the view.

Her eyes darted to the dark green velvet sofas where not one but three famous film stars were deep in conversation. Everyone was too busy being seen to notice anyone else.

Not everyone.

Suddenly aware that she was being watched, she turned, and her breath caught in her throat, her blood freezing.

Louis was standing about ten feet away, an empty glass hanging loosely from his fingers. Like every other man there he was dressed in black tie, but he still hugged all the attention, thanks to his stunningly handsome face.

A face that was currently as still as the mountains outside and about as friendly.

As his eyes locked with hers she felt a shiver of ice and fire flicker over her skin, and her heartbeat tripped over itself like it did when she popped her jumps out on the ice. Her head was spinning again...only this time it was with panic, not alcohol.

For a moment his being there made no sense. He was downstairs in the ballroom...

Except that he clearly wasn't. And just as clearly she suddenly knew that if anyone was going to be at some exclusive private party then it would be Louis.

She swore silently. Why had she drunk those cocktails so fast? Why had she drunk them at all? Louis was the last man she wanted to see, particularly when he was dressed like that.

She stole a glance across the room, her gaze taking in the hard, high cheekbones, the straight, aristocratic nose and teasing mouth. It hurt to look at him. More than that, there was something about him that made her feel unsteady, vulnerable, out of control. And she knew that it was a feeling that had everything to do with bodies and skin and heat.

In other words: sex.

Move, she told herself as he started to weave between the guests towards her. But her legs felt as if they had frozen solid, and she could only stand and stare as he stopped in front of her.

Hoping that her face didn't look as hot as it felt, she glared at him. 'I can't say I'm surprised to see you here.'

'I should hope not,' he drawled. 'I, however, am a little surprised to see you. But perhaps not as surprised as your sponsor would be.' His gaze dropped to the empty cocktail glass in her hand and he smiled mockingly. 'Are you drunk, Santa baby?'

Was she what?

Santa stared at him in outrage. 'Don't call me that,' she snapped, fighting an impulse to slap his handsome face. Ignoring her accelerating pulse, she angled her chin up to meet his gaze. 'What I am is none of your concern, Your Grace. Now, if you don't mind, I'm going to find my friends. Oh, and please don't feel that you have to come over and talk to me again. I really won't be the least bit offended if you don't.'

She had intended to march past him with her head held high, but he stepped sideways and blocked her, his blue eyes locking with hers.

'If you were a man, I'd ask you to step outside for talking to me like that.'

Her heart felt as if it was pounding in her throat. 'If you were a man, I'd be worried. But, as we both know you're a spoiled little boy, now, let me pass or I'll call Security and have you thrown out.'

'Of my own party?'

Staring at Santa's furious face, Louis felt his entire jaw tense, but he barely registered his anger or hers. His head was still reeling from the moment when he'd looked up and seen her standing there. Unsurprisingly, given how they had parted company at the café.

His shoulders stiffened as he remembered her icy disdain. He had never been turned down with such cool, unblinking certainty. In fact, he'd never been turned down. Not to his face, anyway.

Yet here she was. In his suite. Still swatting at him with those imperious, judgemental little smiles.

Some things had changed, though. Last time they'd met she had been wrapped up against the cold. Now...

Pulse accelerating, he looked down at Santa in silence. After she'd stormed out of the café he'd been so frustrated at not having had the last word that he'd ended up looking her up on the internet.

She had started competing as a child. Despite a very promising career, for no apparent reason she had lost form a few years ago. Now, though, not only was she steadily inching her way up the rankings, with several bronze medals and a silver in her last few competitions, she'd also netted herself a sponsorship deal with Bryson's Ices. As their brand ambassador, she'd even had some ridiculous ice cream named after her: the Santa Swizzle, a sickly sounding confection involving a vanilla snow cone dipped in white chocolate with a spun sugar crown.

He wasn't surprised Bryson's Ices had picked her. They were a family brand, run by a devoted family man, and with her shy, serious smile, her wide blue eyes and enamelled cheeks Santa ticked all the boxes.

His gaze swept over Santa. What did surprise him was that dress...

It might have long sleeves and a neckline that modestly skimmed her collarbone, but it was anything but shy, he thought, unable to look anywhere except at the long length of smooth bare leg peeking out from between one of the two thigh-high slits at the front of the glossy dark purple skirt.

He felt his body stiffen, responding to the glimpse of bare skin like a dog to a stick as his gaze travelled down to her teetering red heels.

Why hadn't she just stuck to the rules? She wasn't supposed to be here, dressed like that. Hell, she wasn't supposed to be here at all.

Hardening his gaze to match his groin, he took a step forward. 'You want to call Security? Be my guest. Except you're not, are you? My guest, I mean.' The softness in his voice in no way disguised the taunting note in his voice. 'You're just a gate crasher. Whereas I am the Duke of Astbury.'

Purple was definitely her colour, he thought, his gaze homing in on the berry-stained mouth that was currently pursing into a pout. He watched her fingers curl into fists, and then her outrage bubbled up. He caught another distracting glimpse of her legs as she took a step towards him.

'You are a horrible person.'

'So you keep saying and yet you can't keep away from me, can you?'

Her chin jutted. 'I didn't come here to see you.'

'That's right,' he mocked. 'Because you are—' raising his hands, he made quotation marks in the air '—"not interested" in me.'

'I'm not,' she snapped.

He glanced over at her flushed cheeks and saw the pulse leaping frantically against the delicate skin of her throat. He felt his body grow even harder. He wanted her and he knew she felt the same way. She just didn't want to admit it, to herself, much less to him.

'Then perhaps you need to tell that to your optic nerves.' He accompanied his words with a cynical smile. 'Because you can't take your eyes off me.'

She glared at him. 'You are impossibly arrogant.'

'And you are a hypocrite.' Still smiling, he watched a faint tremor sweep over her body as she fought for control. 'You might not like it. You might not like me. But admit it: you want me.'

Now her cheeks flamed with colour. 'In your dreams.'

Louis stared at her, a beat of heat pulsing down his spine. 'If you want it to be real, baby, you're going to have to ask.'

'What?' Her eyes widened to saucer-like dimensions and she made a noise somewhere between a gulp and a gasp.

'You heard,' he said softly.

Glancing over her shoulder, as if someone else might be listening, she shook her head. 'I'm not having this conversation with you here.'

'Fine,' he said softly, deliberately misunderstanding her. 'Let's go somewhere more private.'

He knew she would never take the bait, but he couldn't stop himself from giving the line a little tug, just to watch her squirm.

Her fingers twitched, and just for a second or two he half expected to feel her hand against his cheek, but instead she made to move past him. Only her shoe caught in the hem of her dress and she stumbled.

He reached for her automatically, his hands sliding around her waist to catch her, and he felt a sharp sting of satisfaction as her breath hitched in her throat. But there was no fear in her eyes, just fire, and he knew why she was so angry.

It was the same reason he was angry.

She felt it too—that sexual pull, that heat and hunger he couldn't remember feeling before. She was just as in thrall to it as he was, and the thought of hearing her confess her desire almost unmanned him.

'Face it, Santa, you want me. You're just too proud to admit it.'

'And *you're* just too used to getting your own way... getting what you want.' Her eyes blazed like marquise sapphires. 'But not every woman finds your charms irresistible, Louis.'

He heard the challenge in her voice, and suddenly nothing mattered more than finding some way to dent her infuriatingly lofty complacency. 'Are you sure about that, Santa?'

For a few half-seconds she stared up at him mutely, wide-eyed, her lips curling disdainfully, and then he pulled her against him with a sudden jerky movement and brought his mouth down on hers.

He felt her hands press against his shoulders and then she leaned into him, her fingers sliding down to grip his biceps. Lust punched him in the gut like a prizefighter.

Now it was his turn to almost lose his footing.

Her mouth was soft, like the softest rose petal, and his head swimming, heart pounding, blood racing, he parted her lips and deepened the kiss.

She tasted so sweet. Dark, like berries and wine. Wanting more, he wrapped one hand around her waist, the other tightening on her hip as she pulled him closer, so that he could feel her small, firm breasts pressing against the muscled wall of his chest.

Her kiss was frantic, almost clumsy, as if she was out of practice, but there was something exciting about her lack of proficiency. It felt real in a way that kissing other women didn't. The blindness of her passion, the way she was melting into him, made him feel harder and hotter than he'd ever been in his life.

His hand slid round to the dip in her back, fingers splaying possessively over the curve of her bottom. Around them, the sounds of the party were fading. He felt the slide of her bare thigh between his legs and his stomach clenched and a savage, clamouring need jackknifed through his body.

'Excuse me, Your Grace.'

Behind him, someone—a man—cleared his throat, and as if a spell had been broken Santa stumbled backwards out of his arms.

The noise of the party hit him like a train.

He stared dazedly down at her, shocked at the sudden and uncontrollable passion that had flared between them. Blood was roaring in his ears.

He had wanted to get under her skin. Instead, she had got under his.

Utterly disorientated, Santa stared up at Louis. Her whole body was pulsing with a hunger that was so powerful she had to struggle not to reach over and grab him by the lapels and beg him to kiss her again.

'I'm very sorry to bother you, Your Grace...' The man standing behind Louis took a tentative step forward.

'Not now, Herr Widner,' Louis snapped, without looking round.

He looked as dazed as she felt, she thought, her heart thumping against her ribs. Streaks of colour highlighted his magnificent cheekbones, and his blue eyes were blazing like a winter sunrise.

'My apologies, Your Grace.'

She watched, her thoughts scrambling for a footing, as Herr Widner gave a nervous smile and Louis finally swung round to look at him.

'But you did ask us to let you know when the security team arrived.'

Louis swore under his breath. 'And now I know. So if you wouldn't mind?'

Santa could tell that Herr Widner was forcing the smile that was stretched so determinedly across his face. 'Of course, Your Grace. But I will need your signature.'

He held out a tablet to Louis, who snatched it out of his hand.

'Fine. Where do I sign?' he snarled.

Santa breathed out shakily. Shock at what had just happened, and the part she'd played in it, was starting to chill her skin and, glancing round, she saw that quite a few of the guests were stealing surreptitious glances at her.

What was she doing? Why was she still standing here? Hadn't she made a big enough fool of herself for one night?

The memory of that night with Nathan was suddenly fresh in her head, and she was struggling to breathe. She certainly didn't need to hang around for any humiliating post-mortem, and before she even knew what she was doing she had grabbed the hem of her skirt and spun round.

She felt rather than saw Louis turn towards her, maybe even reach for her, but by then she had bolted through the nearest gap in the crowd and was skirting the perimeter of the room, moving swiftly, heading for the door.

Only she had gone the wrong way.

No, no, no—it was a bedroom.

Heart thumping, she tapped a woman in a gorgeous sequined dress on the arm. 'Sorry…is there a bathroom?'

'Just there.' The woman swayed, pointing. 'Don't be long, though,' she slurred. 'We're all heading downstairs now.'

But Santa wasn't listening.

Please let it be empty, she pleaded silently.

It was. She shut the door and locked it, her breath coming in panicky gasps. Her hands were shaking, and they felt hot and clammy. She made her way to the sink and turned on the cold tap. Staring at her reflection, she felt her heart thumping against her ribs. Her eyes were huge and dazed and her mouth looked pinkly swollen.

It was like looking at a stranger.

Lifting her hand, she touched her lower lip. She felt like a stranger too, and it wasn't just her lip that felt different. There was an unfamiliar ache deep in her pelvis... an exquisite, tingling warmth that she'd never felt before.

Turning off the tap, she dried her hands, trying to tame her heartbeat, trying to contain, to smooth away, the memory of that kiss.

Only could you smooth away something that had torn a hole in the firmament of your life?

She breathed out shakily.

It was quiet on the other side of the door now. Everyone must have gone downstairs.

And so should she.

But what if Louis was waiting for her?

A shiver of heat ran down her spine. If she saw him again, on his own, she wasn't sure she would be able to resist him.

Maybe it would be safer to wait just a little longer.

She couldn't believe what had just happened. She should have slapped him. Or pushed him away. But she hadn't done either of those things. Instead she had melted into him like butter on a warm knife.

But it hadn't been all her fault.

How could she have known that kisses could be like that? She had only ever kissed one other man, and kissing Louis was nothing like kissing Nathan.

The touch of his mouth had stunned her. It had been a sensual exploration that had made her head swim and her body feel hot and tight with need. A need that hadn't been rational or understandable, yet had felt shockingly, devastatingly compelling.

And it wasn't as if her uncontrollable response had been private...

How many people had seen them kiss?

Her mouth trembled. None that would care. They were

all rich and famous and they all knew Louis. They knew what he was like.

She did too—and that was the worst part. She knew what he was like and it hadn't made any difference to the way she'd acted because she wasn't any different. She was still that same lonely girl who wanted to be special to someone for something other than her skating.

Only here she was...still hiding in the bathroom at a party.

Her gaze jumped across the room, from the huge sunken bath to an alpaca fleece rug that covered half the floor, and then over to the voluptuous curved white sofa beside the window, with its spectacular mountain view.

It was a very palatial bathroom, but a bathroom nonetheless.

She breathed out shakily. The party was over for her. She couldn't face meeting Louis again, and if Merry saw her she would know instantly that something had happened. She didn't want her friend to feel she had to worry about her tonight of all nights. No, it was time to go home.

Smoothing down her dress, she took a couple of steadying breaths and turned the door handle.

She frowned. What was wrong with it? She turned it the other way, then rattled it. But the door stayed stubbornly shut.

'Hello? Is anyone there?' She banged on the door. 'Hello? Can anyone hear me?'

But there was no reply. Because of course everyone had gone to the party.

Biting her lip, she sat down on the sofa. She wasn't going to call Merry—she just wasn't. Maybe she could call Reception. But she didn't really want to have to explain why she was in Louis Albemarle's bathroom.

Feeling suddenly exhausted, she gazed out of the window, watching the snowflakes spiral to the ground.

There was no need to panic. She just needed to think

of the best way out of this situation. Only she felt so tired. Not just tired of being locked in this bathroom, but tired of being so timid, so scared. Scared of kissing and being kissed. Scared of where kissing might lead. And most of all scared of what Louis might say afterwards. Of the look on his face...

She shivered. She hated being this person. Being someone who let fear rule them. Being so cowardly. None of this would have happened if she hadn't been scared of looking into Louis's eyes and finding Nathan staring back at her.

Careless of her hair and make-up, she lay down, pressing her face against the doe-soft Alcantara. It reminded her of her mother's coat, the one she'd always worn to the ice rink. And, feeling a little calmer, she closed her eyes, pressing her hands against the dip of her stomach where she had felt that traitorous, melting thrill.

The night seemed to go on for ever. Every half an hour or so she thought about calling someone and pulled out her phone, only for something to stop her. In the end she just lay there, watching the snow fall and at some point she must have dozed off.

She woke with a start. Outside it was still snowing, but it was no longer dark. Her heart began to pound and, pulling out her phone, she stared at the screen in dismay.

It couldn't be that time.

She couldn't have slept for that long.

Only she had.

Standing up, she almost ran across the room. She began to twist the handle, but as she did so the door abruptly opened.

'What the—'

She heard a familiar deep male voice swear, and then, looking up, met an equally familiar pair of captivating blue eyes.

There was a beat or two of silence, and then Louis said

softly, 'You know, I'm sure there's a perfectly simple explanation for you being here, but please don't feel that you have to share it with me.' His eyes narrowed. 'I really won't be the least bit offended if you don't.'

CHAPTER FOUR

STARING DOWN AT SANTA, Louis gave a careless wave of his hand. 'Oh, and the way out is through that door, just in case you're wondering. You probably missed it last time, seeing as you were in such a rush to leave.'

Spinning on his heel, he turned and walked back into the bedroom, resisting the temptation to slam the door behind him. If he hadn't been so knackered, he would have kept on walking—out of his suite and all the way to the heliport at Davos.

Frankly, it would be the only way he could guarantee that he wouldn't pull Santa into his arms and carry on from where they had left off.

Instead, he crossed the room to the decanter of whisky and poured himself a generous measure. Swearing softly, he picked up the glass, downed it in two mouthfuls and poured another.

He was quite tempted to drink the entire decanter.

A muscle ticked in his jaw. The last few hours had been some of the most baffling and frustrating of his life. If it wasn't enough that Herr Widner had interrupted them, by the time he'd finally shaken off the assistant manager and his tablet Santa had bolted.

His mouth thinned, a beat of anger pulsing over his skin. Even now he couldn't quite believe it.

Women didn't usually flee from his kisses, but Santa

had done just that. One minute she was there in his arms, her body melting into him, her soft mouth fused with his, and the next—

Gone. Disappeared. Almost as if he'd imagined her.

His mouth twisted. Oh, he'd imagined her, all right— before and since. Only in his head she had mostly been naked, and always eager and frantic for his touch, not running from it.

He had been too stunned and proud to ask anyone if they had seen her, and he was only too aware of how it must look to the other guests. Louis Albemarle being stood up by a woman...

It was untenable that anyone should think he cared, or that Santa was in any way special, and so he'd forced himself to act as if she was just an *amuse-bouche* before the evening ahead.

His jaw clenched. By rights that was what she should have been.

Truthfully, he had—in part, at least—kissed her out of curiosity, out of a desire to taste her. But only to prove to himself, and her, that she wasn't special. In the main, though, he had been driven by a devilish impulse to get under her skin, to have the satisfaction of wiping that haughty, condescending look off her beautiful face.

Basically, he'd failed on both counts. And now, as if he needed any reminder of that, she was here in his suite.

Make that in his bedroom, he thought sourly, turning as Santa stalked towards him, her blue eyes narrowing accusingly.

'Where have you been? I couldn't get the door to open. There's something wrong with the lock.'

Draining his glass, he shrugged. 'Why didn't you just call Reception? They would have come and let you out.'

He watched two flags of colour rise along her cheekbones. 'I don't know. I suppose I wasn't thinking straight.'

The words came out in a rush, the colour in her cheeks

deepening as she glanced at the bed, and he knew that, like him, she was remembering those mind-blowing minutes when their bodies had gone into meltdown.

Putting his empty glass down beside the decanter, he rested his eyes on her face, his muscles tensing, his body aching with an excruciating burn of frustration. A frustration that was unlikely to be eased any time soon, judging by the outrage shining in Santa's eyes.

Although, frankly, what did she have to be outraged about? She hadn't been left at a party with a head full of questions and a hard-on.

He gritted his teeth.

'Not thinking straight?' He glanced at his watch. 'Surely it didn't take you five hours to unravel your thoughts?'

That had her lifting her chin, bringing her blue eyes up to his. 'I must have fallen asleep. But I wouldn't have needed to *unravel my thoughts* anyway if you hadn't kissed me. In fact, I wouldn't even have been in your bathroom.'

Shaking his head, he held her gaze, a pulse of irritation and disbelief beating through his body. 'I might have known you'd make this my fault. Go on, then. Tell me,' he ordered, taking a step towards her. 'How am I responsible for any of this?'

She raised her chin, blue eyes flashing like a police car at the scene of a crime. 'Don't be more of a jerk than you are already. You know how... What are you doing?'

Her voice rose to an indignant squeak at the end of the sentence as he sat down heavily on the bed and began toeing off his shoe.

'Are you getting undressed?'

'Why?' He stopped what he was doing and let his gaze fix on her mouth. 'Do you want to pick up from where we left off?'

She drew in a sharp little breath, her blue eyes locking

with his as she shook her head violently. 'No, I do not,' she snapped.

His shoulders tensed at the fierce conviction in her voice. *Not that he cared,* he thought savagely. Wrapped up in that gleaming satin, she might look, and taste, like the most tempting piece of candy, but there were plenty of other less aggravating ways to get a sugar rush.

'Then that makes two of us.' He forced himself to hold her gaze, as if he weren't the least bit affected by the memory of those few heated moments in the room next door. 'I think we're done here, don't you?'

Raging inside, feeling thwarted on so many levels, he began to pull his bow tie loose. He felt wrecked, and not only with alcohol. He was tired—the kind of tired that had as much to do with mood as physical fatigue—and drinking had only worsened that mood. Right now he just wanted this night—day—whatever it was—to end.

She gave him one of those delicate, needle-sharp smiles that cut to the bone. 'There is no "we", Your Grace.'

'Keep telling yourself that if you want, but it won't make it any truer.' Meeting her icy stare, he let a mocking smile pull at the corners of his mouth. 'I might have kissed you first, but as I remember it you were a fully active participant when *we* were kissing.'

And he could certainly remember it, he thought, his body stirring at the memory of how his senses had screamed to have her. Watching her chin jerk up swiftly, he knew she did too, and he let his smile grow.

'In fact, I'd go as far to say that *you* were champing at the bit.'

Two spots of colour spread across her cheeks as she shot him an icy stare. 'You can't help yourself, can you? A decent man would never be so crude, but I suppose I shouldn't be surprised—'

His eyes narrowed on her face. 'You want to talk about

decency? How about we talk about you just up and vanishing without so much as a word?'

'There was nothing to say,' she protested. 'It shouldn't have happened. It was a mistake.'

'You're damned right it was. One I'm planning on forgetting asap.'

Her sharp intake of breath wrenched at something inside him, but he told himself he didn't care. She had hardly minced her words, had she?

'Now, if you don't mind, I think I'm going to quit while I'm behind and get some sleep.'

'*Sleep?*'

Now what? She was staring at him as if he'd suddenly sprouted antlers.

'No, you are *not* going to sleep, Louis.' Her voice was cold and crisp, like new fallen snow, but there was an edge to it too, almost like panic. 'I need to get out of here.'

Santa felt her heartbeat accelerate as Louis looked up at her irritably. 'So go. I'm not stopping you, am I? In fact, let me help you leave.'

Before she could react, he stood up and reached for her arm, and began frog-marching her across the bedroom.

'Let me go.' She shook him off, her anger swept aside by a rush of panic at his touch and her body's instant, indisputable response to it.

Her heart bumped against her ribs. At first when the door had opened she'd simply felt relief at being freed. Now, though, that relief had faded, and there was nothing to filter the impact of his devastating dark looks or the lean, hard lines of his body in that impeccably tailored tuxedo.

Her pulse twitched and she felt her face grow hot as she remembered the urgent press of his mouth and the heat of his hands burning through the fabric of her dress. Remembered, too, her own feverish, uninhibited reaction.

She hadn't instigated what had happened, but she'd come damn close. Another second and she would have reached up and clasped his face, pressed a desperate kiss to his mouth.

Louis was right. She might not like him, but she wanted him.

But even if that was true, what difference did it make?

Nothing had changed. She was still the same woman she had been with Nathan, and the idea of revealing her 'real' self to Louis made her stomach twist painfully.

And yet she wasn't sure she was strong enough to resist this attraction she felt for him.

Taking a step back, she folded her arms in front of her stomach defensively. 'I'm not going anywhere.'

'What are you talking about now?' His eyebrows snapped together and, shaking his dark head, he held up his hands in mock surrender. 'Okay, I'm done with this. Just go back to your room, Santa.' He stepped backwards, his blue eyes narrowed again, his fine-boned features cold and set. 'No need to say goodbye. You can just sneak off when my back's turned. You're good at that, aren't you?'

She hadn't sneaked off. She had run—run from the wild and uncontrollable passion that had flared between them. Or, more specifically, from the humiliating knowledge that she could not sustain or arouse that passion in private.

But she certainly wasn't about to share that with Louis, a man whose sexual prowess was the subject of very public record.

'I can't go to my room.' Santa stared at him, hesitating, her heart thudding. 'I don't have one.' She spoke quickly, trying to outrun the sudden nervousness zigzagging down her spine as his eyes locked with hers. 'I'm not a guest here. I'm staying with a friend. In town.'

There was a long, pulsing silence. 'You have to be kidding me?' he said softly. He covered the space between them in three swift strides, stopping in front of her, his mouth a perfectly executed curl of contempt. A muscle ticked in his jaw. 'No wonder you didn't want to call Reception.'

'I had an invitation to the party,' she said icily.

'Just not a room at the hotel.'

Forcing herself to meet his taunting smile, she straightened her shoulders. 'No, I don't have a room. Which is why I need help to get back to the chalet.'

'So call your friend...?' He let a silence fall between them as he waited for her to provide a name.

'Merry,' she said finally, reluctantly.

'Really?' He raised one dark eyebrow. 'Okay... So call Merry, or one of Santa's other little helpers, and she can come and help you.'

Her stomach clenched. There was no way she was going to call Merry. It wasn't fair to get her friend involved in what was essentially a spectacular mess of her own making. Particularly not when that mess was happening here in the Haensli, where Merry worked.

She scowled at him. 'I can't. That's why I need your help.'

He stared at her for a beat, his blue eyes widening with incredulity, and then he must have realised she was being serious because he started laughing.

'What's so funny?' she snapped.

'You're joking, right?' His smile had transformed into something closer to a sneer. 'Why the hell should I help you?'

The panic and confusion of the last few hours morphed into a flare of anger. Stepping towards him, she stabbed a finger against the wall of his chest. 'Because it's your fault I'm here. And because if someone sees me dressed like this, coming out of your suite, it'll look like I spent the night—' She broke off.

'With me.' He finished her sentence.

'Yes, with you,' she returned icily. 'And you might not care about your reputation, but I do care about mine.'

Louis didn't reply. He just stared at her in silence. And the look of contempt and disgust on his face tugged at a memory she had tried her hardest to erase—a memory that still had the power to make her feel small and stupid and tawdry.

Only why was this *her* fault? Louis was the one who had pressed the play button.

Ignoring the jittery feeling in her legs, she lifted her chin. 'As I remember it, you kissed me in front of a room full of people, so you can damn well help me now.'

His lip curled. 'And what exactly would you have me do?'

'I just need to borrow some clothes. Maybe some shoes.'

He was staring at her now as if she had suggested dressing up as a pantomime horse. 'Great idea. Yeah, I can see *that* not drawing any attention to you.'

Now that she'd said it out loud, it did sound ridiculous. Only she didn't have a Plan B.

'Is that your idea of help? Because—' she began, but he cut her off with a withering look.

'Enough, okay? There's only one possible way you're going to get downstairs without anyone seeing you. You're going to have to use the fire escape. It comes out at the side of the hotel, so you won't have to go through Reception.'

Turning, he began to walk towards the door and she stared after him, stunned by this sudden and apparently flawless solution, and by the realisation that she was finally coming to it. The moment she'd been so sure she wanted to happen.

Only now it was here, the thought that she would never see Louis again was not as comforting as she'd imagined it would be.

'I thought you were in a hurry?'

Louis's voice brought her head up with a snap. He was standing by the door, scowling, and gratefully she felt a clarifying flare of anger.

'I am,' she said.

'Then let's go,' he said irritably as she stopped in front of him.

Her heart-rate picked up as he yanked open the door, and some of her nervousness must have shown on her face because he frowned.

'Look, Santa, it's crazy to worry about your reputation.'

'Is it?' she said stiffly.

'Absolutely.' He nodded, his eyes dropping down to her shoes. 'You're probably going to break your neck in those lethal little red numbers anyway, so it won't matter.'

Louis had been right—*again*, she thought ten minutes later, as she finally reached the bottom of the fire escape. She might find skating as easy as walking, but four-inch heels and ice were not a good combination.

'I can take it from here,' she said, rubbing a hand over her arm.

After the warmth of the hotel the air felt incredibly cold, and she wasn't exactly dressed for snow. But, snow or no snow, she had to get back to the chalet. Straightening her shivering shoulders, she took a teetering step forward.

Louis held her gaze. 'That's good. Carry on like that and you should be there by lunchtime.'

Ignoring his snide tone, she took another step—and gasped as the smooth sole slipped from under her.

Louis's hand pulled her upright. Her heart beat in double-quick time and she jerked out of his grip, almost losing her footing again.

He swore softly. 'You are the most stubborn woman I've ever met. Just take my arm. In fact, take this too.'

Muttering something under his breath, he shrugged out of his jacket and draped it over her shoulders. It was heavy, and knowing that the heat of his skin was now warming her body felt oddly intimate. As she slipped her arms into the silk-lined sleeves she felt suddenly light-headed, imagining how it would feel to have Louis's warm body on hers. Beside her. Inside her.

That thought effectively silenced her for the next ten minutes as they slipped and slid over the snow-covered pavements.

'This is it,' Santa said, glancing up at Merry's small chalet. She could see there were no lights on inside and she felt a flutter of relief. She had done it, and without having to bother Merry.

She shrugged out of his jacket and handed it back to him. The sudden chill made her skin tighten and she felt suddenly ridiculously bereft, as if she had lost something personal and important.

'Thank you,' she said quickly. 'For walking me back."

His eyes locked with hers and for a second they both stared at each other, their warm breath curling through the cool air. Then he reached out and gently touched her earlobe.

She saw it in his eyes at the same time as she felt it low in her belly. A flicker of heat—needle-sharp and impossible to ignore. And suddenly what had happened last night didn't feel like a mistake any more.

'You missed out on your goodie bag. Have it as an early Christmas present on me,' he said softly. 'Just don't tell anyone. I don't want my bad boy reputation ruined.'

Heart pounding, she watched as he turned and walked slowly back down the street.

Inside the chalet it was blissfully warm. Slipping off her shoes, she crept into her room and closed the door. She was incredibly tired and, undressing quickly, she slid under the covers.

But as soon as she lay down she felt suddenly and unaccountably wide awake.

She breathed in deeply. Usually if she couldn't sleep

she worked through her routines in her head, tracing out the patterns on the ice. Only today her head wouldn't co-operate. She exhaled shakily. Instead, and for no good or logical reason, all she could see was Louis's glittering blue eyes, watching her intently as his hands traced patterns on her naked body.

What the—?

Rolling over, Louis grabbed a pillow and pressed it over his head. Who the hell was ringing his room?

Head pounding, he gritted his teeth, waiting for it to stop.

Thank goodness.

As the room fell silent he reached over and irritably pulled the phone jack out of the wall, falling back against the pillow with a grunt.

Only now he was awake.

He kept his eyes closed. He was not ready to wake up and face the world. A world that suddenly seemed very dull.

But why? Nothing had changed.

He was still the Duke of Astbury. He was still the CEO of a global jewellery brand with an A-list clientele. And after the success of last night's goodie bag rollout he was almost certainly one step closer to reaching his goal of being able to buy out the shareholders.

Only for some reason that didn't seem to matter quite as much this morning as it had every other morning for the last six months.

He frowned up at the ceiling. It made no sense for him to feel like that. He'd pretty much curtailed his entire life to make that goal. So why suddenly had his priorities been shifted?

Not shifted, he thought irritably. *Diverted*.

Derailed. By Santa.

Grimacing, he sat up and swung his legs out of bed.

Normally if he wanted a woman it was just a question of when and where and how often. But with Santa the answers to those questions were, frustratingly, *never, nowhere* and *zero*—in that order.

And that was why he was feeling like this. Especially after what had happened last night. Or rather what hadn't happened.

His heart began to pound against his ribs as he remembered how panicky Santa had been about being seen with him.

Could she really be that bothered about her reputation? He felt his shoulders tense sharply. Or was there another reason for her not wanting even a whisper of scandal? Did she have some man at home? A faithful lover waiting in the wings for his skater girl?

The thought of some anonymous man holding Santa in his arms, of her hands splayed over his back, guiding his movements, cut like the flick of a knife.

Not that he cared *per se* about her sex life, he told himself quickly. Santa wasn't special. No woman would ever be that again—he'd learned his lesson with Marina.

Nor was she even his type. She was snippy and stubborn and far too judgemental for him. He knew he could have any woman he wanted. The only reason he wanted her—the only logical reason—was because he couldn't have her.

His mouth twisted. Sexual frustration—that was what this feeling was. And once he'd left Klosters he'd forget all about Santa Somerville and her endless legs, lustrous dark hair and lush mouth—

Scowling as his groin hardened, he stood up and began tugging his shirt free. He'd been too tired this morning to undress before he fell into bed, so was it surprising that he couldn't shake off this mood? He was still in yesterday's clothes—therefore he was still in yesterday's headspace.

But that was nothing a shower and breakfast in bed followed by an hour or two on the slopes couldn't fix.

Wandering back into the bedroom ten minutes later, he felt one hundred percent better. Now all he needed was a plate of Eggs Benedict and some black coffee and he would be ready to take on the windy black run down to the village of Wolfgang.

He was about to pick up the phone and call Room Service when he remembered he had switched off his own phone last night. Nick would probably be climbing the walls.

Should he call him?

He didn't want to ruin his breakfast.

But why should it be ruined? He'd drunk a lot last night, mainly to blot out the pulse of hunger still beating a path around his body. But other than that he'd been a model guest, no housekeeping required. Better still, practically every woman at the party had been wearing Callière diamond earrings—including two princesses and several members of rock royalty.

No, for once, Nick would be singing his praises. And to his surprise he found that he was actually looking forward to speaking to his CMO.

When he switched on his phone, twenty messages pinged into his inbox. Nineteen were from Nick. One was from Donald Muir, the most exacting of his shareholders. Clearly news of his success had travelled fast.

Just as he was congratulating himself the phone rang, and probably for the first time in his life he answered it right away.

'Nick—how are you this fine morning?' Sprawling back on the bed, he switched his phone to speaker. He wanted to hear this loud and clear.

'How do you *think* I am?'

As Nick's voice boomed into the bedroom Louis felt his

whole body tense. He'd been expecting his CMO to sound jubilant—euphoric, even. Instead he sounded furious.

'I thought you'd be happy...' he said slowly. Was this some kind of elaborate joke?

There was a stunned silence at the other end of the phone. Then, 'Happy? Why on earth would I be happy, Louis?'

He heard Nick swear, and immediately he sobered up. No matter how annoyed or exasperated he'd been over the years, he'd never heard his CMO swear.

'You know, I have been your biggest, your only cheerleader. I've made excuses. I've covered your arse. And this is how you repay me—' Losing control of his voice, Nick broke off.

Louis frowned. A flicker of unease slid down his spine. 'What are you talking about?'

'I'm talking about your one-night stand with the ice cream girl.'

'Santa?' He sat up slowly, his heart beating out of time.

'Yes, Santa. The skater. Bryson's Ices. Little Miss Squeaky Clean.'

'I know who she is, Nick,' Louis said coolly.

'I should hope so, given that you spent the night with her.'

'No, that's not—' he began.

But Nick cut him off. 'Save it for someone who doesn't know you, Louis.'

He heard his CMO groan.

'I can't believe you could be so stupid. What on earth possessed you to hook up with that particular woman? And at the Haensli party, of all places.'

'I didn't hook up with her,' he said hotly. 'That's not what happened.'

'So you *didn't* kiss her in front of a whole bunch of people at a party in your room?'

Louis felt his chest tighten. To say that this conversation

was not going as he'd planned would be the mother of all understatements. In fact, it had gone completely off-piste.

'It was just a kiss, Nick.'

'So you didn't see her after that?' his CMO persisted.

'No… Well, yes… But it's not what you think—'

'You don't get it, do you?' Nick interrupted him again. 'It's not what I think that matters here. It's what the shareholders think. It's what the public thinks. Look at the photos, Louis. Oh, and while you're at it you might want to watch the video too.'

Video! His shoulders stiffened with shock. *What video?*

Standing up, he walked across the room and flipped open his laptop. He hesitated, then typed in his own name.

His breathing stalled as he stared down at the screen.

The Duke of Hazard!

That was the caption above a picture of Santa clutching his arm at the top of the fire escape.

No, this couldn't be happening.

What was more, it hadn't actually happened.

Only nobody was going to believe that, looking at these photos.

Somebody must have snapped them with a phone. They were not paparazzi standard, but they were still clear enough to see his face, and Santa's.

He scrolled down the page, his heartbeat accelerating.

Quite a few of them had been taken when they were on the fire escape, with Santa wearing his jacket and the two of them clutching one another conspiratorially. Then there were a few more of them in the street, with her arm tucked under his, and even one just after she'd slipped again, and he had ended up anchoring her against his body.

Most incriminating of all were the pictures of him and Santa outside her friend's chalet. They were standing staring at one another and there was something oddly intimate about their posture, even though in reality the photo must have been taken just moments before she gave him back his jacket.

All of it could be explained away.

But who would believe his explanations?

He found the video easily enough. It had been taken at that party in Cannes—he recognised what he was wearing. But what he was wearing wasn't the problem. It was what he was saying.

'I'm always in love. That's why I'm not married.'

It was his take on the Oscar Wilde quote. He'd been playing to the crowd. But now, playing back the audio, he felt his mouth thin as he listened to the conceit in his voice and the hoots of appreciative laughter in the background.

Even to his ears it sounded bad.

He felt a sharp, unfamiliar stab of panic. 'Have the shareholders seen this?'

But even before Nick's terse affirmation he knew that they had. That was why Donald Muir had called him.

He swore silently.

'What are they thinking?' he asked quietly.

'They can't understand why a man who runs a business that's so inextricably tied to love and romance and marriage would make that kind of remark in public.'

Louis breathed out unsteadily. His heart was beating too fast. 'It was a private party, Nick, and it was months ago.'

There was another silence, this time longer. Then, 'They want you to step down as CEO.'

'No!' The word burst from his mouth. 'No, they can't ask me to do that. They can't make me do that.'

'They can and they will.' Nick hesitated, his voice softening. 'Look, I know how much you care about Callière, but these last few months you've been out of control. They think you're a loose cannon.'

Louis felt his chest tighten. He wanted to explain—to tell Nick why it wasn't his fault. Tell him that his father's death had unleashed something in him…an anger and a pain that was beyond his control.

But he couldn't admit that to anyone.

He couldn't admit the depth of his hurt or his regret at not confronting his father. Or that he needed Nick's help. He could never admit to that.

'There's got to be something I can do or say.'

His CMO sighed. 'You know what, Louis? I think you've said and done enough, don't you? Look, don't answer your phone unless it's me. Don't leave your room. And don't, under any circumstances whatsoever, talk to Santa Somerville.'

As Nick hung up, Louis slammed his laptop shut.

Santa Somerville. This was her fault. None of this would have happened if she hadn't run off and got herself stuck in his bathroom, and then badgered him into walking her home.

For the last ten years his business—the business he had built from scratch, the business that bore his beloved grandmother's name—had been the one constant in his life. After Glamma's death, his need to own it outright had become almost an obsession, and he'd been so close.

Only now it was hanging in the balance.

All those months of being on his best behaviour had been for nothing. Thanks to Santa. And now he had been told to stay in his room like some disobedient child.

A sick feeling balled in his stomach. He'd been here before. And back then he hadn't been able to do it…play the game. He couldn't believe that he was expected to do so again.

His muscles tensed. The memory of that conversation was still raw. How could it not be? It had defined his life. He was still living with the consequences of it now.

But now, as then, he couldn't just sit here and wait for his life to be decided for him.

As for not talking to Santa?

Not going to happen.

He was going to find her and talk to her.

And, whatever it took, she was going to put this right.

CHAPTER FIVE

GAZING UP AT the cloudless forget-me-not-blue sky, Santa breathed in deeply.

She had woken just over half an hour ago, disorientated to discover that it was past lunchtime.

It was the longest lie-in of her entire life, and she had been expecting Merry to already be up, but there was no sign of her friend, nor was there a note, so she must still be sleeping.

A prickle of guilt jabbed beneath her ribs. She had chosen not to knock on Merry's door, telling herself that her friend needed her rest, but that wasn't the reason she hadn't woken her.

The truth was Merry would know in a heartbeat that something had happened last night, and right now Santa wasn't sure she could even explain it to herself, much less anyone else, and particularly not to her best friend.

At the very least she needed a chance to process everything…a few moments alone to decide which parts of last night and this morning she would share with her. So she got dressed, left a note on the kitchen counter saying that she was going for a walk, and then quietly sneaked out of the chalet.

She was glad that she had; it was a beautiful day. The air was cold—refreshingly so—and the sun looked like a giant white snowball, just hovering over the town.

Having forgotten to draw the curtains, she had woken to that same sun, its pure white light pressing against her eyelids and pulling her from sleep.

Not that she had minded. In fact, she had been happy to wake.

A dull heat rose over her face.

Louis might have walked away from the chalet early this morning, but if her dreams were anything to go by he hadn't really left her.

On the contrary, he had been right there beside her, his hard, muscular body pressed close to hers in Merry's small fold-out bed, his mouth on her mouth, his skin on her skin, his hands touching, exploring, teasing her, making her shift restlessly against the weight of the duvet.

The jingling of bells from a horse-drawn sleigh dragged her back into real time and, cheeks still warm, she watched the two grey horses jog rather than dash through the snow, their heads held high.

It was unsettling as well as embarrassing to know that whatever she might have said to Louis's face, her subconscious had been busily undermining her, treacherously unleashing her unfiltered, inhibited desires and wishes during sleep.

But surely that was the point of dreams? They weren't real. And the Louis in her dreams wasn't real either. She had made him up. He was a fantasy.

Her mouth thinned. The real Louis might look like every woman's dream lover, with his floppy brown hair, perfect bone structure and teasing blue eyes, but looks weren't everything, and no woman, no matter how smitten, wanted a sulky, spoiled, self-indulgent boy for a lover.

There was a soft thump as a slab of snow slid from the roof of one of the chalets onto the ground.

She frowned. It must have snowed while she was sleeping, but it was still easier to walk along the pavements now than earlier, when she'd been clinging to Louis's arm to stop herself from falling flat on her face.

Her pulse skipped several beats.

She couldn't believe that she'd had the nerve to do it—that she'd actually come out and asked...no, *demanded* his help. But, with hindsight, what was more surprising was that Louis had helped her above and beyond what she'd expected him to.

Truthfully, as soon as she'd reached the bottom of the fire escape he could simply have left her and let her slip and slide her way home. He hadn't needed to lend her his jacket, or walk her back to Merry's, and yet he had done both of those things—begrudgingly at first, but by the time they'd reached the chalet his mood had shifted. The sulky boy had vanished and his arm around her waist had felt completely normal.

Right.

Perfect.

Her heart clenched.

Just like the kiss they'd shared.

She breathed in sharply, remembering the heat of his mouth and the urgent press of his body. Remembering, too, her own feverish response.

That had been real—

Her throat tightened. Except it hadn't been.

Obviously it had been real in the sense that it had happened, but no matter how mind-blowingly passionate it had been that kiss wasn't who she was. Whoever she had been in those few heated moments...it wasn't her.

The real Santa Somerville was disappointingly clumsy and tame. In other words, a real let-down.

She swallowed, her heart pounding, a shiver of misery snaking down her spine. She even had the photo to prove it, so there was no point in pretending otherwise.

It had been just a kiss, nothing to make a fuss about, and the right and the only thing to do was to put it behind her. Act as if it had never happened. The whole episode, including her shockingly intense reaction, was best forgotten.

Louis was best forgotten too.

And that shouldn't be too difficult, she told herself quickly. There was no reason why she should see him again. They were from different worlds; it was a miracle that they had even met in the first place.

She was lucky they had kissed in his suite. Only a few of his guests had seen them, and they weren't the kind of people who would care, or tell, and nobody knew that she'd spent the night in his bathroom. It was just between the two of them.

Looking up, she frowned. She wasn't sure why, but she had unthinkingly made her way to the hotel. And it looked as if something was happening.

There was a whole bunch of paparazzi hanging around outside the entrance, all blowing on their hands and chattering excitedly. A celebrity worth snapping must be arriving or leaving.

But she'd had enough of the rich and the famous to last her, if not a lifetime, at least until she left Klosters.

And now that she had got her head straight, she was going to get some pastries from one of the little bakeries in town and treat Merry to breakfast in bed.

'There she is… *Santa!*'

She didn't recognise the voice, but jerked her head upwards automatically at the sound of her name. And before she had time to blink the paparazzi turned as one. For a few dazed half-seconds her brain kept telling her eyes that they were looking at someone else, but then they surged towards her, and suddenly everyone was calling her name.

Blinded by camera flashes, she felt as if she had stepped into a film—a terrifying film where nothing made sense.

Everyone was shouting at her, their questions overlapping, jumbling inside her head, so that it was impossible to understand what they were saying, and she was having to concentrate even more than she had earlier that morning to keep upright as they jostled one another to get closer.

She had to get out of there.

It was her last conscious thought before the clamouring pack of reporters and photographers swarmed forward and surrounded her and she acted on it, trying to push her way through to freedom. But there were too many of them.

And then, just as her shock began crumbling into panic, Louis was there, shoving his way through the mob, his broad shoulders making easy work of their cameras and microphones, and even the pushiest photographer falling away from his fulminating expression. He grabbed her hand, shielding her with his body as the hotel's security team swept past them, and then they were inside the Haensli.

'Louis, what is—?'

'Not here,' he snapped, his scowl scattering staff and guests alike as he hauled her through the lobby into the lift.

'Yes, here,' she said, yanking her hand out of his, her panic forgotten, anger sluicing through her veins as the doors closed. 'What the hell is going on?'

'What's going on?' he repeated, staring at her in disbelief. 'How can you not know? Haven't you looked at your phone this morning?'

Her heart was beating heavily in her chest. Outside, she had thought he was furious with the press. In fact, just for a moment, she had actually toyed with the idea that he was rescuing her.

Now, though, staring at his curled lip and taut, stubble-covered jaw, she realised that he was furious with her.

But why? And what did he mean about looking at her phone?

She felt a shiver of foreboding scuttle down her backbone as the lift doors opened and he strode through them into the hallway.

Heart thumping against her ribs, she followed him into his suite. 'No, I haven't,' she said. She had put it in her jacket pocket, but been too busy unpicking the events of the last twenty-four hours to even check for messages. 'Why, has something happened?

'A lot.' He spun round, his blue eyes glittering like polished gemstones. 'While you've been sleeping, my beauty, you and I have become an item.'

What? Santa blinked. She and Louis barely knew one another. They certainly weren't an item.

'I—I don't understand,' she stammered, her voice higher than usual.

His face hardened. 'You will,' he said curtly, picking up a laptop and flipping it open.

She grabbed the back of a chair to steady herself, a slithering panic crawling over her skin. 'Do you think I told someone that you kissed me? Because I didn't. I haven't told anyone—'

He gazed down at her incredulously.

'You think that's why the paparazzi are camped out on the doorstep of the Haensli? Because of one stupid, meaningless little kiss?'

Her fingers bit into the leather edge of the chair and she stared at him, wounded not just by his careless dismissal of what had felt so astonishing and intoxicating to her, but by her own outsized sense of misery that he felt that way.

She let the air out of her lungs carefully, then took another breath. 'But that's all that happened.'

Now he was staring at her as if she had told him she believed in the Abominable Snowman.

'Believe it or not, they don't know about the kiss. But they don't need to know.' He was biting the words off and spitting them out. 'Because—idiot that I am—I agreed to walk you home this morning and now they have something much, much better than a kiss. But if you don't believe me, take a look.'

Louis held up the laptop and, glancing down, everything she was thinking and feeling was swept away.

She felt the room grow hazy around her as she scrolled down the screen.

Snow Queen melts for Duke of Diamonds!

Santa, baby...hurry down my fire escape tonight!

Her head was spinning, a wordless protest building in her throat, and then her phone buzzed, and she clicked on the message, and what she saw made a chasm open up beneath her feet.

She was falling down into darkness...

Watching the colour drain away from her face, Louis swore silently.

In the time it had taken for him to yank on his clothes and slam his hand against the lift button he'd cooled down sufficiently to know that he was acting like a jerk, blaming Santa for the mess he was in.

He'd also begun thinking that, despite what Nick had said, there might be a chance he could swing this just by lying low. Stories like this were tomorrow's chip wrappers. With no new oxygen to feed them, they would quickly die.

His breathing knotted.

Only then he'd seen the paps outside, and everything had suddenly got real, and he'd known that this story was alive and kicking and that once again he was going to be blamed for something he hadn't done.

It was all so horribly familiar, and he had felt the same sickening sense of disbelief and helplessness. His rage and frustration that it was happening all over again, just like it had with Marina, had risen up like a wave, swamping everything.

And now, glancing over at the photos on his laptop screen, he felt an outlet for his anger as his eyes locked on to that expression on her face as if she only had eyes for him.

He was suddenly conscious of the hammering of his heart. How could she do that? How could she look at a man like that and not mean it? He'd thought she was different. She had seemed so different when he'd kissed her... so eager and lacking in artifice.

But she was just like every other woman, and for some reason that hurt a ridiculous amount, so that he couldn't keep the bitterness out of his voice as he met her gaze.

'Do you have any idea what you've done?' he said coldly. 'It's taken ten years, but finally everything was falling into place. I was this close...' He held up his hand, his thumb and forefinger spaced an inch apart. 'This close to being able to buy out my shareholders. And then you came along, with your swishy hair and your ice skates, and messed it all up. And now they want me to take a step back.'

There was a long, taut silence and then Santa gazed up at him. 'I came along and *messed it all up*?' she repeated, the blazing fury in her voice more than matching his. 'You did this. All of this is your fault.' She held up her phone with a shaking hand. 'Bryson's are furious. They're threatening to pull my sponsorship.'

Louis stared at her in silence, his pulse filling his head. He was being pushed out of his own company, the company he had built out of the hard Canadian ground, and she was worrying about her sponsorship?

But there was something in her voice...something in the way she was holding herself—almost as if she had been waiting for the sky to fall on her head—and he didn't like the way that made him feel.

'That's not going to happen.'

Why would it? Unlike him, Santa had never put a foot

wrong, on or off the ice, but he felt obliged to say it...to say something to make her relax.

'It'll be okay,' he said briskly.

Her chin jerked up and she glared at him. 'How? Bryson's made it clear when I signed the contract that my behaviour had to be consistent with their brand image, and your reputation isn't exactly family-friendly.'

Eyes narrowing, Louis stared at her in exasperation. Really? Was this the thanks he got for trying to be nice?

'Well, maybe you should have thought of that when you decided to drag me into your walk of shame.'

Her hands clenched by her sides. 'That's not what it was, and you know it.'

They were inches apart, both of them breathing jerkily. The air around them swirled and swelled with anger and resentment, and something else that seemed to push them closer, so that he could smell the faint trace of her perfume, see the pulse chasing down her throat—

A shrill ringtone broke into the silence filling the room and they both jerked backwards. As Santa stared down at her phone, he watched her face still.

He frowned. 'Who is it?'

She was staring at the phone, stiffly frozen, appalled, as if she was holding a live rattlesnake. 'It's Diana. My agent.'

Before his brain had a chance to catch up with his body, Louis stretched out a hand and grabbed the phone from her. He switched it off.

'What are you doing?' Her eyes flew to his face. 'I need to call her back.'

'And say what?' His frown turned into a scowl. 'That nothing happened?' He gestured towards the open laptop and the picture of Santa wearing his tuxedo jacket, her body leaning familiarly into his in the empty snow-covered street. 'That it was all perfectly innocent?'

'It was.'

For a moment, he almost felt sorry for her. She sounded

defiant, but her face was pale, the muscles taut, as if she were trying not to panic. And he knew exactly how she was feeling because he was feeling it too.

The difference was that he'd been here before, whereas this was her first time, and the first time was definitely the worst.

His stomach twisted. He could still remember now how it had been after he'd jilted Marina at the wedding of the decade. It had been like a crazy dream. For weeks, months, his name and face had been plastered over every news outlet in the world. He'd been hounded, harassed and hunted across the globe.

There was an ache in his chest like a bruise that had never healed. And the people who should have protected him, taken him in, given him sanctuary, had not just turned their backs...they had pushed him into the abyss.

He glanced over at Santa's set face.

But that wasn't going to happen this time.

'You think people care about whether you're innocent or guilty, Santa? They don't. You think they care about whether things are true or not? They don't. All they want is a juicy story.' His eyes found hers. 'And we have given them one.'

'I told you before, there is no "we".'

She met his eyes fiercely, even though he could see from the faint tremor of her body that she was fighting to stay calm.

'There is now,' he said grimly.

'No!'

The word burst from her mouth just as it had done from his earlier, when Nick had told him that the shareholders wanted him to take a step back from the business.

'We just need to tell them to take these pictures down and print a retraction—'

'Who?' His eyes narrowed on her flushed, angry face. 'Who are we going to tell? That's not how the internet works. These pictures have been shared hundreds of thousands of times already.'

Even if they could be taken down—which he doubted—the damage had already been done. Any explanation they offered now was already too little, too late. It might even make them look more guilty.

Not that Santa would accept that.

He could almost see her picking through his words, turning them over and upside down, looking for some kind of loophole that would make all this go away. He felt something pinch inside him as she twisted abruptly away from him.

He swore under his breath. 'Santa—'

She didn't reply, and her silence went on so long that he began to think she had nothing more to say. But then she turned to face him.

'I need this sponsorship, Louis.' Her eyes were very blue. 'I'm not like you. I didn't get handed piles of money just because of who I am. And skating at my level costs a lot of money.'

'Now, you listen to me—' he began. But before he could tell her that, sadly, he hadn't been handed any piles of money in a long time, she cut him off.

'No, you listen to *me*,' she snapped. 'You started this and you're going to finish it. I don't care what you have to do or say to make those headlines go away, but that's what needs to happen.'

'Oh, why didn't you say?' He patted his jacket, as if searching for something. 'If that's all that needs to happen, I'll just find my magic wand and use my special headline-shrinking spell. While I'm at it, I could give the entire world amnesia too.'

Rubbing his forehead, where an ache was starting to build, he watched fury flicker across Santa's face.

'I wish I'd never met you.'

'Likewise!' he flung back at her.

His heart began to thud rhythmically in his chest. What the hell was she expecting him to do? Without access to a time machine, the only way he could make those head-lines disappear would be if and Santa were a real couple—

He tensed, a fragment of a sentence echoing inside his head.

'I'm getting tired of trying to convince the world that your behaviour is the sign of a desperately romantic man searching for the right woman.'

They were Nick's words, spoken sarcastically on the day he'd arrived in Klosters.

But, then again, those words might offer a lifeline...

He was suddenly aware of the woman standing in front of him, and of what he was contemplating with her.

Ten years ago he had jilted the woman he was supposed to marry, leaving her standing at the altar in front of nine hundred carefully selected guests. And he had never re-gretted it—never once considered offering his name to any other woman.

Until now.

His gaze took in her shiny dark ponytail, trembling mouth and furious blue eyes. It was a crazy idea. It would never work. She would never agree to it. He didn't even want to suggest it. But, despite all the objections ringing in his ears, he knew it was the only solution to their problem.

'You said you wanted this to be over...' He paraphrased her words, watching her eyes lift warily to his face.

'I do.' Her reply was swift and clear and unequivocal.

He held her gaze, wanting to see her reaction. 'Care to say that for real?'

'What does that mean?'

He took a breath, trying to check the misgivings clamouring inside his head. 'You want to make the head-lines go away, Santa? Then marry me.'

* * *

Santa stared at him, groping for some way for his words to make sense.

Marry him!

But of course he was being stupid again—mocking her, trying to punish her for what he saw as a problem of her making.

'Good idea,' she snapped. 'Why don't we fly to Vegas? We could get married with Elvis as the celebrant and afterwards we could invite all our new paparazzi friends to the reception.'

His face hardened. 'If you like—although I thought the whole point of getting married was to get them off our backs.'

She felt her face dissolve, her mouth forming an O of shock. He was being serious. 'Are you out of your mind?'

Marry Louis? The idea was absurd, and wrong on so many levels, and yet she couldn't stop a hectic pulse from leapfrogging across her skin, or deflect a sudden vivid memory of the moment when his mouth had fused with hers.

'No!' Shaking her head to clear the image from her head, she took a step backwards. 'I wouldn't marry you if my life depended on it.'

'What about your reputation?'

His voice was cold—but, looking into his eyes, she saw the heat of wounded male pride.

Louis's pride was the last of her worries right now.

'We can't get married,' she said firmly.

'Why not?' he shot back. 'It would solve our immediate problems. Unless, of course, you're already married.'

His eyes locked with hers and she stiffened. 'I'm not married.'

'And you don't have a boyfriend right now, do you?'

Her cheeks were flaming with a shame she hated feeling. 'I would hardly have kissed you if I did.'

Something shifted in his face—something she hadn't got a name for.

'It's not always an obstacle,' he said silkily.

'Only for someone like you.'

'If you say so.'

He tilted his head back, the coldness in his eyes making her shake inside.

'Okay then, as there appears to be no legal impediment as to why I, Louis, may not be joined in matrimony to you, Santa Somerville, let's get married.'

She stared at him, trying and failing to read his expression. No legal impediment maybe, but what about a moral one?

'You can't just use marriage as some kind of sticking plaster to fix this mess.'

He shrugged. 'That's exactly what I want to use it for.'

Her head was starting to spin. *Why was he being so contrary?*

'Well, I don't. It would be dishonest, wrong—'

'It would also be expedient and mutually beneficial. And it's not as if it's going to be till-death-us-do-part. We'll be lucky if we last a month without killing each other.'

And what about kissing each other?

She felt her body still as she imagined what it would be like to share this man's bed, to have unlimited freedom to explore and savour his body—

Except that wasn't going to happen.

'People don't marry to get the paparazzi off their backs, Louis.'

'People marry for all sorts of reasons, Santa. Love...' his eyes met hers, and the blueness of his taunting gaze made her breath catch in her throat '...money, duty, convenience. And what could be more convenient than you and I getting our lives back on track?'

Her heart stopped beating. It was a crazy idea. It would

never work. But what was the alternative? She could switch on her phone and call Diana and tell her the truth... Only this was one of those occasions when the truth would sound even more far-fetched than the lie.

'I don't know...'

She could hear the uncertainty in her voice, feel the lump in her throat as she swallowed.

'Do you have a better idea?'

Louis was staring down at her, his face lightly tanned from winter trips to St Barts, his aristocratic cheekbones gleaming in the afternoon sunlight.

Up close, his beauty was almost absurd—and dangerous. But not as absurd and dangerous as his proposal.

She shivered inside and then, looking into his eyes, shook her head.

CHAPTER SIX

THE HELICOPTER TILTED SHARPLY, climbing above the snow-covered Canadian landscape. Gripping her armrests, Santa shifted in her seat, a pinch of nervous tension tightening her stomach. But her nerves had nothing to do with the bumpiness of the flight.

That shake of her head had been just under forty-eight hours ago, and the reason she felt so nervous was that at some point in between then and now she had not only agreed to Louis's insane plan, she had gone ahead and married him.

And now she was no longer plain Santa Somerville, but Santa Albemarle, the Duchess of Astbury.

As she twisted the plain, gold band on her finger, her gaze flicked across the cabin of the helicopter to where her husband was slumped in his seat, apparently asleep, oblivious both to the helicopter's juddering progress and his new wife's gaze.

But she had a strong suspicion he was faking it, so that he didn't have to talk to her.

He had been like that ever since they'd left Switzerland. Not angry outwardly—he hadn't been that since they had agreed to marry—but she could sense his fury and frustration. And, even though he had sprung the trap himself, she knew he blamed her.

And she blamed him, so they were even.

Except they weren't.

Louis might be able to live with all this drama, but her head was still spinning with shock and disbelief.

Everything had happened so fast. She wondered if the details of all marriages were so quickly and easily agreed upon. Her mouth twisted. Or did that only happen when the bride and groom didn't love one another?

Somehow Louis had conjured up a private jet, and as soon as they were in the air they had each made a few phone calls. Louis had called his chief marketing officer and one of the shareholders. She had rung Diana and her family.

Diana had sounded stunned, and despite their strenuous efforts to sound thrilled she would have had to be deaf or deluded not to hear the bewilderment in her father's and stepmother's voices.

And then Mr Bryson had called her.

Her chest tightened. But of course, Mr Bryson had been truly delighted by the news that she had fallen head over heels in love.

Perhaps remembering her earlier remark, Louis had suggested they marry in Vegas. It wouldn't have been her first choice, but she had no memory of the wedding anyway, other than of how much it hurt to smile when you didn't feel like smiling.

And now they were on their way to Louis's home somewhere near Banff for their honeymoon.

Honeymoon.

Her breath caught in her throat, the word whispering inside her. But before it had a chance to grow louder Louis's eyes snapped open, and he glanced out of the window as the helicopter started to slow.

'We're here,' he said curtly as they landed on the snow.

He soon had the door open and, barely giving her time to gaze up at the beautiful low, linear house, he hustled her across the snow. Inside, a tall, dark-haired woman with a ballerina's poise was waiting in the light-filled entrance hall beside a tall Christmas tree, decorated in minimalist style with just simple white lights and garlands of tiny pinecones.

'Welcome home, sir.' She turned to Santa and smiled. 'Welcome to Palmer's Point.'

'This is Maggie.' Louis turned to look at her, and Santa felt her stomach go into freefall. Aside from at the wedding, it was the first time he had looked at her properly in days, and she had forgotten what it felt like to be the object of that teasing blue gaze.

For a few half-seconds she pictured him stepping closer, his mouth slanting over hers, and the idea produced such a rush of longing that she missed Maggie's reply.

Her heartbeat stumbled.

How had this happened?

How had she ended up here, in this house, with this man? It might only be for a year, but right now that felt like a year too long.

'Maggie, this is my beautiful wife, Santa. Maggie runs the house for me,' Louis continued. 'You need something—anything at all—she's the person to ask. Now, I thought you might like a tour of the house...'

No, what she would like—what she needed—was a few moments away from Louis. A few moments to come to terms with the reality of what she'd agreed to.

She cleared her throat. 'Actually, what I'd really like is to freshen up first. Perhaps you could show me to my room?'

'You mean *our* room,' he said softly.

Santa felt her heart start to beat heavily as his eyes locked with hers momentarily, before snapping back to his housekeeper's face.

'Thanks, Maggie. I think I've got this.'

Grabbing Santa by the hand, he marched her up the wide staircase, stopping as they reached the top step.

'What the hell are you playing at?' he demanded.

'I'm not playing at anything,' she snapped, pulling her hand free.

Only it didn't make any difference. Her skin felt hot where his fingers had grasped hers, as if his touch had left a permanent mark.

She felt her pulse accelerate. Without either of them saying or doing anything she could feel the mood shifting, feel herself softening towards him, the hard, cold shard of resentment and distrust starting to melt.

A rush of panic rose up inside her. She needed that splinter of ice to stay cool and distant, to keep the treacherous possibility of the two of them being transformed from enemies to lovers out of reach.

Louis stared down at her, his blue eyes narrowing. 'Really? Because you seem a little confused.'

She lifted her chin. 'I'm not confused.'

'Then what's with all the "my" room business?'

Santa looked up at him incredulously, her heart throbbing in her throat, his question and all that it implied sending a flurry of small flames flickering across her skin.

'What did you think? That I was going to share your room?' Her voice was fraying, she was almost shouting, and she knew that she sounded a little unhinged, but she didn't care. Better that than for Louis to sense the buzz of excitement that the thought produced. 'That I was going to share your bed?'

'That is generally what husbands and wives do,' he said curtly.

'Not this husband and wife. This is a marriage of convenience, Louis.' Lifting her chin, she held his gaze. 'That means we only act like we're married when we're in public. In private, I have my own room. So either you show me where it is, or I will go and ask Maggie. Your choice, Your Grace!'

Scowling down at his laptop, Louis shifted in his top-spec ergonomic chair and then, swearing softly, leaned back and banged his head in a most unergonomic way against the headrest.

He should be feeling on top of the world.

Nick had practically wept with happiness when he'd told him he was getting married, and the shareholders had been equally delighted. Donald Muir had even sent his private jet to transport 'the happy couple' to their wedding in Vegas.

Even the media had done a complete one-eighty and, despite having portrayed him as an amoral aristocratic heartbreaker for the last ten years, were now enthusiastically recasting him as a lovesick Romeo who had just been desperately searching for his Juliet.

Catching sight of his wedding ring, he felt his scowl deepen. So pretty much across-the-board euphoria, then.

But they weren't the ones trapped in a marriage of convenience.

Nor were they spending the first day of their honeymoon wading through geological surveys.

Not that he'd done much wading, he thought, glancing down at his blank screen. He couldn't concentrate. Instead—and this was a first—his brain just kept worrying away at the thought that he had finally taken a step too far.

Maybe he should have fronted out the scandal like he had in the past. And probably he would have done if it had been just about him. But that would have meant throwing Santa under the proverbial bus...

Picturing her furious, flushed face, he lost the thread of his thoughts for a moment—and then, catching sight of the framed photograph on his desk, his own face tensed, his breathing suddenly uneven.

He wasn't doing all this for the beautiful, angry woman who now shared his name, but for another, equally beautiful woman, whose own legendary hot temper was now just a memory.

His throat tightened. He had other photos of his grandmother, rescued from the Dower House after her death, but this one was his favourite because he could see the fierce, partisan love in her eyes.

She was the only person who had ever truly had his back. Everything he had, he owed to her. And he would do anything to prove to the world that her trust in him had been justified.

His scowl fading, he slammed his laptop shut, got to his feet and wandered over to the window. As he stood and stared, he forgot his anger and frustration and simply marvelled at the beauty and breadth of the view. An open sky, huge frost-tipped firs and a frozen lake that stretched as far as the eye could see.

He'd lived here for nearly ten years, but he still got excited by the scale of everything—and by the snow. Here in the Great White North of Canada the snow was at its whitest and brightest, pure and unsullied.

Unlike his thoughts, which seemed to be a relentless and erotically charged slideshow of images involving Santa's warm, satin-smooth body pressed against his.

Damn it! What was she doing back in his head?

He gritted his teeth as his groin hardened with swift, intense predictability. Only why shouldn't he fantasise about pressing his wife's barely glimpsed body against his? It was going to be the nearest he got to doing so.

His wife!

His lip curled as the words ticked inside his head like an unexploded bomb.

This had been his brilliant idea. And at the time, holed up in the Haensli, with that pack of paparazzi baying in the snow outside and his shareholders holding a gun to his head, marrying Santa had seemed like the best solution.

Expedient and mutually beneficial, in fact.

He frowned. *Yeah, tell that to the ache in my groin.*

Whatever benefits there were to marrying Santa, they

had stopped the moment they'd walked out of the wedding chapel in Las Vegas.

He'd hardly seen his wife since their stand-off at the top of the stairs. She had joined him for a very stilted supper last night and then retired early to *her room*, claiming tiredness. And this morning at breakfast she had treated him to a silence that would have impressed an order of Trappist monks.

As would the vow of celibacy he had unthinkingly but voluntarily signed up for…

Shoulders tensing, he felt a ripple of frustration wash over his skin. Back in Klosters they hadn't actually discussed their sleeping arrangements. In the scheme of things, it hadn't been top of their agenda.

Had he assumed they would sleep together?

Probably.

Had Santa?

Clearly not, he thought sourly.

And that was infuriating too, because she so clearly wanted to—as much as if not more than he did. His breathing stalled, and he remembered that moment on the landing when they were arguing. When it had felt as though it could all start up again…as if they could kiss and keep on kissing—

She had felt it too. He knew she had.

So how could she do that? Get so close to giving in to the pull between them and then claim that *he* was the one who was confused?

He hadn't been confused, but knowing that didn't change the fact that they were going to be stuck with each other for the foreseeable future.

His jaw tightened. After Marina he had sworn he would never marry. Not that he'd needed to make any kind of vow. To get that close or feel committed enough to someone required a trust in people he no longer had. And yet somehow, despite being neither close nor committed to Santa, he was now her husband.

But only in public. In private, he'd signed up to live like a monk.

Which was why the less time he spent with her the better.

His gaze snagged on something at the edge of the lake. A flash of hot-pink that was as shocking and unexpectedly out of place in the winter wonderland as a flamingo.

He stared hungrily through the glass, his heart beating against his ribs and then he saw her.

Santa.

His eyes narrowed as she pushed off across the frozen surface of the lake and, pulse accelerating, he watched her skate backwards, building up speed and then turning her body into a perfectly executed triple Lutz before landing effortlessly on the ice.

Seriously?

Suddenly his breathing was choppy, as if he were out there on the ice, not Santa. He felt a rush of heat tighten his muscles. It shouldn't have surprised him that she was skating—after all, it was basically her life. It was certainly the only reason she had agreed to marry him. And yet he couldn't quite believe that she could be out there, acting as if nothing had happened, practising her damn jumps when he was in here, struggling to get his head straight.

Suddenly, rather than spend as little time with her as possible, he found that he very much wanted to get right up in her face.

It took less than ten minutes for him to pull on boots and a jacket and stalk down to where the lake gleamed beneath a pale but determined sun.

As he stopped at the edge of the frozen water, between a pair of shaggy, snow-flecked spruces, Santa did another seamless sequence of jumps and spins, and he found himself torn between admiration at how they seemed to cost her no physical effort whatsoever and continued resentment that she had so easily tuned out the events of the past few days.

And so easily tuned him out too.

A flurry of ice crystals sprayed up in a shimmering arc as she came to a graceful stop. He felt a jolt of surprise as he realised that she wasn't alone on the ice. His housekeeper's young grandsons, Taylor and Ryan, were there too.

He watched the boys skate after her. Within seconds Santa had them playing tag, and they were chasing one another, the boys' laughter and Santa's giggles rising up through the chilled air.

His heart began to pound. He hadn't seen her like this before. As she smiled, she looked young, carefree, happy. It was like watching the sun break through the clouds on the first day of spring, and more than anything he wanted her to turn that smile his way.

And then, just as if she had heard his thoughts, she did turn—but as she saw him her smile stiffened and the corners of her mouth snapped down.

'Louis!'

The two boys skated across the ice, their faces flushed with excitement and pride. Santa followed them more reluctantly. Her eyes locked with his and he felt something inside him slip sideways as he watched the flare of heat in her glorious glacier-blue eyes.

Dragging his gaze away, he looked down at the two boys. 'Skating's over for today, guys,' he said firmly, speaking over their chorus of protests. 'I want to spend some time with my wife.'

They both watched in silence as the two boys unlaced their boots and headed off in the direction of their grandmother's house, occasionally stopping to throw snowballs at one another. As they disappeared from view, Santa stepped off the ice.

'I thought you might want rescuing. They can be a bit of a handful sometimes,' he offered.

She was staring at him with the cool-eyed hostility of a prisoner of war. 'I do want to be rescued,' she answered tartly. 'But not from Taylor and Ryan.'

His eyes met hers. 'You know, instead of throwing shade at me you could just say thank you,' he said, not bothering to keep the exasperation he was feeling out of his voice. 'If it weren't for me you would have lost your sponsorship. Your future. Your dreams.'

'If it weren't for you,' she retorted, 'I wouldn't have been put in that position in the first place. So before I thank you, perhaps you should think about apologising to me.'

Damn, but she was annoying, he thought, his jaw tensing. Even more annoyingly, he knew she was right.

Picturing the expression on her face when the paparazzi had surrounded her on the steps of the Haensli, he felt his jaw harden. She had looked terrified, like a doe surrounded by a pack of hunting dogs, and he didn't have to dig deep to admit—to himself, at least—that if he was swapped out of her story then it wouldn't have happened.

But it was a long time since he had apologised to anyone for anything. Not so long, though, that he couldn't remember every single word.

His chest grew tight. And not just his own words. He could remember everything his parents had said—and, more importantly, what they hadn't said. In his mother's case that was particularly easy, as she had said nothing at all. He had humbled himself, gone to them expecting... *needing*...comfort and support, and it had all been for nothing. He had lost everything anyway.

And he hated that it still turned him inside out.

Santa was staring at him intently, almost as if she could read his thoughts. Needing to escape her gaze, and defuse the tension gathering in his chest, he said abruptly,

'I didn't mean for any of this to happen, Santa. But we *are* married, and you agreed to that.'

'Only because you didn't give me a chance to think.'

'Oh, right—and you had so many other options,' he snarled.

Her chin jerked up, eyes flaring. 'You were crowding me and I panicked. I thought I was going to lose everything.'

'And you think I don't know what that feels like?' He asked the question before he realised what he was saying...what he might be revealing. 'You're not the only one who had something to lose, Santa. Callière was named after my grandmother. It matters to me as much as skating does to you.'

It was the only thing that really mattered to him any more.

He bit down on his anger, holding on to his temper by a thread. 'I know it isn't going to be easy. But I also know that if we can't find a way to be civilised with each other then it's going to be a whole lot harder.'

Then, before she could reply—before she could quite rightly ask what gave him the right to be so holier-than-thou—he turned and walked towards the house, feeling the burn of her gaze searing into his back.

Santa stared after him in silence. *Civilised?* She almost laughed out loud. Louis Albemarle might be a member of the aristocracy, but he was probably the least civilised person she had ever met. It wasn't just that he said and did such outrageous things...it was that, unlike most people, he refused to be held accountable for them.

So how could he accuse her of making everything harder? He was the one who had feigned sleep on the flight so as not to have to speak to her. And yet, to be fair, he had come up with the only viable solution to their problem. More importantly, she had agreed to it.

Reaching down, she began to unlace her skates.

Of course she had.

It was either marry Louis or risk everything she had worked for her entire life. And it wasn't just about her. Her father and Kate had sacrificed just as much, if not more, re-mortgaging their house and taking staycations long before it had become a thing. Even her little brothers had gone without.

For her.

They had done whatever was necessary without complaint, and those sacrifices weren't going to have been for nothing. She wanted to win. She wanted to make them proud and that meant she'd had to marry Louis.

It was time she accepted that, and not just accepted it. She needed to embrace it as a choice she had made, rather than seeing it as something Louis had foisted upon her. Otherwise she would spend the next year feeling like a victim.

Her fingers stilled against the laces.

Been there. Done that. Got the photo.

And she never wanted to feel like that again—so passive, so powerless. That had been the worst part of what had happened with Nathan. Worse than the names he'd called her. Worse, even, than knowing everyone was talking about her.

Not having a voice. Not having a say in her own life.

She had been helpless, paralysed with shock and shame and hurt. All she had wanted to do was crawl under her duvet and hide.

But she couldn't hide from Louis for a year.

Straightening up, she gazed at the house, her heart thumping. And she didn't want to. She didn't need to.

He might be a duke, but she was a duchess now.

She was his equal. Her needs and wishes were as important as his.

Her shoulders stiffened as she remembered what he'd

said about his grandmother. There had been an emotion in his voice she hadn't heard before, and it was obvious that Callière was more than just a business to him.

It was a legacy.

She understood how that worked. Her mother's dreams had become her dreams, and were all the more important for that.

Perhaps that sense of responsibility was even more true if you were a member of the aristocracy, where your role was to act as a custodian of your family's future.

She felt a pang of surprise that she and Louis actually had something in common, and remorse that she had misjudged him. Clearly they both wanted and needed this marriage to work, and that meant no additional stress, no point-scoring, no spoiling for a fight every time they met.

In other words, a truce.

She glanced at her watch again.

And what better time to inform Louis of her terms than over lunch?

But it was not to be. They had just sat down to eat when Maggie appeared. Bob Arnett was on the phone. There had been an accident at the mine.

Caught between shock and surprise, Santa watched Louis leave the dining room. Back in Klosters, when he'd said all that stuff about the shareholders, she'd thought he was just having a tantrum. That he might be CEO of Callière, but he'd either inherited the position from some family member or been chosen as a poster boy on the basis of his good looks and even better connections.

It hadn't occurred to her that he took his position seriously, or that anyone else might take him seriously either. But there had been a focus and authority in the long lines of his body as he'd crossed the room, and when Maggie reappeared, to make his apologies for not being able to return and join her for lunch, she wondered if she might have underestimated him.

Was he really that bothered?

Did he care that much about the business?

Still pondering those questions later, she made her way downstairs for supper. She had half expected him to be still holed up in his study, but when she reached the dining room he was standing there, gazing through the glass at the distant peaks.

He turned as she walked in, and she felt her pulse twitch as his eyes moved slowly from her face down over her white ruffled top and dark blue jeans and back up to her lips. He had changed too, into dark grey trousers and a cream crew neck jumper that hugged the muscles of his upper body.

She felt a flicker of irritation as he walked towards her. Or maybe it was lust.

He held her gaze, and the sudden intensity in his eyes made her skin sting.

'Sorry about lunch,' he said.

'Don't worry about it.' She smiled stiffly. 'Is everything okay?'

His expression didn't alter, but she sensed something shift beneath his skin like water beneath a frozen pond as he nodded. 'It is now.'

She knew he was talking about the problem from earlier, but something in the way his eyes rested on her face as he spoke made her think it might mean more than that.

'That's good,' she said quickly.

A shiver ran down her spine as he pulled out a chair for her, and then he was behind her, so close she could feel the heat from his body as she sat down.

Maggie's roast chicken was sublime, its crisp, amber skin and the olive-oil-roasted potatoes offset by dandelion greens and a shallot confit. To follow there was a delicious caramelised honey, vanilla and orange panna cotta that melted in her mouth.

'I think we'll take coffee in the sitting room,' Louis

said, pushing back his chair. 'Give Maggie a chance to clear the table.'

Decorated in a muted palette of pale grey and white, the sitting room was a seamless mix of comfort and contemporary style. A fire was burning brightly behind a smoked glass surround and, positioning herself on the edge of one of the huge cream sofas, Santa leaned into its glow as the housekeeper arrived with the coffee.

'If you don't need me for anything else, sir, I'll be heading off,' she said, putting down the tray. 'Have a good evening.'

'Thanks, Maggie. See you tomorrow.'

Santa gazed after the housekeeper. Louis might have his flaws, but he clearly knew how to choose staff. Everyone she had met so far was polite, unobtrusive and exceptionally good at their job.

Her lip pulled into a slight pout. But no doubt choosing top-notch employees was something dukes-in-waiting were trained to do from birth.

'What have I done wrong now?'

Startled, Santa glanced up and found Louis looking at her, his blue eyes resting on her face.

'Nothing…' She hesitated. 'I was just thinking you have a lot of nice people working for you.'

'You seem surprised.'

She felt her skin grow warm as he laughed softly.

'Oh, I get it. You were expecting some entourage of yes-men.' He raised an eyebrow. 'Or maybe yes-women? All rushing around enabling me and encouraging my vices.'

Her cheeks grew warmer as his gaze locked with hers.

'Sorry to disappoint you. *Again*.'

A tingly shiver ran through her body as he flashed her a shadow of a smile.

'But I don't need to be flattered. What I need is people around me I can rely on.'

If she hadn't been looking at him she would have missed the sudden twist to his mouth. But surely as a duke Louis had that anyway? Didn't members of the aristocracy have loyal family retainers?

He was standing by the fire, staring down at the flames, and watching the light play across the stubble stippling his jaw she felt something stir inside her. She had called Louis a boy, but there was nothing boyish about his face. Her gaze dropped to the muscular contours of his chest.

Or his body.

'Tell me something, Santa. I know you think I'm arrogant and feckless and entitled…' he turned, the intentness in his blue eyes accelerating her racing pulse '…but, putting aside all the things you don't like about me, is there anything that you *do* like?'

Whatever she had been expecting him to say, it wasn't that, and her insides tightened, her body responding instantly to his question.

Yes, yes, yes.

His smile. That beautiful symmetrical face. Those glorious summer-sky-blue eyes. His dazzling confidence.

But she wasn't going to let Louis know just how much he affected her. Lifting her chin, she met his gaze. 'You have a nice house.'

He smiled then, one of those devastating, stomach-melting smiles, and suddenly she wished that they were still fighting. It was easier to be around Louis when her anger was acting like a buffer between them.

Only then she remembered what she'd decided earlier and, taking a breath, said quickly, 'And when you're not being arrogant and feckless and entitled, I think you can be compassionate and reasonable. I mean, you could have just left me to face the music on my own at the Haensli. But you didn't.'

She shivered, remembering the moment when the paparazzi had surrounded her…remembering, too, Louis's hand reaching for her.

'I suppose what I'm trying to say is thank you.'

Her heart thudded as he studied her face. 'My pleasure,' he said softly.

Pleasure.

The word rebounded inside her. Staring up at him, she caught the gleam in his eye and felt her stomach flip over. He was a man whose every word, every glance, promised unimaginable pleasures. Even just looking at him made her head swim.

Hoping her face wasn't betraying any of her thoughts, she cleared her throat. 'And I do want to make this work. And for that to happen we both need to stop picking over the past.'

'Fine by me.'

'Obviously once the honeymoon is over we'll be able to spend more time apart,' she continued, 'but for now I think we should set some ground rules.'

He screwed up his face. 'I've never been a big fan of rules.'

Her fingers twitched against the smooth leather. She'd had this conversation all mapped out, but unfortunately Louis was going off-script. 'But you said you wanted things to be more civilised...'

He took a step towards her and, looking up into his eyes, she felt something hot lick over her skin.

'I think this *thing* between us more or less rules out any chance of you and I being civilised for very long,' he said.

She felt her heartbeat falter. Now the conversation was not just changing up a gear, but going completely off-piste into dangerous territory. 'I—I don't know what you're talking about,' she lied.

'Then you must either be very stupid or very scared. And I know you're not stupid,' he said softly.

Louis watched as Santa jumped to her feet.

'I'm not scared of you.'

'No, you're not,' he said, his gaze shifting from her

face to her tightly closed fist. She was clearly angry with him for pointing out the obvious. 'You're scared of how much you want me. But you don't need to be. I feel it too.'

'There is nothing to feel.'

She was shaking her head, but it was the shake in her voice that interested him. And the glitter...the longing in her eyes.

'None of this is real, Louis. We made it up. For the cameras. For Mr Bryson. For your shareholders.'

'And none of them are here.'

Reaching out, he took her hand and pressed it against his chest, against the thundering of his heart.

'But this is real.'

He watched her pupils flare, the black engulfing the blue as he pulled her against the thickness of his erection.

'This is real too. And it's definitely not for my shareholders.'

They stared at one another for endless seconds, faces barely an inch apart, wide-eyed, gazes locked with a simmering intensity that made the blood thicken in his neck.

And then, breathing out unsteadily, she reached up and clasped his face with her hands, pressing a desperate kiss to his mouth.

CHAPTER SEVEN

IT WAS LIKE a dam breaking.

His breath caught, the feel of her lips maddening his senses, and he pulled her against him, wrapping his hand in her hair. Longing rushed through him as he felt her hands curl into the front of his sweater and she pressed her body against his with a desperate, clumsy urgency that made him almost lose his footing.

He'd thought that kissing her would make sense of how he'd been feeling these last few days, but he didn't understand any of this—not her, not himself, not this insane need. All he knew was that he wanted her, and that his whole being was aching for the satisfaction that only she could give him.

'I've been wanting to do this ever since you got into my limo,' he groaned against her mouth. Breathing unsteadily, he kissed her neck, her throat, finding that sensitive spot just behind her ear.

'I wanted you too...'

Her cheeks were flushed, and he thought a man could drown in the glittering blue pools of her eyes. Liquid excitement raced through his body as her fingers wrenched at his sweater, tugging it upwards and over his head, and he felt his skin twitch as she slid her hands over his chest and shoulders, pulling him closer, her mouth finding his, kissing him back, her teeth catching his lower lip, matching his hunger.

Somehow her top came off, joining his trousers on the floor. He breathed out shakily, his groin hardening as she stared up at him, her dark silken hair spilling over her collarbone. She was wearing a simple white cotton bra. No tantalising lace, no teasing mesh, and yet he didn't think he'd ever been more turned on.

And then, eyes dark with passion, she reached behind her back and unhooked her bra, peeling it from her shoulders. Holding his breath, he ran his hands over her body, feeling her shiver beneath his hands as he cupped her breasts.

Her nipples hardened against the soft skin of his palms and, leaning forward, he kissed her abruptly. Then he lowered his mouth to her breast, his lips closing around one swollen nipple, her soft gasp making him hard and hot in all the right places.

Head swimming, he tugged off her jeans, taking her simple white panties with them, and now that she was naked, a primal need to taste her bit deep.

But as he lowered his head she reached out, her unsteady fingers fumbling with his boxers, and then she pulled him free, her hand curling around the hard length of his erection.

The lightness of her touch was almost an agony. He wanted so much more.

For a moment he thought about picking her up and carrying her to his bedroom. But he didn't want to risk a change of pace or derail this head-spinning outpouring of heat and hunger.

And then his thought processes were short-circuited as Santa pushed him back onto the sofa. He sat down and in the space of a heartbeat lifted her in one strong movement onto his lap, breathing hard as she guided him into her body.

Suddenly he was there, inside her.

Her face was soft, her head tipped back, and he felt his self-control snap. Heartbeat raging, he cupped her breasts in his hands, licking first one, then the other, his body iron-hard as she arched into him, almost frantic in her movements.

She was so hot and tight…the feel of her was turning him inside out…

Somewhere nearby his phone buzzed, but frankly it could have burst into flames and he wouldn't have cared. Nothing mattered except the feeling of Santa's flesh against his.

His breathing was ragged now, and he groaned softly. Forcing himself back from an edge he'd never been as close to before, he began to move slowly, surrendering to the sweet bliss of her body gripping his.

And then he felt her tense against him, her body no longer soft and open but still, taut, like an animal sensing danger.

Lifting his face, he stared up at her in confusion, his heartbeat jolting. 'Santa…?'

She didn't reply. Her eyes were wide with shock, and panic, and something else he couldn't name. As if she had woken from a dream.

A bad dream.

'What is it?' he asked hoarsely.

'I'm sorry. I can't do this.'

He was still trying to bridge the gap between her words and her flushed nakedness when she shifted upwards, lifting her weight.

The air felt chill against his skin and he made a noise in his throat. He couldn't help himself. It felt as if she was taking a part of him with her.

'Santa…' he said again. But she was already crouching down, one hand clutching her top in front of her naked body, the other fumbling for her jeans.

Her face was almost unrecognisable from the moment before. Then her eyes had been intent on him—intent with longing. Her cheeks had been flushed with the need and want he knew matched the hunger written all over his face. Now, though, she looked young and lost. And scared.

'I'm sorry.' She was pulling on her top blindly, mechanically. 'I know it's not fair, and I know it's my fault. I shouldn't have kissed you, but I can't do this—'

His brain still struggling to make sense of what was happening, he pushed his erection back into his boxers, his groin twitching in protest. He barely gave it a thought, too distracted by the bruise in Santa's voice and by way she was holding her body as if it was about to fly apart.

She had pulled on her jeans now, and her bra and panties looked small and helpless in her hand.

'It's okay,' he said automatically, his remark pointless and absurd since it so clearly wasn't. Then, even more absurdly, 'I'm not going to hurt you.'

The thought that she believed he might was more painful than the ache in his groin and he got to his feet, wanting, *needing* to say something to make her understand that. But she was already moving, running lightly across the pale wooden floor in her bare feet, her loose hair whipping after her as she reached the doorway and disappeared into the darkness.

He didn't go after her.

It wasn't that he didn't want to…his legs just wouldn't move.

Dropping down onto the sofa, he stared into the glow of the fire, shivering in the vacuum left by Santa's absence. His skin felt cold and clammy, and a pulse was throbbing in his neck, beating so hard that he couldn't swallow, couldn't breathe.

He had been unprepared for her kiss, but nothing could have prepared him for what had just happened. Although right now he couldn't say for sure what that was.

Breathing out shakily, he replayed the evening inside his head.

There had been a moment when he'd first felt her withdrawal... He'd thought she'd suddenly remembered contraception, and in that moment he'd actually been grateful, because for the first time in his life he'd forgotten about it too. He'd been too caught up in Santa and her satin-smooth skin and her soft mouth, and how her body had moulded into his as if it were made for him.

Remembering her face when she'd shifted off him, he felt his stomach twist. He had never had a woman run away from him before. Normally he had the opposite problem: women thinking that sex would somehow lead to something more serious.

His mouth twisted. *Like marriage.*

Only now he was married to a woman who had literally fled from his embrace.

It didn't make any sense. He had felt her response. She had melted into him. And you couldn't fake that heat, that fire, he thought fiercely.

You couldn't fake fear either.

And she had been scared. He'd seen it in her eyes.

So what had happened?

What had scared her?

His shoulders tensed in a sharp, involuntary spasm. He felt as if he might throw up. His whole body was vibrating with a tension he didn't want to feel, but couldn't seem to override.

Of course, while it might be true that nobody had ever run from him before, he had been rejected—banished, in fact.

His parents had turned their backs on him. Not publicly—that would have simply added to the scandal—but he had been stripped of his allowance and forbidden from going to Waverley.

The one and only time he had visited the estate in the

last ten years had been for Glamma's funeral, and he had gone thinking that shared grief might bring about some kind of reconciliation with his parents, hoping that they might talk. But his father had looked right through him as if he weren't even there.

And then he had done the same thing himself, when his mother had called just a week before his father's death. He had heard her voice, and his anger and misery had been so intense that he hadn't been able to breathe, let alone speak. He had hung up. And now his father was gone, and they would never talk again.

In all probability Santa would never talk to him again either. And now, just like then, he was sitting in the darkness alone.

He ran his hand over his face, turning his back on the memories and the vortex of emotion they had momentarily produced, and then, reaching down, he began to pick up his clothes.

His fingers stilled as he spotted a scrap of white cotton. Santa's underwear. She must have dropped them as she fled.

His hand tightened around the soft material as he remembered the moment she had slipped out of them and the heat in her eyes.

So what had happened? Where had it all gone wrong?

He'd been asking himself those same two questions over and over again, but now he realised he'd been asking the wrong thing. What he should have been asking was how could he make it right?

His heart was suddenly beating loudly inside his head, so that thinking was impossible. But it didn't matter. He already knew the answer to that question.

Santa was skating round the frozen lake. Skating in circles round and round, so that the world was just a blur of white. Fleeing from the memory of the night before as she had fled from Louis.

She still had no idea how she had got to her room, but once there she had spent the remainder of the night fully clothed, watching the door, terrified that Louis would knock and demand entrance—or, worse, force his way in.

Not to finish what she had so recklessly started. She hadn't been scared of that…of him. What had kept her rigidly awake had been the fear that he would want answers, an explanation. And she might want to give him one. And she couldn't bear the idea of Louis knowing the truth.

Too miserable to sleep, too strung out to cry, she had waited until it was light enough to see her hand in front of her, and then she had got dressed and come down to the lake.

It wasn't the first time she had skated like this.

When her mother had been killed by a drunk driver she had been having a skating lesson, and Merry's father had come to collect her. She had been only six years old. But when she'd looked up and seen him waiting at the side, she had known something terrible had happened, and so she had skated in circles until finally her coach had taken her hand and led her off the ice.

Inside her jacket, her clothes were damp with sweat, and her legs were aching now, burning as if they were on fire, her chest too, so it was difficult to breathe. But she kept on skating. Round and round the lake. She couldn't stop. If she stopped the pain would start—a different pain…a pain that was all the worse for being self-inflicted.

An image of Louis's beautiful face jumped out at her from the white blur. In some ways the kiss had been the same as last time—the same tidal wave of hunger that had driven out everything but Louis and the fierce, hot press of his mouth and his hands anchoring her body to his.

But in the most obvious of ways it had been nothing like that first kiss, because this time she had kissed him.

Still flushed from her pep talk earlier, she had acted on her desire, wanting to master the past, stupidly believing that for some reason her small act of will might produce a different outcome. That it would be different with him.

That she would be different.

And at first it had been different—wonderfully, amazingly different. Louis was nothing like Nathan, and his touch had unleashed a firestorm through her body, obliterating everything but the flex of his hands against her skin and her own quickening breath.

The pain began again and she skated faster.

She had felt different too. Free and uninhibited and powerful. A woman taking and demanding her pleasure.

And then she'd heard it. His phone. It had been there on the table all along. She had known logically that it didn't mean anything, but she hadn't been able to stop the panic swelling in her throat, swamping her.

Suddenly she had seen herself as Nathan had seen her... as Louis would see her. Clumsy and clueless and embarrassing. A let-down.

A disappointment.

Her eyes were burning now, the tears falling freely, and finally she could skate no more. Just like before, she was going to have to come off the ice and face reality.

Face Louis.

After unlacing her skates, her body aching and exhausted, she made her way up to the house.

She still had no idea what to say to him. Ideally, he would be coldly furious. Then she could take refuge in anger, and that would make everything a lot easier.

Most likely, though, he would simply avoid her.

Or maybe he wouldn't, she thought a moment later as she stepped onto the deck behind the house. Louis was waiting for her.

Her heart bumped into her ribs and she gripped the

handrail tightly as the solid wood beneath her feet seemed to turn into quicksand.

He looked up, his blue eyes resting on her face. 'You missed breakfast.'

It was neither a question nor an accusation, just a statement of fact, and she felt a rush of relief.

He looked pale and his hair was tousled, as if he had been skating in circles for hours too, and then she realised that he wasn't wearing a jacket—just the jumper he had worn yesterday.

'How long have you been out here?' she asked.

'An hour or so.'

'Without a coat? You must be freezing.'

'Careful,' he said softly. 'You almost sounded like a wife then.'

Their eyes locked, and then he shrugged.

'It's okay. I needed to clear my head. Think through some things.'

He left the sentence hanging between them.

'Right.'

It was all she could manage. She didn't want to ask him what he had been thinking about. She didn't need to. She was pretty sure she already knew, and she certainly didn't need to hear him say it out loud.

But evidently Louis didn't care about any of that.

Getting to his feet, he gestured towards the door. 'I need to defrost, and you need to eat, so let's go inside and we can talk while we do both.'

'I don't want to talk.'

His face was unreadable. 'You don't need to,' he said blandly.

Inside, the house was unusually silent and still. 'Where's Maggie?' she asked, glancing round the empty kitchen.

'I gave her the day off.'

She felt her pulse accelerate as he pushed a plate of croissants across the table.

'Fortunately, she made these before she left and, after extensive training, I can work the beast—' he gestured at the imposing state-of-the-art stainless-steel coffee machine '—so I'll make us both an espresso.'

Santa didn't want coffee and she wasn't hungry. But she was too exhausted to argue, and at least eating gave her something to do while Louis fixed the coffee. Picking up the croissant, she broke off a piece and put it in her mouth. It was delicious, buttery and light, with a hint of caramel sweetness.

'Thank you,' she said stiffly as he held out a coffee cup and sat down opposite her.

There was a long pause while they both drank their coffee, and then Louis put down his cup. 'I know you don't want to talk about what happened and that's fine.'

His mouth—his beautiful curving mouth—twisted into the kind of smile you might give a stranger: polite, careful, finite.

'I think sometimes actions speak louder than words, and last night was one of those occasions.'

Her fingers jerked against her cup, slopping hot liquid into the saucer.

'It's complicated.'

And ugly and shaming, she thought, trying to blank out both the tenderness in her chest and the utterly stupid longing to reach over and touch his face, as if touching him might wipe clean the distance in his eyes and magically turn back time to when he had looked at her last night, so fierce and focused on her.

'I can do complicated,' he said softly.

She stared at him, a tiny bud of hope pushing up through her misery. Could she tell Louis? Could she share her shame?

Of course, you can't, she told herself savagely, her eyes

dropping irresistibly to the ring on her finger. He might be her husband, and he might have made vows in front of witnesses, promising to love and cherish her, but theirs was a marriage of convenience.

Louis was staring at her, waiting for her reply, but she didn't nod or shake her head. She couldn't. She was too scared that moving might loosen the tears building in her throat.

For a moment he didn't speak, just kept staring at her, and then he said briskly, 'I know we both wanted it to, but this marriage isn't going to work out. So I think it would be best for both of us to cut our losses and move on.'

She blinked, his words booming inside her head. Her chest hurt. With an actual, physical pain as if he had punched her. 'Move on...what does that mean?'

'Whatever you want it to mean.' His face was a beautiful, blank, impenetrable mask. 'Divorce. Annulment.'

Annulment.

The cup was suddenly a lead weight in her hand.

'Because of last night?' Numb, shaking inside, she stared at him in horror and disbelief.

He nodded. 'Yes, because of last night.'

The room was spinning. 'No...' Her voice was raw with shock. '*No*. I know you're angry, and I understand that, but we can't split up now—not after everything we went through to make this happen.'

She knew she was speaking, but the words jerking out of her mouth sounded misshapen and unfamiliar, almost as if she was a ventriloquist's puppet.

'It's only for a year,' she whispered.

But Louis was shaking his head. 'It's over, Santa.'

'No!' This time her voice was louder. 'It'll look like we made it up.' In other words, it would appear to be exactly what it was. A sham. A lie. A hoax. 'I'll lose everything...' Her hands clenched against the tabletop.

'No, you won't.'

There was a strange light in his eyes. Standing up, he walked over to the coffee machine and picked up a piece of paper and a pen from the kitchen counter.

'Here. I drafted it this morning. I think it pretty much covers all the key points. But, like I say, it's only a draft. If you want to change anything, feel free.'

Silence hung over the kitchen as Santa stared down at the paper. For a moment the print seemed to swim in front of her eyes, as if she had a migraine forming, and then words began to take shape.

She breathed out unsteadily. He couldn't be serious?

'I don't understand...' The paper was shaking in her hands and she let it drop onto the table. 'This isn't what happened. It's not true.'

He shrugged, his eyes fixed on hers. 'It's as true as what we told everyone three days ago.'

Her chest tightened. 'But you're taking all the blame.'

He smiled then, but the expression in his eyes was bleak. 'Won't be the first time. And you don't need to worry about me. I can take care of myself.' Reaching across the table, he took her hands in his. 'This way, you get a Get Out of Jail Free card. You can start over.'

He lifted his hands and, glancing down, she felt her stomach knot. His ring finger was bare, and her eyes burned hot as he placed the golden band on the table-top.

'You'd do this for me?' she said hoarsely.

Now he looked away, staring across the huge kitchen as if he was seeing something more than the stainless-steel range and the clean white units.

'I rushed you...pushed you into this. And it might only be for a year, but I'm not going to hold you to this—lock you into a marriage with a man you don't love or respect or even like.'

'But I—' Santa tried to protest.

Louis cut her off. 'Look, Santa, I know you don't have a very high opinion of me, and that's okay. Most of the time I don't have a very high opinion of myself either.' He sucked in a breath. 'But I want you to know that I would never hurt you, and I'm sorry I scared you last night.'

Her stomach twisted. *No, that was wrong*. This was wrong. Maybe if he hadn't taken that phone call yesterday she might have felt differently, but now she knew he cared about his business. About his staff.

And he was going to lose everything.

Only it wasn't fair for him to be punished for something that wasn't his fault.

She felt her breathing jolt. 'I wasn't scared of you.'

If someone had asked her, she would have said that her brain was a mess, incapable of functioning, and yet the sentence came out fully formed, as if it had been sitting there just waiting to be spoken.

His eyes narrowed on her face. 'You ran away from me, Santa.'

'Not you.' She shook her head, and now that shake was filling her voice. 'It wasn't you,' she said again.

She could feel disbelief radiating from him. 'There was no one else there,' he said, his jaw clenching.

'Yes, there was.'

Blinking back her tears, she pressed her hand against her chest, pushing at the ache of misery, trying to hold everything in. But the words rose up inside her.

'I was there. And that's who I was running away from. Me. The person I am. The person I *really* am.'

Louis stared at her in silence, a pulse throbbing too hard and too fast in his neck. 'I don't understand.'

She was shivering, one hand clenched tightly, the other limp against the table.

'I thought I could do it. I thought it might be different with you—that I could be different. But I'm still her.'

Still who?

He felt his jaw tighten. In the past, if a conversation

had become this intensely and bafflingly personal, he would have changed the subject or walked away. But he didn't want to walk away this time. He wanted to do or say whatever it took to make that haunted look on Santa's face go away.

Watching her eyes slide to the door and the stairs beyond, he was suddenly scared that any pause in the conversation might send her spinning away from him like last night, so he said quickly, 'And that's why you ran away?'

'I didn't want it to be like that with you.'

He clenched his teeth, hearing and hating the ache in her voice. Reaching across the table, he unpeeled her hand, and pressed it against his. 'Be like what?' he said gently.

'A disaster.'

The word sounded both stark and ridiculous in the brightly lit kitchen.

'Why would it be?'

She bit her lip. 'Because it was before. With Nathan.'

His jaw tightened, the name triggering some dull, primitive pulse of jealousy. 'He was your boyfriend?'

She nodded. 'At college.' Her eyes dropped to the floor. 'It was hard for me. I never really fitted in. And when I started winning skating competitions the other kids began picking on me—you know, saying I was stuck up and full of myself.'

He tightened his grip on her hand. 'Kids can be cruel.'

'The teachers stopped it if they saw, but mostly I just put up with it, because I was doing something I loved. And then one day Nathan stuck up for me. I couldn't believe it. He was so handsome and popular.'

Looking at her still, tense body, Louis felt the muscles bunch in his arms. He didn't need to hear the end of this story to know that Nathan had been no knight on a white charger.

'You wouldn't understand.' Her eyes were on his face

now. 'I'm not like you. I need to be out on the ice for any-one to notice me.'

Not true, he thought, remembering that first time when he had spotted her at the heliport.

But before he could correct her, she said, 'I suppose I was flattered. I never had time for all the things everyone else did, like sleepovers and parties and boyfriends, but that didn't mean I didn't want them.'

Louis's heart squeezed tight. It was part of the human condition, wanting what you couldn't have. Worse still was losing it when you did have it.

'Nathan told me I was beautiful. That he loved me and wanted to have sex with me.' Her mouth trembled. 'I wanted that too. And when I went to Sheffield for the fig-ure skating championships we agreed that Nathan would meet me at the hotel afterwards.' Another pause, this time longer, and then a tired smile pulled at her mouth. 'I got a gold medal, and then I went to the hotel and we had sex. And it was a disaster. *I* was a disaster.'

Watching her draw a steadying breath, Louis felt his gut twist. It was all too easy to imagine Santa as a gauche teenager. An outsider desperate to be accepted, to be loved.

'You don't know that.' The adrenaline pumping round his body was making the room shudder in and out of focus.

'I do. And it wasn't just me. He made sure everyone else knew too.'

Sliding her hands free of his, Santa found her phone. The pain and shame in her eyes made him want to smash things with his bare hands.

'Here. I know I'm not in the photo, but they all knew it was about me.'

Heart thudding, Louis stared at the screen. It was a photo of a medal. A gold medal, gleaming in the glare of the camera flash. A filmy red haze was colouring his gaze, but not enough to obscure the comment underneath or the gleeful number of 'likes'.

'I don't know if it's still on the internet. This is a screenshot. I took it because afterwards when everyone found out, I lost form, I just couldn't skate and I wanted—' her voice faltered '—I needed to remember my priorities.'

Rage boiled inside him. And guilt—a searing guilt that he had put her in the paparazzi's firing line. No wonder she had been so terrified...so desperate to find a solution.

'It was your first time,' he said, his voice rough. 'Everyone's first time is a disaster. I know mine was. I barely lasted five minutes.'

Tears were spilling down her face and he moved swiftly round the table, pulling her into his arms, holding her tightly against him.

'When your phone rang,' she whispered, 'I remembered what he did and I panicked...that's why I ran.'

He pulled her closer, stroking her back, her hair. Of course she had run from him. It would have felt like a trap closing around her. Anyone would have run.

Ten years ago he had run from a loveless marriage.

But right now Santa needed him, and he wasn't going anywhere. He held her against him, his hand moving slowly through her hair, until finally her sobs subsided and, breathing out shakily, she eased back and looked up at him.

'He's a troll, Santa,' he said hoarsely. 'A pathetic, spineless troll. I'd like to kill the bastard.'

Her shaky smile tore at his heart. 'I don't think that would go down well with your shareholders, but thank you anyway.'

'I'm sorry.' He breathed out, shocked. Sorry was supposed to be the hardest word—he'd certainly felt so yesterday. But saying it to Santa felt like the easiest and most natural thing in the world. 'I'm sorry for everything. For putting you in this position. For kissing you—'

'No.' She reached up and pressed her fingers against his lips. 'I don't want an apology for that.' Picking up the statement he'd written, she tore it in half. 'And I don't want this either. We made a deal, and we're in this together.'

She held out his wedding ring and he stared down at her in silence, her words and the determination in her voice tangling something inside him.

'You'd do that for me?' he said slowly.

As she nodded, she slid the ring onto his finger.

Her eyes were a soft, clear blue and, feeling a sudden nonsensical urge to dive into them, he dropped his gaze. Only now he was looking at her mouth, at those beautiful, curving lips...

He looked up sharply and his whole body stilled as he realised she was looking at his mouth. Leaning forward, he let his lips touch hers—a fleeting whisper of contact, an unspoken question passing between them.

A second later he felt her answer as she brushed her mouth against his. 'Are you sure about this?' he asked.

She met his gaze. 'I was always sure about you—it was me that was the problem.'

He saw her confidence falter and, shaking his head, reached up and grazed his fingers against her cheekbone. 'You were never the problem. But if you don't believe me then maybe I need to prove it to you.'

'Now,' she said shakily. 'Prove it to me now.'

Bending his head, he took her mouth softly, his body clenching when she parted her lips. Still gently, he deepened the kiss, intoxicated by the sweet caramel taste of her and the warmth of her body. Wrapping his hand around her waist, he felt a heavy throb of hunger pulse through his veins as her body swayed into his and she began to kiss him back, her breath fast against his skin.

Her fingers slid beneath his top, moving over his skin lightly, clutching at his senses, and he pressed into her body, his groin clenching in sharp demand.

'Not here...' he breathed against her mouth as his hip-bone collided with the underside of the counter. He wanted a bed for what he wanted...for what he needed to do with Santa. *'Wait...'*

Pulling out his phone, he tossed it onto the counter, and he felt his body harden to iron as her hands caught his top and she dragged him towards her.

They didn't make it to the bed...

Kissing him urgently, Santa felt her stomach melt as Louis turned them both, his hands burning through the fabric of her top. And then he was walking her backwards into the living room, the two of them stumbling against chairs and tables.

They fell as one onto the sofa, their mouths fused, limbs entwined. Somehow their clothes came off—pulled, tugged, wrenched, discarded—and they were both naked.

Gazing down at his beautiful hard-muscled body, Santa felt her head swim with hunger. She was aroused, but so was Louis—palpably, fiercely...

Last time beneath her desire there had been a fear. Now that was gone. And there was a thrilling power in seeing him so aroused and knowing that she was the reason that made the last remnants of her nervousness and self-doubt vanish.

His hands were moving over her hips and waist in small, maddening circles, and then he cupped both her breasts, pressing them together, his tongue darting between the nipples.

She moaned softly.

Heat was pulsing through her body, shivers of pleasure darting across her skin, and she felt almost frantic in her movements—frantic for him to caress the part of her body that was clamouring loudest for his touch.

As though sensing her need, he caught her leg, drawing it up to bring her clitoris against the hard length of his erection. Her fingers bit into his biceps, her head falling back. The stimulation was enough to send her over her edge. Everything was out of reach, meaningless, except the spasms of her muscles.

As she cried out he shifted backwards, his dark gaze trained on her face. 'I'll get a condom,' he said hoarsely.

'No—' Her hand grabbed his. 'I'm on the pill.'

His eyes found hers. 'And you don't have to worry. I'm careful— I mean, I take care of myself.'

She felt his hands slide under her bottom and then he was lifting her, sliding inside. Of their own accord, her legs wrapped around his hips, pressing him deeper, and he groaned, his breath hot against her face. Then he was thrusting into her, his body tensing and jerking as she arched upwards, her fingers biting into his back, her whole being ablaze and suspended, both of them reduced to a single frenzy.

CHAPTER EIGHT

BLINKING HER EYES OPEN, Santa stared drowsily into the pale grey light. For a few seconds she was utterly disorientated, her brain sluggishly trying to catch up with her surroundings, and then she sat up with a start.

She was in Louis's bed.

Her pulse twitched, the gold band on her finger catching the light as she pulled the sheets up around her naked body, feeling a warm, intoxicating pleasure spilling over her skin.

She breathed out unsteadily. There was pleasure, but also a lightness—as though a weight had been lifted. And in a way it had. Each time Louis had reached for her, his eyes blazing fiercely with passion and need, she had let go another piece of the cold, slippery shame she'd been carrying for years, until finally there had been nothing.

It had taken several attempts for them to actually make it upstairs. Each time either one or both of them had been too desperate, too in thrall to the insatiable hunger between them, to take more than a few steps.

Not that it had mattered.

Outside the window a few stray snowflakes spun gently to the ground and, watching their casual, downward descent, she felt a swift, tiny smile tug at the corners of her mouth. Louis had definitely proved his point…although there were still some things that she wanted to try out…

'You're awake.'

The teasing masculine voice jolted her out of her thoughts and she turned, a pulse of excitement darting across her skin as she saw that Louis was standing in the doorway, a couple of coffee mugs in his hands.

Heart bumping against her ribs, Santa watched mutely as he strolled into the room. His hair was flopping across his face and he was dressed ordinarily enough, in loose dark sweatpants and a white vest. But his aristocratic features and easy confidence made him look as if he was modelling loungewear for some glossy magazine shoot.

'I thought you were going to sleep for ever,' he grumbled, dumping the mugs onto a table and dropping down into the bed beside her.

Santa frowned. 'Why? What time is it? Oh, my goodness—' she said, her eyes widening with shock as he twisted his watch round so that she could see the dial. 'Why didn't you wake me?'

He tilted up her chin and kissed her softly. 'I thought you needed to rest. I mean, we didn't get to bed until three...' his blue gaze rested on her mouth '...and it's not as if we did much sleeping.'

She could feel colour creeping across her cheeks. 'Not much, no.'

Getting to this place had seemed unimaginable before yesterday—but now, suddenly, she was sitting here in bed, with Louis sprawled beside her, the marks of their lovemaking still visible on their skin, and it all felt so much more intimate than sex.

But was it?

Or had what happened last night simply been a mutual but momentary connection?

Two people just needing to assert themselves over the vagaries of fate through touch and passion and release?

The thought that yesterday might have been enough for

Louis made her feel suddenly off-balance, and she pressed a hand against the mattress to steady herself.

Something must have shown in her face because, glancing down at her, Louis frowned. 'What is it?'

'Nothing.' Her eyes dropped to the muscled contours of his chest. 'I just haven't done this before. The morning-after bit.'

He was staring at her, and she felt suddenly stupid beneath the intentness of his gaze.

'It's a bit late to worry about that now,' he said softly. 'I mean, technically, it's the afternoon.'

'I suppose it is...' She bit her lip.

'Hey.' Reaching forward, he pushed her hair behind her ear. His breathing was suddenly unsteady. 'What happened before, with *him*...' he chewed on the word, his voice fierce '...that isn't happening here. Morning, afternoon, evening—whatever time of day or night—I want you,' he said slowly. His hand moved through her hair, his caress warm, measured, precise. 'But perhaps you need more proof...'

It was another hour before they finally managed to make it out of bed. And then, within seconds, a shared shower turned into passion and the soap was dropped, lost, forgotten.

Finally, they were both dressed.

Watching Santa frown with concentration as she pulled her hair into a ponytail, Louis felt his body tense. There was something touching about the careful, precise way she was twisting her hair. It made her seem young and unsure of herself in a way that got under his skin, so that he felt suddenly heart-poundingly angry with the Nathans of this world. Men who used sex and intimacy to bolster their frail egos.

Not that Santa was weak. But, like a lot of talented young people, she had honed one set of skills and in doing so inadvertently stunted the growth of a whole bunch of others.

And yet she was as dedicated and determined as any CEO.

A shiver wound through him as she leaned forward to pick up her watch and his eyes tracked down the line of her back to the splay of her bottom.

She was also a devastatingly passionate woman—and, truthfully, that was what excited him the most. The fact that the poised, immaculate Santa Somerville everyone saw out on the ice turned to flame at his touch.

He liked knowing that she had these different sides to her…liked it, too, that she found it hard to hide behind a mask. It was refreshing and something of a relief. People were complicated, and often contradictory, and life had taught him not to trust anything or anyone who appeared to be outwardly simple and straight-talking.

His lungs felt suddenly too big for his chest.

Not life. Marina.

'What is it?'

Lifting his head, he found Santa watching him. She looked worried, and he felt something pinch inside him. Women liked him, wanted him, but it had been a long time since anyone had cared about him. He didn't count Nick—although funnily enough he *was* pretty sure that his CMO's nagging was motivated by more than self-interest.

But, like he'd told Santa yesterday, he took care of himself. And, for now, he could take care of Santa too.

His chest tightened. She deserved more—far more than that—but that was all he could give her. All he could ever give her.

'Nothing, I'm just starving,' he answered. He took her hand. 'Let's go and see what's for lunch.'

It was lamb, with a bean purée and spaghetti squash. But, frankly, Santa could have been eating cardboard.

She barely registered the delicately flavoured vermouth sauce, or the chocolate praline pinecones that followed the lamb. She was too distracted by their newfound ease with one another.

Her face felt suddenly warm. Obviously, some of that was down to sex. For days now they had both been separately on edge, fighting an attraction neither of them had wanted to feel and, in her case, had been terrified to feel, and now that tension was gone.

Only that wasn't the only reason she was feeling less uptight.

Growing up, she had always been quiet and reserved, but after Nathan she had found it hard to trust people, even harder to trust her own judgement, and what had once been shyness had turned to suspicion.

She had been like a hedgehog, rolling into a prickly ball every time anyone got too close. And she had hated the person she had become but felt powerless to change it.

Until Louis.

Glancing over at him, she felt her pulse quicken. He had been wrong. He hadn't pushed her into marrying him. But he had forced her to face her past, and in facing it she was free to write a different story for herself.

Maybe that was why she was happy…happier than she had felt in a long time.

Picking up her glass, she lifted it to her mouth, using it as a shield to hide a small, swift smile. But she couldn't hide anything from Louis.

'What?' he asked.

He was looking at her intently, his fork halfway to his mouth, his blue eyes searching her face.

'I was just thinking how you're nothing like the person in all those tabloid stories.' She'd started the sentence before her brain had had a chance to catch up with her mouth, and now she floundered to a halt. 'You're different.'

'By "different" I'm guessing you mean even more charming and sexy?' he said softly.

Meeting his eyes, she held her breath. His blue gaze was soft like summer skies, and he was so impossibly, devastatingly handsome it was hard not to simply stare and keep on staring.

She bit her lip, feeling suddenly shy. 'No, actually, I meant nicer.'

'Nicer?' he said slowly, spinning out the syllables almost as if he didn't recognise the word. 'I can live with that.'

For a few seconds he stared at her in silence, and then, leaning forward, he kissed her. The softness of his lips worked on her senses, so that suddenly she was deepening the kiss, letting her tongue dance with his...

'Oh, my apologies—'

They broke apart. It was Maggie with the coffee.

'I'll just leave this here,' she said, a small smile tucking up the corners of her mouth. 'Enjoy.'

Louis grinned. 'Thanks, Maggie.'

Santa knew her face was flushed. 'I think she knows...'

He rolled his eyes. 'Of course she knows. That's one of the givens of having household staff—they know everything about you. The good, the bad and the ugly.' Taking her hand, he raised it to his mouth, his lips brushing against the cool gold band. 'Or, in your case, the unbelievably beautiful.' His gaze held hers. 'Maggie's cool. She's just happy we've got over our lovers' tiff.'

Lovers.

The word whispered through her body, heating her blood, and suddenly she was so hot and tight she felt as if she would melt from desire.

The feeling of being so vulnerable to him was the strangest sensation, and it should have scared her. Two years ago, even a week ago, it would have done. And yet now it didn't. She wasn't scared of her hunger or of Louis.

On the contrary, she felt a previously unimaginable freedom—as if she was on a giant swing, soaring up to the sky, then swooping back down. Every second was more exhilarating and heart-stoppingly thrilling than the next.

'And are you happy about that?' she asked slowly.

He gave her a long, slow, curling smile. 'I couldn't be happier.'

A little while later she was holding his hands, skating backwards, pulling him across the ice. Louis had played hockey when he'd first moved to Canada, but he was definitely rusty on his skates.

'You're having way too much fun,' he grumbled as, laughing softly, Santa tugged him to his feet for the umpteenth time. 'How come you're not covered in bruises?'

'I wear gel pads.' She gave him a quick, shy smile. 'And falling is a skill like any other.'

His eyes met hers. 'I suppose it is,' he said slowly. 'Is it one of those "it's best not to fight it" situations?'

She nodded. 'Pretty much. Basically, just keep your head up. And try not to fall on your knees or your elbows. Or your tailbone,' she added as Louis reached round to rub the bottom of his back.

Grimacing, he shook his head. 'I'll bear that in mind.'

'It's really just repetition. Practice makes perfect.'

'Yes, it does,' he said softly, his eyes locking with hers.

She wriggled free of his grip. 'Which is why I need to practise. And so do you.'

'Ouch.' He grinned. 'And I thought I was doing okay.'

'Well, you've got the basics all in place,' she said, biting into her lip and darting out of reach as he tried to snatch her hand. 'So just keep doing what you're doing while I warm up.'

They spent an hour and a half out on the lake. After warming up, Santa practised her routine, and then she taught him a simple spin, some bunny hops and a Waltz jump.

Later, Louis said, 'You know you're a good teacher.'

They were in bed by then. They had scrambled up the stairs, tearing at each other's clothes, driven by the primitive, carnal need that had punctuated the day like a heartbeat, and now they lay close, their bodies satiated, their muscles relaxed.

'I used to give lessons at my rink. Mostly to children… just to help pay the bills.' She shifted around to look up at him. 'Bryson's pay for everything now, but before that it was hard.'

There was a beat of silence. His eyes were steady on her face, and she remembered what he'd said earlier about why she had married him. But she wasn't ashamed for not having been born a duchess.

'It must have been difficult to fit teaching in, what with school and your training.'

She shrugged. 'My whole family had to make sacrifices, so I was happy to help. And I really didn't do that much—not like my dad and Kate. They worked two jobs a lot of the time.'

He was caressing her hip, and as she spoke his hand stilled against the curve of her bottom. 'Is Kate your sister?'

'I don't have a sister. Just two brothers, Robbie and Joe. Kate's my stepmother.'

It had been a long time since she'd talked about her mother's accident, and she had forgotten all those mundane, normalising phrases about death that had once been so familiar. But everything she had gone through with Louis seemed to have stripped away her usual reserve so that she found it surprisingly easy.

'My mum died when I was six. A drunk driver hit her car. My dad met Kate a couple of years later, so she's pretty much raised me.'

Louis was listening intently, watching her face. 'But your mum taught you to skate?'

She nodded. 'She was a competitive skater. She gave up when she got pregnant with me, but she took me to the rink almost as soon as I could walk.'

His hand tightened against her hip. 'I'm sorry, Santa.'

'It's okay.' She smiled stiffly. 'It all happened a long time ago.' For a few seconds she was silent, and then she said, 'It's worse for you.'

'Worse how?'

There was a tension in his voice that hadn't been there before and, glancing up, she saw a muscle pulsing in his jaw. But that was understandable. His loss was recent, and came with so many other issues attached.

'You lost your father only three months ago. And that would be hard enough for anyone, but you didn't just lose a father,' she said carefully. 'Overnight you became Duke, and you had to step up and take charge of the family business.'

'Callière is *my* business.' His smile was like the blade of a knife. 'It has nothing to do with my family. Or with you, for that matter.'

The vehemence in his voice, coming so soon after the fire and tenderness of their passion, hit her with a jolt. 'I didn't know—'

'Why would you?'

Looking up at him, she felt her pulse stumble. His eyes had frozen over and now his face was hardening, like water turning to ice.

'It's not as if either of us needs to share details about our private lives to get what we want from each other.'

Her heartbeat was filling her head. It didn't make any sense for him to be so cold, so distant, when she could still feel the warmth of his hand against her hip. And yet it made perfect sense, and she knew it shouldn't hurt as much as it did. After all, she had known right from the start that this was a marriage of convenience.

Only just for a moment she had got confused. By the sex, by the intimacy, by that feeling of being so in tune with every shift in his breathing.

But of course that was just a trick of skin and shared sweat. It wasn't real. And if she'd been more experienced she would have known that sex, however incredible, was just about bodies. It didn't mean that she mattered to him as a person.

She didn't. She was, and always would be, just a means to an end, and it was embarrassing to have forgotten that fact.

'I think I'm going to take a bath,' she said, slipping free of his hand.

Blanking her mind to how shatteringly significant it felt to do so, she stood up and walked mechanically to the bathroom. Shivering inside, she closed the door. For a minute or so she just stood there, breathing heavily, and then she walked over to the bath and turned on the taps, staring down at the rushing water, wishing she could follow it down the plughole.

An hour later she was still in the bath, eyes closed, reclining beneath the warm, scented bubbles, when the door opened, sending a ripple of cool air across the room.

She opened her eyes. Louis was standing beside her, fully dressed, his hands shoved deeply in his trouser pockets. He looked tense, unsure of his reception, and for a moment they stared at one another in silence.

'I can go if you want me to,' he said finally.

His voice was taut, as if it cost him to speak, and she stared up at him mutely. He was hurting, and even though he'd pushed her away she couldn't push him away now.

Shaking her head, she said, 'I don't want you to.'

Heart beating out of time, Louis sat down on the edge of the bath. Santa was watching him warily, her blue eyes wide and still, as if he were a tiger that had randomly wandered into the bathroom.

His chest tightened. Given how he'd behaved earlier, he couldn't really blame her.

He had hurt her, and it had been deliberate. He'd needed to stop her talking about his father and his family and feeling cornered, he had lashed out, his anger and fear pushing aside all fairness and restraint.

Of course it had all backfired on him anyway. Feeling her warm body withdraw from his had hurt more than he could have imagined.

But not as much as feeling her retreat from him emotionally.

That pain had been unbearable, and he had known then that he had to do something…say something. He'd understood that he couldn't do what he would ordinarily do and push her away—it just wasn't possible. He didn't fully understand why. Probably there was some kind of equation that would explain it…a law of physics, perhaps. All he knew was that it felt as if Santa and he were joined by an invisible thread.

'Could you pass me that robe?'

He held it out for her, watching as she knotted the belt around her waist. It was his robe, and it was huge on Santa. At least four inches of fabric was pooling on the tiled floor, and the rolled-up sleeves made her hands look tiny.

His pulse stalled. She'd had so much to deal with already in her life. Could he really burden her small shoulders with his problems too?

But not to tell her anything felt wrong, cowardly, and disrespectful to the woman in front of him. She had been honest with him, and now it was his turn to be truthful with her.

'I'm sorry about earlier,' he said as she sat down beside him. 'I don't really talk about my father. He and I… we fell out a few years ago.'

An understatement.

'What did he do?'

What did he do?

Louis stared at her in silence, the shock of her question rendering him not just speechless, but breathless. Nobody had ever asked him that before. They had always assumed that, whatever the situation, he was the one at fault.

For a moment the need to tell her everything—every ugly, gut-wrenching detail—swelled inside him. But he couldn't do it. It was bad enough that he had upended her life. She didn't need to know that she was married to a man whose own parents had disowned him.

He shrugged. 'It's not a secret. I was supposed to get married and...well, I didn't. Only they were more wedded to the idea than I was.'

His smile felt like one of those grimaces on a Halloween pumpkin.

'My father was particularly disappointed in me.'

Another understatement.

'And I was upset by his reaction.'

That made three.

'We argued, and I left. The last time I saw him was at my grandmother's funeral, nearly ten years ago.'

The last time I saw him alive, he thought.

And the guilt and regret that had been an unobtrusive companion for months suddenly clutched at him, so that he had to grip the edge of the bath to steady himself.

'That must have been a difficult day,' she said slowly.

He nodded. 'One of the worst.'

In some ways it had been the worst. He had certainly never felt more alone.

'But even before that we had a sticky relationship. My parents had me late—probably too late. I found him stuffy and autocratic, and he thought I was spoiled and entitled.' Looking down at her, he paused, smiling stiffly. 'If I'd been the spare, I think he would definitely have just written me off, but there was only me so we were stuck with each other.'

Santa hesitated, and then took his hand. 'I'm sorry.'

He shrugged. 'Most of the time I was at boarding school. And when I wasn't at school I stayed in the Dower House with Glamma—my grandmother.'

'Is that the same grandmother the business is named after?'

He nodded. 'She was actually Canadian. This house is built on her family's land. She could have stayed here and married a farmer, but she wanted to go on the stage. And that's what she did. She went to Broadway and became an actress.'

'She sounds amazing.'

'She was.' He bent his head away from the shine in Santa's eyes. 'She was beautiful and smart and tough and I loved her. She always had my back. That's why I named my business after her. To thank her for having faith in me.'

'So how did she end up marrying a duke?'

'She met my grandfather at a polo match. She sat in his seat. Then refused to leave.' His eyes found hers. 'Sound familiar?'

She smiled. 'But it was love at first sight?'

'More like love at first fight. Their marriage was pretty fiery, by all accounts. But, yeah, they loved each other.'

She was quiet a moment, and then she said slowly, 'What about your mother?'

His heartbeat accelerated. Part of him had been waiting for that question, but another part had thought, maybe *hoped*, she wouldn't notice the one person he had failed to mention.

But Santa was an elite athlete. She had spent her whole life noticing every small imperfection because the difference between a gold and a silver medal was in the detail.

And his mother was hardly a detail.

'Oh, I disappointed her too,' he said, making his voice

sound light. 'We haven't had a mother-son relationship for a long time.'

Her fingers tightened around his. 'But that doesn't mean it's too late to try.'

He thought back to his father's funeral. The guests in their black clothes. The glossy dark coffin. His mother's face, pale and despairing and lost.

'It's fine,' he lied. 'I've moved on. What's past is past. It's history. It's over.'

'So why are we talking about it?' she said quietly.

'Because you brought it up.' His whole body was quivering like a stretched bow string. 'Only you don't know enough to—'

'I know you're angry with your parents,' she said, suddenly and bluntly, 'and that's why you cut them out of your life.'

He had a swift, sharp-cut vision of a stone fortress, vast and impregnable, and then, just like that, her words smashed into it like a wrecking ball and everything he had held back for so long spilled free.

'I didn't cut them out of my life, Santa. They cut me out of theirs when I refused to marry Marina.'

Stomach twisting, Santa stared up at him. His eyes were locked on hers, blazing.

'And do you know why I refused to marry her? Because I caught her in bed with another man the day before our wedding.'

'I'm so sorry...' she whispered.

'Don't be. I'm not.'

There was a flat, hollowed-out note to his voice.

'I know now that Marina did me a favour. She forced me to accept how the world works—how it can only ever work for people like me and her. She made me understand that I couldn't expect to marry for love...that marriage would always be transactional.'

He gave her a small, precise smile.

'Maybe that's why it was easy for me to marry you. And I'm glad I did. I'm glad I could do that for you, Santa. But when this is over I won't marry again. I'm better off flying solo.'

His words felt like a blow to the stomach.

Quickly, compulsively, needing to smother her pain, she said, 'Why didn't you tell your parents the truth about Marina?'

She felt her breath catch. He hadn't taken his eyes off hers but something in them had changed, and now she could see not just anger but pain.

'I did tell them. My father said that it didn't matter, and that he was surprised by my middle-class notions about marriage and fidelity.' His smile looked like it was made of glass. 'He told me that it was too late to pull out...that the reputation of the Albemarles was more important than my ego. He said the wedding was a good match, and I should just look the other way.'

Reaching out slowly, the way she might with a cornered animal, she put her hand on his arm. She was shocked by his words...more so by the fact that they had been spoken by a parent to his son.

He breathed out shakily. 'I was stunned—I didn't know what to say. So I agreed to do it...to marry Marina. And then I went to a hotel and started drinking, and I didn't stop until the following evening.'

Her heart felt as if it was about to burst. 'Then what happened?'

'I went home. I knew my father would be angry, but he was beyond angry. He said I'd let him down. Let the family down. I tried to apologise, to explain why I couldn't go through with it, but he wouldn't listen. He told me that I wasn't fit to be Duke and that he wanted me gone. That night. Out of the house. Off the estate.'

She felt as if something jagged was pushing into her chest. 'Oh, Louis, that's awful...'

He gave her a small, taut smile. 'He cut me off financially. I didn't have any income. I didn't have anywhere to live. The press were hounding me. I was exhausted. I kept calling him, leaving messages, but it was like I didn't exist. If it hadn't been for Glamma I don't know what I would have done. She gave me money to live on and the deeds to the land in Yellowknife.'

Santa felt shame rise up inside her. She had believed him to be spoiled and entitled, but the truth was that he had been betrayed by his fiancée and banished by his parents. Parents plural.

'What about your mother?' she asked.

His smile was a swift, wrenching thing. 'Henrietta? She didn't say anything. She just stood there like a statue.'

She felt his fingers tighten around hers.

'After my grandmother died, I changed. I stopped calling my parents and I stopped caring about what people thought. If things got carried away, I just put my hand up for it—I mean, my reputation was shot anyway.'

Santa's stab of pain was so sharp, so vivid, it felt real. 'So that's why you offered to take the blame for what happened in Klosters?'

He nodded. 'And then the business took off, and I just capped the past. Only then one day out of the blue my mother called me.' A muscle flickered in his cheek. 'It was the first time I'd heard her voice in nearly a decade, and it just threw me completely, so I hung up. My father died a couple of days later.'

He looked suddenly exhausted, and without thinking she slid both her arms around him. 'You weren't to know…'

'I just wish I'd spoken to them. To him. Only now it's too late.'

'It's not too late,' she said quietly. 'Not while your mother's alive.'

Louis flinched. It was a reflex response, a tiny involuntary shift in the angle of his shoulders, but her eyes flicked to his and he knew that she'd noticed and that she was holding her breath.

He was too.

But he couldn't hold his breath for ever.

'It would mean going to Waverley.'

He had meant his voice to be expressionless, but he could tell by the way her eyes found his that he'd failed.

'What's Waverley?'

It was everything. Not just a house, but a legacy he had failed to live up to. It was his past and his future. It was the family he'd loved and lost.

His chest tightened. At the time he had been young, and devastated by Marina's infidelity. Now, though, he knew that his pride had been mauled more than his heart, and that what had really cut him to the bone was his parents' rejection.

And, whatever he might have told himself in the intervening ten years, that pain hadn't faded. He'd just been hiding from the truth, holed up here with his past in this beautiful, carefully constructed prison of his own making.

Only now Santa had opened a door and shown him a view that was so beautiful, so brimming with possibilities, it made him breathless.

'Louis...?'

He turned. 'It's the seat of the Duke of Astbury.'

'But *you're* the Duke of Astbury.'

As he nodded, she frowned.

'So who lives there?'

He sucked in a breath. 'Nobody. It's empty. It's been empty since my father died. My mother moved out into the Dower House. But I live here now. I can't go back.'

There was a long silence, and then Santa lifted her chin, something flaring in her eyes. 'Maybe you can't— but *we* can.'

He stared at her, so confused by the fierceness of her

voice that for a moment he didn't take in what she was saying. 'That's not going to happen,' he said finally.

'Why not?'

'For starters, there's nowhere for you to skate.'

She was staring at him, her jaw jutting in a wordless challenge, and he wondered when he had seen that expression on her face before. And then he remembered. It had been just before she'd forced him to help her climb out onto the fire escape.

Suddenly he knew that Santa wasn't going to let this go. Her next sentence proved him right.

'This is my honeymoon. Skating can wait,' she said firmly.

The view that had so excited him moments earlier shimmered in front of him like a mirage. Tempting, but treacherous.

'I just need time...'

She was silent a moment. 'Ten years is a long time.'

He felt something shift inside him tectonically, pushing the past up between them. 'Maybe I need longer.'

'Or maybe you just need to go back to Waverley,' she said quietly. 'Because you might live here, but that doesn't mean it's your home. And maybe it won't ever be your home if you don't fix what was broken.'

Fix what was broken.

She made it sound so easy. But fix it how?

'You need to see your mother...speak to her.' Reaching up, she touched his face lightly. 'Let's go to England, to Waverley, together.'

He stared down at her in silence, his heart feeling too big for his ribcage, his lungs suddenly too small to catch a breath.

'You'd do that for me?'

Her fingers stilled against his cheek. 'We made a deal. We're in this together, remember? You helped me face my past. Let me help you face yours.'

Her words reverberated inside his head.

Face the past? Could he do it?

But it was a rhetorical question.

Ever since his father's death he'd felt as if he was running on empty, and that wasn't going to change unless he stepped up and made it change. Unless he went back to Waverley and finished what he'd started.

He had thought of going back before. But each time something had stopped him. Each time it had been easy to talk himself out of it.

This time, though, it felt different. Doable.

But then this time was different. This time Santa would be by his side, with her chin jutting out and her blue eyes sparking with a fire that would lead him out of the wilderness.

So why not go?

His life was on pause so why not go to Waverley and put the past where it belonged? Say goodbye to the ghosts?

And then, in a year, he would buy out the shareholders, and he and Santa would divorce quietly, and finally he would have everything he'd ever wanted.

CHAPTER NINE

GAZING OUT OF the car window at the familiar English landscape, Santa felt a swift rush of excitement skim over her skin. It was completely illogical—she had been out of the country for no time at all—but it felt like a lifetime since she had boarded the plane at Heathrow on her way to visit Merry.

But so much had happened, she thought, turning to look across the opulent interior of the car to where Louis was staring at the view from his own window.

If somebody had told her when she'd arrived in Zurich that she would meet a handsome stranger and then marry him, she would simply have laughed. But now here she was, returning to England not only married but a duchess.

Her spine stiffened against the smooth leather. Right now, though, she was less concerned with being a duchess and more concerned about what the Tenth Duke of Astbury was thinking and feeling.

She eyed Louis sideways.

Outwardly, nothing had changed since their conversation in the bathroom. And if her body hadn't been so closely attuned to his she might have believed that nothing had changed in reality.

But they had spent so much time together over the past week that where Louis was concerned she was like a barometer. Every breath, every word, every glance seemed to resonate inside her, and she knew that he was playing a part.

It shouldn't be such a surprise. They were both of them acting out a marriage for—among others—his shareholders, her sponsor and the world's media. But this was different. He was playing a part for her. And she hated that. But most of all she hated that life had forced him to be so good at hiding his feelings.

Her chest tightened as she remembered the statement he'd written for the press. Even now she was shocked that he had been willing to do that for her. *Won't be the first time*, he'd said. How many other times had he taken the blame for something he hadn't done? And each time another layer of distrust and despair had hardened around his heart.

She felt the car slow and her pulse accelerated. 'Are we here?'

There was no sign of any gates—just a turning into what looked like a smaller road.

Louis nodded. 'We're going to use the tradesman's entrance. I hope you don't mind, but I'm trying to keep everything low-key.'

He sounded calm and relaxed, but she could see the fine lines of tension around his blue eyes and, smiling up at him, she gave his hand a quick squeeze. 'Of course.'

He had magicked up another private jet, and his household staff had been warned not to discuss their visit. She hadn't even told her family she was coming back to England. She hated doing that, but right now Louis came first.

'Oh, look at the deer.' Leaning forward, she gasped with delight as a herd of fallow deer stopped grazing and lifted their heads with graceful synchronicity. 'Are they yours?'

There was a brief pause and then he nodded. 'There's about three hundred and fifty of them.'

She wondered how he knew. Surely it was impossible to judge that simply by looking.

As if reading her mind, he glanced over at her and smiled. 'Rogers manages the day-to-day running of the estate. He's been keeping me up to speed.'

'What is there to manage?' she asked after a moment.

His lashes flickered. 'The deer, for starters. Then we have tenant farmers, as well as our own herds of sheep and cattle, and obviously with an estate this big there's a constant ongoing maintenance programme.'

She was about to ask him how big—but then the road curved upwards and she saw the house. The sun was low, but even without its rays the pale yellow stone gleamed in the fast-fading light.

'Oh, my goodness...'

She leaned forward again, her mouth dropping open. Her body clock was warped from the switch in time zones, but nothing could detract from the beauty of the huge golden house crouching in the soft green Gloucestershire landscape.

'It's not considered the best aspect. Almost all the paintings of the house are from the east. But personally I prefer this view.'

'How does it feel to be back?' she asked quietly.

His hesitation was so brief it was barely perceptible. 'Like I never left.'

Maggie's English equivalent, a smartly dressed dark-haired woman named Sylvia, greeted them as they walked into the house, and after Santa had been introduced Louis ordered tea to be brought to their rooms, refusing the housekeeper's offer to accompany them.

'Thanks, Sylvia. I think I can still find my way,' he said, with a tilt of his dark head.

If the house had been impressive from the outside, inside it was even more so. The painted ceiling in the entrance hall had to be at least fifty feet high, and there was a life-size bronze statue of a woman holding a bow and arrow.

Santa glanced across at the two huge, elaborately decorated Christmas trees that stood like sentinels on either side of the staircase. In contrast to Palmer's Point, Christmas here wasn't minimalist, but gloriously traditional.

Her pulse accelerated. In Canada, she hadn't really understood how Louis could live in that beautiful, light-filled house and not see it as his home. Now she understood.

Being here at Waverley, seeing all this and knowing that it had been in his family for four hundred years, suddenly made everything click into place.

As they walked up the huge, imposing staircase, Santa felt Louis's hand tighten around hers. She glanced up at the paintings on the wall, looking for something to say that might distract him a little. 'Are these your relations?'

He nodded. 'That one there is the First Duke, and then they follow in order, right up to the Ninth Duke.' His broad shoulders tensed as they stopped in front of a portrait of a man in a dark suit. 'My father. Edward Albemarle.'

Gazing eagerly at the picture, Santa felt her heart punch against her ribs. She had assumed—wrongly—that Louis would have inherited his father's looks just as he had inherited his title. But where Louis was dark and lean, his father was fair, and although he was handsome, in a kind of plump-skinned, well-fed sort of way, his looks were marred by the imperious expression on his face.

Next to her, Louis was silent.

'You have his eyes,' she said finally.

'Luckily. Otherwise he would probably have doubted his paternity.'

He smiled, but she could feel the effort it took for him to do so.

Glancing down at her, he slid a hand under her chin and frowned. 'You look tired. Come on, you can gawp at my ancestors later. Let's go to our rooms and you can have a lie-down.'

She would actually love to lie down. She had slept on the flight over, but woken half a dozen times, and each time she had been aware of Louis, staring out of the window at the dark night sky.

As he pushed open a door he turned and gave her a small, stiff smile. 'Just say if you don't like it. There are another forty sets of rooms, so it's not a problem.'

She nodded mutely. What was there not to like?

The bedroom was huge—and beautiful. She was going to run out of superlatives very soon, she thought, gazing from the vast oak four-poster bed with its lambent Chinoiserie curtains to the view through the window of a sloping lawn, an endless swathe of every possible shade of green.

'Oh, wow...' she whispered.

'You see that line of trees?'

Louis was behind her, the heat of his body warming her skin. She looked to where he was pointing. It took her a moment to find the trees. They were so far away they might easily be in the next county.

'That is the end of our land.'

Our land.

The words, with their implication of something shared, made her throat contract. But of course Louis had been talking about the Albemarle family when he'd said 'our'.

'I'd love to take a look round.'

He nodded. 'Tomorrow. It's going to be dark soon, and besides, you need to rest.' Taking her hand, he led her to the bed.

He drew back the covers and she sat down and toed off her shoes. 'Are you going to join me?'

He hesitated and then, lifting a hand, he stroked her hair away from her face. 'I think that would defeat the purpose of you lying down,' he said softly, and she felt heat flare in her pelvis as he tilted her face up to his and brushed his lips against hers.

As she lay down, a wave of tiredness swept over her. 'What are you going to do?' she asked.

But before she could hear his reply her eyelids closed and she fell instantly and deeply asleep.

Staring down at Santa, Louis felt his shoulders tighten as her question echoed inside his head.

What was *he going to do?*

Breathing out unsteadily, he walked across the room and stopped in front of the window, his eyes narrowing. A better question would be when was he going to do it?

Back in Canada, he had hugged the thought of returning to Waverley close, like a long-lost toy. Now he was here, though, he didn't know where to start.

At the beginning, maybe.

His heart skipped a beat as he remembered that terrible conversation in the book-lined study downstairs. He had been wholly unprepared for the outcome, and devastated, and yet even now he couldn't regret it. Regret simply wasn't an option for something that had seemed so instinctive and necessary for his survival.

But it had torn his life apart.

From that day onwards every single assumption he'd made about his future had changed. And afterwards he had been too shocked, too numb, to do more than put one foot in front of the other and keep walking, hoping that if he kept walking he could leave the past behind, driven onwards by a need to prove his father wrong.

And not just prove him wrong. He'd wanted to rub his success in his father's face—show him that he didn't need what had been taken from him to prosper.

And he'd done that.

Callière was a global brand—albeit one he currently didn't fully own—and for a time he'd convinced himself that was enough. But it hadn't been. There had always been a shadow behind his heartbeat.

And now he had come full circle. The past he had tried so hard to outrun had pulled him back across the Atlantic Ocean.

His gaze locked on to the tiled roof of the Dower House. Here he was in his childhood home, his mother just a stone's throw away, and finally he could put the past to rest.

At some point he would meet with his mother.

He just needed to find the right time…

But first he needed to decompress.

Reaching into one of his bags, he pulled out their wedding certificate. Heart beating, he unfolded it. He still couldn't quite believe that he was a married man, and yet there it was in black and white.

His eyes snagged on Santa's full name: *Santina*.

At the ceremony he'd been too churned up with anger and resentment to do more than parrot his responses, but now he wondered where that name had come from. He would have wondered more if he hadn't spotted something else—something that made his heart beat faster.

Apparently, it wasn't just Christmas they would be celebrating…

The next day the sun shone with unseasonal brilliance, and they spent the morning driving around the estate. Maybe if he'd been alone the experience would have been different, more conflicted, but having Santa there made it easy for him to just sit back in the worn four-wheel-drive and point out various landmarks on the estate.

He knew she was enjoying herself, but he could also sense that she was a little surprised that he was giving her a guided tour rather than going to see his mother. Every now and then he would feel her gaze on his face, and each time he felt something inside him crack open.

His spine stiffened against the worn leather. It was ridiculous. He had travelled four thousand miles to be here, and yet he couldn't take those last few steps.

'What's that?'

Gratefully he snapped off his train of thought and glanced over to where Santa was pointing.

'It's my grandfather's folly.' He gazed up at the octagonal Gothic tower that rose beyond the manicured lawns like a bizarrely distorted inland lighthouse. 'He built it for Glamma for their thirtieth wedding anniversary.'

Santa smiled over at him. 'That's so romantic. It reminds me of the Lady of Shalott.'

Her cheeks were flushed, her skin translucent in the pale English sunlight, and with her hair lifting in the breeze she looked more like some farmer's daughter than an international ice skater.

'Doesn't she die on a boat?' he asked.

She laughed. 'I meant the bit before that.'

He liked hearing her laugh, and knowing that he could make her laugh. Liked, too, the pale curve of her throat—more specifically the times it curved for other purposes. Feeling his body harden, he changed down a gear so as not to give himself away.

'My bad. I read it at prep school, so I think I might have skimmed over that to get to the part with Lancelot.' He glanced at his watch and frowned. 'We should probably be getting back for lunch.'

The morning had gone so fast. Too fast. He liked it best when it was just the two of them.

'Oh, look at that house.'

Santa was leaning forward, her eyes sparkling, and he felt something loosen inside his chest as she turned to him.

'It's the Dower House. Isn't that where your mother lives? Why don't we drop in? Louis?' she prompted.

But he didn't answer. The front door of the house had opened, and panic swelled in his throat as a woman stepped into the sunlight. He caught a glimpse of his mother's beautiful face, pale with shock, and then he put his foot down on the accelerator.

'What are you doing?' Santa was looking at him, her eyes wide and confused. 'Why didn't you stop?'

'Just leave it, Santa, okay?' he snapped, relieved to have found an outlet for the emotions churning in his chest.

Her face stiffened and there was a tiny, fractured pause. Then she turned away.

They didn't speak for the rest of the journey.

Almost before he'd stopped the car Santa wrenched open the door and she was gone, moving so quickly that he had to lengthen his stride to keep up with her.

'Santa—'

His anger had burned away and now he felt exhausted and unsteady. The last time she had run from him he had been worried that it might be his fault. This time he knew it was. He had never felt more lonely or alone.

'Santa, please...'

He caught up with her in their bedroom, spinning her round to face him.

'I'm sorry. I didn't mean to bite your head off.'

She stood in front of him, her chest rising and falling. 'I don't understand. I thought you came here to see your mother.'

'I did.'

'So why didn't you stop?'

There was a beat or three of silence and then he breathed out unevenly. 'Because I didn't tell her I was coming. Because I didn't know what to say.'

Santa felt her stomach knot. His skin was stretched tightly over his cheekbones and there was a tension in his body as if he was shouldering an invisible burden.

'I was scared of what she would say. Or even if she'd want to speak to me.'

She caught his arms. 'She called you that time.'

'And I hung up. She reached out to me and I let her down.' He stared past her. 'All these years I've told myself I didn't care. I told myself there was nothing for me here. But now I'm scared that there really isn't anything left, that there isn't anyone left for me.'

'You have me.'

They weren't just words. She meant it. Every waking thought she had was about Louis. She even dreamt about him. In his arms, everything else ceased to matter. Just looking at him stole the breath from her lungs. He had her body, her heart...

Her heart? She felt dizzy. Her pulse was pounding in her head.

It couldn't be true. Theirs was a marriage of convenience. But knowing that hadn't stopped her from falling in love with him.

In love.

The idea was ludicrous—she couldn't be.

But she was.

Somewhere between getting into his limo and now love had slipped into her heart like a key in a well-oiled lock.

She felt a rush of pure, undiluted joy, clear and bright, like the sun reflecting off snow, and she wanted to share it with him as she had shared everything else.

Only she couldn't do that. He hadn't signed up for love. He wasn't looking for 'for ever'. He had told her himself that he would never marry for love and that he would be better off flying solo.

But didn't he only feel like that because of what had happened with his parents? Surely if he and his mother reconnected then he would feel differently about love?

About her.

She could feel his pulse jerking against her fingertips and she tightened her hands around his wrists. 'I know you're scared about seeing your mother, I would be too, but whatever happens you have me. I'll be there with you when you see her.'

The muscles in his arms were trembling. 'You're a good person, Santa,' he said softly. 'Maybe that's why you're the only person I can't lie to. You make me do the right thing.'

'You're a good person too.' Blanking her mind to the riot of emotions pounding through her body, she reached up and clasped his face, pressed a gentle kiss to his lips. 'And I will be here for as long as you need me.'

He smiled then—one of those devastating smiles that felt like winter sun on her face—and then his hands stole around her waist to touch the bare skin of her neck. Stomach melting, she leaned into him, her hands looping over his shoulders.

'I need you now,' he murmured against her mouth.

His hands tightened around her waist and he picked her up and carried her to the bed. He stripped off his clothes, then hers, his sharp intake of breath telling her more clearly than words how badly he wanted her.

Instantly her own body responded, the hunger that he had unlocked rising up inside like a wave. She pressed closer, brushing her nipples against his chest, her breath quickening as he kissed her shoulder, then the pulse beating at her throat, his lips trailing a path lower still to the taut, swollen tips.

Her fingers slid down to capture his arms. She felt wild with need, her body unravelling against his, and helplessly she arched against him, squeezing her thighs together around the ache that was building there.

She felt his hand move, his wrist warm against her thigh as his fingers slid between her legs, slipping smoothly into the hot, slick flesh, his thumb grazing her clitoris so that the ache was just on the right side of painful.

'Louis...' His name was a noise in her throat.

Clutching his biceps, she raised her hips, oscillating her body against the pad of his thumb. She was so close to losing control… Another second and she would be lost, it would be over, and she wanted to hold on to this feeling for as long as she could.

She batted his hand away and, reaching down to where his erection was pushing into the mattress, took him in her hand.

Louis grunted, his body tensing as he felt her fingers slide over the smooth, blood-hardened skin, her touch bringing him instantly to the point where it wasn't enough. He wanted more. He wanted all she had to give.

Only it was more than wanting. What he felt for Santa was need, raw and unfiltered by ego or etiquette.

He couldn't wait a moment longer. He had to have her now.

Shifting slightly, he rolled her over, pulling her body on top of his, blood roaring in his ears as she helped guide him inside her. Her thighs were trembling slightly and, gripping her hips to steady her, he began to move, thrusting upwards into her.

'Yes…' she whispered, and then she tensed.

He felt a tremor run through the fine bones of her body, the muscles clenching, and suddenly it was too late, and his mouth covered hers, and he was grasping her wrists, their hot breath mingling as her cry mixed with his groan of release.

Later, as she lay wrapped in his arms, he felt her shift against him.

'I meant what I said about being there with you,' she said.

Her blue eyes were focused on his face, soft but steady, and he felt something ignite beneath his skin as she put a hand to his chest.

'I know.' He hesitated. 'But what if it's too late? Too broken? I'm not sure I know how to fix it.'

'You do. I know that you think you're not up to it. But

the truth is your life—everyone you lost, everything you had taken away, everything you've built—has taught you all you need to know.'

She sat up, not bothering to hide her body, and that confidence, that change from the gauche girl who had been ashamed of herself to this beautiful proud woman, made his heart want to beat its way out of his chest.

'You fix your eyes on the prize and you focus, and then you push forward, and you keep pushing forward.'

He breathed out unsteadily. 'I'd like to go now. If you'll come with me?'

She nodded, her smile as soft as her eyes were bright. 'You should have looked at our marriage certificate more closely—then you wouldn't need to ask that.'

'What do you mean?'

'My middle name is Ruth.' Lifting his hand, she threaded her fingers through his. *'"Where you go, I go."'*

CHAPTER TEN

IT TOOK FIFTEEN minutes to walk to the Dower House. Louis kept wishing they could stop and turn back, but Santa's grip never faltered. Finally they reached the smartly painted gate, and then they were standing by the front door.

'Give her a chance,' Santa said quietly. 'Give yourself the chance to be her son again.'

As the door opened, he felt his heart slip sideways.

'Louis.'

His mother was clutching her throat. For a few quivering moments there was nothing but the blood beating in his ears, and then she was pulling him forward, her hands fluttering over his face, tears spilling down her cheeks.

'I'm sorry... I'm so sorry, darling.'

'I'm sorry too. But it doesn't matter any more,' he said hoarsely.

Inside the house, his mother regained her poise and led them into the light, spacious sitting room. He and Santa sat down close to one another on one of the chintz-covered sofas. Her hand was warm and firm in his.

'Did that come from the main house?' he asked, looking across the room at a beautiful mahogany escritoire. He was only asking because he needed to get his voice under control. He knew it did—only how? Why did he remember so much, and in such detail? It was as if he had never gone away...

But then, of course, a part of him hadn't, he thought, looking up into the familiar brown eyes of the woman sitting opposite him.

'You don't mind, do you?' she asked.

He shook his head. 'It's yours, Mama.' The word slipped from his mouth without hesitation, as if it had been waiting there, primed and ready. But he knew that it hadn't. It had been trapped inside him, stifled by the past, and if it had been down to him alone it would have stayed there unspoken for ever.

But Santa had set him free. She had brought him home.

'There's someone I want you to meet...' He turned to Santa, wanting to share this moment with her. 'Santa, this is my mother—Henrietta, the Dowager Duchess of Astbury. Mama, this is Santa, my wife. The Duchess of Astbury.'

He watched his mother reach out and take Santa's hand.

'Thank you for bringing my son home.'

'He was already on his way, Your Grace. He just lost track of time.'

His mother's mouth trembled. 'We both did.' She smiled shakily. 'I wonder, would you like some tea?'

Santa's eyes met his, and he felt her squeeze his hand. After a moment he squeezed it back as she shook her head.

'No, thank you. I need to call my father, and you two have a lot of catching up to do, but I hope to see you again soon.'

'I hope so too.'

At the door, he pulled her close, his mouth seeking hers.

'I can stay,' she whispered.

'No, you're right. We have a lot of catching up to do. But I'll see you back at the house.'

Walking back into the sitting room, he hesitated a moment, and then sat down next to his mother. 'I'm so sorry for hanging up on you.'

'It doesn't matter, darling.'

He shook his head. 'He was right. I let you down.'

Her fingers gripped his arm. 'He regretted it, Louis. What he said...how he acted. He regretted all of it until the day he died. But he was such a proud man—and he thought you would come back, that you would need him...us.'

'I did.' His chest tightened as he remembered the nights when he would barely sleep from missing his home, his family. The loneliness had been like a painful head-to-toe tingling. 'At Glamma's funeral I tried to talk to him, but—'

'I know.' His mother nodded sadly. 'Losing her and you so close together knocked him for six. He had a ministroke and then he changed, became anxious. I couldn't leave him even for a moment. But I should have tried.'

Her eyes met his. They were surrounded by fine lines now, but they were brighter than ever with love.

'I should have stood up for you,' she said. 'I knew Marina wasn't right for you, even before we found out about that polo player.'

He waited for the sting of pain. But he realised with shock that he didn't care. Marina's betrayal felt like a fly brushing against his skin.

A flash of pink fluttered at the edge of his vision and he glanced out of the window, expecting to see Santa, her body arcing in the snow, her blue eyes fixed on the prize, the flawless facets of her face diamond-sharp, impossible to erase.

But it was just a camelia that was defiantly blooming by the gate.

'Why did you think she wasn't right for me?' he asked, frowning up at his mother.

'Because you didn't love her,' she said simply. 'You thought you did because you're like me—romantic. Your heart rules your head every time. But you're also stubborn, like your father, so that you can't see what's right in front of your nose.'

The next day Santa woke late, and for the first time in days she found herself alone. The curtains were still drawn and she sat up, feeling a rush of panic. And then she heard the sound of running water from the bathroom.

It was okay... Louis was just taking a shower.

Pressing her hand against the imprint in the mattress, where the sheet was still warm from his body, she lay back down and stared into the grainy half-light, trying to absorb the detail amid the wider pattern as the events of yesterday swirled inside her head like a carousel.

One particular detail to be precise.

She bit into her lip. How had it happened? How could she have been so stupid as to let herself fall in love with him?

Shivering, she pulled the covers over her body.

More importantly, how was she going to cope when he was no longer in her life? And that day *would* happen—because this arrangement was temporary. A year-long, mutually convenient sticking plaster over the mess they had made in Klosters.

Yes, they had moved the boundaries. Now sex was part of that arrangement. But no matter how passionate or tender, it was still just sex. And that only made her heart ache more.

'Good morning.'

Louis was standing in the doorway, a towel wrapped around his waist, his dark hair damp, droplets of water glistening like diamonds on the smooth, tanned skin of his formidable chest.

'And it's not just a good morning, is it?' he said softly, walking towards the bed. 'It's a very important one.'

Pulse accelerating, she stared up at him mutely. Her

heart might be breaking but her body still reacted to his nearness with unfiltered intensity, so that it was all she could do not to reach up and pluck the towel free of his waist.

He leaned forward and kissed her on the mouth. 'Happy Birthday, Santa baby.'

She blinked up at him. With everything that had been happening, she had lost track of the days. But today was Christmas Eve, and therefore today was her birthday.

'Come with me. I have a surprise.'

Taking her hand, he led her across the room to the window and pulled back the curtains. Outside, the world had turned white.

'It snowed!' She turned to him, her lips curving into a smile. She felt suddenly and inexplicably happy. 'I can't remember the last time it snowed on my birthday. Can we build a snowman?'

In the bleached sunlight, his eyes were very blue. 'As long as you promise not to wear four-inch heels.'

Remembering that early-morning walk through the silent snow-covered roads, his jacket around her shoulders, his hand tight around hers, Santa felt her heart tumble. But just because her feelings had altered, it didn't mean she could alter the past and make it more than it was. He had simply kept her from falling...got her safely home.

'How did you know it was my birthday?'

'The marriage certificate. And I double-checked with your passport.' He grinned. 'Cute photo, by the way.'

She punched him on the arm. 'It was a mistake. I went to a different hair salon and I don't think they understood what I wanted. Besides, no one looks good in their passport photo.'

'*I* do.'

He started to laugh, and then Santa was laughing too, and he pulled her against him, folding her into his body.

'So—I thought we'd have a birthday brunch, and then you get to choose what we do this afternoon.'

She glanced over at the clock. 'What do you suggest we do between now and brunch?'

'Well, I know Sylvia has planned a feast...' His eyes were steady on hers and she felt heat dart beneath her skin like a shoal of tiny fish. 'So I thought it might be a good idea to work up an appetite...'

Two hours later they made it downstairs.

'Don't you want to go and look at the snow?' he asked.

She felt a quick head-rush as he tilted up her face and kissed her on the mouth, his fingers curling into the belt loops of her jeans to pull her closer. His eyes were a glittering, sapphire-blue, and there was an expression in them she couldn't fathom.

Probably he was just fired up with relief at having finally made peace with his mother. Or maybe he was excited about the snow. Robbie and Joe were the same and so was her dad, now she came to think of it.

'Yes, of course I do.'

'You first.'

He nudged her forward and she opened the door, her body tensing with anticipation at the pleasure of the first crunching footstep.

She froze.

A twisting path of rose petals in every shade of pink led away from the house, cutting a brilliant line of colour across the flawless white.

She let out her breath in a little flurry and caught it again. Her heart was galloping like a thoroughbred inside her chest. 'What...? Where does it go?'

He seemed pleased by her reaction. 'Let's find out,' he said softly, taking her hand.

Feeling as if she was walking on air, she followed the trail of petals across the lawn, past the snow-laden topiary hedges of the formal garden—and then she knew where they were going.

The door to the tower was open. Inside, the petals continued up the winding staircase to another door and another smaller staircase. Her fingers tightened around his as she reached the top step.

'Happy Birthday,' Louis said quietly.

Santa pressed her hand to her mouth. Not that there were words for what she was feeling. Nor could she have spoken them anyway.

It was a tiny chocolate box of a room.

There were windows on all eight sides, each with a view of the pristine white landscape. The walls were decorated in a pale raspberry silk, and beneath the tiny, glittering chandelier a log fire glowed orange.

A huge picnic hamper sat on a table by one of the windows, and taking up the rest of the space was a beautiful glossy mahogany sleigh bed, complete with snow-white bed linen.

Trembling inside, she turned to face Louis. 'You did this for me?'

'I wanted to surprise you.'

'Well, you have.'

'Good.' He smiled—one of those dazzling, impossible-to-resist smiles. 'But, much as I'd like to take all the credit, my part was largely limited to making a whole lot of unreasonable demands at impossibly short notice. My long-suffering staff did all the hard work.' His hand slid among the strands of her hair. 'They'll probably all give notice later, so you might have to help me cook the turkey tomorrow.'

He was trying to downplay it, but it had been his idea. He had made it all happen. *For her.*

Her eyes sought his. Hoping, longing to see what was in his heart. But his eyes were a familiar teasing blue and, deciding to focus on what his actions meant rather than on what they didn't mean, she smiled.

'I'll make sure I thank them. But thank you too, Louis.' She kissed him softly on the mouth. 'It's the loveliest surprise I've ever had.' She leaned into him. 'I'm starving. Can we look inside the hamper? Or have you not worked up enough of an appetite yet?'

His body stilled, his eyes sliding towards the bed, then back to her face.

'Now that you've said you're starving, I suppose we'll have to look inside the hamper,' he grumbled, as she took his hand and led him across the room.

They ate by the window, gazing out across the wintry fields.

'My picnics are a little more basic than this,' Santa confessed, as Louis handed her a glass of chilled champagne.

And by 'basic' she meant supermarket baguettes with clumsily cut cheese in the middle, a bag of crisps, a chocolate bar and a piece of fruit washed down with tea from a Thermos.

'My father was a big fan of *al fresco* eating,' Louis said, forking some of the smoked ham hock salad into his mouth. 'He thought it was the truest test of a great country house kitchen. How's the gravadlax?'

'It's delicious.' She glanced down at the jewel-pink slices of salmon with their delicate herb crust. 'So, did you go on lots of picnics when you were little?'

Louis hesitated, his fork in mid-air, as if her question had caught him off guard. 'Yes, we did,' he said finally. 'We used to go down to the lake and row out onto the island. Sometimes we'd get up early and my father would take me out fishing.'

She looked up at him, enchanted by the softness in his voice and by this new openness between them.

She frowned. A phone was ringing. Hers. She glanced

down at the screen. 'Sorry... It's my dad, video calling. I don't have to speak to him now. I can take it later.'

He shook his head. 'It's your father. Of course you should speak to him now.'

Clumsily, she swiped upwards. There was a short pause and then she started to smile, as an enthusiastic rendition of 'Happy Birthday to You' spilled into the room.

'Thank you—that was brilliant.'

'We didn't wake you, did we?' Kate looked at her anxiously. 'We thought you'd be up anyway...you know, to train...but then we worried that you might be having a lie-in.'

'Kate was worried.' Her father grinned. 'I knew you'd be up.'

'I'm actually having brunch...' She glanced over at Louis.

It's fine, he mouthed.

'Hey, there!' Shifting forward, he waved lazily at the screen. 'We thought we'd make the most of the day as it gets dark so early.'

Santa felt her heart twist as one of her brothers leaned forward. 'Do you have a crown?' he asked.

Grinning, Louis shook his head. 'I don't, sadly. But there is the Astbury tiara, which is a kind of crown, and as Duchess your sister gets to wear that.'

Both boys leaned closer to the screen. 'Can we see it?'

Louis laughed. 'Sure, just not right now.'

Instantly the boys refocused on Santa. 'Have you opened your presents yet?'

'Can we see them?'

'Robbie, Joe—that's enough.' Frowning apologetically, Kate pulled them back. 'Sorry, they're just so excited to talk to you both.'

'It's fine, honestly—and, actually, you called at exactly the right time.' Louis looked over at Santa. 'I was about to give Santa her present.'

She stared at him, her eyes wide with confusion. Wasn't all this her present?

'Here.' Reaching into the hamper, he pulled out a beautifully wrapped gift.

'Open it!' the boys chanted. 'Come on, Santa, open it.'

She pulled the ribbon, catching at the delicate paper. Heart thumping, she stared down in a daze. 'Oh, Louis…'

'Okay, we're going to go now.'

Glancing up, eyes burning, she nodded wordlessly at Kate as the screen went blank.

'You shouldn't have,' she said slowly, gazing down at the beautiful diamond necklace.

'I absolutely should. You're my wife.' He hesitated. 'I have a confession. It's not a new piece. It belonged to my grandmother. My grandfather gave it to her on their wedding day.'

It was difficult to speak past the lump in her throat. 'I can't accept this, Louis.'

'I want you to.' His eyes were steady on her face. 'Turn around,' he said softly.

Feeling choked, she reached up and touched the glittering diamonds. 'I don't know what to say.'

'You don't like it?'

He was teasing her—or maybe he wasn't. There was an intentness to his gaze, as if her answer mattered. As if he was asking another entirely different question.

She felt her lip quiver. 'Of course I do. I love it. I love—' She stopped herself just in time. 'I love everything about it. It's beautiful.'

He shook his head. 'Any jewellery can be aesthetically pleasing, but for me, it only comes to life when a beautiful woman is wearing it.'

He made her come alive, she thought, gazing up at him, her heart sliding helplessly free of its moorings. Only she could never tell him that.

But she could show him without words.

Clutching his shoulders, she pulled him closer, moaning softly as his mouth covered hers, her body turning boneless as she felt the hard press of his erection.

Later, they lay together, their limbs overlapping among the crisp white sheets. Pulling Santa's warm body more closely against his, Louis buried his face in her hair, breathing in her clean, floral scent.

He had wanted to give her a birthday to remember. It felt like the least he could do after everything she had done for him. She had not just made him face the past. She had given him back a future he'd thought was lost. Given him back his home. His mother.

But it was more than that. Santa had given him back his self-esteem. When she looked at him, she saw the best of him. And in doing that she somehow loosened everything inside him.

Thinking back to the moment when he had told her about going fishing with his father, he felt his pulse slow. He'd spent so long alternately hating his father or blanking the past that he had forgotten those early mornings out by the water, but suddenly the memory was there, soft-edged and warm, like sunlight fluttering through a veil of leaves. His father's sudden, swift approval as he caught a fish, the measured instructions spoken in that quiet, authoritative voice.

His breathing stilled as he pictured Santa's expression. The softness in her eyes both astonished and scared him. Or maybe what scared him was how badly he wanted to stay here in this tower with her for ever...

'What are you thinking?'

He looked down at her, his head still reeling. But of course it was only natural that he would want to stay in bed with this beautiful woman, he told himself quickly.

'Nothing, really. Just that you have a very lovely family.'

She smiled. 'They're your family now too.' Her fingers tightened on his arm. 'Thank you for this. For everything.'

He glanced at his watch. 'Your birthday's not over yet.'

'I know.' She smiled. 'But it's not just my birthday. It's Christmas Eve too. And that means that tomorrow will be Christmas Day. So I was thinking you might like to ask your mother over to lunch.'

Her eyes found his and he felt his heart stop beating. And then he breathed out shakily. 'I might just go and speak to her now.'

After Louis had gone, Santa sat on the window seat in the tower room, her eyes fixed on the roof of the Dower House that was clearly visible over the snow-topped hedges. She knew that things would be good between mother and son—she was sure of it.

It had taken a long time, but Louis had come home, and she was so happy for him. He was getting his old life back, but it would be a different life too—one with new possibilities.

Her heart squeezed. More than anything she wanted their marriage to be one of those possibilities—a marriage in which their vows were true. And that would mean telling Louis that she loved him. It would mean taking a risk—the biggest risk in her life. But what was marrying a stranger if not a risk? Surely what had happened in Klosters had taught her that in life, and in love, sometimes risks were meant to be taken.

She felt her pulse skip. They weren't strangers now. Nor were they the same people who had squared up to one another in Klosters. She was more rounded, less prickly and uncertain, and Louis was different too. That coiled-spring tension she'd assumed was part of who he was had disappeared, just like it did with her when she came off the ice after a competition.

'There you are.'

He was back, and her stomach flipped over as he strode

across the room and pulled her into his arms. Breathing in the scent of his warm skin, she rested her head against his chest, absorbing the steady stroke of his heartbeat.

'How did it go?'

'Good...' Releasing her, he joined her on the window seat. 'It's not like it was before. It's better. More honest.' His eyes found hers. 'She cried when I asked her to lunch. She was so happy.'

'So she's coming? That's wonderful. I'm so pleased she'll be there for your first Christmas at home.'

'Our first Christmas...' he said softly.

She felt her heartbeat accelerate. If she was going to say something it was now or never.

But before she could open her mouth to speak Louis said quietly, 'She showed me these scrapbooks my father kept. About me...about Callière. There were letters too. Letters he never sent, telling me how proud he was of me.'

She squeezed his arm. 'What matters is that he wrote them, and now you've read them.'

He nodded slowly. 'She gave me this, as well. She said he always intended for me to have it, but he was too proud to reach out to me. And what made him most proud was that I didn't come asking for it.'

He held out a piece of paper: a cheque. She stared down at it, stunned, her heartbeat stalling, her eyes juddering along the lines of zeroes. 'That's a lot of money.'

'I know—it's a crazy amount.' His eyes burned into hers. 'But it means I can buy out the shareholders. I'll finally own Callière.'

Holding herself completely still, she stared up at him, a smile pasted on her face. Of course he should be happy. It was what he wanted more than anything. His prize. Only if he didn't need the shareholders' money then he didn't need to be married, and he didn't need her.

'Hey, don't look like that.' His hand tipped her chin up.

'Nothing's changed. I'm not going to renege on our deal. You don't think I'd do that, do you?'

Feeling sick, she shook her head. She knew he would stick to his word, but his word wasn't what she wanted any more. She wanted his heart. Only that wasn't on offer. The door she had thought was opening wasn't just closed, it was locked, and she didn't have the key.

She never would.

Knowing that made a hysterical bubble of panic fill her throat, and if it hadn't hurt so much she might have laughed.

It wasn't fair. She had thought pretending to the world that she loved Louis beyond reason would be hard, but to look into his eyes every day for a year and pretend she *didn't* love him would be an incomparable torture.

She wouldn't be able to conceal it. She wasn't even sure she could bear it. But she definitely couldn't bear it alone, and suddenly she wanted her family. She wanted to go home.

Only if she told Louis that, then there would be a scene. He would ask questions that she couldn't answer—or, worse, she might end up answering, and it would be mortifying for him to know the truth. Far better for her just to leave without a fuss. At least that way she might find it easier to let go.

'Of course I don't.' Her smile was aching now. 'We have a deal, right?'

A deal that felt like a vice around her heart.

CHAPTER ELEVEN

THAT NIGHT IN BED, she wrapped her arms around his neck, holding him close, trying to remember each quickening breath, trying to commit to memory every second of their last night together.

Afterwards, he fell asleep quickly and completely.

Holding her breath, she dressed in the darkness, and then picked up the bag she had discreetly packed earlier and crept downstairs.

The house was silent.

She had booked a taxi, and the man on the end of the phone had promised her that he would be there before midnight. It was now only half-past eleven, but she couldn't have stayed upstairs a moment longer.

Leaving her bag by the front door, she made her way to the drawing room. There was a good view of the drive, and although the fire was dying it still had a hot orange core. She stood in front of it, shivering. It was as if there was ice in her veins. She didn't think she would ever be warm again, and a part of her was glad. She wanted her heart to freeze and not to have to feel anything ever again.

'You know, you're supposed to be hurrying down the chimney tonight, not out through the front door.'

She turned, her heart hammering in her throat.

Louis was standing in the doorway in his pyjama bottoms. In the light from the fire the blue of his irises looked bruised, and his face was still and unsmiling.

'I'm sorry. I know you wanted me to spend the day with your mother, but I just can't do it.'

'Do what?' He walked across the room and stopped in front of her.

'Lie to her. I just don't think I can do that.'

'Why not? Why particularly not to her? We've lied to everyone else,' he persisted.

'Because she loves you.'

Because I love you.

She almost spoke the words out loud, but something in his eyes stopped her. All of a sudden it was as if none of it had ever happened. As if they had never kissed or made love. He was a cold, distant stranger.

'So you thought you'd just sneak out in the middle of the night? It's Christmas Eve, for—' He swore under this breath. 'And what about saying goodbye to Sylvia? The staff? My mother? What about saying goodbye to me? Could you not do that either?'

Striving for calm, she looked up at him. 'It's not goodbye,' she lied. 'We're going to see each other.'

He took a step closer. 'I'll take that as a no, then.' His eyes fixed on her face, cool and glittering like cut gemstones. 'Is this because of the money? The money my mother gave me? I meant what I said. I'm not going to cut you loose.'

'I know...you said. We had a deal and you're going to stick to it. That's what we agreed, and nothing's changed between us, has it?'

The hope in her voice sounded deafening and her breath caught as he hesitated, seemingly on the point of saying something, but then he shook his head.

'No, nothing's changed, Santa. Nothing at all.'

Of course it hadn't. This was and could only ever be a marriage of convenience for Louis. Anything else was just her overreaching, just like she did out on the ice sometimes. Only this time she had a chance to pull back.

Swallowing past the lump in her throat, she said quickly, 'Look, I'm glad you sorted things out with your mum, and that she's going to be here for Christmas, but I want to go home. To see my family. And then I need to start training again. Obviously, we can still make public appearances together, like we agreed, but this seems like a good time for both of us to move on.'

There was a short silence, and for one beautiful, fleeting moment she thought it would be all right. She actually believed he would stride across the room as he had done earlier, pull her into his arms and tell her that he couldn't let her go, that he wanted her, needed her, loved her, and that she was essential to his life.

'I suppose it does,' he said slowly. 'You know, I actually thought you were different, Santa. I really did. But you're just like everyone else. This was always about you, wasn't it? What you want. Your needs.'

'That's not fair, Louis, we both wanted this—'

'Actually, I don't know what you want. I thought I did, but now I don't think I ever knew you at all. Goodbye, Santa.'

He turned and walked away, and Santa pressed her hand against her mouth, the tears she had been holding back spilling hotly down her cheeks as she grieved for the man she had loved and lost. The man who had never been hers to lose.

Louis stepped into the bedroom, his whole body shaking with shock and a pain like nothing he had ever imagined.

He had woken to find the bed empty, and at first he hadn't been concerned, only then he had realised that it wasn't just the bed that was empty but the room, and that Santa was gone.

Even then he hadn't thought she was *gone* gone, but

then he had made his way downstairs and seen the bag by the door. He still couldn't believe it. He had never felt closer to anyone. Never trusted anyone so much. Needed anyone more.

Loved anyone more?

His heart stopped beating. That couldn't be true. He didn't believe in love. Marina had cured him of that particular myth.

Except he hadn't loved Marina.

His mother had told him that and she was right. But then she knew him better than anyone.

'You're like me—romantic,' she'd said. *'Your heart rules your head every time. But you're also stubborn, like your father, so that you can't see what's right in front of your nose.'*

His mother was right about that too. He hadn't seen what was right there in front of him, but Santa had.

Only now she was gone. It was too late.

Glancing up at the sky, Santa blinked. It was snowing again. Heavier than before. By morning, Waverley would be cut off from the world. But for her it would always be out of reach.

The thought almost undid her, and she stopped and swiped at the tears spilling down her cheeks. It was difficult to walk when you were crying. Harder still when your heart was breaking in two.

'Santa!'

For a moment she thought she was imagining it, hearing voices, footsteps crunching on snow. Only then, turning, she saw that Louis was there beside her, dressed now, his breath white in the air, his eyes blazing in the darkness.

'You have something of mine. You need to give it back before you leave.'

She sucked in a breath, hurt, horrified, the momentary flicker of hope that had flared in her heart instantly snuffed out.

'I didn't take your grandmother's necklace. I know how important it is to you and your family. I wouldn't do that. I left it upstairs.'

'I'm not talking about the necklace.' His voice seemed to stall in his throat, and then he reached up and touched his chest. 'I'm talking about my heart, Santa.'

For a moment she thought she must have misheard him. 'I don't understand—'

'You have my heart.'

She stared at him, deprived of both speech and breath, as his hands slid around her body and he pulled her closer.

'Ever since I met you I haven't felt like myself. I couldn't work out what was wrong with me. And then, literally a moment ago, I realised there was nothing wrong, and the only reason I didn't know what I was feeling was because I've never fallen in love before.'

Her heart was speeding now, heat blooming over her skin. 'You love me?'

Breathing out shakily, Louis nodded. 'I'm crazy about you,' he said softly. 'Completely smitten. And I'm sorry it took so long for me to realise that.' His arms tightened around her. 'I don't want you to leave. Not because of some stupid deal, but because I love you and I can't live without you.'

He looked down at her, everything he was feeling shining from his eyes. Framing his face with her hands, she kissed him fiercely. 'I love you too, Louis.'

As snowflakes fluttered onto their faces the sound of bells rang out across the blanketed fields and Louis pulled her closer. 'Happy Christmas, Santa baby,' he whispered, and then he kissed her.

EPILOGUE

ALMOST EXACTLY THREE years later, Santa stepped out of the shower and wrapped a robe around her damp body. Today was Christmas Eve—but it wasn't just Christmas Eve. It was Christmas Eve at Waverley, and a very special private anniversary.

Obviously she and Louis celebrated their wedding day, but this was the day when their marriage had stopped being one of convenience and become instead a marriage of love.

A love that had only grown stronger and more precious with every passing year.

Her heartbeat fluttered as she touched the delicate diamond bracelet around her wrist. Louis had woken her with breakfast in bed and a kiss—which, as usual, had turned into passion. They had made love slowly and tenderly, taking their time, letting their pleasure build until neither of them had been able to bear it any more.

Afterwards he had given her this bracelet, but she had decided to wait just a little longer before giving him her gift.

She dressed quickly and made her way downstairs. Louis was in the hallway, gazing up in satisfaction at the two immensely tall Christmas trees.

'You're not still gloating, are you?' she said, biting into the smile curving her lips.

He grinned. 'Definitely taller.'

She rolled her eyes. For some unfathomable mascu-

line reason that she and Merry didn't understand, every
Christmas Louis and Giovanni competed over who had
the tallest tree. Last year Giovanni had won by an inch.
This year Louis had trumped him by half a foot.

'I'm sure Giovanni has got more important things on
his mind this Christmas. Like being a dad,' she teased.
'Besides, size doesn't matter.'

Louis pulled her into his arms. 'I think we both know
that's not true,' he said softly.

She felt a prickling of heat dance across her skin as his
blue eyes drifted over her face and down her body.

'But maybe if you're having doubts we should go back
upstairs…'

Her stomach tightened, her breasts suddenly aching.
She wanted to. Her need for him was as strong as his for
her. But…

He groaned. 'I know, I know… I said I'd walk down to
get my mother and I can't be late.'

Leaning into him, she kissed him slowly, hungrily. 'No,
you can't be late. But there's always later.'

Louis stared down at her, savouring the hunger rising inside him. He truly believed he was the happiest man on
earth. Marrying Santa hadn't just changed his life, it had
changed *him*. And for the better.

He was stronger, calmer, kinder.

She had made him grow up and face his fears, and
with her by his side he knew that anything was possible.

'Not too much later, though,' he said, sliding his hand
through her hair and pulling her closer. He grimaced.
'Talking of my mother, I need to get Sylvia to help me
wrap the portrait. You do think she'll like it, don't you?'

Looking at him, Santa nodded, her heart swelling. 'She'll
love it.'

The painting was a surprise for the Dowager Duchess.

The first official portrait of the Tenth Duke of Astbury and his Duchess.

'I still think you should have been wearing your medals,' he said.

She laughed. 'They're not that kind of medal.'

His blue eyes flared. 'Maybe—but you still earned them, and I'm so proud of you, baby.'

'I know.'

And not just proud—he had been so supportive. Waking early to come to the rink and watch her train, attending every round of every competition.

Her dream had come true. She had won gold and Louis had been there with her.

She felt her face grow warm. Maybe it was time to give him his present.

'But the painting is finished now,' she said.

He frowned. 'It can be changed. We can change it. Do you want to change it? I could call Andrew. He only lives thirty minutes away. I'm sure I could persuade him to drop round this afternoon.'

Her heart skipped a beat. She had been hugging her secret to herself since yesterday, dithering over when would be the perfect time to tell him. Now, though, she knew that there was no need to choose.

Every moment with Louis was perfect.

'That won't work…' She stood on tiptoe and gently kissed his beautiful curving mouth. 'The baby won't be here until June.'

* * * * *

THE
GREEK SECRET
SHE CARRIES

PIPPA ROSCOE

MILLS & BOON

This book is for my sister, Kate.
I would not be where I am without her.
I would not be who I am without her.
Love.
Always.
xx

PROLOGUE

Last night...

THERON THIAKOS STALKED the damp London street, cursing the rain. It just never stopped. How could people live like this? he angrily asked himself, longing for the piercing heat and pure bright sun of Greece, the glittering blue sea that sparkled enough to make a person squint. The cloud-covered night gave the Mayfair street an air of mystery as he came to stand before the impossibly exclusive private members club, Victoriana.

Before him, two men stood either side of a door with such thick black gloss the paint looked like running water. The Tuscan columns supporting the portico spoke of riches and a sense of history that struck a nerve. Theron bit back a curse. This was exactly the kind of superior, expensive establishment that would appeal to Lykos's ego. Theron made to step forward when, shockingly, one of the men raised his hand to stop him.

'I'm here to see Lykos Livas,' Theron stated, not bothering to conceal the distaste in his tone. He had neither the time nor the patience for this. The anger in him was overpowering and he wanted someone to blame. *Needed* someone to blame. And he knew just the person.

The other doorman nodded, holding the door open and

gesturing Theron towards a woman wearing some sort of strange green tweed trousers that cut off at the knee and a waistcoat. Lykos had always had a flair for the dramatic, but this was so... English. *Old* English.

The immediate press of warmth that greeted him after the cold London night was a blessed relief. His mouth watered at the thought of the whisky he'd fantasised about for the entire drive down from the Soames estate in Norfolk where he'd left Summer standing on the stone steps, unable to face the look in her eyes as he drove away.

He'd lost everything. Absolutely everything.

Theron followed the hostess weaving her way through a surprisingly large establishment, completely decked out—as one would imagine—in furniture and furnishings from the Victorian period. And, despite the negative bent of his thoughts, he couldn't help but be impressed by the bar that stretched the entire length of the main room. Two houses, at least, must have been knocked together to create such a space.

He caught sight of his quarry, sitting at a booth of deep green leather with a woman no less exquisite than to be expected in Lykos Livas's company. Theron's gaze barely touched the brunette, his mind instead seeing rich golden hair, hazel eyes and lips that were ruby-red when full of desire and pale when devastated.

His fingers pulsed within his fist as Lykos finally turned to acknowledge him.

'This is all your fault,' Theron charged, his tone firm and bitter.

Lykos stared at him for a moment, his gaze so level Theron wondered if he'd even heard the accusation. Then he blinked that silvery gaze. 'I'd say it's good to see you but—'

'We are well beyond niceties, Lykos, so I'll say again, this is all your fault.'

'That depends on what "this" is,' Lykos said over the rim of his glass before taking a mouthful of his drink.

Inhaling a curse, Theron turned to the brunette. 'Leave us.' He hated being so cruel but he was at his wits' end.

'That is hardly necessary,' Lykos protested half-heartedly.

'It's not as if you won't find someone else to play with,' Theron said truthfully, turning his back on the girl as he looked for the hostess. 'Whisky?' She nodded and disappeared into the bar's darkness.

'True,' Lykos replied with a shoulder shrug, watching his companion leave in a huff before narrowing his eyes at Theron. 'I see you once in ten years and now you won't leave me alone?'

It was a relief to speak in his native tongue again. It had been—what?—a week since he'd left Athens and found himself in that hellhole in Norfolk. Some found the Greek language harsh, but to Theron it flowed like *tsipouro* from Volos and tasted like honey in *loukoumades*.

'This is not the time for jokes, Lykos.'

'You never did have a good sense of humour,' he groused.

Theron's drink arrived and he slipped into the now empty seat. He palmed the glass, staring at it as if he hadn't spent the last three hours wanting it.

'You'd best bring the bottle, *glykiá mou*,' Lykos said, leaning well into the server's personal space. Not that she seemed to mind. At all.

'What are you doing in London anyway?' Theron asked before challenging himself to only take a sip of the liquid he wanted to drown in.

'I like it here.'

'I don't believe you. I don't believe that any Greek worth their salt would enjoy all the...*grey*,' Theron said with such distaste it was as if the colour had taken up residence on his tongue.

'Grey? I'm not quite sure I've seen London during the daytime hours. Is it that bad?' Lykos asked, appearing to sincerely ponder it.

'Yes. But Norfolk is worse.'

Lykos's silver eyes narrowed and Theron's dark gaze held the challenge. 'Is that so?' Lykos asked.

'It is. They've even named a paint after it.'

'What, Norfolk?'

'Yes. It's grey.'

Lykos sniggered into his glass, before sobering and then sighing. 'What did you do?'

Theron clenched his jaw at the accusation. For just a moment it had been like it had always been between them. The banter flowing freely from the bone-deep knowledge of each other. But that was before Lykos had walked away from their friendship.

'If you're looking for absolution,' Lykos warned, 'you've come to the wrong damn place,' he went on before eyeing up the bottle of Glenglassaugh the waitress had placed on the table as if he wasn't sure he wanted to waste such good alcohol on Theron.

Theron shook his head, frustrated with the man who'd once been like a brother to him. 'I don't need absolution. I need to know why you called me a week ago.' Theron knew with absolute certainty that he was involved in all this somehow, but he needed to hear it from Lykos.

'To taunt you, of course,' Lykos said with a smile that had more than likely charmed women right out of their underwear. 'When your holiday fling turns up at my door—'

'Watch your mouth,' Theron growled.

'Ooh, touchy.' Watching Theron from the corner of his eye, Lykos continued. 'When the lovely Ms Soames arrived at my door trying to offload a fifteen-million-pound estate in the country for a third of the market value, I just wanted to brag. I've always wanted a castle.'

'It's not a castle.'

'Oh?'

'And it's rundown. There are holes in the walls and it's freezing. All the time. And the damp...' Theron threw his hands in the air as if in despair.

'Oh, well, that wasn't in the sales pitch. Is that why you're here? To talk me out of buying the estate?'

Theron thought about it for a moment too long. 'Buy the estate,' he said tiredly. 'And it's worth the market value, Lykos. Don't take advantage of a vulnerable woman.'

Lykos slammed his glass down on the table, ignoring the stares it drew from the other guests, his eyes shards of ice but the burn in them white-hot. 'There's a line, Theron, and you are skating dangerously close to it.'

Theron wanted to bite back, wanted the anger Lykos threatened. His pulse pounded and he welcomed it, his breath audible now as his lungs worked hard. They stared at each other, while Theron waged an internal war and Lykos waited to see what he would do.

Gritting his teeth, Theron decided it was better to leave than to cause a scene and got to his feet.

'Oh, sit down before you break down,' Lykos bit out.

Theron stared at the doorway long enough to realise that he didn't have anywhere else to go.

'Break down?' he asked.

'I can practically feel the tears from here. Drink that,' Lykos said, passing him a large measure of whisky, 'before you start weeping all over the place. *Then* have the kindness to leave before you scare off the rest of tonight's entertainment.'

'You're a real piece of work, you know that?'

'Theron, as hard as this is to believe, I really don't care what got your knickers in a twist.'

'You would have once.'

'And you chose Kyros,' Lykos growled.

'No,' Theron shot back. '*You* left.'

'And you could have come.'

'And how would that have repaid the man who gave us *everything*?' Theron demanded.

'That was always your problem. What could ever be equal compensation for what he did for us? What could you give him that would repay such a thing?'

Theron turned away from the demand in his oldest friend's gaze and stared into the whisky, trying to ignore the feeling that he might have finally found something worthy of such a debt.

His heart.

And his child.

'Fine,' huffed Lykos. 'You may explain, if it will take that look off your face.'

Summer paced before the fire in the Little Library. Back and forth, back and forth as her eyes went from wet to dry, red to pale. But her heart ached as if she'd never stopped crying.

This room had become her sanctuary in the last two months, every inch of it as familiar to her as if she'd lived here all her life. But instead of seeing books that would make the British Library jealous, she saw eyes, dark like coals, making her shiver from the heat. Eyes that had laid her bare, exposed her soul. Her heart pulsed and her core throbbed as if taunting her, reminding her of the night before, as he'd thrust into her so deep and so deliciously she *still* ached from the pleasure. She turned and paced back past the fireplace where flames danced joyously as if there was nothing wrong, as if her world hadn't just shattered into a million pieces.

She brushed her hair back from her face. Six months ago she had been a naïve third-year geophysics student whose only worry was how to pay her sisters back for working all hours to pay for her to go to university. And now?

She was pregnant.

And yet she couldn't afford to think about it. She couldn't think about Theron Thiakos or even her father, Kyros. Now she *had* to think about her mother and sisters. About finishing the treasure hunt she, Star and Skye had been sent on by the grandfather they'd never met. The task? To find the Soames diamonds, hidden over one hundred and fifty years ago by their great-great-great-grandmother from her abusive husband. Clues had been found, coded messages translated, and her sisters had travelled the world to track down the elements needed to find the jewels.

It had been easy to hide her baby bump three weeks ago, when Skye had flown first to Costa Rica and then to France to locate the map of secret passageways that led throughout the Norfolk estate. And Star had been so full of romance when she had left for Duratra in the Middle East, searching for the one-of-a-kind key made by joining two separate necklaces that her sister had missed all signs of Summer's pregnancy too.

Meeting the terms of the will, she had been forced to stay behind. She had scoured their great-great-great-grandmother's journals, searching for clues about exactly *where* Catherine had hidden her family's jewels, but hadn't been able to find any. But if they did find the jewels, the sisters would have met the terms of their inheritance and be able to sell the estate in order to pay for their mother's lifesaving medical treatment. That was *all* that mattered right now. The jewels. Her mother's health. She couldn't think of anything else.

Especially not a man with eyes as dark as obsidian and a heart protected by granite. A granite, she thought with a sob, she'd hoped to have chipped. She placed her hand over the crest of her bump, reassuring both herself and their baby that they'd be okay.

'It will all work out in the end,' she whispered. 'It's what Auntie Star is always saying. And Great-Great-Great-Grandmother Catherine? Trust, love and faith,' Summer assured her child, wiping away the last of her tears.

The sound of the ancient doorbell ricocheted throughout the sprawling estate that looked—at least on the outside—like Downton Abbey. On the inside? It could have inspired Dickens. For five generations the men of the Soames line had let the estate go to ruin, fruitlessly looking for the Soames diamonds. And the last, their grandfather, in his madness had been driven to knocking great holes in the walls. The irony was how close he had actually come to finding them.

Summer took a deep breath, swept another reassuring hand over her belly and whispered, 'It's time to meet your aunties.'

Summer opened the front door and was instantly pulled into a tangle of arms that squashed and hugged and she didn't need to see her sisters' faces to know she was *home*. It didn't matter where they were in the world, as long as they were together. Summer breathed them in. She had missed them so much.

'Oh my God, it's so good to see you,' Star rushed out in one breath. 'And oh my God, we have so much to tell you, and oh my... *God, what is that?*'

Summer found herself thrust back as Star stared wide-eyed at her stomach. Over her shoulder, Skye's delighted smile followed Star's gaze down to Summer's waist and her eyes sparked with shock.

'Surprise!' Summer called weakly just before she burst into tears again.

As if the spell had been broken, Summer was instantly pulled back into her sisters' loving embrace and given soothing declarations of support and reassurance. Unfortunately, this only made her cry harder, until Skye took charge and guided them off the steps and into the estate.

They held her all the way to the Little Library, Skye on one side, Star on the other, words of love filling the cold damp estate and easing Summer's hurt just a little. Once they had seen her settled in the large wingback chair, Skye put another log on the fire and ordered Star to make a cup of herbal tea from the kettle they'd set up in the library almost two months ago.

Skye crouched down and levelled her gaze at Summer. 'Are you okay?'

Summer nodded, blushing furiously now that the crying had once again stopped.

'Is the baby okay?' Star asked from behind her sister.

Summer nodded again, her hand soothing over the crest of her bump, and when she looked back up she saw the most beautiful smiles on her sisters' faces—joy lighting their eyes, pure and bright. Summer sniffed and Star passed her a tissue, keeping one back for herself and wiping at her eyes. Summer smiled as she could see Skye trying to suppress an eye-roll at their romantic middle sister.

'Can I ask—?'

'I don't want to talk about it. Now you're here—'

'Summer,' Star chided.

'I don't,' she replied, shaking her head resolutely. 'Besides, we have to find the jewels.'

'But I thought you found the jewels?'

'I haven't actually seen them. I was waiting for you both.'

As if quickly weighing up the importance of things, Skye seemed to come to a decision. 'The diamonds aren't going to disappear overnight,' she insisted gently. 'They can wait. *You* are more important right now. And we're not going anywhere until you tell us what's going on,' she said firmly.

The kettle reached boiling point and clicked off, all the sisters' gazes called to it, and a sudden silence blanketed the room until Star laughed. 'Okay, let's have some tea, take stock and, you know, breathe.'

Skye and Summer shared a look.

'Okay, who are you and what have you done with Star?' Skye demanded.

Star smiled. 'We have a *lot* to catch up on.'

And for just a moment they enjoyed the silence, enjoyed being back together again, reunited after the longest time away from each other. Then, as Star made the tea, Skye told them about her fiancé Benoit and the cottage in the Dordogne they had been staying in for the last few weeks. Star asked a few questions before telling her own tale about the oasis the Prince of Duratra had whisked her away to before his ostentatious proposal and how much she wished she had some *qatayef* to share with them as they had their tea. It was as if they sensed that Summer needed time just to let the heavy emotions settle. Warmth finally seeped into her skin and wrapped around her heart and finally both Star and Skye looked at her expectantly.

'I don't know where to begin.' Summer shrugged helplessly.

'At the beginning, of course,' Star replied, as if she were talking to her primary school class.

Summer took a deep breath, the words rushing out on a single exhale. 'I found my dad.'

'Wait...what?' Skye asked, clearly not expecting that to be where Summer's story began.

'In Greece. I found my father.'

'But I thought Mum didn't know his name?' said Star, frowning. 'Which was why she could never find...' She trailed off, as if suddenly understanding.

'Oh, no,' Skye said. 'Really? She knew the whole time?'

Summer nodded, the ache of all those missed years, of all the questions unanswered for so long, that missing part of her... She understood *now* why her mother had done what she'd done but, with a child growing within her, she knew that she couldn't have made the same choice.

'Why didn't you tell us?' Skye asked gently.

'I didn't want you to think badly of her. *I* didn't want to think badly of her.' Summer shook her head, trying to find the words to explain why she'd hoarded that information, hoarded that hurt from her half-sisters. Skye's father had started another family after he and Mariam broke up, Star's father had died tragically when she was just months old. But Kyros? He was *her* father and a part of her feared they wouldn't understand the need she'd felt to meet him. The need in her to connect with a man she'd never met. And perhaps beneath that, deep down, the thing she hadn't been able to admit...that if he rejected her then she wouldn't have to tell them. No one would have to know.

'I... I wanted to meet him first,' Summer said.

'And did you?'

CHAPTER ONE

Five months ago...

YOU CAN DO THIS, Summer told herself as she stepped out of the air-conditioned arrivals hall in Athens and was hit by a bank of heat that nearly knocked her back. Looking out at the wide road and the bus stop, she squinted as the sun bounced off the pale concrete floor.

She stared at the instructions from her hotel—a hotel that was within walking distance of Kyros Agyros's office building—and after gazing longingly at the line of taxis she steeled herself and found the ticket machine that thankfully had an English language button.

Less than five euros and ten minutes later she was on the bus, with half her mind on the stop announcements and half a mind on her father. An ache bloomed in her heart, one that had been there ever since she'd found the photo of her parents tucked away in the attic amongst all the old albums and family documents. Mariam had always told her that she'd never known her father's last name.

Oh, she'd told Summer many other things—that his name was Kyros, that, just like her, he had a little mole on his collarbone. That he'd made her laugh, made her believe in love again, even through her grief, and, despite how brief it had been, they'd had a wonderful, magical relationship. And Summer had never doubted it. Until, when looking for her passport, she'd instead found a picture of her mother staring deep into the eyes of a handsome man—and on the back, written in her mother's handwriting, the name Kyros Agyros.

Her already shaky foundations had been rocked by the secret Mariam had kept from her and, no matter how much she wanted to ask her mum about it, she couldn't. Because Mariam Soames was ill. Very ill. Words like stage three and cancer sent tremors through her and Summer dashed away a tear that threatened to fall. So no. She couldn't ask her mum about why she'd lied about knowing her father's identity. So that only left her one other option.

'Syntagma Square,' a robotic voice announced, and Summer grabbed her large rucksack and made it off the bus just in time.

She had planned to find her hotel first. It was, according to the guide, less than a ten-minute walk south of the square. But when she turned and saw the Parliament building behind her, she lost her breath on a gasp. On the opposite side of a wide road, white columns gleamed against the burnt yellow brickwork and towered magnificently over the square. Behind her, steps led down to a fountain where kids were playing and screaming and splashing water at each other. Off to the side were rows and rows of canopied tables and chairs, the scent of coffee hitting her all the way to where she stood.

In an instant she was filled with something she could hardly explain. Her geophysics professors and fellow students certainly would have laughed if she'd tried to explain it to them, but her heart swelled and she was brimming with something warm and thick and sweet. This was part of her culture, her heritage, her identity.

She walked across the length of the square, taking it all in. The heat, the people, the colour, the noise—it was so different to what she was used to. She was about to try and find the road that her hotel was on when she followed the sleek lines of a gleaming office building into the sky, shocked to see a bright red illuminated sign bearing her father's name.

She'd known his office was near here, but…an entire building? Her heart started to race and she rubbed her suddenly damp palms on her trousers, resenting the physical manifestation of a hormonal shift in adrenaline and cortisol. As if in defiance, Summer hitched her rucksack higher onto her shoulder and pushed her way through the circular doorway into a large atrium.

Instantly she found herself gawking as she looked up at the ceiling that reached thirty storeys up, feeling a strange sense of vertigo. The press of the air conditioning cooled the sweat slicking her skin and she resisted the urge to shiver. Summer looked to the reception desk where a beautiful dark-haired woman was waiting, her smile a slash of bright red lipstick.

'May I help you?' she said in perfect English as she approached, without Summer even having to do the awkward *Do you speak…?* dance.

Summer bit her lip, releasing it only when she finally had the courage to utter the words, 'I would like to see Mr Agyros, please.'

The receptionist hit her keyboard with a few furious strokes. 'I see, and do you have an appointment?'

'Unfortunately, no. Could you tell him that… Mariam Soames would like to see him?'

The receptionist looked at Summer, a little confused. 'I'm afraid that won't be possible.'

'I'm sorry, I know I don't have an appointment but it really is quite urgent that I speak to him.'

'I *appreciate* that, but it's not possible because he's not here. He is away with family.'

Family. The word sliced through Summer and, although she knew it was just a word, knew Kyros Agyros would have a family, it hurt unaccountably. He was supposed to be here. She'd done her research.

Her expression must have betrayed her because the receptionist was looking at her as if worried. 'Is there someone else I can put you in contact with?'

'No, thank you,' Summer said, shaking her head. 'Do you know when he'll be back?'

'I'm not at liberty to say,' the receptionist said, not unkindly.

Summer left the building feeling utterly shocked. She'd checked—he was supposed to be at a conference here in Athens according to several press releases and two different websites.

Back out on the street, the wave of heat made her feel nauseous and she sank onto the stone wall surrounding the building, trying to ease the seesawing motion the world seemed to suddenly take on. She felt so *lost*. She had wasted almost her entire savings on this trip. Savings that she'd planned to use to pay back her sisters. So *foolish*. Did she really think that...what—she'd come all the way here, head into his office, introduce herself and he'd welcome her like the long-lost daughter he'd always wanted?

The online research she'd done on Kyros had shown a lifetime of financial success stories and philanthropic endeavours, but very little about the man himself. He seemed to have kept himself out of the public eye as much as possible and the few articles she'd found indicated that he protected his privacy with two things: ruthlessness and a man called Theron Thiakos.

And as she looked up at the entrance to the building the man himself emerged from the revolving doors and Summer put her hand to the stone to steady herself. He stopped a few feet from the building to take a call. There, in the middle of the pavement, he seemed utterly heedless of the people having to swerve around him, an innate authority signalling his superiority.

She had seen pictures. Vague impressions of dark hair and formidable expressions, but at the time her attention had been on her father. Now, as she took in the entirety of Theron Thiakos, Summer lost her breath, as if the full Technicolor image was too much for her brain to handle.

Angles. Sharp, clean angles she wanted to trace with the palm of her hand. That was what Summer saw first. The wedge of his shoulders, the slant of a determined brow, the sharp cheekbones and the slash of his lips. They made her want to touch. She'd *never* felt like that before. She shook her head and tried to appraise him clinically, like the scientist she was.

He was tall, at least six foot.

Sleek. Fine.

She frowned at the useless descriptors, but they wouldn't stop coming.

Dark. Brooding.

She slowed her breathing, hoping it would help calm her erratic pulse, forcing her online research to mind. Thiakos was only six years older than her and, at twenty-eight, he had achieved a status and security that some could only dream of. He had graduated from a *very* prestigious school that counted the children of princes and diplomats amongst its alumni.

Elite.

Summer bit her lip at the rising heat on her cheeks.

After excelling in his national service with the Greek armed forces, staying for longer than the allotted time period, he had walked straight into a high-level position in Agyros's company before branching out with his own security company. Agyros had been Thiakos's first contract, but was by no means his only client. But nothing in her research of Theron Thiakos had prepared her for...*him*.

She looked down at her hands and noticed that they were fisted against her trousers, before shaking them out. By the time she looked up she couldn't see him any more. Panic rushed through her as suddenly what felt like her only connection to her father had disappeared.

The receptionist hadn't been able to tell her when her father would be back, but Theron Thiakos might.

She jumped up, blood rushing to her head as if she'd been holding her breath, and ran across the road, ignoring the blaring of car horns behind her. Careening round a corner, she caught sight of him again and the wave of relief that struck her was so powerful she sagged against the nearby building. Forcing her legs to move again, she took measured breaths, trying to slow the pulse raging in her ears, and focused her gaze squarely on his back. Her eyes tripped along the inches of his very broad shoulders and danced downward to lean hips and...

The sound of a laugh cut through her thoughts and, although it was still early, she noticed that all around them bars and cafés were bustling with people and animated conversation, the air electric and infectious. Everyone looked glamorous and sophisticated, bright and colourful and Summer felt the opposite of her namesake in black cropped chinos and a white and black striped boatneck top. But she had learned a long time ago not to draw attention to herself. Each of the Soames girls had. It wasn't the 'done thing' to have children by three different fathers and, while no one had said anything to their faces, the whispers and drawn curtains and judgement was evident from parents, teachers and neighbours alike.

And then choosing to study science? Worse, a subject like geophysics. The first and only time she'd worn anything remotely bright to class it was as if she'd thrown potassium into water. God only knew what would happen if she'd dared to wear make-up. Or—heaven forbid—a *skirt*.

Theron Thiakos turned into a bar on the corner. Large windows had been folded back like a concertina and people spilled onto the outside seating area. It was like everything Summer had encountered so far, colourful and riotous. She watched as he was greeted by a group of friends, shaking hands and kissing cheeks, and she barely resisted the urge to rub at her own tingling cheek.

'Good evening, are you looking for a table?'

Summer's focus on Theron was such that the waiter had to repeat his question before she realised he was speaking to *her*.

'Yes.' The word jerked out of her before she could change her mind.

'Theron, what are you doing here?'

It was the second time someone had asked him the same question and, unsurprisingly, his response was the same. A tight smile reminded them that not only was he their boss and the owner of the hugely successful international company they worked for but that he didn't have to explain himself to anyone. As expected, the person who had asked the question scurried off into the crowd.

He was here precisely because he didn't want to be. It was good for him to keep himself *and* his staff on their toes. But as he accepted a drink from the waiter he couldn't block out the conversation he'd had with Kyros's niece that morning.

It's just family. I'm sure you understand.

Just family.

Family.

Four hours ago, Theron had ensured an irritated Kyros boarded the boat kept docked at Piraeus, which took him away to the 'surprise' family gathering that the Agyros clan had organised. It had been pitched as a celebration, but it was so close to the first anniversary of Althaia's death that neither man had been fooled. Kyros had left to commemorate the loss of his wife and Theron hadn't been invited.

He had watched the boat sail out from the harbour, ignoring the devastating ache deep within and instead feeding the belief that he was better off alone. Repeating that thought like a mantra in his mind, he tuned back in to the sounds of the bar. Over the low hum of voices, glass shattered, a woman screamed in delight and a man laughed. His head snapped up.

It was the tone of their laughter that gripped him. It poked and prodded at a memory from Theron's childhood—from the orphanage in the days before he'd met Kyros. From before his life had changed irrevocably. It was snide, conspiratorial, mean and it cut him like a knife.

He turned to search out the source of the laughter amongst the bar's patrons. Noticing the two younger men standing on the brink of the outdoor seating area, he followed their gaze towards a blonde rolling her shoulder as if working out a tight muscle.

His gaze stuttered over her and a sudden rush of incendiary heat poured over him. A heat that felt without beginning or end, but one most definitely with her at its focal point. She glowed, a golden halo of hair, her skin warm like the first blush of life and her lips…the kind of fresh luscious red that money couldn't buy. Hungrily, he consumed what he could see of her, gorging himself so quickly he could only take in broad strokes. He almost stepped back to sever the power of his reaction.

He forced his gaze back to the two men and it was clear. She was their intended target.

Picking up his drink, Theron pulled out his phone as if checking an email and slowly closed in on the men.

'I bet you one hundred euros that she'll spend tonight in my bed.'

'Her? Why?'

'Why not?'

All three men turned to look at her as she thanked the waiter in English and the second guy grinned. 'Two hundred says she'll be in mine.'

'Three hundred with photos,' the first said with a leer that made Theron see red.

He forced himself to loosen his grip or he'd break his mobile. And he'd much rather break something of theirs.

He watched as the first guy made his approach, the way they tag-teamed it made Theron fear just how many times this had happened before. Surreptitiously, he took photos of both the men before putting his phone away, looking up to check the girl's reaction. They had chosen her because she was on her own, English, a tourist, a *target*.

The word ricocheted through him, bouncing off different memories from the past. In those first few months in the orphanage, he had seemed like a target to the other kids too. But he had learned and paid attention and used everything available to him so that no one considered him a target ever again. Him or those he cared about.

Through the haze of his thoughts, he felt her eyes on

him, pulling him back to the present, and an unholy need exploded into being deep within him, like a punch to his gut. She held his gaze as if she was there with him, standing in the eye of the storm of need, and it was an experience unlike any he'd ever had.

And then one of the men moved between them, cutting off Theron's line of sight and taking a seat at her table. By the time he could see her again, she was smiling, her face open and curious and wholly unaware of the danger she was in. Theron rejected any further prevarication.

'Darling,' he called loudly in English as he made his way towards her table, his purpose in reaching her quite clear. A few heads at surrounding tables turned to him and as she looked up her eyes widened to near comical proportions—only there was nothing funny about the gold and green that glittered in her hazel eyes. It was such a sight he nearly stopped. But didn't.

'Sorry I'm late—forgive me?' he asked as he rounded the table and placed a kiss on her head. He felt her flinch beneath him, but he didn't give her the time to question what was going on. 'You have company?'

'Mr Thiakos,' said the first man, half rising out of his chair —to greet him or run away, it seemed the man himself wasn't sure. It wasn't unusual for strangers to recognise him, and in this instance it would make things considerably easier.

Theron held his hand out and when the man reached his out, Theron's grip would have crushed walnuts. The second man in the chair beside him rose and Theron placed his other hand heavily down on the man's shoulder and pushed him back into his seat.

'Gentlemen,' he all but snarled. To the outsider they looked like a group of friends meeting for a drink, but the undertone was as dangerous as a riptide. 'Allow me to explain,' he said in rapid Greek. 'I overheard your little *bet*.' The guy beside him jerked beneath his hand, but Theron simply held him in place. 'Now, as you can imagine, the man who wins this bet, who takes this lovely young woman to bed, will have to contend with me. Or not? I suppose, then, it could be said that *I* will win this bet, no?'

The first man paled considerably, and Theron waved off the verbal fountain of apologies that streamed forth. 'The money?' he demanded. The man's eyes flashed with anger, but Theron had seen and been worse. He simply nodded, forestalling any further objection.

The first guy reached for his pocket and pulled out two hundred euros as the second guy did the same.

'I believe it was three hundred. I have *photos*,' he said, offering his phone and displaying their images, the threat clear. After a reckless moment of deliberation, each man finally handed over three hundred euros and left.

Theron watched them until he was sure they were gone and turned back to find the blonde watching *him*. Again. As someone used to being the observer, it was a novel experience.

'Theron Thiakos,' he said, holding out a much gentler hand in greeting, wondering if she had any idea how close she'd come to a very dangerous situation.

She looked up at him with huge wide hazel eyes, not once glancing at the six hundred euros on the table. She reached out her hand and, as it slipped into his, the smooth skin gliding against his flashed the most indecent images into his head.

'Summer,' she said by way of introduction.

Heat. Warmth. The feeling of the sun against his skin.

It wasn't her name that conjured such impressions. It was *her*. He needed to leave. Theron nodded to the money on the table. 'That's yours,' he said and got up to leave.

'Why?'

It was the way she asked. As if it was completely foreign to her that she would be given something for nothing. 'It was a con,' he bit out.

'I don't understand.'

'They had a bet as to which one could sleep with you tonight.'

The colour ran from her face, leaving her looking pale and shocked.

'They were being perfectly nice,' she said in the way that people did when they didn't want to believe they were victims.

'And take the photos to prove it,' he explained.

'And the money? That you took off them?' she demanded as if she wanted to see all the workings of what had just happened before she could believe him.

'They'll only learn if it hits them where it hurts.'

And if Theron delivered the photos to his investigative team to see if there would be enough evidence to take to the police. This probably wasn't their first time. He had turned away and was about to leave, determined not to give her another thought, when he heard what she said next.

'Thank you,' she said, sounding a little unsure if that was what she meant.

Against his will, he turned back to her. He came from a world where *thank you* was a forgotten word and the conclusion of business was the payment of an invoice. But she was looking at him as if he sat on a white horse and had just slayed a dragon. And he didn't think *anyone* had looked at him like that before.

Before he could leave, a waiter arrived with three drinks, oblivious to the disappearance of two of his customers, mainly because he was eyeing the pile of banknotes on the table. Theron resumed his seat and waited for the server to leave.

He gathered up the money and passed it to *Summer*. Her name in his mind did things that he didn't want to look at too closely.

'Please. Put this away before you draw even more unwanted attention.'

She took the handful of notes from him, blinking as if only now realising just how much it was. 'I can't take—'

'You can,' he said firmly.

The dim lighting made it impossible to tell, but he thought she might have blushed when his fingers met hers. The women he encountered didn't blush. Oh, he would leave them flushed. And panting. But…blushing spoke of innocence. An innocence he shouldn't even be in the proximity of.

'He knew you?' she asked, as if finally processing the events that had happened. 'He *recognised* you,' she said, a statement this time.

He shrugged off her apparent realisation of his notoriety, instead finding focus once again in her features. Her thoughts had furrowed her brow, drawing his attention to a nose that was distinctly 'button-like'. From there it was impossibly easy to drop his gaze to her lips and he was forced to stifle the sound of his swift inhalation.

Her lips looked swollen, as if recently kissed and thoroughly so. It wasn't a pout, and it wasn't the exaggerated bee-stung puff that silly people paid ridiculous amounts for. It was a natural fullness that he wanted to bite down gently on. There wasn't a slick of lipstick on them, yet their colour was as rich a red as his favourite Limniona. He could almost taste the wine on his tongue, the scent of the herbs and cinnamon spice in the air about them.

'What are you doing here?' His question surprised them

both and for the first time in a long time he felt the white-hot sting of embarrassment. Never before had he shown such a shocking disregard for self-control as to give voice to what definitely should have been a passing thought.

'I'm... I was supposed to be meeting someone.'

Her answer pierced the haze she had plunged his mind into. 'Oh, my apologies,' he said, frowning. He wasn't used to misreading situations, given that his career depended on it. 'I'll—'

'Oh, no, it's not like that,' she said, the words rushing out just like the hand she placed on his forearm. 'I... Family. I was supposed to be meeting family, but he's not here.'

Summer was quite aware that she was staring, but she couldn't help herself. And it had absolutely nothing to do with whether Theron Thiakos had access to her father, and everything to do with the fact that she had never seen anyone like him before.

He was impossibly good-looking. Carelessly so. Although his body was angled away from her as if he was desperate to leave, he seemed as unable to break the strange connection between them as she was.

Which was why she noticed the minute tremor that rippled beneath the surface of him when she had mentioned family. To some he might have appeared relaxed, but there was a tension formed deep within him and she didn't need a seismograph to know it. He reminded her of dolerite, the rock formed from pressurised molten lava.

'You are on your own?' He didn't seem to like the idea.

'In Greece? Yes,' she confirmed.

He turned back to his friends, his gaze snagging on the exit to the bar and then back to her, and something in her curled as she realised he didn't want to be there. With her. Shame. Embarrassment. Frustration?

She looked down as she saw him press a business card along the table with his index finger.

'Just in case you get into trouble.'

'I won't need it,' Summer said, no matter how desperate she was to accept the link to him, to her father.

He smiled, a painfully civil press of his lips that she felt around her heart. 'Maybe, maybe not. But take it so I will be able to sleep tonight.'

And with that he disappeared.

For a moment she sat, stunned, watching him leave. And only then did she realise she hadn't asked him when her father might return.

CHAPTER TWO

SUMMER HAD BEEN awake for a while without realising it. Staring up at the ceiling, her mind had continued to play out her dreams from sleeping into waking. And if it had just been a matter of images she might have been able to shake off the strange fantasies that had rolled out through the night hours. But it was the feel of them that had shaken her.

She could have sworn on the Bible that she knew the weight of his hand on her thigh, the press of his lips against her neck, the warmth of his body against hers, the safety she felt within his arms. A safety, a presence that made her unaccountably sad. The kind of deep sadness that felt familiar, that felt *old*.

Loneliness.

She realised it with a sense of confusion. She blinked at the ceiling and then approached it with a rationality that she was known for. Clearly it had more to do with missing Kyros Agyros than Theron and any such emotional reaction was surely understandable. Perhaps it was because she was in Athens alone that made it seem more...powerful.

She blinked back the threat of tears and threw herself into the shower, making plans as she washed the entirety of last night from her hair.

She didn't know when Kyros might return from wherever he was, but she had to hope that it would be before she left in a week's time. She decided to pass by the Agyros building later that afternoon and if there was a different receptionist she would try her luck again. If he hadn't returned in three days, then she would *have* to call Theron and somehow force the conversation onto her father. Until then she wanted to see as much of her heritage as possible.

After breakfast she left the hotel and decided just to walk. The streets ranged from hidden cobbled passageways littered with coffee tables, fuchsia bougainvillea and old men playing backgammon, to wide city streets that stretched for blocks and shops with expensive fashion labels and jewellery.

She wondered what her father was doing now. Was he still here in Athens? Or had he left for some other part of the world just at the exact moment she'd arrived looking for him? She tried to imagine what it might have been like to grow up here and was pierced by a sharp prick of guilt. She would never exchange what she'd had growing up with Skye and Star and her mother. Whenever she thought of Mariam her mind skittered over itself. As if she wasn't able or ready to think about how she had lied to her.

It hadn't taken much research to discover that Kyros had been married to a woman called Althaia. She had died twelve months ago and Summer had felt a strange grief on behalf of a father she had never met for a woman she had never known. They had married before Summer was born, so clearly her father and mother must have had an affair. Summer didn't know what to think about that, but wondered if it was why Mariam had never told her the name of her father.

She went to buy a bottle of water at a kiosk, pulled out her wallet and felt her eyes widen at the sight of the six hundred euros from the night before that she had completely forgotten.

Should she give it to the police? She took the change from the man at the kiosk and clamped her bag a little more tightly under her arm as she took a sip from the bottle of water. It wasn't exactly stolen though. She bit her lip and frowned. The thought of spending it made her feel a little hot around her neck—as if it were wrong. Yes, she could use it to pay for her flights or the hotel, or even a little treat, but it made her stomach squirm.

She and her sisters had always been frugal with money. They'd had to be. Mariam had provided love and security but not always consistency and over the years all three sisters had been there to fill in the gaps. But in the last few years Skye had worked as a secretary for a local builder and Star as a teaching assistant at the local primary, sharing a flat so they could help pay for the expensive tuition fees for Summer's geophysics degree. And she was determined that when she graduated and got her dream job she'd be able to give back to them.

Summer's part-time job meant that she had *some* savings so the lure of ill-gotten gains waned considerably. And only when she saw the animal shelter on the corner did her heart ease a little and she knew what she had to do. Five minutes later and six hundred euros lighter she felt *good*. For the first time since leaving her father's office she felt...*happier*.

She passed beneath a bright white and yellow awning, absentmindedly looking at the display in the window, and stopped, staring at the most beautiful yellow dress she'd ever seen. The long-sleeved ankle-length dress was deceptively simple and utterly elegant. A button-lined deep V-neck reached tantalisingly low and hugged the torso, flaring out at the legs and making it eminently cooler than what she was currently wearing. The design was pretty but it was the colour that really caught Summer, the kind of bright sunny yellow she'd always been told that blondes could never wear. *Should* never wear.

Beyond her reflection, she saw a woman smiling at her and beckoning her into the shop. Summer was about to shake her head regretfully when she saw herself meeting her father in a dress like that. Looking beautiful and accomplished. And not like…*her* as she was now. Crumpled old clothes in muted colours. *Invisible* colours.

She did have her savings…

You can't, she told herself.

Unbidden, Theron's voice from the night before replied, insistent and final.

You can.

All morning Theron had stared at the Parthenon from his office window when he should have been answering emails, phone calls, running last month's figures or doing *anything* but thinking of an English girl waiting for her family.

He could blame it on the fact that he hadn't been with a woman for nearly eighteen months, but that would only be a half truth. Ever since he'd bought the apartment at Althaia's insistence, he'd not been able to bring a woman back there. Before her death, Althaia had asked him to stop living in the short-term rentals that had made up most of his adult life thus far. Beneath that had been the silent censure about his short-term pastimes of the female variety, but she'd been too kind to call him on it.

Stability. Kyros and Althaia had always known how important it was to him. How it was more than a desire, but a need in a life that could very much have gone the wrong way, like so many others in the orphanage had. For just a moment, a memory of the first night in that place slipped through his defences and his entire body turned to stone. In a heartbeat he'd shut it down but that tension still held in his shoulders, in his jaw.

It will be good for you, she'd said.

All the while Althaia had been trying to give him stability, knowing that her death would rob him of it. She'd even tried to get him to reach out to Lykos, but that had been a step too far.

As he looked up the hill once again, he cursed. He needed coffee. Despite his assurance that he would only sleep well if she took his number, his dreams had been fevered images of Summer wrapped in his sheets, heated, flushed and utterly debauched. And as frustrating as those images were, he much preferred them to thoughts of the past.

Stalking from his office, he ignored the confused look of his assistant, blanked the question from his second-in-command and went for the stairs instead of the elevator, hoping to work off the nervous tension thrumming through his veins. Theron took them two at a time, his sense of urgency gaining rather than decreasing with the action.

He burst onto the pavement, sending a couple of pedestrians scattering, and made his way to the best coffee cart in the whole of Athens. He caught the eye of the mean old man who worked the cart every day of the year, rain, shine and even the occasional snow. He'd had the same coffee here every day for ten years and the old goat still growled, 'What do you want?' at him every time. It might have had something to do with how he and Lykos had once stolen a whole tray of muffins from his cart and, although he was fifteen years and several million euros away from the kid he'd once been, Theron had the sneaking suspicion that the vendor remembered it.

The rich smell of chocolatey coffee hit him and soothed this strange aimless fury unsettling him. He rolled out his shoulders and waited at one of the cheap metal tables that despite its apparent frailty—much like the coffee vendor—had somehow lasted the test of time.

His fingertips tapped out an impatient tattoo on the table top. The old man was mean, but he didn't usually make Theron wait. He turned just as the most incredible flash of yellow caught his eye. He fought against it, he tried *so* hard not to look, but the impression of supple curves outlined in gold was seared immediately and indelibly into his mind. The woman had her back to him, affording him an exquisite—if illicit—view of the way the material caressed the sweep of her backside and swayed gently as she leaned towards the coffee vendor, who looked as if he'd just fallen in love.

Theron couldn't *not* trace the arch of her spine and wonder whether the space between her shoulder blades would fit his outstretched palm perfectly. Blonde tendrils had been swept up to reveal a neck pink from the sun, but no less tempting to his lips and tongue.

She looked around too quickly for him to turn away and his gaze crashed into a gold-flecked hazel stare that instantly widened with surprise. A surprise he felt himself, down to his very soul. Her name sounded in his mind as if he hadn't already thought it a hundred times that day. But his name on her lips sent a surge of fire through his blood.

Her footsteps faltered and she came to a stop in the middle of the tables, staring at him while Theron sat there, hypnotised by the sight of her, so beautiful he felt changed by it.

Finally, he stood, pulling himself to his full height. 'Summer.'

She looked back to the coffee vendor, who shooed her

in Theron's direction explaining in broken English that he'd bring her coffee over. Looking decidedly uncomfortable, she picked her way through the tables, the sway of the yellow material he wanted to feel beneath his fingertips gently billowing in her wake.

'I didn't know that you'd...'

'My office is just round the corner.'

'Of course.' The moment she said it she blushed and he couldn't quite fathom why she would think that his office would *of course* be round the corner.

She stood beside the chair he had offered her, looking at him in that way she did, until the vendor arrived with his coffee and her frappe. Theron ignored the side-eyed glare from the old man that warned him implicitly not to upset the nice English lady, and waited for Summer to sit.

He looked out to the street, but even the cars and tourists couldn't wipe the sight of the deceptively provocative V of her dress from his mind. As he turned back, he caught her averting her eyes and smiled at this strange dance happening between them.

'So. What do you do?' she asked, biting her lip immediately after the last word was out of her mouth.

And then he registered her question with slight surprise. It had been a while since someone had not known who he was, what he did. Had not known him to be joined at the hip with Kyros. It was novel.

'Security,' he replied, his natural disinclination to talk about himself cutting his words short.

'Financial?' she asked, a slight pink to her cheeks.

'No.'

The light seemed to dim from her eyes a little and he silently cursed. He was so unfamiliar with flirting. Was that what he was doing? In the past it had seemed much easier, the women more knowing and determined and he just as willing to go along with the simple sexual exchange. He had the suspicion that there was nothing simple about Summer.

'What have you done today?' he asked and she seemed relieved.

'I went to the Acropolis today. It was...' she shook her head, her eyes lit with excitement and pleasure '...incredible. The sense of history there is quite amazing. And the way that the underlying rock formations have developed...' She trailed off, biting her lip as if to stop herself from continuing.

'Yes?'

'Mmm?' she replied, as if asking a question.

'The underlying rock formations?'

'Oh, shall I continue?' she asked, surprised.

He couldn't help but laugh a little. 'Are you in the habit of pausing mid-sentence and changing the subject?'

'Well, yes, actually,' she answered honestly. 'Usually when I start to talk about rock formations, people's eyes glaze over,' she said, sweeping a loose corn-coloured tendril back behind her ear.

'Are my eyes glazed over?' he asked and held his breath as she leaned forward across the table to look more closely at his eyes, squinting and assessing and smiling as if he'd delighted her somehow.

'No,' she replied, trying and failing to contain a gentle laugh.

He gestured for her to continue, picked up his coffee and sat back in his chair to listen to her talk on, of all things, rock formations.

'It's actually quite interesting really, because the limestone capping the Acropolis—the ground on which the Parthenon is built—is Cretaceous Age Tourkovounia Formation. But the layer beneath that, the Athens Schist, is from nearly thirty million years *after*. So the upper rock layer is older than the lower, which is a perversion of the principle of superposition.'

He nearly choked on his coffee at the way she said perversion and he felt like a naughty schoolboy. He didn't think he'd *ever* felt like that, even when he had been at school.

'And because the schist is more susceptible to weathering than the upper layer of limestone, it's being nibbled away over time from the sides. But essentially it's an erosional remnant of a much larger...'

'Larger...?'

'Thrust sheet,' she said, blushing, and as much as he tried, he really couldn't help the smile that pulled at his mouth. 'I'm sorry, I should shut up,' she concluded.

'Why?' he asked, genuinely intrigued why she would regret something that brought her to life in such a way— even if he'd been amused by her accidental double-entendre. 'This is your work?'

'I'm a geophysics student. It's the study and analysis of the physical properties of the earth and space around it.'

'And your interest is in...' He had never had to work so hard to get a woman to talk to him. Instinctively, without question, he knew Althaia would have loved her.

'Well, most people go into oceanography, but I'm quite interested in engineering.' She shrugged helplessly. 'It's—' her eyes sparkled '—it's fascinating to me, but boring to most people.'

He frowned. He might not have understood all of it but her enthusiasm and expertise had been electrifying. 'Boring or intimidating?' he asked.

'Well,' she said, giving it that same kind of focused consideration he was beginning to appreciate about her, 'perhaps it's just harder to relate to,' she said, shrugging. 'Or to talk about,' she concluded.

'Or they're just not taking the time to understand why it's important to you?'

Summer's mind went completely blank. No one outside her course could relate to it and while her sisters loved her greatly and made obliging sounds and supportive gestures, they didn't know *why* it was important to her. It was something she'd never really told a soul. But the way that Theron was looking at her…expectant and…and…as if he were challenging her not to disappoint.

'I never knew my father.' His eyes flashed for a second, as if surprised at the direction of the conversation. 'It…it made me feel less…tethered. As if I wasn't quite sure of the ground beneath my feet. I have a wonderful mother and two incredible sisters, but there was something about having half of my history, my identity, hidden that made me need to know that everything around me is…'

'Safe,' he finished for her.

'Yes.'

He nodded. And for just a second she thought he understood. That he knew that feeling too.

'What you do is important,' he stated and the ferocity shining in his eyes painted her skin in sparkles, the assurance of his words vibrated in her chest, making her feel glorious. But then he blinked and it was too late to ask him about the hurt she had seen beneath the burn in his eyes. He had covered it so quickly, if she hadn't been so used to observing and recording she might have missed it. 'Everyone in Greece knows that.'

She linked his two statements and made the connection. 'Of course. Your earthquakes here are—'

'Almost daily.' He seemed dismissive.

Summer nodded, feeling a little less shiny. She had waited so long to find someone who was impressed by what she did, but when it had happened, when Theron had said those things, all she'd wanted was for him to be impressed by *her*.

She leaned back in her chair, trying to shift away from the gravitational field that seemed to pull her to him. She took off the straw's paper wrapping and plunged it into the coffee the vendor had assured her she'd like. The moment the cool, sweet, creamy coffee exploded on her tongue she couldn't help but moan. In her peripheral vision she saw Theron's jaw clench and pulse. Perhaps he believed that iced coffee was for children, she thought, but she didn't care. It was delightful.

He checked a watch that could only be described as obscenely expensive and glanced at her quickly, as if checking it was safe to do so. 'You've eaten?'

The question caught her as slightly strange. As if he didn't quite care, but wanted to make sure that she was looking after herself. She was tempted to lie, but found herself shaking her head when he returned his eyes to hers.

Then a gaze that had been distracted, as if he'd been at war with something in his thoughts, cleared and the creases at his eyes softened. 'Would you have dinner with me?'

Her mind skittered to a halt, quickly running over the last few moments. She might not be well versed in dating, but had he intended 'You've eaten?' to be an invitation? She couldn't help but smile a little at the discomfort he was hiding fairly well as she kept him waiting. A hundred reasons to refuse ran through her mind against the one that connected him to Kyros. But that wasn't the reason she placed her hand in his.

It was a little awkward at first as they made their way out of the square, past cafés and bars, weaving between pedestrians, but after a few minutes it eased and became comfortable. And then comfortable became something warmer, softer...something intangible that Summer couldn't explain or quantify, but could most definitely *feel*. She smiled and when she turned to see him casting a glance her way, the hint of something soft curling the corner of his lip, she felt it in her chest. A thud. A beat. A pulse.

When he asked, she explained a little about her family, what it was like to grow up in the New Forest, focusing on her siblings rather than her mother. The ache in her chest from the hurt and confusion over her mother's lies a bruise she gently protected. Theron was now talking about the way the different areas in Athens had changed over the years, and she wondered what he would think if she told him about Kyros. Her conscience stirred, warned her that by not telling him the truth, not telling him why she was there, she was lying to him. But, for the first time in her life, Summer ignored the rationality of her mind and followed the beat of her heart.

The sun was low in the sky by the time she saw the first glimmering shimmer of the sea. And soon they were walking along a pathway that bordered the thin strip of sand between them and the sea, towards a small white-fronted building with blue and white checked tablecloths.

'Is this where you bring all the girls?' she asked, forcing her tone to be light, but genuinely curious.

'No, I've never brought a woman here,' he said, looking as surprised by the answer as she was.

He was greeted like royalty by the staff and customers, who he waved off good-naturedly, and eventually they were led to an outdoor area where lines of fairy lights created an illuminated canopy above. She sat in the chair that Theron had pulled out for her and, before she could even take a breath, a carafe of wine had been placed beside large glasses of iced water. The waiter said something to Theron in Greek before leaving.

'You're hungry,' Theron determined.

'Starving,' she confessed. And within minutes nearly ten different plates had filled the table. Some she recognised, some she didn't, all smelling absolutely divine. Not knowing where to start, she followed Theron as, plate by plate, he dipped some of the gorgeous warm pitta into each dish.

He hardly ate a thing, while Summer seemed to taste and test everything, returning to ones that she liked in order but leaving her favourite until last—the one that made her eyes drift closed and her shoulders lower as if finally relaxing.

All afternoon he'd known that he should put her in a taxi and send her back to her hotel. But then she'd say something to make him laugh and he honestly couldn't remember the last time that had happened. Or she'd ask a question and the next thing he knew it was an hour later. Or she'd look at him in a way that convinced him she was the most innocent person he'd ever met. Everything was there on her face, each new delight, concern, question, joy, desire...

'Thank you,' she said, putting the fork down, her gaze low and her smile small but satisfied. 'So, why here?' she asked.

'The food is the best in Athens,' Theron said, speaking God's honest truth. It was also about two miles from the orphanage he'd grown up in and would probably still be leaving out food for the kids had he and Kyros not funded a soup kitchen two corners over eight years ago.

'You must have been coming here a long time.'

'I have,' he confirmed, watching her look around at the humble restaurant in awe.

He speared some of the *xtapodi*—his favourite dish—
and was just about to open his mouth when she asked, 'Did
you come here with your family?'

The sharp sting cut him from head to toe. He hadn't expected it. He usually didn't get this far in conversation with
anyone, let alone a woman. He blinked to wipe the haze
from his eyes, mind and heart. 'No,' he said, trying to find
his way back to the present. 'They died when I was five.'

Her eyes flashed to his, a sudden fierceness in her gaze
as if she could personally hold back his grief, standing
between him and it. Her sympathy was active, alive and
pulsing and it shocked him to his core.

'I'm so sorry for your loss.' Even her condolence was
defiant almost, rather than the muted sadness he'd had
from others.

'It was years ago,' he dismissed and as she held his gaze
something fresh came into his mind.

It was twelve months ago.

His eyes widened in shock. The sudden, completely unbidden realisation that Althaia's death had hit him just as
hard as that of his parents gutted his heart. He mentally
shook his head and excused himself from the table. As he
stalked out towards the rear of the restaurant, he ordered
himself to get a grip. When he got back to the table he'd
send her on her way. He couldn't be around her. She prised
things from him he usually kept locked tight. And he didn't
have to be told how innocent she was. She'd blushed at the
word thrust, for God's sake. He should send her home and
head back into town and find someone to lose himself in.

Summer felt a presence coming towards the table, but instinctively knew it wasn't Theron.

'Good evening.'

She looked up to find a man even taller than Theron

standing at a respectable distance away, as if not wanting to interrupt.

'Lykos Livas,' he said, holding out his hand for her to take. 'I'm an associate of Theron's. I hope you don't mind,' he said, placing his free hand on his heart in a gesture she was sure would have charmed a large percentage of the population. It might have worked on her too, if her mind wasn't already on *another* handsome Greek man. Her mind and her heart.

'It is sacrilege to allow a woman as beautiful as you to be here on your own,' he concluded.

The sheer ridiculousness of the line made her laugh and, to her surprise, rather than being offended, Lykos Livas seemed strangely pleased.

'Does that usually work?' she couldn't help but ask.

'Yes, actually,' he declared.

'Tourists?'

'Always,' he affirmed happily.

Summer shook his hand and felt...nothing. Not the tingles that shot up her arm every time Theron accidentally brushed her hand. Not the heart pounding, breathless feeling in her chest when she caught him looking at her that echoed deep within her until she felt as if she might explode.

'So, you work with Theron? With Kyros?' Summer asked, trying not to flinch as she said her father's name.

Lykos's silvery gaze sparkled as he held her gaze for a little too long. 'No,' he finally replied with a deadly smile. 'My millions are my own.' He looked behind him as if checking for Theron and reached into his jacket. He handed her his card. 'Just in case you ever need anything.'

'Why would I—?' she said, taking his card and, before she could stop him, he had swept up her hand, bowed and pressed his lips to the air just above her skin in a kiss right out of one of Star's historical romances.

'It was nice to meet you, Ms Soames,' he intoned and vanished as quickly as he had appeared.

Summer was still staring after his retreating form when Theron stalked over to the table with such fury she reared back.

'What did he say to you?' Theron demanded.

'What?'

'Livas. What did he say?'

'Nothing,' she said, folding Lykos's card in her palm. 'He just asked if I was alone. When I said no, he left.'

Theron stared at her, then threw some money onto the table. 'And the kiss?'

'What kiss?'

CHAPTER THREE

THERON KNEW HE was overreacting, knew absolutely one hundred per cent that he had regressed several millennia into caveman behaviour, but he couldn't help it. His blood rushed in his veins, pounded in his ears, and his inner voice had howled out the word *mine* the moment he'd seen Lykos bent over her hand.

He hadn't seen Lykos for ten years and Theron hated that his first reaction had been one of joy. And then he'd remembered. The way that Lykos had left, the argument they'd had, the demand Lykos had made. The betrayal he'd felt. He hadn't even been there for Althaia's funeral.

'He didn't kiss me—my hand, I mean.'

'I know what I saw.'

'Or you saw what he wanted you to see,' Summer replied, watching him closely. 'And, even if he had, it was just a kiss,' she said with a shrug.

'Just a kiss?' Theron demanded, horrified. 'There is no such thing as *just a kiss*,' he said, wondering what inept individuals she had been kissing to say such a thing.

And then she blushed and looked down at the table. And he knew. *None*.

How was it possible? This beautiful, vibrant, incredible woman and no one had kissed her? He stared at her as she tried to gather herself, understanding that she was embarrassed, and glared off into the ocean to give her a moment's privacy.

He cursed himself mentally. He'd known she was different from the women he had associated with in the past, but this? This was an innocence that should be well beyond his reach.

Coffee was placed on the table along with plates of baklava and Theron wavered. He desperately wanted to leave, return Summer to her hotel and never look back. But he couldn't leave her looking like that.

'He likes you,' he said to her. When Summer raised eyes full of questions, he explained. 'The owner. He only ever gives out one piece,' he said, pointing to the two squares of baklava on her plate.

His answer took away some of the hurt in her eyes and he was thankful. But he still marvelled at her innocence. How she could—

'The town I grew up in is quite judgemental and, my sisters and I, we have…we have different fathers. So…' she shrugged, as if that would make all the preconceptions, judgement and sadness he imagined she must have battled as a child just disappear '…for the most part people avoided us.'

'For the most part?'

She frowned, making him want to smooth away the little furrow in her brow. 'When I was about thirteen, a boy—*the* boy—at school asked to meet me after class.' She smiled sadly at herself as if she should have known better. 'I overheard his friends talking about it. How they wanted to see if I was just like my mother.'

Theron clenched his fists under the table, feeling the anger he'd banked ignite instantly, her experience with bullies and teasing melding a little with some of his own. The fights he'd had, before Lykos.

'I left him waiting and ignored him and his friends for the rest of the year.'

He tried to let go of it—the anger—the way she seemed to have done.

'It was easier to stay away from boys like that. And at uni the guys on my course... Well, they tend to be more interested in...'

'Igneous rock formations?' he asked, thinking of her studies.

She laughed, as if it was funny that she had so little experience of receiving attention, and his heart broke a little. 'Yes. Exactly,' she affirmed.

He nodded. 'Eat your baklava,' he commanded.

'Yes, sir,' she replied with a smile.

From the first mouthful of the sweet, nutty, sticky dessert she had fallen instantly in love. And through every subsequent bite Theron had sat back in his chair, sipping at his coffee, never once taking his eyes off her.

At first it had made her self-conscious. Her forkfuls had been small, dainty and her eyes low on the table. But then she had lost herself in the tastes and textures of each mouthful, caught herself stifling a moan of sheer delight and risked a glance at Theron, who seemed almost carved from stone. Almost, because there was nothing inert about his eyes. They flashed, sparked, flared, flickered... There was such movement in them she could look at them for ever. She felt them graze over her face, her shoulders, her hands where they picked up the fork, her chest when she sucked in a breath, her neck when she leaned forward to take a sip of coffee, her lips when her tongue smoothed over a drop of syrup. Every single action made her aware of her heart beating in her chest and the low pulse between her legs. Something was building within her, a yearning, a need, and she felt as if she might jump out of her own skin if it wasn't let loose. She might never have experienced it, but she knew exactly what it was. She put her fork down, giving up on the unfinished dessert because that wasn't the kind of hunger she felt now.

She knew it. And so did he.

Theron reached across the table and picked up her hand. He brought it towards him and her heart shifted. He cradled it within his palm, the pad of his thumb smoothing imaginary lines on the back of her hand as if slowly, inch by inch, he was erasing the memory of one man and imprinting himself in its place.

He lowered his head and she felt sparks ricochet in the air between his lips and her skin, the vibrations getting quicker and quicker until her heart felt as if it might burst from her chest. As his lips pressed against her skin, her heart missed a beat, her fingers curled in his palm, tightening around his hand and her thighs pulled together. She bit her lip and felt unaccountably angry when he finally released the press of his lips and looked up at her.

Just a kiss?

He had proved her wrong. They both knew it, but in doing so he'd opened a door that she'd never walked through before, never wanted to before. And now...now she feared he might close that door before she'd even tried.

Now *she* was angry. With him because she knew Theron wanted to walk away. With her father for not being there. Angry for him and for the loss of his parents. Angry with her mother for being ill. With everything *not* going to plan.

She lurched up from the table, startling him and the other customers with the scratch of the chair legs against the floor, and turned, running down the stairs and out onto the walkway illuminated solely by the light of the moon.

She called herself all the different kinds of fool she

could think of. How had she let this happen? She pressed the back of her hand against her lips, as if somehow she could superimpose his kiss onto her mouth. But it only left an aching emptiness inside that hurt even more now she knew what it was like to feel filled with need and desire. Her breath sobbed against her hand and she tried to hold in the tears that wanted to be let free.

She drew to a halt, staring out at the inky black sea merging with the night, wishing for something she couldn't put words to. Fingers wrapped gently around her wrist and pulled her round and when she refused to look up into the dark expressive eyes she knew would be there, a finger hooked her chin and tilted her face to his. Eyes flickered back and forth over her face, as if trying to read thoughts that were incoherent even to her. She felt as if he were turning the pages of her mind, reading the words of her heart: desire, need, desperation, sadness, fear, yearning, permission, consent. It was there, all of it, and she just wanted him to—

He moved so slowly she thought she'd imagined it at first. She'd expected him to crush her to him, like the romances her sister Star was always swooning over. But he didn't. And somehow it was so much *more*.

She was sick with want and it took her a moment to realise it wasn't just her that felt that way. He reached up to brush a lock of hair back behind her ear, his fingers shaking ever so slightly. The moment he noticed it he clenched his fist and looked at her accusingly, as if demanding to know what she was doing to him.

Before he could take it back or change his mind, Summer closed the imperceptible distance between their lips—a space that felt like a heartbeat between before and after and…

Oh…

That was what it was like.

She'd expected his lips to feel firm and a little cool perhaps, but they were soft and so warm and sent fireworks shooting through her entire body. It was such a shock that her mouth opened on a gasp just as he began to kiss her back and the feel of his tongue gently pressing against the curve of her top lip made her breath hitch and her hands curl and, before she knew it, she had risen up onto her toes and pressed herself against the length of him and leaned into everything she was feeling.

But it was nothing compared to what she felt when he took over the kiss.

He'd given her a chance to explore, to feel, to touch, slide and press her way through it. And then he moved. His hand cradled her neck as his fingers threaded through her hair, sending the band holding it in place flying and the tendrils of her long hair falling down her back.

His other hand cupped her jaw, angling her head and her mouth in the most perfect way. Her chest rose to meet his, wanting to feel him against her, skin to skin—needing to. She reached up to clutch the lapels of his jacket, pulling them closer together. His hand slipped from her neck to her back, his fingers stretching between her shoulder blades, and she felt him sigh.

He pulled back from the kiss and pressed his forehead to hers, their rushed breathing buffeting the air between them.

This was it. This was the moment he would leave. Summer's fingers clenched reflexively. She swallowed the hurt she felt already.

'I should take you back to your hotel.'

'Should you?'

'Summer—'

Unwelcome nausea swelled in her stomach, her inner voice already howling at what he was taking away from her.

'Is this the bit where you tell me that I'm too innocent to know what I want?' she demanded. He pulled back, searching her face, and she raged at him for underestimating her. For denying her something she could see that he wanted too. 'The bit where you tell me that you're not good enough for me?'

His eyes darkened, whether in defiance or defence, she couldn't tell. And then he let her go, turned back onto the walkway and began to disappear into the night. Summer clenched her jaw, all the feelings within her bubbling up to the surface, hot, angry and aching.

'You're not that much older than me, you know,' she called after him. 'And...and...' He paused, as if wanting to hear what she was going to say. 'And you were a virgin once too!' she yelled, shocked by her own audacity.

He spun round and ducked slightly, as if to avoid the words, and closed the distance between them in seconds. '*éleos*, will you keep your voice down?' he growled, casting wary glares left and right. He looked like an angry schoolboy, a dark curl having fallen onto his forehead and a ruddy streak on either cheek. It was comical, the laugh rising up in her chest cutting through the darker emotions from just moments before.

'Are you blushing? Was it the word virgin?' she demanded, incredulous.

'Oh, for the love of—'

He kissed her then, the way she'd thought he might but could never have expected. The crush of his lips, his body dominating hers, overpowering her and it was incredible. It was all she could do to hold onto him and not be swept away into the sea.

'You're going to ruin me, aren't you?' he asked between kisses.

'Isn't it supposed to be the other way round?' she asked,
the breathlessness of her voice causing his pupils to flare.
She loved being able to see the reaction in him, to know
that she was the cause.

'Come with me?' he asked.

The drive they took back to his apartment was short but
interminable. Nothing was said, but it was far from silent.
Sitting beside her in the back seat, Theron watched her for
the entire journey, his eyes conveying more than words
could as they touched every part of her in a caress that she
could feel. It stoked an arousal within her so strong, so
pure, and the curve of his lips told her that he knew *exactly*
what he was doing. Was purposely doing. And Summer
gave up any concerns or embarrassment, his clear desire
of her as sure a thing as she'd ever known.

He paid the driver and led her through the foyer and
into the elevator, up to his apartment, and gestured for her
to pass the threshold first. All the while her eyes were unseeing and her senses heightened.

He stalked her through his apartment. He hadn't turned
on the lights, so only the glow of the moonlight pouring in
through the glass walls spanning the length of his corner
apartment illuminated her path. She was breathless with
delight and dizzy with need, adrenaline coursing through
her veins making her pulse trip. The gleam in his eyes
told her he felt it too. Fed from it even. Summer kicked
her shoes off and into the corner of the living area as she
rounded the sofa and her jaw dropped as Theron simply
stepped up onto the cushions and over the back, reaching for her, but she twisted and spun away from his hold
with a laugh.

She reached out to the door frame of another room and paused on the threshold as she realised it was his bedroom. Her heart pounded in her chest as she felt him behind her. He leant against the frame, his hand just inches above hers, the warmth from his body crashing against hers in waves as she took in the sight of the large bed. The throbbing of her heart radiated outwards through her entire body and she was filled with desire and need.

'We don't have to do anything you don't—'

She turned and kissed him. To stop his words, to stop the awkwardness she feared was replacing the delighted fizz from mere moments ago. She felt the curve of his lips through the kiss and he gently pulled away, softening his retreat. She couldn't quite explain the writhing emotions twisting in her because it wasn't that she was unsure, it was as if she felt embarrassed by it, even though rationally she knew she shouldn't be.

'Summer, consent is an important conversation to have,' he said, his words whispered into her ear, brushing against her neck and filling her with want. 'It's not embarrassing. It's respectful. You have as much control in this as me, and if you want to spend the entire evening making love I will. And if you want me to stop I will.' He shrugged as if it were that simple.

Summer turned, touched so deeply by his words, his assurance not only sweeping aside the awkwardness she'd felt but making her want him more, making her feel protected and cared for in a way that was somehow more than just moments before. She knew then she'd never regret tonight.

'This is something I want very much,' she said, reaching up to cup his jaw. 'And something I've only ever wanted with you. So, I do want you to stop...' she said, Theron's nod swift and sure against her palm, '...

talking,' she finished and pulled him to her in a kiss that took him only a second to take over.

His hands settled over Summer's body, reaching for her waist and lifting her up above him so that her hair fell about them. He locked his arms around her thighs and walked them back to the bed, turning so that when they fell he was beneath her, cushioning her as she became a tangled mess of laughter and legs and arms that turned into kisses and sighs and touches that made his heart soar in a way he couldn't remember ever having felt.

'You are so beautiful,' he said, reaching up to tuck a long blonde tendril behind her ear so he could see the golden flecks in her hazel eyes. 'You should always be in this colour.'

She bit her lip as if embarrassed by his observation, but the blush on her cheeks, the widening of her eyes... He'd pay her compliments until she got used to them, until she welcomed each and every one of them as her due.

He reached for the zip he'd noticed at the side of the dress and slowly pulled it down, his fingers impatient, dipping between the opening and casting circles over smooth skin. She was exquisite. Every touch new, every taste incredible, and if this was ruin then he would go to it willingly and gladly.

She shrugged out of the top of her dress, her arms slipping through the material while holding it to her chest. He could see her nerves but he could also see her desire, her determination and when she let the top go, revealing herself to him, it made him feel so damn honoured. She bent down at the same time as he reached up towards her and they met in an axis point of pleasure and need, and as she rocked against him his pulse roared and his heart leapt.

His arms wrapped around her waist and he pulled her

beneath him, drawing the dress down her hips and away
from her ankles. He made quick work of his own clothes,
hating to leave her even for that short time, but the way
her eyes flashed and flickered all over his body was worth
every second.

It was as if she were studying and analysing every inch
of him and he let her, beginning to understand that it was
part of her process, working through variables and col-
lecting data. He retrieved the condom from his wallet,
tore across the seal and rolled the latex over himself, her
hot eyes not leaving him for a second, turning him on
even more.

He placed his hands on her thighs, gently sweeping ca-
resses inch by inch towards the apex of her legs. 'This may
hurt.' She nodded, her expression serious, understanding
that it wasn't his intention to. 'And know that I will stop
at any time. Any, okay? Nothing is too late, or too far.'

She nodded again and he almost groaned out loud. The
look in her eyes was his undoing. He leaned forward and
pressed open-mouthed kisses to her neck. 'I need to hear
you say it, *agápi mou*,' he whispered.

'Yes, Theron. Yes. Please... I want...' she trailed off and
the yearning in her hazel gaze exploded like starbursts '...
everything,' she finished, as if confused by her own desires. He wanted that for her. He wanted to scoop up the
world and give it to her.

He kissed along her collarbone, his gaze snaring on a
mole about two inches from her clavicle. He pressed his
thumb over it, something jarring in his mind, before she
shifted beneath him, beckoning his touch to the valley
between her breasts. He kissed back up the long column
of her neck and positioned himself between her legs. He
longed to taste her, but this wasn't about his wants. He
trailed his hand over her thigh and between her legs the

evidence of her need, the slickness dampening the curls made his heart stop.

He bit his lip, grounding the need for control with every ounce of his intent, and as he locked his longing gaze on hers he slowly pressed into her, consuming her gasp with a kiss. He held himself still as she tensed, her eyes flaring wide with the shock, and his eyes held only regret and hope that it would pass for her quickly. She blinked slowly, breathing through it, her body beginning to relax around his. He pressed kisses against her skin, showered her in words he had no hope of her understanding, and slowly began to move within her. Bit by bit her body began to move with his, her thighs hitching around his hips, her ankles crossing behind him, pressing him closer to her, and his heart began to pound. He braced himself, his hands either side of her on the mattress, his muscles beginning to shake as he fought to control the desire that was spinning out of his reach. As if Summer felt it too, her sighs became cries of pleasure, urging him to some impossible point. Sweat-slicked and on a knife's edge, he held them at the absolute pinnacle until her release urged his own and, together, they fell deep into the night.

Summer woke the next morning encircled in Theron's arms and decided there was no better feeling than that. A blush heated her cheeks at the way he had drawn from her a pleasure she'd never known existed. She ducked beneath the covers, hiding the smile that felt private yet utterly full of joy behind the cotton. It felt…magical to be with Theron here, in this way.

But, as wonderful as it was, she knew she'd not be able to get back to sleep, so she slipped out from under his arm, tiptoed to the bathroom and turned on the shower. She threw a look in the mirror, wondering who the beautiful woman staring back at her was. The one with pink cheeks, bright eyes and thoroughly kissed lips.

Ducking beneath the powerful spray of the water, she wondered what they might do today. Maybe Theron could take her to somewhere only he knew. Maybe, she thought, she could tell him about Kyros. It was crazy to think that she could trust him with her body, but not that...

Theron was still asleep when she came out, so she grabbed a shirt from his closet, her dress now completely crumpled on the floor, and quietly stepped out of the room. She went to the kitchen and spied a very fancy coffee machine that only took her fifteen minutes of opening drawers, pressing buttons, cursing under her breath and one hair pull to produce a decent espresso.

She took the cup over to the large window that led onto a beautiful balcony, staring at the way the sun swept up from the sea, casting the sky in orange and yellow hues that had her so mesmerised she didn't hear the key in the door before it was too late.

She spun round, nearly spilling the coffee over the borrowed shirt, and stared.

'Theron!' yelled the man with shocking white hair, deeply tanned, lined skin and a scowl. 'Theron?'

Summer didn't recognise the rest because it was in Greek, but she certainly recognised the man. It was her father. Two steps brought Kyros Agyros into the apartment enough to see her standing by the window and close enough to break her heart.

The look he cast her was barely a sneer, the distaste in the gaze he raked over her cut her deeply and brought a sheen to her eyes that she feared might fall down her cheeks. Turning her back to him, she bit her lip so hard from trying not to cry out, she tasted blood. Her breath shuddered out of her lungs as she heard Theron emerge from the room, throwing back to Kyros whatever response was needed. She tried to tell herself that her father didn't know, that she didn't feel mortified, humiliated or shaken, but she couldn't.

Summer held her breath through the short exchange and let it go only when Kyros had left the apartment. But something had changed. Something irrevocable. She turned, blinking away the sheen, to find Theron standing there in his trousers from last night and nothing else. He was staring at her and, no matter how much she tried to hide it, he'd seen enough.

'Care to explain to me what that was about?' he demanded, doing up the button above his trouser zip without taking his eyes off her.

'I don't know—'

'Don't lie to me.' His voice might not have been a shout, but the tone was cold and harsh in a way she'd have thought impossible after last night.

'It's hard to explain,' she replied, suddenly realising how it might look to Theron. She'd thought she'd have time. Time to explain herself.

'You are articulate and intelligent. Try.'

Summer breathed deeply. 'He's my father.'

Every single emotion that had been shining in his eyes was immediately blanked. He uttered what could only be a curse and sent a glare her way. 'Don't be ridiculous,' he all but spat.

'He is,' she insisted. 'I—'

He threw up a hand, cutting her off before she could explain. 'Of all the schemes and lies you could have told to have me even *half* believing you?' His gaze was frigid, disgusted and horribly like the one Kyros had spared her.

He shook his head. 'No. That is the one that would *never* work. Kyros was absolutely one hundred per cent committed to his wife and family. I *know* this to be true. I have seen it with my own eyes.' His accent grew thicker and heavier the more vehement he became. 'So, what, this was a shakedown?' he demanded.

'No!' Summer cried, appalled at how he'd interpreted the situation.

'A money-making scheme? Coming here after his wife's death—'

'I didn't—'

'And sex with me was—what? A perk? An in?' Theron yelled, before slamming his mouth shut as if to prevent anything worse from coming out. Not that Summer could even begin to imagine what that might be.

'Did you know who I was?'

Shock pooled the blood in her stomach, leaving her face cold. 'Theron—'

'That first night in the bar. Did you know who I was?' he said, taking one step towards her and then holding himself back.

The anger, the betrayal, the pain. She could see it. Familiar as it was to the way she had felt when she'd discovered her mother had lied to her about her father. Regret and hurt washed over her in a tidal wave, threatening to pull her under.

'I tell you what,' he said, sniffing and walking past her to the coffee machine. 'I'll give you fifteen minutes to get out. And that is purely a *professional* courtesy. You were incredibly convincing last night, *agápi mou*, I must say. I am man enough to admit I fell for it,' he said, his back to her, before turning and clapping his hands together slowly.

'Well done. Now get out.'

Last night…

The noise of the bar in Mayfair cut through the haze of anger that Theron felt as if it were only yesterday rather than five months ago.

Lykos cursed. 'That was low, Theron. And, coming from me, that's saying something,' he said, disgust heavy in the air between them.

Theron felt the thick slide of shame in his gut and he took a mouthful of whisky to drown it out, not sure that it was any better than the rage he'd felt burning a hole in his heart when she'd left his apartment in Piraeus five months ago. Or the devastation he'd experienced four hours ago when she'd stood on the steps of an estate in Norfolk, staring at him in the rear-view mirror.

'I thought she was trying to get to—'

'Your precious Kyros. I know,' Lykos said as if tired of repeating himself.

'It's my job!' Theron growled.

'You keep telling yourself that.'

'What's that supposed to mean?' Theron demanded furiously.

'It means that you've always put him on a pedestal. You've idolised him. And you'd do anything for him, no matter what it cost you. And that's not the way to live a life, Theron.'

'He stayed. Not even *you* did that,' Theron accused.

'I asked you to come with me, Theron. You made your choice. Do us both a favour, be a big boy and live with it, okay?'

'I want you to tell me what Kyros did that was *so* bad that it erased all the money, time and effort he chose to pour into us? He gave us somewhere safe from looking over our shoulder every two minutes, he gave us an education, somewhere with food we didn't have to steal.' Theron stared at Lykos, searching his features for something other than anger and disdain—searching for a trace of the man he'd grown up with, the man he'd once called brother. Before he had left him without a second glance. 'All I know is that one day you were working for him, and the next you were telling me you were going to leave. What happened? What did he ask you to do?'

But Lykos just shook his head, holding and hoarding his secrets, as he always had. He signalled to the waitress and turned back to Theron. 'So let me guess. Summer left your apartment and you went back to work as if nothing had happened, right? Did you even tell Kyros?' Lykos asked.

'What, that I had let some con artist into my bed? That as the owner of the company he uses for security, I had nearly left him open to that?'

Theron felt Lykos's silvery glare through the darkness of the bar. 'And you didn't suspect anything beyond that?'

'I didn't think of her at all,' Theron lied. 'Until you called.'

'Here,' Star eased the cup from Summer's shaking grasp, put it on the floor and took her hands in her own. 'I'm so sorry that happened to you. That you shared something so special with Theron and that he didn't believe you...'

'I'm calling Benoit. We'll do a background check on him or something. Find a way to—'

'It's okay,' Summer interrupted with a watery smile and a sad laugh. 'I'm not finished yet.' Star reached for a couple of blankets as Skye threw another log on the fire and they settled in. 'I went back to uni, not telling anyone about what happened in Greece. I thought it would be better if I forgot the whole thing and I decided I never wanted to see my father again.'

'Oh, no, Summer, you can't hold that one moment against him. I'm sure there was something else going on,' Star said, ever hopeful, always loving.

She shrugged. 'I couldn't forget the disdain in his eyes. He barely even looked at me. And what proof did I have, really? A name, a photograph, the story of a matching mole?'

'There are DNA tests that we could get,' Star offered.

'Well, that wasn't the test I ended up doing back then,' Summer confessed, remembering sitting on the bathroom floor of her room in the university halls, her back against the door and her knees pulled up to her chest, numb with shock, staring at the little blue tick.

She'd thought it was the flu. She'd felt rundown, achy, nauseous. It could have been any number of things. And then one of the guys in her class had made a stupid joke about nausea and pregnancy and, as she'd stood there smiling while everyone laughed, she'd been doing the maths. She'd been working out just when her last period had been and her world had morphed into something she barely recognised.

She'd bought a pregnancy test immediately after class and taken it the moment she'd got back to her room. Waiting for the results, she'd wanted to call her sisters...but also hadn't. She'd thought about calling Theron, but his slow clap had rung in her ears as the seconds passed. She'd left his apartment that day, eyes blinded by hot tears and cheeks stained red by hurt and guilt.

Guilt because he'd been right. She had lied to him, she had intended to use him to find out about her father. But that had been before Theron had looked at her and she'd felt *seen*. So to have that taken away when he'd refused to believe or even hear her about her father had felt like an eclipse. A sudden absence of light. And ever since she'd left Greece there had been an ache in her heart that she'd tried to blame on the disappointment of meeting her father, but she'd known that was a lie.

And in that instant she'd made a promise to her unborn child. Never would they feel rejection. Never would they feel the shame and confusion and sadness that she had experienced. And, sitting on the cold laminate floor as the blue cross had appeared, something had stirred deep within. A maternal instinct she'd never known she had. It was fierce and true and surer than anything she'd ever felt before. And it had only grown bit by bit each day since. There had not even been a second when Summer considered anything but having her child. But that didn't mean it hadn't plunged her into a state of worry and confusion.

'And within days of finding out, we were told that the NHS were unable to offer Mum's cancer treatment, Elias died and we came here for his funeral. And then, when his will dictated the search for the Soames diamonds...'

'Did you call Theron?'

'I wanted to. But I was pretty sure he'd want a paternity test and I didn't want to risk any harm to the baby. He thought the worst of me already, so I was going to wait.'

'Going to?'

'It didn't quite work out like that.'

CHAPTER FOUR

Six days ago...

THERON FISTED HIS HANDS in his trouser pockets and stared up at the Acropolis, thinking of hazel eyes, blonde hair and a yellow dress. His notoriously lethal focus had drifted in the last few months and Kyros had noticed. Theron had felt a wave of guilt each time he'd avoided the older man's probing questions. Guilt and shame that he'd been taken in by such a con. But each night as he reran the events of that morning through his mind, he came back to the same question. Summer had admitted that she'd known who he was with the same open expression as when she'd insisted Kyros was her father. An open honesty that had bewitched him from the first moment.

Had she been telling the truth?

It had driven him mad in the days and weeks following. And more times than he'd care to admit, he'd been on the verge of asking Kyros about it. About her. About whether Kyros had cheated on his wife while she'd been on her sickbed. The thought made him more furious than he'd been in years. But still, he couldn't risk it. Kyros was everything to him. He'd given Kyros his word, his loyalty, and in return Kyros had given him stability, security and a home. Theron owed Kyros that trust.

A knock on the office door cut through his thoughts, causing him to turn.

'I'm sorry, Mr Thiakos, you didn't answer your...' His secretary appeared, red-cheeked, reluctant to call him on his ineptitude. 'Mr Livas on line two for you. Would you like me to tell him you're not available?'

Lykos hadn't been in this building for nearly ten years but his reputation still stalked the halls. Theron frowned, something swift and sharp twisting in his side. Whatever it was, it couldn't be good. He picked up the phone.

'What do you want?' Theron demanded as his secretary retreated from the room.

'Lykos! Great to hear from you after all these years! You well? I *am*, thank you, Theron. And how are you? Oh, can't complain. Can't complain.' Lykos performed his one-man show through the earpiece replete with intonations worthy of an Oscar.

'Really? This is what you waste my time with?' Theron bit back angrily.

'Is it so surprising that I might want to check in on my oldest and bestest friend?' Lykos's saccharine tone made Theron's teeth ache.

'Given that it would be the first time in nearly ten years? Yes,' Theron admitted.

'Well, I've just been presented with an interesting business opportunity but... I don't know, there's something about it...'

'You're worse than a cat with a mouse. Stop toying with me and spit it out.'

'But where's the fun in that?'

'About as much fun as me hanging up on you,' warned Theron, preparing to do just that.

'Wait!'

Theron didn't say anything.

'It's a business opportunity in Norfolk.'

'You're in America?' Theron asked, confused.

'No, Norfolk, England. An acquaintance of ours brought it to me.'

'We don't have mutual acquaintances,' he growled, his voice one hundred per cent sure, but his mind flashed onto Summer looking up as Lykos bent over her hand. How had he forgotten that?

'Oh. My mistake. I must have been confused.'

'Stop being coy. You don't get confused,' Theron bit, a dangerous edge to his voice now.

'Small, blonde. Very pretty—positively *radiant*. Must say, fits her name perfectly.'

Theron gripped the phone. 'What is she doing with you?' he demanded, shocked by the phosphoric fury burning in his veins.

'Get your mind out of the gutter. It was a business proposition,' Lykos replied, distaste heavy in his tone.

'And you never mix business with pleasure?' Theron scoffed.

'Oh, all the time,' Lykos replied easily. 'I just don't mix *my* pleasure with *yours*.'

Theron breathed his heartbeat into submission. 'Has she mentioned Kyros?'

'Not once. Why?' Lykos replied.

'Are you sure?'

'It's possible that it slipped my mind,' he taunted.

'What was the business?'

'She has a twelve-million-pound estate in Norfolk she wants to sell for a third of that value.'

Theron cursed. 'She's a student. Where the hell would she get an estate from?'

'If you want to know, go ask her. Though might I suggest, before you go in there bashing down the front door—'

'No,' Theron interrupted, the sudden need to find out exactly what was going on, intoxicating. 'I don't know what the hell you're getting out of this, but I know you have an angle here somewhere. So, no, you can't suggest a thing. I'm going to get to the bottom of this *right now*. And you will *not* buy that estate,' Theron commanded.

Less than twenty-four hours later, as Theron put the rental car into park, he told himself that his pulse was pounding because of the near miss with a scaffolding lorry, *not* because Summer Soames was hiding somewhere inside the estate in front of him. What was her angle here? Had she moved on from Kyros? Was she now targeting Lykos? He could have her.

No!

Everything in him roared denial at the bitterly careless thought. He could lie and claim not to have dreamed about her every night since she'd left his bed. He could try to tell himself that he'd put her out of his mind as the money-grabbing con artist he'd accused her of being, instead of remembering the devastation in her eyes that morning, first with Kyros and then with him. But he wouldn't lie to himself about how much he'd wanted her with every single fibre of his being since that morning.

So, no. Lykos couldn't *have her*. Because Theron wasn't done with her yet. He needed to know what she was doing and whether it had anything to do with the man he would protect with his life if need be.

His shoes crunched on the gravel as he got out of the car. He had to crane his neck to take in the sprawling building, little more than a dark outline against the dusk. In the evening's gloom it was clear the estate was in need of some serious repair, but it was still a thing of beauty, faded or otherwise. There was a sense of something more,

though, tugging at him, drawing him closer...but he shook
the silliness out of his head as he took the steps two at a
time, reaching the semi-circular dais at the top in front of
a very large wooden door.

He pounded on it, wondering whether he had a hope in
hell of her hearing it. As the minutes ticked by, Theron became increasingly frustrated. He stepped back off the steps
and peered up at windows caked in grime and cobwebs.
He frowned. The building looked deserted. Abandoned.
Anything could happen here and no one would know. An
icy tendril wound its way up his spine and he was worried. Worried about Summer. The suddenly frantic beat of
his heart infected his thoughts and his mind quickly became a jumble so that when the door opened and he saw
Summer standing there it took him a moment to breathe.

And he forgot. Forgot about Kyros and about her insane
accusation. He forgot the anger that had so cleverly laid
over the hurt. The ache that she'd fooled him. That she'd
used him. And instead he just took her in.

A wave of relief washed over him, and a feeling he
barely recognised and dared not name was left on the shore
of his heart. Summer's eyes widened in recognition, and
for just a second he thought he might have seen something
like hope spark in her eyes.

As if tethered to her he approached her with one step.
And then another. And another until somehow he was
within an inch of her and his hands were reaching to frame
her face and his mouth was claiming hers and he felt as
if he was *home*.

A moan sounded on the air between them and he
couldn't be sure if it had been hers or his. Her lips tasted
of honey and opened beneath his and a shocking heat unfurled within him, his heart in his mouth and realisation
on his tongue. He'd been lying to himself for months. He'd

not put her out of his mind, he'd kept her there, the memories of her locked away, and the moment that he'd seen her again they were all unleashed. This was what he'd needed, just so he could breathe, he thought as he pulled her flush against his body and...stopped.

He opened his eyes to find hers staring at him, shock and something horrifyingly like fear sparking to life in them. He pulled back and reached out at the same time, his hand unerringly finding the curve, not of her stomach but a bump. Just about the right size for a...

Summer closed her eyes. It had taken her only seconds to consume the sight of him. The thick wave of hair, so dark it looked velvety, the stubble on his jaw, the breadth of his shoulders, the way his forearms corded beneath rolled-up shirtsleeves—everything about him made her want to touch. Her breathing hitched and she felt utterly betrayed by her body as it throbbed and pulsed just at the sight of him. And the thread of hope she'd barely admitted to herself during the last weeks and months sprang to life. But when he'd reached for her, hopes, fears and fantasies had disappeared and she'd melted into him as if nothing else mattered.

She'd forgotten. That was the power he had over her. For just a second of madness, she'd forgotten. Until Theron had reared back, the look of shock on his features indelibly marked across her heart.

'No.'

The word severed the spell he'd cast over her, bringing her back to reality with a painful jolt. She was surprised that it hurt so much. His denial. It wasn't as if she hadn't expected it. Neither could she blame him—she'd had that moment too. The moment when in less than a heartbeat her mind had travelled through infinite possibilities and futures, all twisting and turning out of reach in light of the shocking fact that she was now going to be a parent. But she'd also seen futures in which their child was the most precious, beautiful part of her life.

But the look in his eyes—the one he was trying so desperately to mask—was all too familiar to her and just as painful as it had been in Greece. That moment of rejection, that feeling, compounded by her father's dismissal, fired a kiln that forged steel within her. She would not subject her child to that now or ever.

'You are pregnant?'

'Yes,' she said, waiting for some kind of indication that he had realised that he was a father. But where once she had marvelled at his impenetrable, stone-like qualities, now it just felt cruel. As if it made her even more conscious of their differences. She felt soft and sore and emotional and he seemed hard, cold, tough and it made her hurt even more. What kind of father would he be for their child?

'What are you doing here?' she asked, her thoughts making her voice a whisper.

Theron blinked, looking around as if he didn't know how to answer that question. He went to say something and had to clear his throat. 'Lykos…'

Summer rolled her eyes. She should have known the Greek billionaire friend of Theron's wouldn't have kept his mouth shut. Not that she'd had much of a choice. It wasn't as if as a geophysics student she knew *that* many billionaires. And when she and her sisters had realised they would need to sell the Soames estate, and sell it quickly, Summer had remembered what Lykos Livas had said when he'd handed over his card. *Just in case you ever need anything.* Lykos had been there for her when she'd needed it, not Theron. Not the man who had tossed her from his apartment in such a cruel way.

Hurt fired her fury as she focused back on Theron, who was staring at her stomach. 'I don't have time for this,' she said around his silence. 'I don't have time for *you*. You can go,' she dismissed, her heart breaking as she turned blindly down a hallway, not caring where she went.

'I'm not going anywhere.' The tone of Theron's voice was all the warning she got before he pulled her round to face him and in an instant she was overwhelmed with the memory of the first time he'd kissed her. She looked up just in time to see the flare of his pupils as if he too was lost in the same thought. But then he blinked and once again she was shut out and the icy-cold stare he levelled at her made her shiver.

'Ask me,' she demanded.

For a second he looked confused. 'Ask you what?'

Summer shook her head, blinking furiously, praying that she could get through this before the tears came. She looked up at him, her heart breaking. 'Ask me if it's yours.'

Shock slashed angry red marks across his cheeks and gutted his chest. That was what it felt like. As if everything inside him had been scooped out and exposed.

He was more certain that she was pregnant with his child than anything he'd ever known in his entire life. The question hadn't even crossed his mind, let alone formed into a sentence, and the thought that she'd believe he'd question such a thing burned his soul.

You were incredibly convincing last night, agápi mou, I must say. I am man enough to admit I fell for it.

This time the slow clap that echoed in his mind was for him and him alone.

Of course, she had doubted he would believe her. What on earth had he done to make her think otherwise?

'Summer—'

'Ask me,' she repeated, her voice raised this time but stronger.

'No.' The word clawed against his throat.

She cocked her head to the side and his heart pounded. He knew where this was going and he wanted to stop it. He wasn't prepared for this.

'Why not?'

'Because I don't have to.' He knew that wouldn't be enough and that she'd be right to demand more. Because he saw it now. She'd had the same look on her face the morning of the argument. 'Because I know.'

'Know what? That if I said it was yours that I'd be telling the truth?'

He nodded, shame, anger, guilt making him nauseous.

'I want to hear you say it,' she said, her voice trembling.

He gritted his teeth. It was the least she deserved and, if he had his way, the first of everything. 'I believe you.'

He cursed mentally, knowing the truth of it. Knowing that the child was his, but more than that—Summer was Kyros's child. She had been telling the truth the day he'd kicked her out of his apartment, treating her no better than a...

He fisted his hands. He didn't want to know, but the question was burning a hole in his empty chest. 'Were you going to tell me?' He couldn't look at her as he asked the question. He didn't want to see what her expressive features betrayed.

But she was hell-bent on making him work for his answer. It was only when he met her gaze that she responded.

'After. When a DNA test would have been safe.' Her eyes told him that she'd wanted to lie, wanted to say never, but she wasn't like that. Why hadn't he seen that then? Why hadn't he believed her?

A phone ringing in the distance cut through the mo-

ment. Summer looked behind her and then back to him.
'I have to get that.'

'We will talk about this,' he warned.

'Fine. But... I just... I need to get that.'

She disappeared into the bowels of the building before he could argue and suddenly Theron felt dizzy. He
turned, with no idea where he was going, just knowing
that he needed to get back outside. The corridors were
too dark, the house too damp, empty... It was lifeless and
he couldn't breathe. Bursting through a door that led out
from the back of the house, he bent over, his hands on his
knees, pulling air into his lungs.

Had he missed it? The mole on her collarbone? No. He
remembered putting his thumb over it, remembered the
strange sense of recognition stirring within him. Something sure and strong tightened in his gut. Kyros had the
same mole. He was proud of the strange family trait. Every
Agyros had it. Theron remembered it, because once as a
teenager Lykos had found him trying to draw one on his
clavicle and mocked him mercilessly for it.

Theé mou. How could she be Kyros's daughter? The
old man had been faithfully married to his wife—his incredibly sick wife—hadn't he? Theron had never known
Kyros to leave her side. He'd never spent a night away
from her, never had anything but love in his words and
actions towards her.

But Theron had only known him for fifteen years. Perhaps something had happened before that? Summer was,
what...early twenties?

Early twenties and pregnant. He tried to cast his mind
back to that night. How many times had they made love?
How many times had they used protection? That he
couldn't quite remember was damning enough. He'd been
utterly mindless in his desire for her.

A desire that hadn't been misguided. He'd thought himself a fool for thinking her so pure and so bright that night. But he'd *not* been wrong. He hadn't misread her, been fooled or tricked. Summer was absolutely all of the things he'd thought and wanted that night.

He pulled himself up and tried to fill his lungs with oxygen, but he feared they'd never fill again. He was going to be a father. Something primal, instinctive roared to life within him. A possessive, determined, living need welled inside him with such ferocity it almost scared him.

Was this what his own father had felt? And his mother? Had his birth been planned or, as with him and Summer, had the pregnancy been a shock, a surprise?

He had no one to ask these questions, no one to tell him about his parents, their relationship, their lives, their hardships. Both Kyros and Althaia had tried to help him find someone who was connected to his life, but they hadn't been able to find anyone who had known his parents.

And now he was going to be a parent himself. The vow didn't even form words in his head before he felt it in his heart. His child would *never* have questions about their heritage. His child would never feel the losses that he had experienced. It would never want for a single thing. And instinctively he knew Summer would feel the same. It was there in her determination, her challenge to him.

Ask me.

It had been as much a demand as it had been a test.

One he had already failed.

There was only one possible way forward now.

Summer found him sitting on the old stone steps at the back of the house, shrouded by the night. She'd hung up after talking with Star, who had left Duratra and headed into the desert to find the second half of the key to wherever and whatever held the family's missing diamonds. A part of Summer quivered with fear that Star might not find it, and that she herself might not find this hidden location where her great-great-great-grandmother had placed the family heirloom. And without the diamonds they wouldn't meet the terms of their grandfather's will and be able to sell the estate to Lykos, so that they could pay for their mother's treatment.

The other part was trembling because of a certain Greek magnate staring into the sky, looking as if he had no plans to leave.

I believe you.

If he'd said it immediately, freely even, she might not have trusted him. But he'd said it as if it had cost him something and she couldn't understand what that might be.

Kyros was absolutely one hundred per cent committed to his wife and family. I know this to be true. I have seen it with my own eyes.

'What is my father to you?' Summer had been so busy putting the pieces together that she'd spoken before she'd thought. And the look in his eyes when his gaze rose to meet hers made her wish she hadn't.

The tangle of hurt, resentment, love, protection...all these emotions knitted together in his eyes.

'Everything,' he replied, turning back to look up at the stars. 'I still...'

She flinched, knowing that words of disbelief would have finished that sentence.

'I do believe you,' he said, as if he'd felt rather than seen her hurt. 'It's just *hard.* I've known him since I was twelve.'

And I've never known him, she thought as something twisted in her heart.

'He gave me everything that I have today and I would do anything for him.' He said it simply, easily, like floating on water, but she felt the words like a stone, weighing and pressing him down. Maybe he couldn't see it.

'What happened? How…?' He asked as if she held the answer to understanding a shocking mystery.

'I don't know. I was hoping to ask him.'

'And…your mother? What does she say?'

'I can't ask her,' she replied past the hurt in her chest.

'Why not? Surely she'd—'

'She's not well,' Summer said, cutting him off, the stubborn jut to her jaw putting an end to his line of questioning. His eyes softened, and she didn't want to see it. Things had been much easier when he'd been an ocean away and ignorant. She'd hardly thought of him at all.

Liar.

'Does she know about the baby?' he asked quietly as if, without being told, he knew that darkness stalked the fringes of their conversation. Loss. And possibly worse.

'No.'

He nodded once. 'Well, we can stay here until you're ready.'

'Ready for what?' she asked, not quite sure what he was talking about.

'To return to Greece.'

'Why would I return to Greece?'

She couldn't understand why he was looking at her as if she had lost her mind, or memory, or something.

'Because that is where we'll live.'

'What?' she demanded, heat creeping up her neck and twisting in her belly.

'When we're married.'

'*What?*' she said, louder this time.

Theron's hands were cold and he felt as if he'd swallowed stones. He clenched his jaw, stifling the desperation he felt lest it show in his tone when he next spoke. He was used to people simply doing what he said. Managing his business like an army. It was how he'd achieved what he had in such a short time. Supreme self-confidence and determination. But Summer was like a live wire, twisting and turning, and he never knew what she would do next.

'We will marry,' he announced and this time she laughed.

'No.'

'What do you mean, no?' he demanded, shocked by her response.

'What do you mean, we will marry?'

'Well—' he frowned, confused '—exactly that.'

'Yeah. Me too. So *no*.'

Theron frowned. Opened his mouth. Closed it again. He'd not foreseen this. He stood up, feeling that he needed the height advantage, and regretted it as she seemed intuitively to know he'd done so on purpose. He realised this the moment she took two steps back to meet him at eye level.

'I don't know you,' she growled softly.

'I hardly think that matters,' he replied, mentally batting away how much her statement had hurt.

'Really?' she demanded. 'What *does* matter then?'

'That you have my name and my protection,' he insisted.

'I'm happy with my name, Theron, and I don't need your protection.'

Her response was so damn reasonable, when he felt anything but. He wanted to shout, to yell, to roar against this strange sense of everything he'd never known he'd wanted slowly slipping through his fingers. He tried to get himself under control before he made things worse, but Summer seemed to be one step ahead of him at every turn.

'Look,' she said, striving for a calm that felt impossibly out of reach. 'Clearly we have to talk, but it's late. Why don't you go and come back tomorrow, or...?'

'Never? Would you prefer that?' he demanded, cursing himself and his own anger when he saw her eyes flare in defiance. She made him so…*emotional*. He took a breath. 'I'm not going anywhere,' he explained, keeping his tone as calm as possible.

'You can't stay here,' Summer replied with a shake of her head.

'It's not as if there aren't any free rooms,' he pointed out.

She held his gaze for a moment, an explosion of wicked sparks in her eyes. 'By all means, take your pick.'

She'd known, he realised half an hour later, as he lay down on a dusty mattress that was sure to give him allergies in a room that probably hadn't been heated for one hundred years. She'd done it on purpose, leaving the choice to him, knowing there was literally no good option. This was the sixth room he'd tried and he was too exhausted to care any more.

The wind howled down an empty fireplace and reduced the room's temperature by another degree or two. It was definitely the least he deserved and if there was more, Theron swore to himself and his unborn child, then he'd do whatever it took. Because they were now—whether Summer liked it or not—his family.

CHAPTER FIVE

THERE WAS SOMETHING in the walls. Theron didn't believe in ghosts, yet he would have sworn that he'd heard footsteps. But when he'd stuck his head into the corridor it had been empty. And then, after returning from the most unpleasantly cold shower he'd had in at least ten years, he'd thought there was someone actually in the room, even though it was obviously empty.

He threw his trousers on and rubbed his hair dry with a towel, thinking back over last night. The way he'd reacted, the way he'd demanded she marry him...

An explosion crashed through the estate and adrenaline instantly drenched his body as he ran towards the sound.

'Summer!' His heart pounding, he tried to figure out where the sound had come from, searching left and right. 'Summer!' he yelled again. He cursed in Greek and careened around a corner to find a slowly dissipating cloud of dust. In the middle of it was Summer, dressed in jeans, a jumper stretched over her belly, dust in her hair and on her face, coughing.

'What the hell is going on?' he demanded, striding forward, grasping her arm and pulling her from what looked suspiciously like a giant hole in the wall.

Summer sucked in huge lungfuls of air and shook her head, sending little bits of centuries-old plaster flying.

She coughed once more, fanning her watery eyes and then looked up at him, her eyes seeming to clear.

'Are you okay?' she asked.

'Me?'

'Yes. You've gone quite pale,' she stated before marching off, patting down her clothing as she went.

'Stop!' he commanded, regretting it the instant she turned with a raised eyebrow. 'Don't give me that look,' he growled. 'You emerge from a *hole in the wall* as if it were nothing, and I don't have a right to know what's going on?'

'A right? No. You don't have a *right*. But if you would *like* to know, you could change your tone, lower your voice and ask nicely. *That* might work.'

He stared after her for a moment, floored. Althaia had been the one and only woman to put him in his place and he couldn't shake the feeling that she would have definitely been on Summer's side.

'Can we start again?' he called after her.

He could have sworn he heard a huff of laughter.

Summer rested her head against the tiled wall of the shower as water rushed over her head, neck and shoulders. She'd done her best to keep the surprise from her face as Theron had found her emerging from the hole in the wall. She'd been on her way back from searching the last of the secret tunnels in the east wing when she'd caught her shoulder on a bit of protruding battening which had knocked her centre of gravity and she'd fallen against the hole already there from Elias's search and it had collapsed. She'd managed not to fall, but the mess it had created was impressive.

She eased out the kink in that same shoulder as she reviewed her progress. So, the jewels weren't hidden in the east wing's secret passageways. Summer had now thoroughly searched all of them. The ones around the main section of the building appeared to be more functional, serving as shortcuts through the building, which left just the secret passageways in the west wing.

She had the map from Skye, could only hope that Star was close to retrieving the key…but none of it would matter if she couldn't locate where Catherine had hidden the jewels.

But the look in Theron's eyes kept bursting in on her thought processes. Unwanted but determined—just like the man himself. He'd been worried about her—because she hadn't missed that. She couldn't have missed it. It had shone from his—admittedly angry—eyes, but the worry was what had pinned her heart.

He'd stayed last night, which was more than she'd expected of him. He hadn't browbeaten her, ridiculed her or threatened her last night. Not that she'd expected that of him—or at least not what she knew of him from their time in Greece before he'd kicked her out.

She sighed in defeat. She owed him an explanation at least and, in all likelihood, a lot more. But before she could change her mind, she turned off the shower, dressed and went to find him.

He was looking out of the large library window, his profile outlined by morning sun, the rest of him cast in shadow. His profile made her heart soar inexplicably. She hadn't realised how lonely she'd felt in the last few weeks in the estate on her own. But, if she were honest with herself, she'd felt it ever since returning from Greece. There was something about Theron that had made her feel…seen. Briefly, at least.

He turned and for just a moment she felt the burn of his gaze, the power he had to simply light up her body as if she were hackmanite, left to glow in the dark even in his absence. And then he blinked and she shivered.

'It's a long story,' she said, half hoping he'd tell her to skip to the end.

'I have time. And breakfast,' he said, pointing to the table, where fruit, toast and tea were all gathered. Her stomach growled at the sight and she realised she'd forgotten to eat that morning. He smiled wryly, snared an apple before taking a seat.

She sat in the opposite chair, swept her legs up under her and picked at the buttery toast. 'Just before I went to Greece, Mum had been diagnosed with stage three cancer. We were waiting to hear back on the treatment plans.'

'Summer, I… I'm so sorry.'

She nodded, gritting her teeth against the wave of nausea that always came when she thought of her mum's illness. It swept at her ankles and feet, threatening to topple her sense of up and down. But, strangely, Theron's words anchored her. Their sincerity surprised her and touched her. 'Thank you.'

'Is that why you were looking for Kyros?' he asked.

Her stomach churned, making the nausea acidic. She pressed a hand against her sternum to hold it back. 'I didn't…it wasn't like that.' She shook her head, fearful that he believed she was trying to replace one parent with another. 'Kyros wasn't a backup or—'

'Summer.' His tone was firm but gentle. 'That is not what I meant. At all. I know that's not what you were looking for.' The way he said it, the current that swirled beneath his tone, pushed back the ache just enough for her to feel thankful that he didn't think the worst of her. She breathed, but it was full of sadness as she remembered the fresh hurt laid over the rejection of both Theron and her father.

'When I came back from Greece, we found out that the treatment Mum needed couldn't be offered.'

'Why not?'

'Different areas in the UK have different access to certain treatments. We didn't live in the right area for the treatment she needs.' She shook her shoulders free of the tendrils of hurt and fear that still reached for her now. And if she concentrated she could hear the tick-tock of time running out. Every time she thought of her mother, the illness, it prompted a wave of helpless fear that made her need to find the jewels feel like claws scratching at her ankles.

'That's…' the look on Theron's face was incredulous '…barbaric.'

She nodded, agreeing with him completely. 'Just over two months ago, Skye got a call informing us that our grandfather had passed away. We never knew him,' she said quickly, forestalling his sympathy, 'and I don't think I would have wanted to. He clearly wasn't a pleasant man, having cut his daughter from his life and financial support. Still, he left me and my sisters the estate and everything in it—on one condition. That we find the Soames diamonds that have been missing for over one hundred and fifty years. No one searching for them had discovered their hiding place in all that time.'

'But you have?'

'Sort of.' She nodded. 'We uncovered a collection of journals, a photograph and a necklace hidden here in the library. In the journals was a coded message, explaining that our great-great-great-grandmother had hidden the jewels from her undeserving husband after her marriage.'

'In the walls…?'

Summer couldn't help but laugh. She supposed it did sound a little crazy. It was, after all, a one hundred and fifty-year-old treasure hunt. 'The estate suffered some fire damage in the mid to late eighteen-hundreds and was re-built by a French architect named Benoit Chalendar.'

Theron frowned. 'As in Chalendar Enterprises?'

'Mm-hmm. He put in a secret recess behind the shelves over there,' she said, pointing behind him. 'And also built secret passageways behind the walls here in the estate for Catherine Soames's amusement. They turned out to be a sanctuary for her. And somewhere within the passageways is a room, or a box, where the diamonds have been kept safely locked away.'

'So, you have the key?'

'I *think* so,' she said, desperately hoping that to be the case. 'Star is in Duratra now and says that she knows where the necklace is.'

'What does a necklace have to do—?'

Summer scrunched her nose, realising she was telling this all wrong. 'Sorry. The necklace we found here in the library interlocks with a necklace that the royal family of Duratra have been protecting. Together, they form the key to where the diamonds are.'

He frowned, as if mostly keeping up. 'So you have a map of the tunnels, the key is nearly here, but you don't know *where* in the passageways the diamonds are locked?'

Summer nodded.

'And you won't inherit the estate if you don't find the diamonds?'

She nodded again.

'But if you find the diamonds, inherit the estate, then you can sell it to Lykos, so that you can…pay for your mother's treatment,' he concluded, understanding finally dawning in his eyes.

'Exactly.'

'Summer, I can give you that money,' Theron insisted.

She bit her lip and shook her head. 'In exchange for?'

'What? No, there would be no strings,' he said. For a moment he appeared offended that she had thought such a thing. But he'd said it as if he actually believed it.

'Oh, so maybe when we have a disagreement about me having a home birth—'

'A home birth?' he choked.

'Or the name of our child, or where I live with our child, or—'

'We *will* be getting married.'

'Or *whether* we marry... Theron, if I take your money for my mother's treatment it will always be there. We are going to be parents together. We are going to look after a baby, a child, a teenager and a young adult. We *have* to be equals in this. I could not spend the rest of our lives in your debt.'

It was probably the only thing she could say to cut through the fog of his indignation and incomprehension. Because Theron knew the weight of such a debt. He felt it every single day. Even now, thinking of Kyros, he felt the hot ache of guilt. Coming to England had been the first time Theron had ever lied to him. A new client. The words had stuck in his throat when he'd lied to the man who had given him so much that no repayment could ever be compensation enough. Theron should have never kept this— kept *her*—from him.

'I will stand for nothing less, Theron.'

'You shouldn't,' he agreed, swearing to himself that he would never do such a thing to her. The pride he felt seeing her determination, seeing the spark of golden fire in her hazel eyes, was bewitching. In that moment he knew that she would be fierce as a mother, protective, sure and powerful. It humbled him.

And then it scared him. What kind of father would he

be if his first act had been to cast out the mother of his child and accuse her of…? His heart pounded in his chest and he clenched his fists, trying to refocus himself as a cold sweat broke out at his neck.

'How long have you been searching the tunnels?' He forced the words out, trying to distract himself.

'Skye sent pictures of the map about a month ago.'

He cursed, his mind moving from himself to her in a heartbeat. 'You've been searching these tunnels on your own for a month?'

'We're all doing our bit,' she said defensively. 'Skye is in France with Benoit—they're figuring out a few things through the engagement and Star is in Duratra trying to get the key back from Sheikh Khalif Al Azhar. And I'm supposed to find the jewels, except I can't.'

She sounded so lost he wanted to help. Needed to.

'How did you find the map and the key?' he asked, genuinely curious.

'There were coded messages in the journal entries we discovered, and the last message said, *You will find them when the map and the key are brought together.* Which is fine, but we don't have the time to wait. If the diamonds are here then I *should* be able to find them. Yet I've been through the passageways and the journals and I can't see where they might be hidden. Catherine writes so much about faith and love and truth, and *trust,* but…'

'That is not quite your area of expertise? Because you like touching and knowing and understanding?'

She looked up at him as if surprised that he recognised that about her, but then his words incited a different understanding. Her cheeks heated, raising his own temperature, the pulse of desire catching and flashing the entire length of his body.

Mine.

But it was more than desire. It was more than recognising someone as sexually compatible. This time it was primal, animalistic. He'd never felt anything so powerful in his entire life. She was his and carrying his child. The cry of possession, loud, insistent and undeniable, tolled through his entire body.

The fierceness of it scared him. Because already to want that much, to need it…it was spinning out of his control and he was *never* out of control. He'd never been out of control. Before her. He drew in a lungful of air to stop the way the ground seemed to shimmer beneath his feet.

'Let's get out of here,' he said, rising as he spoke, surprising them both. His skin itched and he felt half suffocated by his thoughts and by this estate.

'That wasn't my fault,' Theron growled, wondering how quickly he could book a dental appointment back home. His molars were getting a pounding from the clench of his jaw.

Beside him in the car, Summer slowly exhaled. 'That was most *definitely* your fault. You're too far out in the road.'

'What road? It's little more than a dirt track,' he replied, outraged.

'Do you want me to drive?' she asked, not wholly sarcastically.

Theron actually *felt* the look of utter disbelief on his features and tried to ignore the way she bit her lip to stop herself from smiling.

Following the satnav directions on the postcode he'd plugged in, he tried not to become distracted by the slashes of verdant green stretching along the horizon in ways he'd never seen before. But from the corner of his eye he could see Summer's fingers twisting in her lap.

'I want to apologise.' The words fell from his lips urgently, before he could change his mind.

Summer flicked a confused glance at him. 'What for?'

It was a valid question. There were quite a number of options. He saw her bite her lip just before he returned his eyes to the road.

'The way I...behaved,' he said, the words twisting, hot, guilty and painful, in his gut. 'The way I treated you in Greece.' He shook his head. 'Sorry doesn't change it, but I am very and truly sorry.'

He felt the press of her gaze against his skin, checking the road before turning to look at her, hoping that she saw the truth of his words. But it cost him dearly, because he saw the depth of her hurt from that day. He turned back to the road only after she nodded.

'Where are we going?' Summer asked after a few minutes. 'Only I don't like being away from the estate too long.'

Theron paused for a beat. 'When was the last time you actually left the estate?'

She pressed her lips together and looked out of the window. Clearly she hadn't left. He frowned. From what she had said, they had arrived for the funeral nearly two months ago and her sisters had left nearly one month ago. All that time with nothing but searching for the diamonds to distract her from her worry about her mother.

Waiting for the inevitable, hoping for a miracle.

He knew that feeling well. It had been written on his soul during the days he'd spent with Kyros beside Althaia's bedside in the hospital room as the monitors beeped down to a flat line. Theron had hurt with Kyros, cried with him, paced with him and held both his and Althaia's hands. He'd realised in that hospital room that Kyros and Althaia had been in his life longer than his own parents had. The love he had borne witness to in those weeks, and over the years, had made it so hard for him to believe what Summer had told him in Greece.

How ironic then that as he looked at Summer now he suddenly saw Kyros in her. It wasn't the mole on her collarbone or the shape of her face. It was her eyes. The way that she faced the future with a sense of inevitability. As if braced for hurt.

He remembered that feeling. Waiting for the next blow, emotional or physical, it didn't matter. He'd had to cut himself off from feelings, he'd had to embrace a numbing to live through that and he didn't want Summer to experience that. He wouldn't let that happen.

He turned off the main road and cut down a track, wincing as the car's suspension took a pounding. Perhaps he should have rented a four-wheel drive.

He was focused so hard on the road and the car that he hadn't looked further until he heard Summer gasp. Having grown up in Piraeus, practically on the beach, Theron was faintly dismissive of her reaction to what was presumably a small strip of blue. Until he looked up.

'Oh.'

The car rolled to a stop and they stared out at the incredible stretch of sand and the ribbon of blue bisecting the horizon. It was as if he were looking at an optical illusion. Both far and near, impossibly wide yet completely attainable. It made him feel small, as if he were the tiniest speck of sand in the universe.

Summer got out of the car and he followed, watching her eyes grow round with awe and surprise. 'It's beautiful,' she exclaimed as she pulled her coat around her, walking towards the path to the sea.

The wind whipped across his face as he followed her, drawn to her like the tide was to the land. The pulse of the sea had been like an echo of his heartbeat; it was the most constant thing in his life. To hear the crash of waves on a quiet day brought him peace. The same kind of peace, he realised now, that he'd felt in Summer's company that night back in Greece.

As the pathway opened up to the beach, the stretch of sand before them was endless. They drew to a stop and unaccountably his fingers found hers, their palms touching and easing the tension in his chest for the first time since the day before. The sun was warm on his face, taking a little of the sting out of the wind's bite, and he closed his eyes for just a moment.

Unbidden, the memory of his mother's laugh came to him on the wind. The press of her lips to his cheek, the warming of his heart, something soft that he couldn't quite place…and then it was gone. He breathed through the hurt, forcing himself forward towards the water. He felt Summer's gaze on his skin and he resisted the urge to reach up and capture it, to hold it there.

'You like the sea,' she observed.

He nodded. 'Lykos and I spent nearly every evening at the beach. We'd sneak out of the orphanage after lights out and just sit there. The sea, the stars… My father was a fisherman and being out there, I felt…' he sighed '…connected, I suppose.' He could feel her silent questions pressing against him and owed her that much at least. 'I was five when they died. The earthquake, it was a six point zero,' he said, shaking his head. 'Devastating. It killed over one hundred and forty people and injured thousands.' He no longer saw the sea, the English horizon.

The sound of the tide became a roar, a rumble, the shift of the sand beneath his feet became a tremor. His heartbeat pounded in his ears. In his mind he put his arm out to the doorframe to brace himself. He was screaming for his mother, for his father. They were on the other side of the house. He was all alone and tears were blurring his vision, the whole room was shaking. Where were his parents? Then he saw him—his father, he was coming to get him, his mother following just behind. They were coming for him and they would all be okay. He wouldn't be alone and...

Theron clenched his jaw against the hot press of tears against the backs of his eyes, refusing to let them fall. He focused on the sound of the waves, their gentle sweep across the sand somehow making it easier for him to speak the hurt of his past, as if it took his words and brought them back changed. 'A ceiling beam came down on top of my father and caught my mother. She died later in hospital.'

'Theron—'

He squeezed Summer's hand gently. He knew. He felt her sympathy. 'I was taken to an orphanage. Neither of my parents had family, so that was where I ended up. And where I met Lykos,' Theron said, shaking his head, unable to help the smile pulling at his lips. 'He was... I had lost my family, but I found a brother,' he said, realising just how hard the last ten years had been without him. Even though it still felt as if Lykos was in his head sometimes.

'But when I met him in Greece you seemed more like business acquaintances.'

'We had a falling out,' Theron stated.

'Did it have something to do with my father?' she asked.

Theron kept his features neutral, even though the mention of her father still twisted a knife. Theron should have called Kyros last night. He was torn between loyalty to the man who had been like a father to him and the woman who carried his child.

'Yes,' he said, finally answering her question about Lykos but reluctant to delve into it further.

'How did you meet Kyros?' Summer asked, as if sensing he wasn't going to say any more.

'He found us running scams on the streets. We were picking pockets, raising hell, the usual wayward stuff,' he said, a smile pulling at his lips. They were some of the best memories he had. 'Lykos had picked his pocket, but when he saw the photo in it he said we had to give it back.

'The photo was of him and his wife dancing.' It was only later, when Theron had met Althaia and realised how badly the multiple sclerosis had ravaged her body, that he'd realised the significance of the photo. Kyros eventually told him it was the last time they had danced. 'He wanted to reward us for returning it to him. Lykos,' he said, smiling broadly at the memory of the then fifteen-year-old's audacity, 'demanded one hundred euros. Kyros laughed, insisted that he wanted to give us something much more valuable than that.

'He paid for our education at one of the most exclusive schools in Athens and promised us that if we graduated then we would come and work with him.'

Theron looked out at the endless sea, marvelling at what an incredible gift they'd been given—the opportunity to be more than a statistic, a failure. They hadn't been stupid, even then he and Lykos had known. Life half on the streets, half in the orphanage, little education or hope even after that…it didn't paint a pretty picture. For all that life had been fun with Lykos, it also had nights full of terror, days full of worry—where was the next beating going to come from, where was the next meal…? Life hadn't existed past that.

'We stayed at the orphanage, but went to a good school. It was a little rough at the beginning—a few kids trying it on—but Lykos put a stop to that immediately. It helped that he was a couple of years older and a hell of a lot bigger. Kyros putting us in that school got us off the streets, gave us an education we would never have had. On Sundays we'd go round to Kyros's house for dinner. He'd ask us what we were learning, how our week had been, and he'd tell us about his business. We didn't realise, but even then he was preparing us to work for him.'

'And Althaia?'

Theron looked at Summer. Her hazel eyes had dimmed, the green clearer in them than ever. She'd lost some of the colour he liked seeing so much in her cheeks and for the first time he wondered how Summer would have felt about the woman her father had chosen to be with.

CHAPTER SIX

'SHE JOINED US on the days when she could. Which wasn't often,' Theron said, squinting in the bright sunshine piercing the blue-grey sky that seemed to blanket everything. 'The form of MS she had affects a small amount of people, but the symptoms were difficult and devastating. She was bed-bound for the last two years of her life and constantly battling infections and the slow deterioration of her body.'

Summer's heart hurt for them all and what they'd been through. 'What was she like?' she asked, half wanting to know, half not.

'She was…loving, kind.' He shrugged. 'As interested in us as Kyros was, but often distracted and in pain. Her diagnosis was progressive and it made things very hard for her. Hard for them both.'

Summer wondered if that was why Kyros had strayed—to have one moment outside of the impossible heartbreak he faced. She wondered whether her mother had known, and couldn't quite work out how she felt about it, hating the idea that one thing in her mother's past could change the way Summer saw her. She shook her head, her heart hurting.

'So you both went to work for Kyros when you finished school?' she asked, half changing the subject.

'Yes. For a while.'

Summer frowned, sensing his hesitancy but not the reason why.

Theron took a breath. 'Lykos was two years older than me, so he had gone to work for Kyros before I joined the company. But when I was eighteen, Lykos turned up and told me he was leaving.'

'Why?' she asked.

'I don't know.' Summer didn't know whether he'd realised his hand had tightened around hers, but she soothed her thumb over the back of his hand and his grip loosened. 'He never told me. We had an argument and...we have only spoken once since that day.'

His jaw was clenched so hard that Summer could see the flare of his muscle. She thought he was done, but he surprised her by carrying on.

'He wouldn't tell me why he was leaving, but he wanted me to go with him. I said that we couldn't. That we'd promised to work with him after school. Lykos accused me of choosing Kyros over him and... I couldn't deny it.'

He turned to her, his eyes filled with hurt and pain, warring with that decision all over again.

'I remember every word he said. "It's not real, you know. This little family you've created in your mind from Sunday dinners with Kyros and Althaia. You'll never be part of their real family. You'll be the dog that they feed scraps to for the rest of your life. Because you'll never find a way to repay that debt of yours, will you? *I'm* your family, not them. Come with me".'

'I'm sure he didn't mean it,' Summer said.

'He did,' Theron said, looking out at the sea, the stoicism in his expression heartbreaking for her to see. 'But all I knew was that I had somewhere I felt safe. Somewhere I felt I belonged.' He turned to Summer and she knew, even if he didn't say it. With Kyros he'd found a home. A family. 'I owe Kyros my life. I know what happened to some of the boys at the orphanage. I know what some of them did, what they had to do and where they ended up because of it.'

He lifted the veil holding back his feelings then and she could see it. See it all. The honesty, the fear that it could have been him, the dread of truly horrible things that she could barely conceive of. She might not have had Kyros in her life, but she'd had her mother, her sisters, a roof over her head and a sense of constant security. She understood the awfulness of his childhood, the shock of losing his parents, of being placed in an orphanage—and then being presented with what Kyros was offering. She could see so clearly how impossible it would have been for Theron to have left with Lykos.

'My debt to him will never be repaid.'

Something inside her curled in on itself, as if it recognised something final, something horribly conclusive. She pushed past it to try to see what he wanted her to see.

'Is that why you sent me away in Greece? Because you were trying to pay your debt?' she asked.

'I am in charge of his security. Summer, you're not the first person to claim to be the illegitimate child of a very rich man.'

'He looked right at me—'

'Summer—' he said, as if about to defend him.

'He looked at me and saw nothing.' The words hurt as they poured out of her, her throat thickening with pain.

Theron took a breath. 'He doesn't know about you,' he said simply, with horrifying ease. 'He's not looking for you in young women around him because he doesn't *know* to look. If you were to take a DNA test you could prove it to him. It's a mouth swab. It won't hurt the baby.'

'But it could hurt *me*!' she cried, remembering the pain

she'd felt when he'd dismissed her with a glance. *Or you*, she thought, already beginning to see how precarious his position was with Kyros. If she proved herself to be Kyros's child, she couldn't see how that could be any kind of good for Theron. Not with how things stood.

That thought, that realisation, made her frown. 'Is that why you proposed?' Nausea swirled in her stomach.

'Is what why I proposed?'

'Because I'm his daughter. Because—' she shook her head '—I can't imagine how getting your mentor's illegitimate daughter pregnant with an illegitimate child would go down particularly well.'

'I proposed because family is everything. I learned that from him. I cannot allow you to have our child, unmarried.'

'My mother was unmarried when she had me, so don't you dare—'

He held his hands up in surrender.

She shook her head in disgust. 'Kyros might have taught you about family, but my mother taught me about love. And love isn't a debt you can repay.' Her heart ached, her soul felt heavy and her tongue thick with grief. 'Don't ask me again to marry you,' she ordered, before storming off down the beach.

He'd felt it. For just a moment, the softening between them. He'd hardly dared to ease into it, a softness that felt both strange but familiar. Like a half-forgotten song. Until she'd asked why he'd proposed.

Love isn't a debt you can repay.

Her words had echoed in the silence of the journey back to the estate and it felt as if they were eroding his foundations—the very things that he'd clung to for security for all these years. He searched his heart and had to admit the truth. There had been a part of him that sought to appease a future he could see on the horizon. A reckoning with Kyros that he'd perhaps always sensed coming in one form or another.

But it wasn't the only truth. And that was the thing that scared him the most.

After their return he had spent a couple of hours in the room he'd taken as his, answering work emails, concluding business with one client and reassuring another, before going to look for Summer.

As he rounded the corner to the kitchen, she was drawing various ingredients from the fridge that he registered with disgust.

'What is that?' he demanded.

'Dinner.'

'It is no such thing,' he replied, taking steps towards the monstrous selection of food she had gathered together. She turned on him, and had to lean back to peer up at him. He hadn't intended to get so close that he could smell the faint traces of salt and sea air still clinging to her clothes and skin. But he wouldn't retreat. Couldn't.

'There is nothing wrong with a cheese sandwich,' she said defiantly.

'"Dinner" is supposed to be *hot*. And it should most definitely have a vegetable in there somewhere.'

'Fine. Cheese and tomato then,' she snarked. Only he wished she hadn't, because the gold flecks in her eyes sparkled and danced when she did.

'Tomatoes are a fruit,' he dismissed. She had to step back as he went to the fridge to see what there was and sighed heavily. 'Is this an English thing?' he demanded.

'What?'

'A horrible relationship with food.'

'No. It's just that…well…' He turned to find her looking

uncomfortably at the floor and he bit his tongue. He hadn't meant to shame her. 'Skye cooked. For us,' she clarified, 'when we were growing up. She always cooked.'

'Mariam can't cook?' he asked, more gently this time.

'She can. Actually, she's a great cook,' Summer said, her shoulders tensing slightly at the mention of her mother. 'It's just that…she was a bit scatty when it came to meal-times. She'd always be lost in a sunset, or her yoga or… like, right now, she's focused on her candle magic and…' She trailed off and Theron hoped to God the confusion he felt wasn't on his face this time.

'You've done it again.'

'Done what?' she asked.

'You've stopped mid-sentence.'

'Oh, well, I was expecting some kind of commentary on candle magic.'

Theron frowned. It might not be his thing, but who was he to judge? Althaia had insisted on reading his cof-fee grains whenever he had visited on a Sunday morning. 'Nope. I don't have any. But I'm curious how you and sci-ence fit with such a free spirit.'

'Not easily,' Summer said, and he wondered if she was aware of the tension in her voice. 'I sometimes felt too se-rious for her, but I always felt loved.'

He doubted that she realised how much she defended her mother to him. As if it was important to her that he thought well of Mariam. He gestured for her to take a seat as he finally figured out what he could do with the limited ingredients in the fridge, pulling the potatoes out before he went looking for a pan.

'You cook?' she asked.

'Yes,' he stated.

'I thought you'd be more of a restaurant kind of guy,' she said, shrugging.

He smirked. 'I do that too, but...' He sighed. 'Althaia taught me. On Sundays, when we'd visit, she'd teach me a new recipe and we'd eat it together. *Not like that*,' he echoed, his hand coming down in the air in a cutting movement. *'Like this,'* he said, smiling as he repeated the gesture at Althaia's 'correct' angle. But then he remembered the days she hadn't been able to help so much. She'd sat in the corner of the kitchen, rattling off directions like an army general.

'I'm sorry,' Summer said, and he frowned. 'She clearly meant a lot to you.'

He nodded and poured boiling water over the potatoes and then pulled flour down from the shelf.

'What are we having?' she asked, eyeing the potatoes and flour suspiciously.

'*Gnocchi.*'

'Really?' she asked incredulously. 'You're just *whipping up* some *gnocchi*?'

'Yes,' he replied, and a touch of pride flashed through him as the gold in her eyes sparkled.

He opened his mouth to ask the question that had snared in his mind earlier, but he hesitated, reluctant to broach it. And he wouldn't have if he hadn't thought that Summer needed it. Her mother was important to her and, whatever was holding her back, she would never forgive herself if anything happened while she held onto that hurt.

'Why are you angry with her?' he asked gently.

'Who?'

'Your mother.'

'I'm not.'

Theron just managed to stop himself from contradicting her, choosing instead to wait her out.

Summer pressed her lips together and stared at her hands until her shoulders sagged ever so slightly.

'She told me she didn't know who my father was.'

Summer watched as he filled the pan with water and put it on the lit stove. He was waiting for more, she recognised that in him now. Waiting for her to say what she needed. She liked that about him. It would make him a good father, she realised with a jolt that hurt her heart a little as she realised just how much she'd missed.

'Mum told me that they'd met, that the time they'd shared had been magical, but that they hadn't exchanged names, so she'd never been able to tell him about me. Over the years there might be slight variations, a few extra details, or some that changed. But it had always been an almost mystical holiday romance. As if it had been outside of time and incredibly special, but entirely contained within that bubble.

'But that was a lie. She could have reached out to him. Even if Kyros was married, even if it was difficult, even if he'd said he didn't want anything to do with me,' she said, the words rushing out on a shaky breath, 'I would have preferred that to...'

'To?' he nudged gently.

'To growing up searching every face, every person, for the thing that I felt I was missing. Not knowing, it was a physical pain for me. An ache for something I couldn't even name.'

A sense of security—was that what a father gave? Summer wondered. A template for how men should behave, how they should treat her as a woman? Was *that* what she'd missed? A safe haven, somewhere to turn, no matter how hard or bad or difficult things got? She loved her mother fiercely and with her whole heart, but keeping her father from her had hurt her and shaped her in ways Mariam could never have realised.

And in that moment, in that half breath between that thought and her next, she realised something that would change her life irrevocably. She could never do that to her child. No matter what happened between her and Theron, no matter what, her child would know their father. They would be a part of each other's lives if she had to move heaven and earth to make it happen.

She looked up and blinked back a shimmer of tears as Theron's gaze searched hers as if he wondered where her thoughts had taken her. She shook thoughts of her child from her head, memories of her own childhood in her heart. Now wasn't the time for that conversation with Theron. There was so much more to speak of first. She bit her lip and looked out of the kitchen window at the night sky beyond.

'So yes, absolutely, growing up without a father hurt. But it was a hurt that I had made peace with. Until I found the photo.'

Theron put down the pan and walked to where she sat.

'Before then, it wasn't anyone's fault. It was a horrible *absence*. But finding the photo... She'd lied to me and I can't even tell her that I know. She betrayed me and I have so much... I'm so *angry*.'

He reached her on the first sob of breath and pulled her out of the chair on the second. 'Oh, God,' she half cried. 'What if we don't find the diamonds? What if Mum doesn't get the treatment and what if I am still angry with her when she...?'

She couldn't bring herself to even say the words.

Theron held out his hand. 'I'd like to show you something.'

Summer followed Theron as he led her down a hallway and through a door to the garden that had become devastatingly overgrown. In a strange way it reminded her of the roses around Sleeping Beauty's castle.

The evening air was surprisingly warm and the sky was a blanket of stars, shockingly bright and clear. The sight of it burned away some of her anger, but not enough. She could still feel it roiling, barely a millimetre beneath the surface. She hated it. She wasn't this person. She was practical, not emotional. Logical, not irrational. But ever since her mother's diagnosis, ever since the discovery of her father's identity, ever since *Theron*, she'd been behaving completely out of character.

She inhaled the scent of honeysuckle and frowned. She'd not seen the beautiful fragrant plant out here. In the dark, Theron seemed to be looking around.

'Neighbours are quite far away?'

'Yes. Why?' she asked, very confused now.

'Good. No one will hear you.'

'You get how that sounds, right?' she asked, unsure whether to laugh or back away.

He looked at her in all seriousness and then a smile broke out across his face, lighting his eyes and making him look his age for the first time since she'd met him. 'Yes. That's the point. You are going to scream.'

'Okay, enough with the psycho talk,' she said, turning back, before he caught her arm to stop her.

'No. I'm serious. All this anger. You're going to scream it out.'

Summer stared up at him, finally understanding what he wanted. 'I don't think—'

Theron sighed. 'That's the point. You *do* think. You think far too much. Screaming? It's visceral, it comes from here,' he said, pressing his hand to her diaphragm, just above the round of her stomach. There was a slight pause, a flare in his eyes, before he masked it. 'You need to let it out because it's damaging. So, scream.'

Summer was so tempted. She could imagine it. How it might feel to release all the emotions bottled up inside her. But she was embarrassed. She'd sound stupid, she'd probably get it wrong, and she'd look—

Every thought stopped as a thunderous bellow cut through the night sky. She turned to Theron, eyes wide and shocked.

'That's how you do it. Your turn.'

She frowned, still unsure.

'Hold on,' he said, placing his hands over his ears as if he understood her concern, as silly as it might be. 'Go.'

She huffed out a laugh, but he didn't move, just waited for her to get on and do it. Finally, she took a deep breath, looked out across the mass of brambles and stars…and *screamed*.

She winced through the first awkward second or two, but then it rushed out of her, gaining power and volume just at the end.

'*Naí.* Good. Again,' Theron commanded.

Her heart pounding and the pressure in her head and chest beginning to flow, she screamed again, the sound, the anger, the tension, the constant fear she'd been holding in, all purged from her body in one long howl. She nearly choked when she heard Theron join her.

Her blood fizzed in her veins and there was a lightness in her chest that she hadn't felt since Greece. 'People are going to think we're crazy,' she said, laughing.

'That's okay.'

She looked up at him, outlined by the stars in the night sky, his eyes blazing more fiercely than the moon. And then she remembered. That night on the beach. She'd tried to force it from her mind because of the intensity of the feelings, the emotions it brought. Her fingers itched to reach up and brush the stray lock of hair that had fallen across his brow.

Because she wanted to see him. All of him. She wanted so damn much. But she was scared. And that was why she turned back to look out across the garden.

'Was it Lykos who taught you that?'

There was a beat of silence before he answered.

'No. It was Kyros.'

And suddenly it hurt. Hurt that her father had given him this…*thing*, had spent years with Theron, while she'd had nothing. It made her feel mean and angry all over again. But most of all it made her sad.

Once again, he stopped her before she could turn to leave. His hand was at her wrist, a gentle clasp that she could have easily broken, but didn't. Couldn't because of the way she felt alive beneath his touch.

'I remember a similar feeling,' he said, his voice quiet but breathing sincere emotion into the night air between them, 'to the one you described. That anger. At the world, at my parents for dying, at Lykos for leaving. It's as familiar to me as the blood in my veins. And if Kyros hadn't intervened, things might have been very different. But he did.

'Do you think it's possible,' he asked, looking down at her, as if trying to read the eyes she kept hidden from his gaze, 'that Kyros taught me, all those years ago, so that I might be here with you now, showing you?'

The idea behind his words, the intent, was all too much. She felt like a raw nerve, exposed and vulnerable, and she wanted to feel powerful. She wanted to feel confident—all the things she had embraced the night she'd spent with him in Greece. And, before she could stop herself, she reached for him, her hands threaded through his hair, clasped at his neck, pulling him down towards her, and when his lips finally met hers it was as if she could breathe again for the first time.

For just a moment he didn't move and she thought he would pull back, feared that he would leave her breathless and wanting. And then he groaned helplessly against her lips as he deepened the kiss, thrusting his tongue into her mouth at the same time as pulling her against his body and everything in her exploded. Open kisses, tangled tongues and pounding heartbeats were all Summer knew for blissful endless moments that rolled into each other.

She breathed in the scent of him, salt from the sea mixing with honeysuckle and cedar. His hand settled between her shoulder blades and the other swept up her side, perilously close to her breast, but not close enough. Her nipples tightened in anticipation, in need and then—

The harsh, bright ring of the doorbell cut through the night.

Theron reared back, dark slashes of crimson on his cheeks, matching—she was sure—those on her own, his hungry gaze consuming hers until the doorbell rang again and he stepped back. Summer hugged her arms around her body, pulling the edges of her shawl around her shoulders before turning away from the look of…what, regret? Frustration? She didn't want to know.

Hurrying down the corridors, she called that she was coming to whoever it could be at the door at this time of night. The doorbell rang again, spiking her adrenaline for some reason, the urgency of it scratching against her delicate nerves.

She pulled open the door, the heat she felt from Theron hovering in the dark corridor behind her giving her a sense of safety.

A small, bespectacled man stood blinking up at her,

frowning as if she were not what he'd expected. Behind him was a long sleek town car with three dark-suited men who, at the sight of Theron looming behind her, came to stand tall, puffing out their chests as if to meet power with power.

She refocused on the man in front of her.

'Ms Summer Soames?'

'Yes.'

'Can I see some identification?'

'Why?'

He inhaled, as if frustrated by her response. 'What I have is—I've been told—of great importance to you and your family and I will not give it into the wrong hands,' he said, his voice imperious. 'It is from Ms Star Soames. I have brought it all the way, in person, from—'

'Duratra! It's the necklace!' Summer cried, making the bespectacled man wince, the suited men around the car start, and Theron draw one step closer. 'Don't go anywhere! Don't move! Theron, please make sure—'

'They don't leave. Got it,' he said as she disappeared into the bowels of the house to retrieve her wallet. She ran, the whole time her pulse racing, but never as wildly as it had when Theron had kissed her.

It was the key. It was here. Finally.

So why did her thoughts keep veering back to the kiss? Why did she stop in the middle of the corridor to bite her lip where his lips had touched, to try and hold that sense of him to her, instead of rushing to retrieve her identification? Her breath juddered in her chest and she put her hand half out to steady herself. But then she steeled her spine.

It was the key. It was here and she needed it. Now.

She returned to the front of the house with her passport and showed it to the man, who bowed low and when he righted himself presented her with a package as solemnly as if it were a crown jewel.

The man eyed Theron suspiciously, then snapped his fingers and he and the suited men disappeared into the car, which turned in a slow arc before grinding down the gravel path away from the estate.

Last night...

Lykos howled with laughter. 'I still can't believe you took a convertible to Norfolk. Even *I'm* not that ridiculous.'

'The English can't drive. It was not my fault.'

'You keep telling yourself that,' Lykos said with a smirk on his lips. 'Drink up.'

Theron took the last mouthful of his whisky and pulled on his jacket as Lykos palmed an obscene number of notes off to a very happy-looking waitress. As he shrugged into the sleeves of his coat, he could have sworn he still smelt the salt of the North Sea.

'You remembered it wrong, by the way. *You* saw the photo and forced me to agree that we should give it back,' Lykos stated as they stepped out of Victoriana onto the wet pavement, throwing his collar up against the rain, ignoring the man with an umbrella and stalking towards the sleek town car waiting for them.

Theron stood on the steps, staring not at Lykos, holding the door open for him, or the black cabs and yellow lights of London, but the way Summer had run off into the house after receiving the package from Duratra, her focus so all-consuming.

'Look, get in the car, don't get in the car. Not my concern. Whatever you're going to do, do it,' Lykos said, sliding into the back of the car, leaving the door open.

He got in and closed the door, turning to Lykos, scanning his phone for something.

'There's nothing wrong with my memory,' Theron said. 'I ought to sue you for misrepresentation.'

Theron waved him off. After a while he couldn't help himself. 'What are you doing?'

'Looking for that *gnocchi* recipe,' Lykos answered, eyes still glued to the screen. 'Since you clearly turned into a domestic goddess—'

Theron reached for the nearest thing, which happened to be a rather creased newspaper, and threw it at him.

Lykos caught it without looking up, a smirk across his lips.

As they made their way through the city at night, the faint glow of Lykos's screen illuminating the back of the car, Theron spared a brief thought for what Lykos had been doing all these years. Because of his job, Theron had access to as much information on people as he'd ever want. But he'd never looked Lykos up.

'Okay, fine,' his old friend said, putting away his phone just as they pulled to a stop. 'Right, I've got it. Maps, secret passageways, hidden jewels, treasure hunt. Blah, blah, blah.'

'I'm beginning to think you're more interested in me and Summer.'

'No idea what you're talking about,' Lykos hotly denied. 'My only interest is in whether I can get my hands on that castle or not.'

'It's an *estate*,' Theron growled, getting out of the car and staring up at the building it had pulled up in front of. He frowned. He had expected to find Lykos staying in some sleek and impossibly expensive penthouse. And while this definitely ticked the impossibly expensive box, the Regency terrace in a tree-lined road in the heart of

Knightsbridge was altogether something *other*. He looked from the house to Lykos and back to the house again as his old friend passed through the wrought iron gate, pressed his thumb against an electronic keypad and pushed open the front door.

'But it *was* the necklace from Duratra, right?' Lykos asked, not bothering to look back as he stalked into the living area, tossed his suit jacket on a chair and went straight to a drinks cabinet to pour himself a whisky. Belatedly, he turned, gesturing to Theron, who nodded and accepted the glass Lykos then gave him.

'Yes, it was the necklace.'

CHAPTER SEVEN

Three days ago...

THERON PACED THE tiled floor of the kitchen.

That kiss.

It had been just like the one on the beach in Piraeus. It had knocked him off his feet and made him lose his mind. Only it hadn't been enough. Not nearly enough. He knew *exactly* what would have happened if they hadn't been interrupted. His body did too and was still clamouring for it. Needy for it.

He shook his head in swift denial of his thoughts and his body. He needed to get a grip and put it to the back of his mind. Summer and her sisters had been searching for the jewels non-stop for nearly two whole months. Dancing to the tune of some now dead relative in order to save their mother. She now had within her grasp the ability to help save her mother's life.

What would he have done for such a chance?

Anything. The answer was swift and sure.

He could see in an instant how nothing would be conceivable for Summer until she found the diamonds. No thinking about the future, no decision, nothing. Her mother's health and her and her sisters' ability to secure it would have, and clearly had, eclipsed all else.

But there would come a time when they would have to sit down and talk—about their future, their child's future and what that would look like. And before they could do that he needed to know what *he* thought, what *he* wanted it to be.

His mind flashed back, not to Sunday dinners with Kyros and Althaia, not laughing with Lykos on the beach, terrorising tourists and local vendors for money and food, but to sitting in his mother's lap in a room he could barely remember, hands clasped around her neck, cheek to chest, feeling nothing but safe, nothing but love.

That was home. That was what a parent gave a child— what *he* wanted to give *his* child.

But could he give that to Summer?

The sound of water bubbling over the edge of the pan drew him back to the *gnocchi*. Seeing that they were ready, he tossed the potato dumplings into the frying pan with the sauce and finished with salt and pepper, before dividing them between two plates. He found a tray from somewhere and put the plates, some water and cutlery onto the tray and took a deep breath before heading to the library.

As he'd expected, Theron found Summer hunched over the small table where she'd gathered all the journals, her hand resting on the necklace's velvet pouch while the index finger of her other hand traced the handwritten instalments in leather-bound journals that looked exactly what they were: decades old.

He turned on the overhead light, causing Summer to momentarily sit up, blink, and then go back to the journals. Her concentration was fierce and impressive—it must be, to study what she did, to think the way she did—but he worried about the toll it took on her. He placed the food on the table beside her and took his to the chair by the fire.

Over the next few hours Theron came and went and

Summer barely moved. He took away the plates, washed up, added logs to the fire, looked at the rows of books on the shelves, but none of the titles caught his eye.

He frowned, looking over at one of the journals Summer had discarded and snagged it from the table without her noticing. Gently, delicately, he fingered the pages, frowning at the tightly curled cursive handwriting, passing dates that spanned months through the late eighteen-hundreds. Unable to resist, he turned to the final page.

I have heard it said that life is lived forwards, yet only to be understood backwards. I believe I know a little of that.

Theron recognised the Kierkegaard quote as one of his favourites, marvelling at how forward-thinking Catherine had been. And then he smiled, realising that he shouldn't be surprised. The Soames women were impressive, and his heart warmed with the hope that their child might be a girl to carry on those same indomitable traits.

Finally, he turned back to Summer, just to watch her. She had fallen asleep, her arm folded beneath her head and her hair falling free, the flames from the fire flickering over the golden rope-like twists. She made his heart expand. He couldn't understand it. Couldn't explain it. But she did.

He stood, rolled his shoulders. Everything was about to change. And he needed to change with it or risk losing everything. He walked over to the table, reluctant to wake her. Beyond the curve of her neck, he could see the map of the estate with the details of the secret passageways that ran just behind the hallways.

The map itself was a thing of beauty. Over one hundred and fifty years old, the detail was incredible. A filigree border surrounded the map and in the light of the fire it looked as if there were two pale gold lines leading down towards the map of the estate, but they stopped just before there was a sense of where they might lead. He peered over Summer's shoulder at the necklace. It was a strange design with two chains. He'd never seen anything like it. He remembered Summer telling him how the two necklaces would fit together to form a key, but it was still a beautiful piece of jewellery.

Then another set of faint gold lines caught his eye and he traced them with his fingertips and smiled. If he were to place the necklace chains along the four gold starter lines, then the pendant would come to rest in the north-west of the estate. He smiled to himself, feeling a deep satisfaction, which he tempered. Whether he had just found the location of the diamonds or not, Summer needed to rest. They would not disappear by the morning.

'Summer?' he whispered gently. He rubbed her shoulder, not wanting to disturb her too much. She shifted in her seat, the hold of sleep strong, and he gently pulled out the chair. Reaching down, he placed an arm beneath her legs and lifted her into his arms. Her eyes fluttered briefly but closed immediately and she leaned against his chest trustingly.

For a moment he stood in the library, Summer in his arms, and felt humbled. And then he turned into the corridors that would take him towards her room and, pushing open the door with his foot, walked to her bed and placed her gently onto the mattress. But as he went to stand, he noticed she had fisted his shirt in her hand. He tried to loosen her fingers, but instinctively he knew that she would wake. And then she'd probably yell at him for taking her away from her search for the diamonds. To avoid such a thing, he toed off his shoes and lay beside her on the bed.

As if sensing his capitulation, she crept closer and pressed into his side. The fine material of his shirt and the thick material of her cardigan were not enough to stop him from feeling the press of her chest against his side, the heat of her body and the scent of cinnamon and spice that he wanted to drown in. He took swift and harsh control of his body before it could spin out of control. He didn't care how much his body wanted or needed, *craved* hers, Summer needed sleep. And it was then that he felt it, stronger than anything he'd felt with Kyros. The bone-deep knowledge that he would protect Summer from anything and everything.

Summer opened her eyes, her fist clenched around an invisible tether she'd felt all through her dreams. It had been like an anchor to something safe, something secure, and she didn't think she'd ever felt peace like it. She opened her hand and smoothed the sheets next to her, frowning slightly at the indentation but deciding that she must have turned in her sleep.

She looked at the clock and started. Nine a.m.! It was *nine*! Suddenly yesterday came crashing through her memories like strobe lighting but all jumbled out of order. The kiss, the beach, the necklace, the library.

Her heart pounded in her chest, her mind torn between the kiss and the necklace.

Necklace first, she decided and threw off the covers, surprised to find herself still in yesterday's clothes.

Swinging her legs over the side of the bed, she shrugged out of the cardigan, pulled her T-shirt over her head. Shower now? Shower later? If she was going into the secret passageways she might as well shower later, she decided, standing up and tugging at the clasp of her bra at her back.

She yelped as Theron rounded the corner and she

grabbed the blanket, covering herself as he stepped into the room, frowning at her as if she were behaving strangely.

'I brought you...' Theron trailed off as he stared at her beneath a very furrowed brow. She was behaving like a child, she knew it, but she was practically topless. 'You know I have seen you naked before, right?' he asked, as if trying to keep a laugh from escaping.

'That was before.'

'Before?'

'Before...*everything*,' she said, unable to quite express the magnitude of *beforeness* that had changed since they'd spent that life-changing night together.

'Right,' he said, as if it were normal for her to be so inarticulate. 'So, I brought you breakfast and—'

'Okay, you can leave it there. And go,' she said, inching her shoulders beneath the blanket and closing her eyes against the state of her room. It was a mess. She'd never had a man in her room before—even if it wasn't technically *her* room but simply the room she was staying in— and there Theron was, and she was so embarrassed.

Why wouldn't he just leave?

'Actually,' he tried again, 'I—'

'Theron, *please*?'

'Please what?' he asked, unable to hide a laugh of incredulity. 'I have brought you breakfast and I have something important to tell you and you act like I'm beneath consideration or...or...' He trailed off, struggling to find the word.

'I've never had a man in my room before, okay? And it's weird. The room's a mess, and I'm embarrassed, and I don't even remember how I got here last night, and—'

'Summer? Breathe.' He locked his eyes onto hers, as if specifically *not* looking around her room, and she did as he asked. Breathed. 'Here is some breakfast. I want you to eat it before I show you something.'

'Can I get changed first?' She thought she saw the ghost of a smile curl the edges of his lips, but he nodded so she couldn't see it. She waited, but he stayed there. 'Turn around?' she asked.

'Really?'

'Yes!'

He laughed again, but did as she asked and turned around. She waited a second, as if he might still turn back and catch her in her underwear, but he didn't so she dropped the blanket and grabbed for her clothes. She was being silly because he'd certainly seen more of her the night they'd spent together in Greece. But she felt different now. Her body was different. She reached the wardrobe and grabbed a pair of trousers that she wouldn't mind getting dirty and a shirt so old it felt like silk on her skin. It was cream and pretty and she loved it.

Theron was whispering but she couldn't make out the words.

'What was that?' she asked, slipping her hands through the arms of the shirt.

'You don't want to know.'

'I do, or I wouldn't have asked,' she corrected.

'I said, "Please no more grey…please no more grey".'

Summer pulled up short. 'No more grey?' she repeated.

Theron turned and she sent him a glare, but not before she saw his eyes snag on the yellow dress hanging in the wardrobe, next to a vivid green one from the same shop. A look of deep longing passed over his features. It was so strong Summer blushed, as memories of the dress, how he had taken it from her body, what he had done to her crashed through the mental barriers she'd placed around that night.

'You shouldn't wear any more grey. Or black.' He shook his head, as if awkward. 'You should always dress in colour,' he said, nodding to the two dresses in the wardrobe. 'I'll be in the library.'

With that he turned on his heel and disappeared, all trace of his gentle laughter gone.

Biting her lip, Summer made her way into the library after eating the toast he'd brought her. Okay, one piece, but it counted, she told herself. She wasn't quite sure what to make of what he'd said about her clothes. If she was honest with herself, she knew they needed to have a proper conversation about exactly what kind of relationship they had and would have in the future. But all that could wait. The diamonds—her mother's health? That *couldn't*.

He was leaning over the table she had sat at last night, studying the map, and she had a sudden image, half memory, half wish, of him behind her, the heat of his skin against hers, as if they had been cheek to cheek. Unconsciously, she raised her hand to her face and he looked up, something passing across his gaze, making her drop her hand. His eyes went to the scarf, back to her face and down to the map without a word.

Awkwardness. She hadn't felt it before…before the kiss.

'So you've searched the east wing and you don't think it's in the central secret passageways?' he asked, still not looking at her.

'Yes. But, even so, there must be one final clue to the precise location because the secret passageways stretch for miles.'

'Well, I think you're right. And I think I know what it is.'

'What?' she demanded, rushing to the table, staring at the map and the necklace that seemed strangely placed over it.

'Can you see these faint gold lines?' he asked, nudging one of the four gold chains attached to the interlocked pendant. Summer nodded as she saw the finest of gold lines on the map. 'If you line up the chains with the lines then the pendant hangs, not in the centre of the map as you might expect, but here, amongst the west wing secret passageways.'

She leaned over to where he pointed, trying to focus through the scent of cedar from his aftershave, making her lick her lips. He pointed to where the pendant hung. The block handle of the key formed by the two intertwined necklaces created a large rectangular hole through which the chains threaded, allowing the entire key to sit flat against the map. However, the rectangular shape also had a circular cut-out, showing a small and very specific section of the map.

Summer moved the necklace out of the way to see where on the map it had pointed to, but there was nothing there. She tried again, but still she couldn't see anything but the secret passageways that had always been on the map.

She threw up her hands in frustration. 'There's nothing there!'

'With all the hidden journals, the secret maps and the far-flung corners of the world that your sisters have had to travel to, I hardly believe there would be a giant "X marks the spot".'

He was so calmly rational about the whole thing she wanted to scream.

'You've read Catherine's journals a million times. She must have said something in them about the final part of the treasure hunt.'

'It's not a treasure hunt.'

'It kind of is.'

She huffed herself into a chair, wondering why she was fighting this so hard.

'Summer?' Theron asked, coming to crouch in front of her. 'After all the searching and all the stress of the last two months, it's completely understandable to fear that it might all come to nothing.'

Summer angrily wiped at the tear that told them both he was right. She clenched her jaw against the threat of any more tears. 'I'm not this person, Theron. I am rational, deductive, sure.'

'And why is it not okay to be the opposite of those things?' he asked gently. 'Why can't you be all those things *and*…this?'

'Because I'm not the emotional one. That's Star. And Skye's the one in control. So…'

'So, then you are the best of both,' Theron announced as if it were as simple as that. She looked at him and wondered how he could see her as the best of anything. She'd been nothing but trouble since she'd entered his life and couldn't see how she'd be anything less for the rest of it. 'In the meantime, I can't believe that your great-great-great-grandmother would be so meticulous as to plan all this for it to completely fall apart at the end.'

'You can't?'

'No, I have faith.'

Summer huffed out a slightly teary laugh. 'Faith… *Faith!*' she yelled, springing up from the chair and grabbing the journal with the last entry in it.

'Where is it, where is it…yes! Here. Listen. *Faith that all will be well and, most importantly, faith that you will find not just what I have left for you, but what you truly need. For the thing about faith is that while it cannot be seen, it can be felt.* You're right. Faith in what cannot be seen!'

Summer placed the necklace back over the map as

Theron had done and carefully made a pen mark in the space in the necklace's ball. She gently swept the necklace out of the way and laughed, rolling her eyes at herself. 'Of course,' she groaned. 'Look,' she said, beckoning Theron to the map.

'What? I don't... Wait, is that—?'

'Catherine's room. It's in the secret passageway just behind Catherine's room.'

She stared up at him, not realising how close they'd become and for the first time not caring. Her heart was soaring with excitement, her pulse racing, and she swept her arms around him and clung on for dear life. Hope, relief, shock and excitement all warred within her and Summer rode out the storm in his embrace.

Theron was sure he could be forgiven for expecting a sliding bookcase or a vase on a table that swung open, rather than the hole in the wall, with fine wooden slats and bits of plaster crumbling onto the floor.

He wanted Summer wearing a face mask. *He* wanted a face mask. There would be at least a century's worth of dust in these passageways, surely. He followed the shadowy outline of Summer created by the beam of her torch as she made her way along the narrow corridor constructed within the walls of the house. The design was ingenious and the construction infallible. He wondered at Catherine, who had made all this happen, and was beginning to think it wise not to underestimate the Soames women.

Summer was trailing her hand against the wall when she came to a stop, and Theron had to pull up quickly to prevent himself from crashing into her. She ran her hand back and forth along the wall on the opposite side of the corridor, frowning, until her eyes widened in shock.

'What is it?' he whispered, not quite sure *why* he was whispering.

'Here, feel this.' She grabbed his hand and he ignored the burn he felt from her touch. It was a heat that his body welcomed, and his heart struggled with. Spreading his fingers beneath hers, she gently pressed them against the wall and he felt it.

The metal rectangle with a small impression where a key might go. Even he felt a childlike glee at the thought that they might have found the hidden treasure.

'You've found it!' he exclaimed.

She bit her lip, but failed to disguise the smile of pure joy spreading across her features. '*We* found it.' She produced the key and placed it into the lock. The metal slid into place as if it had been used only yesterday. He inhaled in expectation and then...

Nothing. Summer didn't turn the key.

'Summer?'

She leaned forward, pressing her forehead against the door. 'My sisters should be here for this.' She shook her head against the door. 'I can't... I need to wait for them.'

Theron understood. *Family.* He knew why that couldn't be him for Summer, not in this. Star and Skye had gone on this journey with her. It was as much their right as Summer's.

But it didn't stop the twist of hurt slice his heart.

He reached up to where her hand still held the key in the lock and pulled it gently back, taking the key from her loose fingers and hanging the necklace around her neck.

'It's time for you to call them home then,' he said.

CHAPTER EIGHT

SUMMER WANTED TO bottle what she was feeling. She didn't think she'd ever been so excited. Here in this half place where she knew where the diamonds were but hadn't yet seen them. She was on the brink of infinite possibilities and anything and everything she'd ever wanted could happen. Her mother healthy and well, her sisters back with her, she even felt for just a second that she might want to meet her father. That perhaps somehow, being with Theron, they could smooth over old hurts and together they could create something beautiful for the future. She could pinch herself.

There was something about the way that Theron had said she should call her sisters back *home*. Until that moment, the estate had been in the way. It had concealed the one thing they needed to truly help their mother. It had been broken, dusty, old, damp, full of her grandfather's ugliness and his father's, and his grandfather's—Anthony Soames. The man who had married his unwilling cousin for the estate and some jewels, abused her terribly and been miserable until the day he died. There was so much sadness and anger and neglect in this estate.

But there was also Catherine. And Benoit with his secret passages, and even Sheikh Hātem, who Catherine had met in Duratra, had become as much a part of the fabric of the estate as his family had been integral to finding the diamonds. So this time, as she walked through the corridors, instead of the gloom and darkness, she saw the beams of soft sunlight through hazy windows, she saw the potential that was there, just beneath the surface of dust and chaos.

She shook her head. Renovating and repairing the damage to this estate would cost millions and take years. But, even as she discarded the completely impossible idea, her imagination soared as she picked and discarded various styles or materials that could restore the series of problems in the east wing. Her mind jumped ahead to wonder whether Skye's fiancé might be interested and able to help. Then she laughed, wondering what incredible fantastical decoration Star would delve into, what inspiration she would return from the desert with... And in a heartbeat an impression of the estate, restored beyond its former glory to something that honoured both Catherine's history and the Soames sisters' futures, formed in her mind like a miraculous mirage and a longing so deep, so hard took root.

She paused, peering down one of the hallways, and could have sworn she heard the faint echo of children's laughter. She placed a hand over her bump and just for a moment let herself imagine what it might be like to raise her child here. With Theron.

And she could. She could see it so clearly, feel it so powerfully, it made her heart hurt. And it scared her because she'd never wanted anything more in her life.

She found Theron sitting at a table in the garden, leaning back in a chair, his face turned up towards the sun, his features relaxed, and he looked, for the first time, his twenty-eight years. He inclined his head just a little towards her and she realised that was his way of telling her he knew she was there.

She took the seat beside him. 'Do you miss it?' she couldn't help but ask. 'The sun. Greece,' she clarified.

'God, yes. I don't know how you do it. It's...*unhealthy.*'

The laugh tumbled out of her. She was not in the least offended by his over-exaggerated negativity towards England, or Norfolk. It was playful, the teasing. Not mean or cruel. And the idea of him not being able to withstand a bit of English weather was exactly that: laughable. Because there was something incredibly strong, immovable about him. She had—back in Greece—compared him to dolerite and now she realised how fitting that was.

Its powerfully strong properties were what made it so suitable in protective barriers and construction. That was what she felt about Theron. That, no matter what, he would protect her. Perhaps whether she wanted that protection or not.

'So how does it feel?' he asked, cutting through her thoughts. 'To have found a treasure that's been hidden for over one hundred and fifty years?'

Summer smiled, her heart soaring once again. 'Incredible. But knowing that we'll be able to sell the estate and pay for our mother's treatment is...' She shook her head, trying to find the words that could express the relief, the joy, the hope... 'I know it's not a guarantee that the treatment will work, or that she'll be okay, but it feels as if we've won half the battle at least,' she said truthfully. Although she couldn't quite explain why the thought of selling the estate dimmed her joy a little.

'Catherine Soames must have been a very impressive woman,' Theron mused. 'I can't imagine the thought, determination, the...'

'Faith?' Summer asked as she smiled at him.

'Faith,' he acknowledged with a nod, 'to plan something like this. It must have taken years.'

'I don't know what I'm going to be doing in five years, let alone...' Summer's careless words trailed off and her smile fell as she realised that she would have a four-year-old child. That *they* would have a four-year-old child. She swallowed. She knew they needed to talk about this, but until now she'd been so focused on the diamonds, her mother, even Kyros... Had she thrown them all up as excuses to stop this very conversation? 'I didn't plan for this,' she said, trying to explain.

'I know,' Theron said, looking intently at his hands.

'No, I mean... I had *plans*. Always. Skye was the one who looked after us, Star was the dreamer, the romantic, and I was the one who was going to get *the job*. The one who would make sure we were all going to be okay. Financially.' Summer squinted and it had nothing to do with the gentle sun's rays and everything to do with trying to pierce the shrouds of time to a point when she'd *not* had plans. 'My *plan* was to go to university. Take my fourth year abroad. Finish my degree and find a job in the environmental engineering sector. Get settled. Save money. Look after Mum and the girls.' Summer took a breath, wondering how many years she'd clung to that plan. Nearly ten, maybe? 'And then everything started to fall apart when I found out about Kyros. I deviated from my plan and went to Greece and...' she broke off, laughing bitterly '...and he wasn't there. And then, when he was...' Her heart hurt so much at the memory of his dismissal. She'd never felt such rejection. Until Theron had said what he'd then said. She tried to close the door on that hurt.

She now understood why he'd behaved the way he had. Theron had thought she was a threat to Kyros—the man who had been more of a father to him than he'd had the chance to be to her. And she also had to face the fact that she could have stayed. She *could* have. Theron hadn't the power to kick her out of Greece. Her plan had gone wrong and she'd left because it had been easier than staying and confronting her father.

'The point is,' she pressed on, 'I was making plans. And now I'm not. Because they don't work and I'm not sure what to do any more.' She slowly exhaled the breath that had built in her chest and wondered if anything she'd said had made sense.

Theron held her gaze when she looked at him. It was open, accepting and understanding. And suddenly she didn't want it. She didn't want his understanding. She wanted him to tell her what to do.

'Plans are not *wants*. Plans are what we do to get what we want. So, until you know what you want, you can't make a plan. What do you want?' he asked.

'I want you to tell me what you want,' she hedged.

Theron smiled ruefully and narrowed his eyes as if considering what to say. 'I want you and our child to be safe and happy.' But he said it in a way that sounded sad. As if he was separate from it. And in that moment Summer didn't have the courage to challenge him on it.

So, what did she want?

The answer was there, beating in her heart. She wanted the strong, patient, protective man who had not laughed at her mother's esoteric leanings, who had not dismissed her job or her interest, who was stubborn and sometimes sulked like a teenager, but who felt so deeply he didn't always have the words to describe it.

But something was holding him back. And until he was able to face that, Summer felt a little too vulnerable to voice the truth in her heart. So instead she thought of what she wanted for their child and the answer flew from her lips.

'I want you to be there. I want you to be all the things that my father wasn't or couldn't be. I don't want our child to hurt the way that I hurt, to feel the inability or yearning that I felt. I want them to know who their parents are and be absolutely sure that they are safe. That they are loved. So,' she said, taking a breath, 'I need you to promise that you'll be there.'

When she looked back up at Theron she noticed that his hands were fisted and his knuckles were white, his mouth was a fine tight line, and her heart broke a little. She felt foolish for speaking so freely, but knew that her words had been right and true and she would stand by them for her child.

He nodded once. But to let her know that he'd heard her or in agreement, she couldn't tell. And then he was gone. Just like that. As if he'd never really been sitting there.

Theron paced the length of his room, passing the empty fireplace and unseeing of the dust and damp that had horrified him on his first night here. He felt as if creatures were crawling up his body, scratching against his skin, and he couldn't stop it.

I want you to be there.

She'd had no idea what she'd said, how her words had poked and prodded at the open wound in his heart. He clenched his jaw at the sudden rush of memories, all piling in on each other. Lykos walking away from him, the loss of Althaia, Kyros leaving him behind as he left for the island without him. As if he'd never been a part of the Agyros family. His hand fisted and he wanted to lash out. To punch something. To have a physical pain that would be easier to bear than the chaotically sprawling emotions he couldn't seem to control.

I want you to be all the things that my father wasn't or couldn't be.

He looked at his phone, staring at the five missed calls

from Kyros. Theron dropped down onto the mattress and put his head into his hands. Summer still held so much hurt from not knowing Kyros. And what of Kyros? He couldn't imagine what pain it would cause him to have been kept away from his child for so long. He couldn't put it off any more. He had to call Kyros, no matter what it cost him.

Even as he picked up his mobile, Theron couldn't shake the feeling that everything was about to go horribly wrong, just when he needed it to be right.

An hour later Theron stalked through the halls of the estate, knowing that he had to find Summer but feeling utterly out of control. He wanted a tether. He needed her. She had anchored him since the first time he'd seen her. Pulled at his unconscious like a magnet. From the first time he'd got up to leave and sat back down, he'd felt as if he was constantly returning to her, would always return to her, somehow.

She wasn't in the kitchen, or the library. The garden looked empty and he hoped that she wasn't in the secret passageways again. He was about to go back to the upper floors when he thought he heard something being dragged across the floor. It was faint, but there. He followed the strange sound. Whatever it was seemed heavy, which worried Theron. Summer had a habit of biting off more than she could chew.

He turned down a corridor he'd not visited before, running parallel to the back of the house, seemingly all the way to the other side. The sound finally began to grow louder and the end of the corridor began to throb with light, firing his curiosity. Treading softly, he made his way towards the light, peering around the corner, hoping to remain hidden, but what he saw made his jaw drop.

A floor of aged white and blue tiles stretched down

the centre of a large glass-roofed structure attached to the main house. At the far end two thin-paned glass doors were thrown open to the setting sun and in between were huge, deep forest-green plants of all shapes and sizes. Thick, broad leaves bent open like palms, thin, spindly, pale green tendrils coiled and curled, and some kind of climber hung beneath the peeling white ironwork of the ceiling, through which the sun shone beams of dappled light back onto the ornate floor.

'What is this place?' he wondered out loud as he passed into the glass chamber.

'It's the orangery. As the only place utterly ignored by our grandfather, it has—unsurprisingly—thrived,' Summer replied from behind him.

He turned to find Summer hauling an impossibly large sack of compost across the floor. 'What on earth are you doing?'

She peered up at him, huffing a long blonde tendril from her eyes. 'Making a roast dinner. What does it look like I'm doing?'

She was angry. She had every right to be, he knew that, but he felt it too. Anger, frustration. The sense that everything he wanted was right there within his grasp... but not quite.

'You shouldn't be trying to move that,' he declared over his chain of thoughts.

'I *moved* it. I wasn't *trying*.'

Theron suppressed a growl. 'You don't have to do it all yourself, you know.'

'You don't get to do that,' she said, dropping her hold on the enormous plastic bag of compost and rounding on him. 'You don't get to come here, out of nowhere, and suddenly be everything.'

'Be everything?' he asked, the anger in Summer's tone igniting his own.

'I meant be every*where*,' she lied badly. She stepped towards him. 'You might find this hard to believe, but I was fine without you.'

'Yeah?' Theron demanded, taking a step towards her, closing the distance between them like pieces on a chess-board. 'Well, so was I,' he gritted through his teeth, the lie like iron on his tongue, with the realisation that he'd not been even remotely fine until meeting her, even as his mind scrabbled to take the thought back. And that vulner-ability, that weakness only angered him more.

His eyes caught hers, the golden sparks firing against the green evidence of her own internal war. And then, as if static electricity arced between them, linking them, draw-ing them together, he couldn't fight it any more.

They moved together at the same time, lips crashing, hands reaching and curling, hearts beating, breath hitch-ing, caught and held. All of it, he wanted to hold all of it— Summer, their child, the past and the future, in one single breath. To consume it and keep it safe for ever.

She moved against him, her hands reaching around his neck, holding him to her as if worried he would stop. She was like fire, twisting and turning in his arms, and he Pro-metheus, as if he'd stolen her from the gods themselves and he couldn't help but fear what his punishment would be.

But when she opened her mouth to his, when her tongue thrust against his, all thoughts were lost to sensation. Her fingers moved from curling in his hair to his chest, one hand pulling and the other pressing as if she couldn't tell what she wanted more.

Theron had no such confusion. He wanted everything. The thought roared through his veins, beating like a drum in his chest. He placed his hand at her back, fitting it between her shoulder blades, loving how he could stretch his palm between them, pressing her against him, feeling her chest and thighs against his.

His other hand slipped beneath her shirt and the moment his skin touched hers his heart missed a beat. He thought he felt her gasp against his mouth as his fingers swept around her waist to her stomach, and when his palm pressed against the gentle slope of her abdomen he paused. Gently, she pulled back and gazed up at him—a moment of calm in the madness. A moment just for them that healed a hurt he wasn't sure he'd known was there. But, as they gazed at each other, peace turned to hunger, turned to need, and desire became impossible to resist.

Summer inhaled once swiftly, her eyes inflamed, and she drew him back into her kiss.

She tugged at his jumper, dragging it from him as he tore at the buttons of her shirt. Her hands went to the button on his trousers and his went to her thighs and he lifted her up into his arms. He swallowed the squeak of surprise with his kiss and drew her up his chest, the friction sending enough sparks to consume them both. She shifted endlessly in his arms, and he could have held her there for eternity, but he wanted to touch, to taste, to tease. He backed towards the chaise longue he'd seen—the ancient piece of furniture fitting the faded dignity of the room and completely at odds with what he wanted to do to Summer. He wanted her indecent, he wanted her incandescent, he needed her as mindless with pleasure as he was every time he touched her.

He wanted to hear her scream his name and know that no other man would be able to do that for her. He wanted… The backs of his legs met the cushion of the lounger and he sat, bringing her with him, the air knocked out of their lungs at the impact.

He groaned out loud, not from the fall but from the exquisite pleasure of having her in his arms again. He felt completely lost to her, his heartbeat racing, an urgency in him that he couldn't quite account for. As if time was running out for them and he greedily wanted everything he could take, every memory he could make. It was as if Summer could feel it too. He could sense it in the way she searched his gaze, the way she held onto him so tightly, the desperation that seemed to make their hearts beat together.

Summer had never felt anything like this. As if all the want and need she'd tried to deny had boiled up and escaped and was now coursing through her veins. She was drunk on lust and she felt out of control, as if she honestly didn't know what she would do next. She wasn't this person, she was considered, rational, calm, but right now she was mindless, incoherent and wild. Here in this beautiful orangery, with deep green plants curling up to the ceiling, she felt elemental.

The thought struck her and stuck.

Elemental.

It was as if the word unlocked something within her that freed her from any further doubt, debate, any last vestige that would stop her from doing and taking what she wanted. It was just like it had been that first time in Greece. There was some strange alchemy between her and Theron that seemed to alter her DNA. And that change, that new element that rose within her filled her so completely it took over with the power of a crashing wave.

She pulled back from his hold and slipped her arms from the now damaged shirt, from where he had pulled it apart and sent the buttons flying. Her eyes were on his as his gaze scoured every inch of her skin, flicking back to her every other second as if making sure she was still there. That it wasn't all a dream. She knew how he felt.

She reached for the clasp of her bra and released it, her heart soaring at Theron's swift inhalation and the slash of crimson on his cheeks at the sight of her. She felt glorious. She felt beautiful and womanly and empowered all at the same time. Backing up off the chaise longue, she undid the buttons of her jeans and pushed them from her hips, kicking them out to the side with her bare feet.

He bit his lip and clenched his fists as if he was trying to restrain himself from reaching for her and she loved that she wasn't alone in the madness. Her thumbs hooked in the waistband of her high leg briefs and the gold in his eyes flared. In a second he was half off the sofa, his hands pressing against hers stopping her as she was about to draw them down her thighs.

He looked up at her from a half crouch and her breath caught in her lungs. She felt worshipped. He batted her hands gently aside and slowly, inch by inch, drew the cotton down her thighs. The intimacy of it was overwhelming. As her legs began to tremble he placed a supporting hand against her hip, his fingers sweeping around, and once again she felt cared for and desired at the same time—a combination she'd never experienced before.

She stepped out of her briefs and Theron tucked them into his pocket as if they were something too precious to kick to one side. There she was, naked and vulnerable, while he was dressed only in his dark trousers, the button at the waist she'd undone what felt like hours before.

He gazed up at her as if he were more than happy to stay there at her feet for as long as she could ever wish it, but that stirring of need, that impatient desire unwound thick and fast in her chest and she reached to pull him up.

When he reached his full height she had to crane her

neck to look up at him to take him in, to understand what arcane language their bodies were using to communicate. She wanted to spend the rest of her life learning it, using it and exploring it. She barely had time to register that thought when he swept her up in his arms and took her back to the chaise longue, laying her gently down on it.

He looked at her as if he couldn't get enough. His gaze covered every inch of her and she smiled at the errant thought that he might even turn her over and inspect her back too. The thought brought a blush to her cheeks, one that his keen gaze didn't miss. He opened his mouth as if he was about to ask her, but then shook his head as if he forgot what he'd intended, lost in the sight of her, his eyes glazed with the same desire and lust that she felt coursing through her body. Rather than the frantic desperation of moments before, the thick heavy thump of need pulsing in her veins became slow and languorous, as if they had both been hypnotised by the same thing.

He leaned back on his heels and reached for her foot, picking it up gently and bending to place kisses along the arch. Unconsciously, she pulled her leg back slightly, the sensation driving a laugh from her lungs and drawing him towards her and exposing her in a way that caught her breath. His hands swept up her thigh, his kisses following, open-mouthed and deliciously decadent as her heart thundered in her chest and he gently pressed her thigh to the side.

Her back arched off the mattress the moment his tongue pressed against her, and her hand fisted over her mouth to prevent herself from crying out. She had barely caught her breath when another long sweep of his tongue drove the oxygen from her lungs and her back into the air once again. She cursed, unable to stop herself, and she swore she could tell that he was smiling.

He pressed gently against her pelvis, angling himself and her into a position that allowed him to—

Her mind completely blanked. She couldn't have said what he did, she didn't know, other than it was amazing and incomprehensible and in the space of a heartbeat she was completely overcome by an orgasm that she felt broken by.

She came back round to the feel of gentle kisses around her abdomen, something about them bringing a sweet tear to her eye that she dashed away before Theron could see.

Eventually, as if reluctantly, the kisses began to move up her body, along her ribcage, Theron's head gently nudging at her side, causing her to shift onto her side so that he could slip behind her and place more kisses on her shoulder blades as his hands wound around her protectively.

The hot humidity of the orangery was the absolutely perfect temperature to be there naked in his arms. Her heart felt light, happy but scared, as if this moment was precious only because it might not last.

She felt his forehead lean against her shoulder.

'I don't have a condom,' he said, his tone regretful but not more than that.

She sighed, unable to help the smile curving her lips. 'I think it's a bit late for that, Theron.'

There was a pause before he replied. 'There is no risk from me. I have not been with anyone since you.'

She swallowed, realising the thought of risk hadn't crossed her mind. Even in this, she marvelled, he was protecting her. 'Me too. I...' Her words trailed off as his fingers entwined with hers, reassuring, loving even. She turned back to look at him, his gaze burning bright and intense. And, just like that, want and desire ignited in a firestorm and she reached for him, knowing he was the only thing that would quench her need.

They made love until the stars disappeared from the night sky and the sun peered at them from over the horizon. A gentle yellow glow filled the glass-walled room, warming the jasmine until its perfumed scent filled the air. Summer pulled the large throw Theron had found at some point during the night over her shoulders and burrowed deeper into his embrace. She thought he was asleep, but a new tension filled his form, an energy that ignited her own and for a moment she indulged in it. A moment where heady desire, expectation and promise were just there in the next heartbeat, if she could only—

In the distance she could hear the ring of Theron's mobile and they stilled, holding their breath, as if instinctively they both knew.

Knew that something was about to happen that would change everything.

CHAPTER NINE

THERON WAS WAITING in her room for her when she came out of the shower. Her steps faltered when she saw his broad shoulders outlined by the early morning sun. He appeared to be looking out of the window, but she was half convinced it was to protect her modesty.

'You should wear the green dress,' he stated without looking at her.

And in an instant the fury that she'd banked with cool water from the shower reignited. 'Calling Kyros was bad enough. You don't get to tell me what to wear too,' she threw at him.

Theron's shadowy outline bowed his head. 'He needed to know.'

'Will you always put his needs before mine? Before yours?'

Frustration bloomed over anger like a watercolour painting. They had just been getting somewhere. There were things they still needed to say. But now Kyros was twenty minutes away her thoughts had completely scattered.

'You sound like Lykos.' Theron's tone was dark, but not bitter or resentful.

Summer felt seasick. She just wasn't sure what she should be feeling, where her allegiance should be. With Mariam? Her father? Or the father of her child? The man she knew she was falling in love with. Nerves tickled her soul.

What if Kyros didn't like her? What if he became angry with her mother? What if she didn't like him? Theron clearly respected him, loved him even—he'd cared for his wife throughout her illness and part adopted two teenage tearaways. So he couldn't be *bad*.

But she couldn't shake the feeling that meeting her father would cost Theron something. Cost *them* something. No matter what happened, it would definitely alter his relationship with the man who had been like a father to him for longer than his own parents were alive. And Theron had still made the call to Kyros.

For her, she realised. It was a sacrifice he'd made. For her.

'Theron—'

The sound of a car on the gravel drive turned both their heads towards the window.

'He's here,' Theron announced needlessly, and he looked back at her before leaving. 'The green dress. You will look beautiful in it.'

Theron made it to the doorway as the sleek racing-green Jeep pulled to a stop in front of the stone steps. He felt numb. As if he'd gone into shock ahead of some great trauma, as if protecting himself from what would come.

Kyros stepped out of the vehicle and straightened his tie. Despite the fact that his hair and beard were shocking white, they were thick and vital. No one ever mistook Kyros for a weak old man. At full height they stood shoulder to shoulder and, despite the immense power he wielded, Kyros had always been quick to laugh and his heart was huge.

But it was a heart that, once wounded, rarely recovered and when Kyros looked Theron straight in the eye, Theron knew. Any hope he might have entertained that they could survive this, that their relationship would survive, was gone.

Kyros looked at the house and for a fleeting moment he seemed scared, before he returned his steely gaze to Theron.

Theron opened his mouth to speak but was cut off.

'We will speak later. My daughter?' Kyros demanded, wanting to know she was here.

Theron nodded, but before he took Kyros inside he needed to know. Theron forced the words out through clenched teeth. 'She is pregnant.'

Kyros's steely gaze turned glacial. 'Yours?'

'Nai.'

With nothing left to say, Theron led Kyros into the house. Summer had said that she'd be in the library and each step towards her felt inexplicably as if it were taking him away from her. He had to put a hand out to steady himself, vertigo hitting him as if he'd entered an Escher painting.

Summer had hastily slipped into the green dress and pinned her hair up, let it down and put it back up again in the time since Theron had left her room. She was in the library now, finally deciding on hair up because she was so hot and flustered she needed it off her neck. To stop herself from pacing she'd sat in the chair, but the moment she heard footsteps in the corridor she lurched up, her hands clasped before her.

Suddenly she wanted to cry. But she fisted her hands, ordering herself to be strong. She was aware that two men stood in the doorway, yet she only had eyes for one. Kyros—her father—looked so familiar she had to sit down.

Kyros covered the room in strides as if worried that she was unwell, his arm at her side, ready to support her, which she gratefully took.

'I'm sorry,' she said, embarrassed by her reaction.

'There is *nothing* that you could be sorry for.' His reply was strong and sincere, his eyes wide as if he just couldn't look at her long enough. She knew the feeling because it was exactly how she felt. He pulled up a seat so he could hold her hand. '*I* am the one who is sorry and I cannot even begin to ask for your forgiveness. I only hope that you believe I truly did not know of your existence.'

Summer smiled through a watery gaze that hungrily consumed every single inch of the man who had fathered her, yet not been her father. 'I know. Mum always said that you didn't know.' She pressed her lips together at the mention of her mother. She didn't miss the way that Kyros's blue gaze sparked, but not with anger, something more like surprise before it was quickly mastered.

'We have so much to talk about,' Kyros insisted, pulling his chair closer to hers.

'We have time,' Summer said, a slight pinprick of hurt cutting deep at her heart, wondering whether the same could be said for her mother. She couldn't stop staring at him. Her eyes raked over him, wondering that he was really there. Wondering at this strange sense of connection she felt branded into her heart in an instant.

'Your mother, Mariam. How is she?' Kyros asked in a way that made Summer think he already knew. Summer turned to the doorway, wanting to see if Theron had said anything, but he wasn't there.

She frowned, but returned her attention to Kyros and took a deep breath. 'She is not well.' Her father seemed to clench his jaw, as if bracing himself. 'But we are soon going to be able to get her the treatment she needs.'

'We?'

'Yes,' Summer said, her smile wide and full of love. 'Me and my sisters.'

Kyros nodded. 'You have sisters. That is good. You have…' he seemed to search for the words '…you have had a good life?' he asked tentatively.

'Yes. So very good,' she said sincerely and reassuringly. 'I never blamed you. Mum made it very clear that you would have moved heaven and earth if you'd known about me. But…' Summer hesitated, not wanting to paint her mother in a bad light '…she…she told me that she didn't know your full name and how to find you.'

Confusion passed into realisation in her father's gaze and a nod that reminded her of Theron seemed to conclude his thoughts.

'I would like to tell you how we met,' he began. 'I don't want to…contradict or say anything your mother wouldn't want you to know, but… I want to be honest,' he said, shrugging into the words as if feeling his own way through this strange situation.

Summer nodded and as they huddled together he explained how he had met Mariam Soames.

'I was on one of the islands. I had gone there by myself in order to figure some things out. My wife, Althaia—I loved her greatly. We had been together since we were sixteen and twice that many years later our love was still strong. It was a soft, gentle kind of love, but one that was unbreakable.' His eyes misted for a moment and Summer put her hand on his. 'We had just found out her diagnosis and our world had been shattered. Althaia had asked me to leave to give us both some time to process how we felt.

'I was…devastated. Selfish. Hurt. Angry,' Kyros admitted, shaking his head at himself. 'Your mother, Mariam. She…burst into my life at that moment and, somehow, took it all away. Before I even knew her name, I—' He clenched his jaw, seemingly to stop himself from saying more. 'I told your mother. Everything. About Althaia and her diagnosis, our marriage. She told me about the loss of the partner that she was still grieving, about her daughters and the love she felt for them. She was so…bright and fierce. She was like a whirlwind and I couldn't help but be drawn in. Somehow, together, we found more than solace in each other, and I need you to know that what we shared…it was incredibly special to me.' Summer looked at him as his gaze clouded with memories and unspoken moments, before it cleared enough for him to carry on. 'We agreed, nothing more than that one week together, but it's important that you know it changed my life.

'The moment I returned home I told my wife about Mariam. Althaia's understanding was as surprising to me as my short time with Mariam. Althaia understood the kind of love we shared was different and that the future we would have was not for a moment what anyone could ever imagine or choose. But I did. Each and every day, I chose that life and her love and I would do it again in a heartbeat. But it was your mother who helped me make that choice.'

He gazed at her with watery eyes, the sincerity and truth shining in them warming her through.

'Mari and I—'

'Mari?'

He smiled, as if embarrassed by the name he had given her mother. '*Mariam*—' he stressed for her benefit '—and I knew that what we shared, even for that brief moment, was special but could not be. I had Althaia, she had her daughters… We felt as if it had been a gift of sorts. One that we could carry within us for ever, but not something to be revisited.

'I thought at one point…' He trailed off and Summer

searched his face for a conclusion, until Kyros shook his head and any possible ending away. He sighed deeply. 'But I am here now. And so are you!' The exclamation lifted his features from darker memories and she thought she recognised some of herself in him once again. She lifted her hand to sweep aside a tendril of blonde hair that had fallen from the band and Kyros's eyes caught on her collarbone. 'Oh.'

She immediately pressed her hand over it, protectively rather than secretively.

'You have the family birthmark?' He laughed, surprised and pleased.

'Yes. It was how I first realised you were my...' The word, so strange and unused, sat on her tongue.

'Father. Yes, Summer. I am your father.'

She had waited her entire life for those words, half convinced she'd never hear them, never feel this bond that welled up between them, surrounding them, binding them together, and tears brimmed in her eyes.

'You were in Thiakos's apartment. Five months ago?'

'Yes.'

'I...' His head hung down. 'I am ashamed. I did not know who you were. An urgent business deal had brought me back from the island and I—'

'Please. You don't have to explain. What happened with Theron—'

'No. Let's not discuss that now. I will deal with him later.' Summer frowned, worried, but not wanting to contradict or push things with Kyros when things were so fresh and new. He took her hands in his and held them tight. 'There is so much I want to tell you. So much history you have back home in Greece. Perhaps, when things are settled, you could come and visit.'

'I'd like that very much,' she replied, feeling a wetness

against her cheek that he reached up to brush away. His
hand paused and he looked to her, seeking permission, and
when she nodded his thumb swept away the tear and she
leaned into his palm as if it had always been there.

Theron looked out across the impossibly flat Norfolk horizon that seemed incredible to him. It gave the sky so much
space that it seemed further away than ever, so untouch-
able that it made his chest hurt.

He was unused to the silence and it was unnerving. It
gave rise to too many thoughts—thoughts that were on
the future now. Summer had her father. When she and her
sisters found the Soames diamonds and sold the estate,
Summer would be more than financially secure. She had
their love and support. She would be protected by them,
her family. And Kyros would make sure that she never
wanted for a single thing.

But not him.

Because he couldn't give her the one thing she wanted.
It ate at his soul, scratched and lashed out like a living
thing, breathing fire and burning everything it touched.

I want you to be there.

Bitter breath fell from his lips. He hadn't even been
there for Kyros. He'd lied to the old man, kept him from
his daughter. He had taken her virginity and kicked her
out of his life as if she were less than nothing. And now
she was pregnant.

Theron fisted his hands, impatient for Kyros to return,
because he knew what was coming. He'd seen it when the
old man had looked at him as if he were a stranger. Family meant everything to Kyros. And he was not part of
Kyros's family.

She is your family.

He rejected the thought that sounded far too much like

Althaia, making his heart hurt all the more. He felt torn between the absolute desire, a need so powerful it rocked his foundations, to be there for Summer. With her and their child. But he couldn't. He couldn't make that promise. Even the thought of it tore his heart, his pulse pounding, a cold sweat tickling his neck.

The breath left his lungs, burning as it did, as he thought of what he would miss. Watching Summer grow big and round with their child. The quick change of her temper, from ridiculous anger to tears, to a laugh so pure it healed everything. The way she'd look at the world as if everything was wondrous and worth study, worth investigation. He'd miss the moment of her success when she was able to find the jewels with her sisters. The moment that her mother would receive the treatment she needed, and the moment Summer realised that it had worked. That it had all been worth it. In his mind's eye, Theron saw her future, full of love and laughter and sunshine. And he wasn't in it.

She had everything she needed now. Her father. Her mother. The diamonds. There was nothing for him to give her other than promises he couldn't keep.

The sound of the Jeep's engine firing drew Theron back to the present and he looked up to find Kyros standing at the top of the stone steps.

'She's incredible,' Kyros said, as if in wonder at his daughter.

'She is,' Theron agreed.

'I looked for her mother once.'

Theron frowned in confusion.

Kyros sighed. 'I…thought you might have known because of Lykos, but this surprises you?'

'I had no idea. I didn't…' He clenched his jaw, hating the words he forced from his lips. 'I didn't believe her. When she first told me.'

Kyros nodded, looking out over the estate's long drive-way, squinting in the sun. And, without another word, he got into the Jeep and drove away.

Summer was looking for Theron. Meeting her father had been beyond anything she could have imagined. It had healed a part of her that had ached since first finding the photo and soothed a part of her that had hurt for years.

She had just got off the phone with her mother and felt strangely as if everything was falling into place. Mariam had been shocked, yes, but Summer hadn't missed the hope and the yearning in her mother's voice. As if she still thought of Kyros, still cared for him. Mariam had been desperate to explain that she had kept Kyros's identity secret out of respect for his wife. It had been her decision to embark on that affair and she had hated the thought of Summer or Althaia suffering because of it. And even though she'd hated lying to Summer she had honoured the promise she had made to him. Mariam told her that she had always intended to tell her one day, but somehow that day had just got further and further away. She'd peppered Summer with questions about Kyros, and was startled by her response.

'He will be in England for a while and I was hoping that you would come up to Norfolk. We have some news and I would like you and Kyros to be part of that.'

Her mother had agreed instantly, but Summer had been distracted because she'd seen Theron through the window, looking out at her father's car driving away.

As she turned towards the estate's entrance Summer decided that she didn't want to be like her parents—two people who clearly had strong feelings for each other but had missed so much. She was happy that Kyros had stayed with Althaia, that the love they'd shared had accepted and moved beyond his affair with her mother. But the thought of that lost time was like a pull on her heart.

She didn't want that with Theron. She didn't want to miss another minute with him. Because, even when they were arguing, he seemed to understand her. Even when he teased her, he taught her something about herself. And it was more than that…it was *him*. She wanted to know *him*. She wanted to help soothe the hurts she felt were just beneath the surface. His insecurity about his place with Kyros, the loss of his relationship with a man who was still like a brother to him even after ten years of silence— and the deepest pain of the loss of his parents. She wanted to help him heal. She wanted him to see what she saw in him. She wanted him to see…how much she loved him.

She drew to a stop, her hand covering her mouth in shock. *She loved him.*

The man who yelled at her for trying to drag compost across the floor, the man whose eyes didn't glaze over when she talked about her work, who could see how important her independence was, who understood her need to be responsible and accountable to and for herself. The man who had brought her to dizzying heights of pleasure, the man who was the father of her unborn child. He had asked her to marry him once and she had said no. But now it was all she could think of.

She burst through the front doors of the house, hoping that he would still be standing where she had seen him from the window, but he wasn't. She turned, looking out to the road, her heart thumping with the need to see him, to tell him. Not just about what had happened with her father, but her feelings for him. Her love.

She was teary from happiness and she couldn't wait to share it with Theron. He had brought this to her. He had

brought her father to her and given her hope and a sense
of more than she could ever imagine.

A little voice in her head told her to slow down, to hold
back, to pull back from the edge, when all she wanted to
do was hurl herself over it with blind faith and love. Maybe
her head had been turned by Catherine's journals, a treasure hunt and what she secretly believed was a reunited
love between her parents, but all this…*happiness*…she
didn't think she'd felt it before.

Theron was at the table they had sat at yesterday and,
when he saw her, his eyes raked over her hotly as if he'd
never seen anything more beautiful and she felt so utterly
precious. Until he blinked and the look was gone. She
frowned, rubbing her arms against the sudden bite to the
westerly wind, and her steps slowed as she approached. It
was as if a cloud had passed over the sun and she resisted
the urge to shiver.

He sat there, unmoving, as if he were cut from a piece
of dark marble, eyes watching her in one long gaze, taking her in completely. She halted on the other side of the
table, suddenly uncomfortable. She could see his jaw flex-
ing from here.

'Theron—'

'How was it?' he pressed out through teeth she was
sure were clenched.

She looked about the garden, trying to find signs for
why it felt as if everything was strange all of a sudden.
Off-kilter, as if she were in a dark, twisted, kaleidoscope
version of her world.

'It was…amazing,' she hedged, not able or willing to
lie. 'He…is beyond what I'd hoped. He wants to see Mum,'
she admitted, unable to prevent the hope in her voice. 'And
I can't thank you enough. For calling him. Bringing him
here,' she said, hoping that the sincerity in her voice, the

truth of it would penetrate this strange, hard outer shell he seemed to have retreated behind. Her stomach twisted as she realised that something bad must have happened between him and Kyros.

'Theron, did something—'

'It's good. That he wants to see your mother.'

She frowned at his responses, his actions, all just a little delayed. She felt out of step with him in a way that she'd never done before. Giving up all pretence, she rushed round the table and went to him, kneeling on the floor, her hands reaching for his, uncaring of how desperate or needy she might look.

'Theron, in the last week…' She struggled to find the words. His lack of response, the way he looked at her as if he couldn't comprehend her behaviour, was awful in comparison to how she'd always felt understood by him. She huffed out a breath, shook her head a little and said, 'Theron, ask me to marry you again.' The smile pulling at her lips, the sparkle she could feel in her eyes hung on a heartbeat. And as if she could sense him withdrawing even in her silence, she leant upwards, reaching for him, and pressed kisses against firm, unyielding lips.

It was then that she realised her heart was already breaking. It had cracked just a little each minute since she'd seen him sitting at the table. And still she kissed him. Again and again, hoping that he'd open beneath her. Wishing that he'd let her in.

Finally, he reached up to her hands to pull them free from his neck and leaned away from her, that dark hollow look in his eyes. And this time she wasn't able to prevent the shiver that trembled through her body.

'Ask me to marry you,' she whispered. 'Please, just—'

'No, Summer.'

And her heart shattered.

'Why?' she asked, not quite sure she wanted to know the answer.

'I could ask the same question,' he said, his tone devoid of emotion. She stood up and frowned at him, stepping away from him, wondering why the sun she felt against her skin wasn't warming her.

'What?' she asked. 'Why I want you to ask me to marry you?' He nodded. 'Because I...' The words felt silly now. Strange. Even though in her heart she knew it was the truth, saying them to him now when he was being like this felt wrong. 'I want us to be a family,' she replied eventually.

Her stomach dropped as she looked at his face, and she knew somehow that she'd said absolutely the wrong thing. But, before she could take it back, Theron stood from the chair and turned his back on her as if unable to look at her any more. The ground beneath her feet shifted and Summer couldn't work out what had happened. When had everything gone so wrong?

'You have a family, Summer. Your sisters, your mother... Kyros.'

'Is that what this is about? My father?'

Theron took her question and turned it in his mind. Was it about Kyros? It might have started out like that, trying to protect Kyros from Summer and then to protect the old man from Theron's own mistake.

Liar. You were protecting yourself then, just like you are now.

No!

Theron knew how much growing up without Kyros had hurt Summer, he knew what she wanted, what she needed. Stability, safety, security...she'd asked him to make that promise and he just couldn't. A part of him knew that he was being irrational, but the feral part, the animal instinct was flooding him with the need to flee. It felt visceral and all-consuming and he shook with the effort to fight it.

I want us to be a family.

He'd wanted that for so long. For ever. But he couldn't… Images of his parents' fear-filled eyes, of Althaia's, full of pain, of Lykos's hurt and anger, turning away from him, and his heart turned in on itself.

'No,' he said, having to clear his throat, finding the strength for what he needed to do. 'This has nothing to do with Kyros,' he said, turning to hold her gaze, surprised at the numbness settling over his body. 'You have what you need now, Summer. You have the diamonds, your mother will receive her treatment and you will be supported by your family. Kyros will ensure that none of you will want for anything ever again.'

'But I want *you*,' she said, her words bouncing off the barriers around his heart. 'I *love* you.' A distant part of him recognised the panic, the hurt flooding her expressive features, but that numbness was too strong. 'Can't you see that?'

'You can't see love,' he retorted.

'Neither can you see faith,' she returned instantly.

'So you think you love me? In a matter of days?' he scoffed, wondering at his own cruelty.

'In a matter of *moments*,' she replied determinedly. As if somehow his dismissal of her had only made her stronger. 'From the moment I saw you I—'

He shook his head, the act cutting her off mid-sentence. He was glad. He didn't want to hear the rest of what she had to say. He knew instinctively that he would bring out those words to torture himself in years to come. When he thought of her. When he thought of their child.

Would his child feel the same sense of loss as Summer

had done? As he himself had done? The ground beneath his feet jerked, but he ignored it. No. She and Kyros would make sure that the child wanted for nothing, including love.

As if her thoughts began to follow the same path as his, her hands flew to her stomach as if to protect it from their words. Their hurt.

She looked up at him, her eyes watery but glinting with something else. Something fearfully like understanding.

'I think…' she said, her breath shuddering through her words as if she were fighting to say them. 'I think…' she tried again '…that you are scared.' His scoff gave her pause, but she pressed on. 'I think that you have experienced great loss and hurt over the years and that…that the idea of family is terrifying to you.'

'Summer—' he warned.

'I think that this family is something you want so much that it terrifies you.'

He turned away, unable to look at the truth shining in her eyes as she spoke. From over his shoulder, he heard her words.

'So I don't need a promise from you that you'll be there for me. I'm promising to be here for you.'

He took a step away from her, the anguish in his heart so severe that he feared he'd never recover.

'I will *always* be here for you,' she said as he took a second step and a third. And just as he reached the car he could have sworn that he heard her say, 'I love you.'

'Oh, Summer, when did this happen?' Skye asked.

Summer held back a sob and looked at her hands. 'A couple of hours ago.'

'Oh, hun!' Star cried, pulling her into a hug that Skye quickly added herself to.

Summer let herself sink into her sisters' embrace for

a moment, indulging in their comfort. She'd meant what she'd said to him. She did have faith that he would come back to her. That he loved her. But there, in their arms, she allowed herself to accept the possibility that he might not be able to overcome the traumas of his past.

'You're sure he's going to come back?' Skye asked and Summer nodded, blinking away the tears.

'And if he doesn't?' Star tentatively asked.

'Then we will be fine,' Summer insisted, pulling her head up from the hug to speak and lock eyes with her sisters. 'Mum raised us all on her own. And I have you both. And we'll find these damned diamonds and sell the estate to Lykos and Mum can be receiving treatment as quickly as the beginning of next week. And then—*then* I can make a plan.'

'What about uni?' Star asked, her eyes glistening with sympathetic tears.

'I'll take a few years' sabbatical,' Summer replied, her own eyes glistening. Not with regret, but determination. 'This is the twenty-first century, and I can and will have my child, my education *and* my dream job.'

After a beat, her sisters sent up squeals of delight and cheered, Star started to dance and when Skye turned to watch her, laughing, Summer allowed herself just a moment of hurt that Theron wasn't there to witness her family's joy for her. Because now the ache in her heart wasn't just for herself, it was for him. It was for the damage done by his childhood that held him back from being all that he could be, feeling all that he could feel.

As she looked up at her sisters, celebrating her pregnancy, the culmination of their journey to find the Soames diamonds, their heritage, their mother's future health and the love that had inspired it all, Summer felt and saw the richness of life. She understood why Catherine had protected the jewels from a husband who would most likely have sold them. She understood too how Catherine had embraced the love she had felt for Benoit and Hātem, despite the heartache. How she had used it to give her the strength she'd needed in her marriage and her motherhood. Summer looked around the room and felt the Soames heritage rise up, as if generations of Soames women were here to witness and celebrate yet another of their line.

She allowed a tear at the thought of having to sell the estate to roll down her cheek—she would give it that—knowing that she would take their heritage with them forward into their new future, with their mother's health secured and her sisters' happiness assured.

'Let's do it,' she announced.

Skye frowned. 'Do what?'

'Find the diamonds!'

'What, now?' Star asked. 'It's five-thirty in the morning,' she replied as if Summer had lost her mind.

'We've been talking all night?' Summer asked, shocked.

'Yes!' Star and Skye announced together, laughing.

'I'm so sorry,' Summer said, thinking of how tired they would all be.

'Don't be,' Skye said. 'It's been a while since we stayed up like that. I've missed it.'

'And I've missed you,' Summer said, looking between Skye and Star. 'The last couple of years, it's felt a little like we've all been drifting apart.' She'd been scared to say it, but breathed a sigh of relief as she saw on their faces that her sisters felt the same way. She reached for their hands, a smile of joy pulling at her lips. 'And now you're going to be living in France, and you in Duratra… Everything's changing,' she said, her voice soft with wonder. 'But that's okay. We don't always have to have a plan, we don't always have to see our path. Sometimes, we just need a bit of faith.'

This time Star laughed. 'Who are *you* and what have you done with Summer?' she demanded.

'I am your sister,' she said, the tears welling once again. 'And I'm going to need both of you to help me so much in the next few years.'

'Whatever you need,' said Star.

'Whenever you need it,' said Skye.

Staring into the flames of the fireplace in Lykos's London townhouse, Theron bowed his head, his fists clenched against the pain that still rocked his body from Kyros's dismissal of him from his life. From his own personal exile from Summer's life. But this time, instead of fighting it, he chose to feed the anger instead. The fury coursing through his veins at what had happened after and at what had happened so many years before collided, and he glared up at Lykos.

'You knew,' Theron growled.

Lykos's silvery gaze narrowed ever so slightly before he nodded firmly, confirming the accusation.

'You knew that Kyros had an illegitimate child—*Summer*—and that is why you left all those years ago?'

Lykos looked away, as if debating how to handle him.

'No, I'm done, Lykos. No more evasions, no more lies or witty rebukes. No more. I want the truth. All of it.'

Lykos turned his steely gaze on Theron, the anger burning like phosphorous in his eyes. 'You want the truth? Fine. When I was nineteen, Kyros asked me to go looking for Mariam Soames. He didn't tell me why, but I wasn't stupid. A Greek billionaire tycoon looking for a young Englishwoman and all he had was a faded photo?' Lykos got up out of his chair and stalked over to the window, the sun beginning to rise across the London skyline. 'He had betrayed Althaia! He had betrayed his family!' Lykos raged.

Theron might have flinched but his own anger was simmering. 'So you discovered Summer's existence, and what—just abandoned them?'

'No. Over the years, I have checked up on them. Made sure they were okay.'

'Really? So, Mariam Soames' stage three cancer diagnosis just slipped through the gaps then?' Theron demanded. 'The way that Summer constantly worries about money, about paying her sisters back for all they have sacrificed for her to attend university?' Theron spat before rising out of his chair to face Lykos. 'A girl who thinks that spending one hundred euros on a dress for herself is an extravagance she doesn't deserve, Lykos. You've drunk more than that this evening alone!'

'I didn't know about the cancer,' Lykos roared back. 'I'm going to buy the estate!'

Theron shook his head in disgust. 'Were you? Why did you call me, Lykos? The truth this time.'

'I recognised her, that night in the restaurant. I knew who she was. But what I didn't recognise was the way you looked at her. Because I've *never* seen you look at a woman like that. And I know—or I *thought* I knew—how you would feel if she were pregnant.'

'What do you mean, *thought* you knew?'

'I believe it's time for you to tell me just what the hell you think you're doing here with me instead of being with *her*,' Lykos spat disdainfully. Theron could see it as Lykos paced back and forth in front of the fireplace—the anger that he had been keeping at bay all evening.

'What is it to you?' Theron demanded, wanting it. Relishing it.

In the blink of an eye, Lykos spun round, grabbed

Theron by the shirt collar and shoved him up against the wall. 'You walked away from them!' he roared, the fury in his eyes blazing as strongly as the hot coals in Theron's gut. 'You know where we came from and you *walked away*?'

Theron shoved both palms into Lykos's chest, pushing him back, but not as far as he'd have liked. 'Yes!' he roared back, stepping forward and closing the space he'd just created between them. His blood pounded in his veins, his hands fists already and desperate for a fight, for the sting of physical pain to overshadow the emotional wound that he'd opened up in himself and he feared would never heal.

'How dare you?' Lykos growled.

Theron shoved again and the look on Lykos's face was thunderous. But also knowing.

'What does it matter to you, Lykos?' he demanded.

'Because your parents *died*, Theron. But mine left. They—as you have done—*chose* to leave.' The disgust written on his face was so much worse than his anger. 'And you have *no* idea what that feels like.'

'No? Like when *you* chose to leave?'

'I asked you to come with me. *You* chose *him*.'

'I chose family, Lykos. I chose Althaia and Kyros. And…' Theron clenched his jaw, a wave of grief hitting him hard and threatening to pull him under '…you didn't even come to the funeral.' His eyes felt hot and wet and he had to turn away.

'I was there.' Lykos's words were a low whisper. 'I was there, Theron. I just…didn't come close enough for you to see. How could you think I wouldn't be?'

'Because everyone leaves, Lykos. Everyone. My parents, you, Althaia. And when Summer asked me to promise to be there—to give her the one thing her father had not been able to give her... I just couldn't. I've hurt enough. It's easier to let her go.'

'So she was right. You are scared? Theron—' Lykos started, but Theron interrupted, not wanting to hear what his friend had to say.

'No. I'm done. With the lot of you,' Theron said, turning away and grabbing his suit jacket.

'Then you are not the man I thought you were,' Lykos accused.

Theron paused. Jaw clenched, hands fisted, all that anger and hurt so very close to the surface.

'I called you because I knew she was pregnant. I called you because I knew how much you cared for her and I knew how much you would love both her and your child. But love isn't anything without faith. And I was hoping she'd have taught you that.'

'Faith?'

The words so familiar, bound up in a one-hundred-and-fifty-year-old treasure hunt that had nothing to do with him, struck a chord and held him still.

'Faith that it's worth it. Faith that her love for you is more powerful than the hurt that you *might* feel,' Lykos demanded.

While faith can't be seen, it can be felt.

Theron shook the words from his memory.

'And you love her?'

'Yes, of course,' he admitted, his head bowed.

'Then you are a fool and you don't deserve her at all.'

Theron rounded on Lykos, fury spreading through his chest.

'No,' Lykos pressed. 'You don't get to have it both ways. You can't love her and turn your back on her and your child because you're scared, Theron. Be better than my parents. Be better than me, dammit, and I swear...if I have to say one more soppy thing to get you to realise that you need to go back and fight for her, I'll kill you myself,' he finished, angrily throwing his hands into the air and turning to pour himself another drink.

Theron couldn't help the laugh that launched from his chest, cutting through the tension and the anger. It cracked something within him, letting something free. Something powerful, strong, bright and healing.

'I'm not joking, Theron. If you tell anyone what I've just said, I'll hunt you down,' Lykos threatened, pointing at him with his whisky glass. 'Sit down,' he ordered.

'Why?'

'Because you need a plan.'

'A plan?'

'Do I have to do everything for you, brother? To win her back, of course.'

The sisters crept through the tunnel, Summer in the lead, jumping at every little sound, and laughing at themselves.

'Why is this so creepy?' Star asked in a whisper.

'Why are you whispering?' Skye asked, also in a whisper.

Summer felt the childlike giggle rumble in her chest. She felt drunk. Drunk on love and excitement—all the more sweet for the underlying ache that felt as if it would always be there until Theron came back to her.

If.

No. She wouldn't think like that.

She held the key in one hand and the torch in the other and came to a stop, her sisters stumbling a little.

'Aren't we on the other side of Catherine's bedroom?'

'Yup,' Summer confirmed with a smile.

'All this time!'

Skye shushed Star as Summer found the lock and re-

trieved the key. The last time she'd been here was with
Theron. He had been so close she had felt—

'Summer?'

'Sorry.' Summer shook the memories from her head
and pushed the key and turned, this time gently pressing
against a door that swung inward as easily as if it had been
used only yesterday. She cast a glance to her sisters and,
holding out her hand for Skye, who held out her hand for
Star, they made their way through the door.

The torch illuminated a room large enough for them all
to stand, albeit slightly hunched. There were shelves on
the walls lined with books that Star was instantly drawn
to, and Skye's torch beam passed thoroughly over every
inch of the room as if properly inventorying the space.
But Summer was drawn to a table beneath a once-white
dustsheet and when she gingerly lifted the sheet she saw
three velvet-covered boxes on it.

'Summer?'

She removed the sheet and her sisters huddled around
as Summer lifted the first box, the smallest of the three.
At her sisters' encouraging nods she raised the lid and in
the torch's beam three diamonds sparkled so much that
she had to blink. Perched between the folds was the most
beautiful ring she'd ever seen, pristinely preserved and
absolutely breathtaking. All the sisters lost their breath
simultaneously. Gingerly, Skye reached for the second
box and Star the third, as Summer placed the torch on the
floor facing up to illuminate the small space better. Star's
box was deeper and narrow, and when she lifted the lid she
gasped at the sight of the large diamond in the centre of an
exquisitely detailed diadem. And when Skye opened the
box she held to reveal a stunning necklace the rush of air
from her lungs drew the gazes of her sisters and they each

sighed, as if stunned by the sheer opulence and beauty that Catherine had hidden away.

A longing rose in Summer's chest, a want that rivalled the way she felt about Theron, but different. Sadder. She would love to have kept these pieces. Not because of their financial value but their emotional one. It was as if each of the sisters was taking a moment, remembering the journeys that had brought them here. All they'd wanted was to fund their mother's treatment, and now they would be able to do that.

But Summer had sensed a change in her siblings. Their journeys had done more than bring them here. They had changed, and not because of the men they'd met and now loved, but because of the women they had become. Women who were worthy of this inheritance, as Catherine had known they would be. And it was there, in a secret room created by their great-great-great-grandmother, she felt as if something had been righted in the world, felt the sigh of relief that came when something had found its true home.

She allowed that feeling to fill her, even as she knew that within hours, after meeting Mr Beamish, the estate lawyer, she would be arranging for the sale of the estate, and it hurt. A layer added over the ache caused by Theron. Summer knew that it would likely get worse in the weeks to come, that hurt and pain, if he didn't return to her as she'd hoped. But for the moment she focused on the plan. Even if his voice whispered in her ear.

Plans are not wants. What do you want?

Summer wanted him. She wanted this. She wanted the future that she could see just beyond her reach. And with a hand around the curve of her bump, she wondered if she had the faith to make something magical happen.

CHAPTER TEN

FOUR HOURS LATER and the world looked impossibly different. Summer's head was spinning at the shocking plans she had put into motion. Her sisters looked at her, eyes wide, round but utterly thrilled.

'Are you sure you want to do this?'

Summer was so tempted to shake her head. She was terrified but also excited, as if she were on a roller coaster and never wanted to get off. So she nodded, quickly and surely. 'Yes. I am.'

'You're crazy,' Skye whispered in awe. 'But I love it.'

'Good. Because I'm going to need Benoit's help. And lots of it!'

'Duratra has incredible metalworkers. They made the necklace. I'm sure that they could help too.'

'I would *love* that, Star. I think Catherine would have too,' Summer said, the press of tears, happy ones for now, against the backs of her eyes.

They were in the office where Skye, Star and Summer's journey had started just under two months ago. Of all the rooms and corridors Summer had searched, she'd never come back to this one, knowing that the hard-faced portrait of Elias Soames sent shivers down her spine every time she caught sight of it. But somehow, at that moment, it felt poignant, *right*, that they had come full circle to end where it had all begun.

Summer sat between her sisters as Mr Beamish imperiously scrawled on the paperwork—a witness following his every signature—seemingly thankful that the whole sorry mess of the Elias Soames estate was soon to be behind him. Star peered over her shoulder at the room off to the side, where Mariam Soames and Kyros Agyros had been sequestered for the last hour.

'Do you think they're okay?' Star asked.

'He's very handsome, your father,' Skye said with a smile.

'They have a *lot* of catching up to do,' Summer said, her heart warming.

'Did you see the way she looked at him?' Skye asked. *Fireworks*, she mouthed and Star let out a snort.

'Even though it's Mum, that's still a bit—'

The door to the room opened and all three sisters squeaked and turned away as if naughty schoolgirls being caught out. Mariam Soames was blushing like one herself, and the twinkle in Kyros's eyes was something magical to Summer.

'And that concludes our business, I believe,' Mr Beamish announced, calling their attention back to him. 'The estate, the entail, all yours now that you've found the Soames diamonds.' Summer felt a sigh of relief, no longer expecting someone to magically appear and snatch it all away from them. 'Congratulations. I hope that—' he broke off, looking around at the dark, damaged house with barely concealed disgust '—you are happy here.'

The girls couldn't help but laugh as he hightailed it out of the estate with his assistant and the witness as quickly as humanly possible.

'And you are sure that this is something you want to

do?' Kyros asked his daughter, everyone seeming to hold their breath.

'Absolutely,' Summer replied resolutely. 'I—*we*— couldn't be doing this without you, though. And we can't thank you enough.' Her sisters' agreement rose in the air, but Kyros seemed to shake them off, the swift jerk of his head reminding her bruised heart of Theron.

Mariam Soames looked to Kyros. 'But after Althaia…'

Summer could sense it—her mother's sadness, guilt even, about Kyros caring for another sick lover.

'It is the least I can do,' Kyros said, taking her hand in his and gazing into her eyes, 'and the least I want to do. The treatment will start the day after tomorrow and I will be there with you every second of it. And when you beat it, you will come with me to Greece and recuperate in the sun, on my island.'

Star's eyes bugged out. 'He owns an island?' she whispered, and Summer smiled.

'You own a country,' Skye chided.

'Well, not *own* and not *yet*,' she replied, fanning herself as if the thought was suddenly quite overwhelming.

'And I own an estate,' Summer said in wonder as her sisters looked at her with joy and excitement for her.

'Yeah, you do,' Skye said, gently bumping her shoulder against Summer's shoulder.

It unfurled within her, this sense of rightness and excitement. She would restore the building using the latest and safest technologies and ensure that Catherine's heritage, *their* heritage, would stand for a very, very long time.

Once again, she could have sworn she heard the sound of a child's laughter disappearing into the estate, and, whether it was prescient of the future or an echo of the past, Summer felt comforted by it. A gift, given to her by her ancestors.

The sound of wheels on gravel drew the group's attention to the windows.

'I'd hoped Beamish had left,' Skye said, failing to suppress the shiver of dislike that ran through her body.

'He must have forgotten something,' Summer said, standing from her seat.

'I'll go,' Star offered.

'That's okay,' Summer said, stretching out the slight ache across her shoulders. 'I'm sure I'll only be a moment.' She left the room before there could be any more protests. It was a strange feeling, but after weeks on her own in the estate, with her parents and her sisters here it suddenly felt crowded, a little claustrophobic even. A part of her wanted to be alone, to feel all the things that had happened to her in the last twenty-four hours. If she thought about it too hard her head started to spin.

The sound of the car grew closer and closer as she reached the front of the house and she pulled open the door in time to see a black behemoth pull to a stop. It looked like something from the army.

She frowned, a little worried now, as the passenger door opened and she heard the tail-end of an argument in heavily accented English, 'At least it's better than a convertible!'

The slam of the door drew her attention to the tall form stepping down from the beast of a car, long legs easily reaching the distance to the ground and turning on the gravel. From the handmade shoes to the expensive superfine wool trousers moulding powerful thighs, the leather belt at lean hips she had clung to, the broad expanse of chest that made her pulse trip, she knew every inch of the father of her child and would never tire of seeing him, even if he had shattered her heart.

The sensuality of his lips was inflamed by the determined slant to them, the flare in his gaze as he drew to a sudden halt, seeing her standing in the doorway at the top of the stone steps. For moments they just stood and stared, as if gorging on the sight of each other.

They both moved at the same time, starting towards each other and stopping again.

'*Gia ónoma tou Theó...*' Summer shot a glance over Theron's shoulder to see Lykos Livas standing against the monstrous vehicle with his arms crossed over his chest and an almost childlike look of irritation on his features. Summer had to suppress a smile, guessing at the translation from the obvious impatience in Lykos's voice.

Then she saw him flinch as Lykos looked over her shoulder, and she turned to find her father and mother standing behind her with her sisters off to the side. Lykos and Kyros stared each other down, before Lykos purposely cut his gaze away.

Summer frowned, wondering what had happened there but knowing that was a story for another time. Paying no more attention to them, her gaze hungrily returned to Theron. Hope bloomed in her heart and she gazed into his eyes, knowing that something was different. She'd been waiting for the shutters to come down to mask his feelings, but they didn't and she began to believe that they might never come down again.

He opened his mouth as if to speak, then stopped. She moved a step forward as he did and then stopped again.

'I love you,' he said, and her legs trembled. 'There are things I was supposed to say. A *plan*. But... I love you.'

She couldn't help but laugh gently as she repeated the words he'd once said. 'Plans are not wants.'

'I *want* you,' he said helplessly. 'With every single fibre of my being. I want you. I always have. You need to know that. But now, and for ever, I want to *be* with you. To hear you laugh, to help you cry, to be the vent for your anger, your frustration. I want to argue with you, I want to make up with you, I want to care for you, protect you, grow old with you. I just… I want to love you and be loved by you. Any plan, now or in the future, will always be for you and our child. Whether I'm with you in the same room, house or even country. Whether—' he paused, as if swallowing some deep emotion '—you want me or not.'

Her love-filled gaze cleared enough to see his sincerity, but his words brought back the memories of their argument and, despite the joy she felt at his declaration… it wasn't enough. She needed it and their child needed it. 'What changed?' she asked, shrugging helplessly.

Theron stood to his full height, never once taking his eyes from her, drawing strength from the earth beneath him to say what he needed to say, desperately hoping that Summer would know the truth of his words.

'I left because I was scared,' he said, his throat thick with emotion, the shame and hurt filling his chest. 'You asked me to be there for our child,' he said, stopping himself from explaining why. He cast a glance to where Kyros stood beside an older version of Summer and two younger women who could only be her sisters. He refused to shame either Mariam or Kyros for their choices, but he knew Summer would know the depth of her request. 'And I… that terrified me. You were right.' He shook his head, hating the way his heart trembled in his chest. 'I've lost so much family. My parents, my brother,' he said, casting a look back to Lykos, who raised a wry eyebrow. Smiling slightly, Theron realised that Lykos would always be his family. He knew the hand that Lykos had played in this, in leading him to Summer, guiding him back to where he needed to be.

He took a breath and thought of the other person he had loved and lost. 'Althaia,' he said, unable to meet Kyros's gaze. 'The thought of losing you, the thought of anything happening to you or our child… I couldn't bear it. I still can't. But even just a night without you was more painful than anything I've experienced,' he pressed on truthfully. 'And if there's even a chance that you'd consider letting me prove to you how much I love you, then please tell me. Give me hope.'

The sheen in her eyes told him there might be, but he would settle for nothing less than her words. Her heart. Even if it took him a lifetime. Behind him Lykos cleared his throat and he suddenly remembered.

'No matter what happens, though, I want you to know that the estate is yours.' He watched as her brow furrowed in confusion and he silently cursed himself. He was messing this up. 'I've spoken to Lykos and I will buy the estate.'

She stared at him, her thoughts hidden from him. 'It's not for sale,' she said quietly.

'What? You didn't find the jewels?' he demanded, shocked, a thousand fears going through his mind at once.

'We did,' Summer said, her head tilted to the side, a smile pulling at her lips. He was distracted for just a second until her words penetrated.

'But your mother's treatment?'

'I am handling that,' Kyros announced from the steps behind Summer, his arm around the woman who Summer resembled so very much. When Theron looked at Kyros this time, there wasn't disappointment or rejection, there was pride, love and a determined glint that warned Theron not to mess this up. He felt it. A blessing. One that he would never take for granted. He turned back to Summer, trying to read her gaze.

'So you're keeping the estate?' Theron asked, instinctively knowing how much she would like that.

'I still want a castle!' Lykos groused in the background, pulling smiles from both Theron and Summer almost against their will.

Summer nodded. 'Benoit and Skye will help with the redesign and Star and Khalif will arrange for help from Duratra on the large amount of metalwork I'd like done. I want to put my studies to use on the renovations.'

There was more to it, Theron knew. He could see it burning in her gaze. 'You have a plan,' he said, knowing instinctively that it would be marvellous.

'But I also have a want,' she whispered, stepping closer to him, a spark of something deliciously wicked in her eyes.

A tendril of hope unfurled in his heart and heat soaked into his bones. 'Tell me,' he demanded.

'I want you to ask me to marry you,' she said, closing the distance between them to inches.

He searched her gaze, the sparkle in her eyes, the mischief, the promise.

And his heart crashed.

He pressed his forehead against hers as an ache of sad frustration coursed through his body. 'I don't have a ring. We left London at six-thirty in the morning. I...' he bit back a curse '... I want to do it properly. I want to give you everything you deserve,' he said, his voice rough with emotion.

She bent her head back, her hazel eyes sparkling with gold. 'Is that all?' she said with a smile, though what she could possibly find to smile about he had no idea. Until she looked back to her sisters, the taller one he imagined was Skye, who smiled broadly and threw something small towards Summer, who caught it and presented it to him.

'It's perhaps a bit unorthodox, but I think Catherine

would approve,' Summer said, passing him the small ring-shaped box.

'The Soames diamonds?' he asked, and she nodded, her eyes and heart seeming as full as his own felt.

He took the velvet box, warm from her touch, in his palm and pressed it against his heart. But he wanted one last thing. He would propose no matter what, but this felt right. Felt just.

He looked up to where Summer's family had gathered by the front door of the estate, catching Kyros's eye first, then Mariam's.

'Ms Soames, Kyros, I would very much like to ask for your daughter's hand in marriage. I want you to know that I will protect her and our child unconditionally, I will love her and our child unconditionally, and I will—'

'We get the idea, Theron,' Lykos said, rolling his hand as if to say get on with it. The smaller sister with red hair hid a laugh behind her hand and the older one bit her lip as if to stop herself from smiling. The love and happiness shining from Mariam was one of the purest things Theron had ever seen. She looked up to Kyros and back to him and nodded.

'You have my blessing, *yié mou*,' Kyros said, the words *my son* miraculous to hear after all these years.

And then absolutely nothing could have pulled him away from Summer.

He took her hand in his and slowly bent to one knee, unfeeling of the bite of gravel through his trousers. Wonder and awe coursed through his body as he looked up at the woman who made him feel complete. Whole. The woman he would spend the rest of his life loving to distraction.

And there, surrounded by people bonded by blood or by choice, he knew *this* was his family: Summer and their child and the people who loved and cared for them, all brought together by Catherine and the Soames diamonds. Wetness pressed against his eyes as he looked up at the love of his life. 'Would you, Summer Soames, do me the greatest honour and be my wife, my confidante, my love, my family, my *home*?'

'Yes,' Summer said as tears rolled down her cheeks and her sisters screamed and yelled, and even Lykos seemed to clear his throat of emotion. 'Yes, I will,' she said, pulling him up from the ground and bringing him into a kiss that branded his soul as hers.

'I love you,' she whispered between presses of her lips. 'I will always love you,' she promised and Theron knew that, no matter what happened in the future, the love that he felt in that moment would fuel the rest of their lives.

EPILOGUE

Five years later...

SUMMER WAS JUST finishing her journal entry. She'd been hurrying to get it done in time, looking as the clock ticked down the minutes until—

'Mummy! Mummy? Where are you?'

Right on time, she heard Katy's not so dulcet tones calling for her, even as a smile full of love pulled at her mouth. Theron always tried to keep their mischievous daughter occupied in the kitchen for at least half an hour after dinner so that Summer could have this time, knowing how important her journalling was to her.

Quickly she put down the journal, turned off the light, closed the door to the secret room, slipped through the passageway and back into the master bedroom just before Katy burst into the room.

'Mummy, where are—' Katy descended into a fit of giggles as she realised she'd been shouting when Summer was standing right there.

'Mummy, that's naughty,' she accused. It was Summer's daughter's latest delight. Although Catherine was the name on their daughter's birth certificate, they had called her Katy from day one.

'What's naughty, sweetpea?' she asked.

'*You* are!'

'*I* am? *I* am?' Summer demanded, all mock outrage as she chased her daughter with tickle fingers and they both ended up in a hysterical heap on the bed. She didn't think that there was anything more pure, more beautiful than the sound of her daughter, out of breath from laughter.

Summer pushed a dark curl from her daughter's forehead, so happy that she had her father's deep dark eyes. But the sparkle? That was *all* Soames.

'Where are my girls?' Theron's voice boomed into the room.

'Here, Daddy. Mummy's being naughty again,' Katy said, bursting into laughter as Summer's quick tickles found her.

'Oh, really?' Theron demanded as he came into the room, staring down at them with a glint in his eye that Katy was thankfully far too young to recognise. He smiled and Summer felt it in her heart.

Summer didn't know how, but he was able to do this thing where he'd look at her and time would just *stop*. She'd feel an infinity of love in an instant and knew that she could never want for anything more.

He sighed, before checking his watch, as if he'd felt it too. His eyes widened and then he pulled a grimace. 'Katy, we have to get dressed. The others are going to be here in twenty minutes.'

Katy scrabbled up on the bed and started jumping up and down, crying, 'The others are coming!'

Even as Summer put her hand out, just in case, Theron was by the bed in an instant, plucking his daughter from the air mid-jump.

'Come on, my love. You have your new dress to—'

The scream of delight from their daughter was so loud it could have burst his eardrums but he didn't flinch, didn't loosen his hold even for a second. Cradling her to him, Theron bent over the bed, Katy now giggling at being horizontal, and kissed Summer quickly but lovingly and took their daughter off to get ready for the day.

Summer watched them go until she checked the time and jumped off the bed and threw herself into the shower. Fifteen minutes later, she was showered, dry and opening the wardrobe door, marvelling at the array of colour that was on display. She passed the teals, the beautiful bright yellows and the verdant greens. There was only one colour to be worn today.

As she came down the stairs, the beautiful scarlet silk swirled around her calves, matching the red stilettos she knew that her husband would appreciate, even if she didn't last the *full* day in them. Her fingers tripped over the red velvet ribbon Katy had insisted should wrap around the banister, and the scent of pine trees and spiced orange rose up from the lower floor. Everywhere she looked was sparkles of tinsel, rich green foliage and deep red velvet. Theron, apparently, loved Christmas as much as their daughter.

An impossibly tall spruce stood proudly in the hallway to greet every member of the family as they arrived. Giant red bows, little silver bows and American candy canes hung from the boughs while sparkling cream lights twinkled between the fronds. There was a giant silver urn on the side table with mulled wine and glasses ready for their guests.

Summer inhaled deeply and rolled her shoulders free of any stiffness, relishing the excitement and anticipation of the day ahead. In the last few years it had become her favourite part of the year because it was the one time that everyone was guaranteed to gather together. At any other point, they were spread as far and wide as Greece, Dura-tra, France, Costa Rica and wherever else Skye could en-tice Benoit to wander.

But everyone came home for Christmas.

Although Kyros hadn't been happy about it, Summer and Theron had waited until Katy was three years old be-fore marrying. By that point, Skye had married Benoit exactly a year on from his proposal in a gorgeous outdoor wedding in France, the Soames diamond necklace as her something old. And no one had minded one bit when lit-tle Katy had burst into beautiful laughter as the priest had asked for anyone to 'speak now or forever hold your peace'.

Star had married Khalif in a stunning ceremony in Du-ratra's capital, where the celebrations had lasted for days and Katy had been treated like a little princess and loved every minute of it. Star had worn the Soames diadem and the interlocked necklace in honour of both Catherine and Hâtem. The joining of the two families felt fated.

But Summer's wedding to Theron had been a little closer to home.

Two years ago today, Summer had walked down these very same stairs in a wedding dress of oyster-coloured silk. The design had been similar to that of the yellow dress she had bought all those years ago in Athens. And although everyone proclaimed her to be the most beauti-ful bride they'd ever seen, she only had eyes for Theron.

In front of their families, those of blood and those of friendship, Summer had sworn to love her husband for eternity and a day and Theron had promised to be by her side and never leave. The glint in his eye as he'd finally made the promise that had terrified him so much was more than Summer could have ever asked for.

In a mixture of Greek and English, wreaths and rings, their love had been celebrated and cemented in the estate in Norfolk that had been in her family for hundreds of years, and Summer couldn't shake the feeling that Catherine had been watching over them that day.

Before she could round the corner, Theron appeared at the bottom of the stairs and Summer couldn't help the burst of arousal from deep within her at the sight of her husband dressed in a suit that fitted him to perfection.

As if he were feeling the same way, his eyes flashed for just a moment before he blinked. But while the intensity in his gaze had been banked, in the last five years and all their years to come his thoughts and feelings were never hidden from her again.

To her surprise, he bent to one knee.

'What are you doing?'

'Asking you to marry me.'

'But—' she broke off to laugh '—we're already married,' she said as she drew closer and closer to him.

'I know. I just want to be able to promise you that I'll never leave your side in front of our family and friends as many times as possible.'

'We don't need a lavish ceremony just for that.'

'*Just* for that?' he demanded in the same way he'd once demanded what 'just a kiss' was supposed to mean. 'If I want, I will have a hundred ceremonies to tell you how much I love you and to make unending promises to the most beautiful wife a man has ever had.'

'Theron, don't let Lykos hear you say that, or he'll be offering a *thousand* ceremonies to his wife.'

Theron laughed, standing to his full height. 'I still can't quite believe that he actually ended up with a castle,' he said, fitting her to his side and placing his hand between her shoulder blades as he liked to do. He guided her to a stop and took her hand in his, pulling her round to face him.

He slowly inched forward, his lips hovering a hair's breadth from hers, pleasure and anticipation rising within her as she held onto the tease, waiting to see which one of them broke first this time.

The moment was broken by the peal of the doorbell.

Theron smiled and whispered, 'You owe me a kiss,' into her ear before he turned and braced himself against the screams of her sisters and nieces as they rushed the couple with hugs, laughter and love. Through the chaos Summer saw Benoit following through the entrance, talking to Khalif about the incredible memorial project for his brother and sister-in-law and she couldn't help the tendril of professional curiosity getting the better of her. Theron caught her eye and understood her desire, enticing her sisters and nieces away to meet Katy, so that she could catch up on how the bridge and conservation area between two kingdoms in the Middle East was coming along.

Before long, Katy came running to find her and pull her back to the living room, where piles and piles of presents were being unloaded to her mounting horror.

'I thought we said only one present each,' Summer said, feeling a little worried.

Star laughed gently. 'We did. And we stuck to it. But we wanted to take some gifts to the children's ward at Norfolk and Norwich Hospital. The boys are going to take the girls there this afternoon.'

Understanding dawned in her eyes and she nodded, feeling a spread of love for the generosity they were able to share, but also the tug of a promise they had made when Mariam had first started her treatment.

Five years on and Mariam had received the all-clear and was officially cancer-free. The celebration planned for that evening, after Mariam and Kyros flew in from Greece, would be incredible. But no less important than the personal moment the sisters had planned for that afternoon.

Over a leisurely late brunch, that Skye argued with Theron was more lunch, and Lykos, who had arrived with his wife, rolled his eyes and complained about, saying the English didn't know anything about food, which Theron wholly agreed with, Summer felt love for her family rise up around her and fill the house completely.

In her wildest dreams she couldn't have imagined such a future. And it was all thanks to Catherine Soames. She caught her sisters' eyes and, as if they all felt and thought the same way, they quietly excused themselves from the table. Their husbands, understanding, kept the children distracted and soon Summer heard the entire group getting into their respective cars and heading out to the hospital for the family tradition that had started the year after Skye's little girl had spent a terrifying three months in hospital over Christmas. She could see that Skye was torn, wanting to go with them, and Summer put a hand on her arm for comfort.

'It's okay,' Skye insisted. 'There will be plenty more years for that. *This* is something I want to do.'

'It's something we all want to do,' insisted Star, and Summer led them to a section of wood panelling beside the master bedroom that they hadn't seen before. 'Wait… what…?'

Summer smiled and shrugged mischievously. 'Well, we were renovating so many of the areas and I thought that just because they were secret passageways doesn't mean they have to be *grim* passageways.'

Skye's eyes grew round, staring at the panelling and finally seeing the faint impression of a secret door. 'You didn't! Benoit didn't say anything,' she chided.

'We wanted it to be a surprise,' Summer replied.

'Naughty,' Star teased.

'You're the second person who's said that to me today,' she said, confused. 'I don't think I'm naughty at all.'

Skye made a face and Summer gently nudged her with her shoulder.

Star looked up impatiently. 'Well, what are we waiting for?'

Summer laughed. 'You.'

'Me?'

'Yes. The key.'

'But that's for the… Wait. Oh, Summer!'

She smiled as Star produced the key and found the lock on a door that looked like part of the mahogany panelling beside the master bedroom.

The key slipped in as if it had been used only the day before. Which it hadn't. Summer had a secret entrance from the master bedroom to Catherine's hidden room, but she'd wanted separate access for her sisters whenever they wanted to use it.

The door opened to a gently lit corridor, grained wooden flooring and smooth plastered walls. The corridor wrapped around the bedroom and all the way to the small room Catherine had hidden the Soames diamonds in. A room which had also undergone a bit of a transformation.

Skye and Star looked around, wide-eyed, at the little room that now contained shelves and three chairs and was cosy and beautiful.

'This room is now separate from the rest of the secret passageways,' Summer explained. 'We thought that the girls might enjoy being able to use the other passageways when we're ready to show them. The renovations have made them safe and secure and I have promised Theron a thousand times that they won't get lost in them,' she assured her sisters. 'But this room is separate and can only be accessed by us. For the moment.'

Skye and Star nodded. 'It's perfect,' they said together, each taking a seat in one of the chairs.

'Have you brought them?' Summer asked.

The girls produced little velvet boxes and placed them on the table in between them. Star had brought the diadem she had worn on her wedding day, Skye the necklace and, with a little bit of a heart-wrench, Summer twisted the beautiful engagement ring from her finger, before replacing her wedding ring.

For the last five years, Summer and her sisters had been talking about the idea of returning the Soames diamonds and Catherine's journals to the secret room that had kept them safe for so many years. Unaccountably, each of the sisters felt strongly that it was the right thing to do and had decided to leave their own journals and letters for future generations of Soames women.

For a while the sisters talked, caught up, shared the stories of their lives, laughed, cried and loved, until a text from Theron announced their return. The women placed the Soames diamonds in a box on the shelf next to Catherine's journals, and their own diaries. In the years to come, those shelves would become full with the writings from generations of Soames women, each telling their own story of adversity and triumph, loss, but most of all love.

But, for now, Skye, Star and Summer left the room, locking it behind them and returning to their families, ready and waiting for Mariam and Kyros's arrival.

Later that night, as Summer got ready for bed, Theron came out of the bathroom, a towel slung low on his hips and drying his hair with another, and she marvelled at just how handsome her husband was. Not once had their attraction dimmed, even through their occasional arguments and their even more occasional hurts, and Summer wanted her husband with the same ferocity as she had on the beach at Piraeus that first time.

Theron's gaze flickered from her eyes to her ring finger and back again.

'I'm sorry, I should have said—'

He smiled, knowing and loving, the look in his eyes cutting her off mid-sentence. 'You didn't need to, *agápi mou*,' he said, kneeling on the bed, tossing the towel back into the bathroom and reaching into the drawer of his bedside table. He produced a small white box she'd not seen before. 'I know. I see you. And I love you. More than anything in the world, Summer Soames. I am the proudest man alive that you chose me and I will spend every day being worthy of it.'

Love bloomed in Summer's heart, strong, powerful, fierce and determined. He opened the box to reveal a stunning diamond engagement ring. It was different to the Soames diamond she had worn, but it was just as special to Summer.

Before reaching for it, she placed her hand on her husband's. 'Five years ago I went to Greece, looking for a part of me that I knew was missing. A part that had felt missing my entire life. And there, in Athens, I found it. Not Kyros, not my father. But you, Theron Thiakos. You are the other half of me and you will always have me and my heart, in yours.'

That night they made love until the sun crested on the horizon and not one of their family minded that they missed breakfast. Apart from Lykos, who grumbled about it for the rest of the day.

* * * * *

COMING SOON!

We really hope you enjoyed reading this book.
If you're looking for more romance, be sure to
head to the shops when new books are
available on

Thursday 1st December

MILLS & BOON

Coming next month

ONE SNOWBOUND NEW YEAR'S NIGHT
Dani Collins

Van slid the door open and stepped inside only to have Becca squeak and dance her feet, nearly dropping the groceries.

"You knew I was here," he insisted. "That's why I woke you, so you would know I was here and you wouldn't do that. I *live* here," he said for the millionth time, because she'd always been leaping and screaming when he came around a corner.

"Did you? I never noticed," she grumbled, setting the bag on the island and taking out the milk to put it in the fridge. "I was alone here so often, I forgot I was married."

"*I* noticed that," he shot back with equal sarcasm.

They glared at each other. The civility they'd conjured in those first minutes upstairs was completely abandoned—probably because the sexual awareness they'd reawakened was still hissing and weaving like a basket of cobras between them, threatening to strike again.

Becca looked away first, thrusting the eggs into the fridge along with the pair of rib eye steaks and the package of bacon.

She hated to be called cute and hated to be ogled, so Van tried not to do either, but *come on*. She was curvy and sleepy and wearing that cashmere like a second skin. She was shorter than average and had always exercised in a very haphazard fashion, but nature had gifted her with a delightfully feminine figure-eight symmetry. Her ample breasts were high and firm over a narrow waist, then her hips flared into a gorgeous, equally firm and round ass. Her fine hair was a warm brown with sun-kissed tints, her mouth wide, and her dark brown eyes positively soulful.

When she smiled, she had a pair of dimples that he suddenly realized he hadn't seen in far too long.

"I don't have to be here right now," she said, slipping the coffee into the cupboard. "If you're going skiing tomorrow, I can come back while you're out."

"We're ringing in the new year right here." He chucked his chin at the windows that climbed all the way to the peak of the vaulted ceiling. Beyond the glass, the frozen lake was impossible to see through the thick and steady flakes. A gray-blue dusk was closing in.

"You have four-wheel drive, don't you?" Her hair bobbled in its knot, starting to fall as she snapped her head around. She fixed her hair as she looked back at him, arms moving with the mysterious grace of a spider spinning her web. "How did you get here?"

"Weather reports don't apply to me," he replied with self-deprecation. "Gravity got me down the driveway and I won't get back up until I can start the quad and attach the plow blade." He scratched beneath his chin, noted her betrayed glare at the windows.

Believe me, sweetheart. I'm not any happier than you are.

He thought it, but immediately wondered if he was being completely honest with himself.

"How was the road?" She fetched her phone from her purse, distracting him as she sashayed back from where it hung under her coat. "I caught a rideshare to the top of the driveway and walked down. I can meet one at the top to get back to my hotel."

"Plows will be busy doing the main roads. And it's New Year's Eve," he reminded her.

"So what am I supposed to do? Stay here? All night? With *you*?"

"Happy New Year," he said with a mocking smile.

Continue reading
ONE SNOWBOUND NEW YEAR'S NIGHT
Dani Collins

Available next month
www.millsandboon.co.uk

LET'S TALK
Romance

For exclusive extracts, competitions
and special offers, find us online:

📘 facebook.com/millsandboon

🐦 @MillsandBoon

📷 @MillsandBoonUK

Get in touch on 01413 063232

For all the latest titles coming soon, visit
millsandboon.co.uk/nextmonth

MILLS & BOON
Desire

Indulge in secrets and scandal, intense drama and plenty of sizzling hot action with powerful and passionate heroes who have it all: wealth, status, good looks…everything but the right woman.

MILLS & BOON

HEROES

At Your Service

Experience all the excitement of a
gripping thriller, with an intense romance
at its heart. Resourceful, true-to-life
women and strong, fearless men face
danger and desire - a killer combination!

MILLS & BOON
MEDICAL
Pulse-Racing Passion

Set your pulse racing with dedicated,
delectable doctors in the high-pressure
world of medicine, where emotions run
high and passion, comfort and love are the
best medicine.